PRAISE FOR WEINA DAI RANDEL

The Last Rose of Shanghai

"*The Last Rose of Shanghai* is a powerful story of the relationship between a Shanghai heiress and a Jewish refugee, set against the backdrop of a nightclub in China on the eve of the Second World War. Weina Dai Randel skillfully shines a light on a little-known moment in history through the lens of two vividly drawn characters whose unique and unexpected relationship is one readers will never forget."

—Pam Jenoff, *New York Times* bestselling author of
The Woman with the Blue Star

"Set in Japanese-occupied Shanghai, this is an unforgettable, page-turning tale of an impossible affair between lovers from two cultures. Randel casts an unflinching eye at the horrors of wartime Shanghai, where refugees starve while the wealthy and privileged continue to drink and dance, and where daily threats of danger and death only serve to fan forbidden passions to a blazing climax."

—Janie Chang, bestselling author of *Dragon Springs Road* and
The Library of Legends

"*The Last Rose of Shanghai* vividly depicts the clash of East and West as Jewish refugees flee Hitler's Berlin for faraway Shanghai, where they struggle to survive amid the uneasy coexistence of Chinese magnates and Japanese invaders. Sophisticated heiress Aiyi knows she is taking a risk when she hires Jewish pianist Ernest to play jazz in her nightclub, but she has no idea that she will be risking her heart, her family, and everything she holds dear as a forbidden love blossoms and Japan's hold on her beloved home city tightens. Weina Dai Randel's poignant, sweeping love story paints a vibrant portrait of a little-known slice of World War II history. Not to be missed!"

—Kate Quinn, *New York Times* bestselling author of *The Rose Code* and *The Huntress*

"A sweeping novel that transports readers to 1940s Shanghai, *The Last Rose of Shanghai* is a must-read for historical fiction lovers. Filled with page-turning suspense and a poignant and unforgettable love story, Weina Dai Randel wholly immerses the reader in this richly detailed and powerfully drawn story."

—Chanel Cleeton, *New York Times* and *USA Today* bestselling author

The Moon in the Palace

"A must for historical fiction fans, especially those fascinated by China's glorious past."

—*Library Journal* (starred review)

"A very successful and transporting novel that beautifully captures the sounds, smells, and social mores of seventh-century China."

—*Historical Novels Review* (Editors' Choice)

"*The Moon in the Palace* depicts Empress Wu's sharp, persistent spirit but does not neglect to make her believably naive and vulnerable, an untried girl among ruthless women. The intrigue and machinations of the imperial court come to life under her hand, a vast and dangerous engine with each piece moving for its own reasons."

—*Shelf Awareness* (starred review)

The Empress of Bright Moon

"A full-immersion, compulsively readable tale that rivals both Anchee Min's *Empress Orchid* (2004), about the dowager empress Cixi, and the multilayered biographical novel *Empress* (2006) by Shan Sa, which also features Empress Wu."

—*Booklist* (starred review)

THE
LAST
ROSE
OF
SHANGHAI

ALSO BY WEINA DAI RANDEL

The Moon in the Palace (The Empress of Bright Moon Duology #1)

The Empress of Bright Moon (The Empress of Bright Moon Duology #2)

THE LAST ROSE OF SHANGHAI

WEINA DAI RANDEL

Published by Lake Union Publishing, Seattle

www.apub.com

Amazon, the Amazon logo, and Lake Union Publishing are trademarks of Amazon.com, Inc., or its affiliates.

ISBN-13: 9781542032872
ISBN-10: 1542032873

Cover design by Shasti O'Leary Soudant

Printed in the United States of America

Dedicated
to
my mother (November 1950–March 2018)
and
Raymond Randel (January 1933–June 2017)

AUTHOR'S NOTE

Though this story features historical events, this is a work of fiction. Names, characters, organizations, events, dates, and incidents are products of my imagination or used fictitiously.

1

FALL 1980

THE PEACE HOTEL, SHANGHAI

I'm sixty years old, an entrepreneur, a philanthropist, and a troubled woman. I've dressed carefully for the meeting today, wearing a black cashmere cardigan, an embroidered yellow blouse, black pants, and a custom-made shoe. I hope, with all my heart, that I look refined and humble, just as an easygoing billionaire ought to appear.

I turn my wheelchair around, moving from one octagonal table to another. It has been a long time since I last came here, and the hotel seems to greet me like an old friend: the chestnut wood–paneled walls, the black-and-white prints, and the golden chandelier hung on the ceiling like a blazing bird nest. In the air, of course, there are no familiar jazz tunes, or angry shouts, or his steady voice. After all, it has been forty years. Our past—my light, my tears—is gone, forever out of my reach. But I hope after today it will be different; after today, I'll be at peace.

I've decided to donate this hotel—this iconic landmark built by a Briton, controlled by several governments, now under my ownership— to an American documentarian whom I'll meet today. I'll ask her to do only one thing: make a documentary. This is an unusual deal, a poor deal on my part, but I don't care. The documentarian has flown across the ocean to meet me, and I'm eager to meet her.

At a black table near Corinthian columns, I park my wheelchair. I shouldn't be nervous, but my heart races. Did I forget to take my medication this morning? I don't remember, and I can't seem to move, either, caught in the crack of memories.

2

JANUARY 1940

AIYI

About two years after the fall of Shanghai, four months after the war started in Europe, I was twenty years old, and I had a problem. My nightclub, a million-dollar business, was running out of liquor due to the wartime shortage. My visits to the breweries and trading companies had yielded no luck, and the customers had taken notice of their adulterated wine. At my wits' end, I went to see the last person in the world I'd ask for help: my business rival, the British businessman Sir Victor Sassoon.

He lived in his hotel, located in the heart of the International Settlement near the Huangpu River. Close to the building, I asked my chauffeur to park my brown Nash sedan so I could get out and walk the rest of the way. My scarf around my face, I passed squeaky rickshaws and rumbling automobiles, my head bent low, praying no one would recognize me.

It was late in the afternoon; a great storm had blown through, the sky looked gloomy, and the sun lay behind the clouds like a silver coin. The air, chilly, smelled of perfume, cigarette smoke, and the fried dumplings from the racecourse a few blocks away. When I reached one of the hotel's entrances, I saw ahead of me a jeep crash into a man on a bicycle—a local Shanghainese, I could tell—who held his leg, screaming, his face bloody. From the jeep jumped a Japanese soldier in a khaki uniform. Smirking, he stepped up to the poor biker, took out his pistol, and shot him in the head.

The loud gunshot pierced my ears and my heart, yet there was nothing I could do but look away. We had lost the city to the Japanese; now, sadly, all of us Chinese in Shanghai were like trapped fish in a sunless marsh. To avoid the hook of death and go on living, we had no choice but to remain unseen under water.

I quickened my pace, went up to the landing at the hotel's main entrance, and stepped through the revolving door. A gust of warm air roared to greet me in the lobby. Letting out my breath, I unwound my scarf and took in the rich Persian rugs, gleaming marble floor, luscious burgundy leather chesterfields, and bouquets of fresh roses and carnations nestled in tall indigo vases. I loved this hotel. Before the war, I had often pampered myself by booking the Jacobean, one of the hotel's extravagant suites that featured unique French decor.

I didn't see Sassoon, but a blond man on a chesterfield, clad in a gray flannel suit similar to one my fiancé owned, was frowning at me. Near him, three men in blue American Fourth Marines Regiment uniforms, who must have heard the gunshot, stopped smoking their cigarettes and turned to me as well. They looked annoyed, as if I were an intruder who had just broken into their dining room.

I wondered if they thought I had something to do with the shooting outside, but most likely they were displeased because I was the only Chinese guest in the lobby. I had to be careful. Everyone knew the Chinese and foreigners were like salt and sugar that must not be mixed, since the foreigners in the Settlement viewed the locals as a nuisance and we shunned them as enemies. These men in the lobby didn't know me, but people in Shanghai, including Sassoon, held me in high regard.

And I had come in my usual finery: a tailored red dress with a slit near the thigh and a luscious black mink coat with a tuxedo collar, accessorized with gold leaf earrings, a gold necklace, and an expensive purse. There were not many girls in Shanghai like me—young, fashionable, wealthy, dare I say beautiful, and skillful from years' experience of running a nightclub. I knew how to handle all kinds of people.

I didn't sway my hips like a flirt, didn't lower my eyes like a servant, didn't smile like someone for hire. Instead, I raised my free hand, gave them a polite nod like the businesswoman I was, and said in perfect American English, "Good afternoon, gentlemen. How are you?"

No reply was given. That was fine with me. I walked past them to the other side of the lobby, waving off the bellboys in beige uniforms offering their help. Sassoon, living in the penthouse on the eleventh floor, had said to meet him in the lobby but hadn't come down yet. I was glad, for his notorious hobby of photography and his request still lodged in my mind, and I also needed a moment to subtly ask for a favor without appearing abject.

I headed to a chair near the elevator, where two white men, holding bottles of Pabst, staggered out. They were drunk, their faces sweaty, their eyes glazed. The one with a shaved head peered at me. A mutter, in English, hit me: "Dogs and Chinese are not allowed in this hotel."

Had this been my club, I would have had the man escorted out. I fixed him with a glare, switched my purse to my left hand, and walked to the Jazz Bar at the end of the lobby. I had just taken two steps when a bottle flashed in the air and struck my head. A violent bout of laughter burst in my ears; I felt dizzy, but I could see, in the light-adorned lobby, everything was normal and no one was concerned. Not the blond in the flannel suit, who raised a magazine to his face, not the American Marines, who disappeared into the Jazz Bar, and definitely not the fat-necked old man, who clapped as though he were watching an amusing show.

I wouldn't need their assistance anyway. Keeping my perfect composure, with one hand on my waist, I felt my throbbing forehead with the other. There was something viscous. Panic ran through me—my looks meant everything to me. "You hit me! I'm going to call the police."

"Go ahead. They'll take you to jail." The man who'd struck me snorted, and then they chanted, "Jail, jail, jail."

I hated to be threatened, but everyone in Shanghai knew this too—the Settlement's Sikh policemen were biased, and we the locals, the losers of the war, couldn't rely on them for any sort of justice. Forget about Sassoon. I just wanted to get out of there. I turned around, but somehow my high heels slid over a pile of shards and I dropped to the ground with a thud. It was mortifying.

"Let me help you," a man said near me, his hand outstretched. It was an ugly hand with gnarled knuckles, the pinkie curled up like a question mark, and a web of jagged scars and snaky welts on the back. But grateful for the help, I let him pull me up, and I was glad, too, that the man seemed to be able to read my mind—he steered me away from the glass shards, away from the snarling ruffians, and rushed through the revolving door.

On the landing, the chilly wind pawed at my face. I pulled my coat tight around my chest, relieved, stunned. I had never been attacked before, and now I owed a debt of gratitude to the man with a scarred hand. I looked at him.

He was a young man, tall and wiry, wearing a black double-breasted coat with creased lapels, no gold watch or necklace—he was not the type of person I usually dealt with. His facial features were distinct: full lips, a strong jaw, and a prominent nose that seemed to tell the world he had a purpose for his life. But I would still have thanked him, had it not been for his eyes—a striking shade of blue.

Another white man.

"There they are! They assaulted us. Arrest them!" Through the revolving door, like a bad omen, the two thugs came out, accompanied by an enormous Sikh policeman wearing a turban.

What nerve they had. I swept aside my bangs to show the policeman my bleeding forehead, and in English, in my easy business voice, I said, "Look what they did to me, sir. They're lying. But let's forget about this, shall we? There's no need to arrest anyone."

This Sikh, a bull of a man, put his hand on the Webley in his holster. "Miss, I'm trying to do my job."

Just a typical policeman in the Settlement, for any unbiased policeman would know a woman like me was more likely a victim.

"She's telling the truth, sir," the blue-eyed foreigner said beside me. He was holding my purse and scarf I had inadvertently dropped in the lobby. I would like to have them back, but prudence told me to keep a distance from him.

"Arrest them, arrest them." Loud protests burst from near the revolving door, and the Sikh stomped closer.

"Sorry, miss." He grabbed the front lapels of the man who had helped me.

It happened so fast: The foreigner pulled away, dropping my purse and scarf, and stumbled backward. Unaware of the staircase behind him, he missed a step, fell, and rolled off the landing to the street. The Sikh policeman lunged after him, those hateful attackers roaring with laughter.

I rushed to pick up my purse and scarf and hurried down the landing to my Nash on the street. Only after I reached my car did I look back. In the distance, among the mass of speeding rickshaws, long-robed pedestrians, and crawling black automobiles, not far from the biker's body, was the enormous Sikh policeman, who clutched the hands of the foreigner, the innocent man, behind his back, and led him in the direction of the police station.

3

ERNEST

Fresh from the boat, now fresh heading to jail. This was not the new life Ernest Reismann had envisioned in Shanghai. He struggled to loosen the grip of the giant policeman but with no success. The man was frustratingly strong, and he muttered something about Ernest being stupid to get caught with the hooligans, his voice surprisingly gentle. No foul racial slurs or vicious threats either. A relief. So he would not be imprisoned for his religion in Shanghai, but in this new city where he was determined to build his future, he'd rather not be imprisoned at all.

Ernest had to think fast. They were turning onto a crowded street with shops selling jars of pickles and bags of roasted chestnuts and dried mushrooms, and he was being pushed around by the jostling long-robed men weaving through the bicycles, carriages, and one-wheel wagons.

"Sir, what are those called?" Ernest tossed his head in the direction of a skinny fellow who raced past pulling two poles attached to a vehicle shaped like a baby stroller. A diversion. He had seen these vehicles earlier, the pullers perspiring profusely while their customers sat with their legs crossed as if it were the most enjoyable ride. That transportation, perhaps, was the strangest sight of all things in Shanghai. He felt sorry for the pullers, the human oxen.

"Rickshaws." The Sikh steered him away. "New to Shanghai? This way."

"You seem like a good man, sir. I'm sorry about this." He thrust hard into the Sikh's chest with his elbow, pulled away, and ran. He raced past a carriage, a row of rickshaws, and then a man plodding along, carrying a pole with a basket at both ends, each holding a small child. A shout came from behind Ernest: the Sikh, at his heels, had crashed into a basket, and the children had dropped to the ground. Murmuring an apology, Ernest passed a red double-decker bus and raced into an alley behind an art deco building. At a building with red bricks, he looked behind. The policeman was not in sight.

He smoothed his coat, ran his fingers through his hair—he had lost his hat—and put on his glove, the glove for his scarred hand, which he had taken off to shake hands with the hotel manager earlier. He did not care about fashion, but the glove was the only accessory he couldn't part with. Without it, he often felt as if he were walking naked in public.

Spinning around to check once more that he wasn't being followed, he submerged into the tide of the crowd on the street. He'd had a rough start looking for a job. Not a big deal. He should try again.

Ernest Reismann, a Jew fleeing from Nazi Germany, had just landed in Shanghai on an Italian ocean liner hours ago. After he was transported from the wharf to the Embankment Building, the temporary shelter for Jewish refugees, he had left his suitcase on the bunk bed with his sister, Miriam, and gone out to look for a job without changing his clothes.

He didn't want to waste time. The twenty Reichsmarks, all that he'd been permitted to bring out of Germany, had been spent. He planned to find a job as quickly as possible and then settle down in an apartment so Miriam would have a place to stay.

He had gone straight to Sassoon's hotel, located at the bustling waterfront where the ocean liner had docked. The wealthy Briton, Ernest had heard, was most charitable, having given an entire floor of his Embankment Building, free of charge, to shelter the refugees so they could get on their feet in this foreign city. But Ernest was unable to meet the man, only the bespectacled hotel manager who scrutinized him through his glasses and said they were not hiring. Disappointed, Ernest had been passing through the lobby when he saw those schmucks throw bottles at the girl. He had rushed to help, memories of pogroms, violence, and pain fresh in his mind.

He had never seen a Chinese girl in Berlin. The one today had been fascinating, a creature of beauty. She'd had an oval face, flawless pale skin, expressive black eyes, a small nose, and red lips. Her hair was short, reaching her shoulders, her bangs evenly trimmed and meticulously curled, framing her face. She seemed about his age, but her mannerisms were sophisticated, distant, with a strong sense of aloofness.

He hoped, with all his heart, that he would see her again.

Suddenly feeling exhilarated, Ernest looked around. He was standing in front of a five-story building in smooth art deco design, near a classical building graced with a statue of a Greek god and a neoclassical edifice crowned with a dome. And Sassoon's towering hotel with a green pyramid was a few feet away. It seemed in his escape he had circled back to the bustling waterfront area again. He began to walk, searching, peering at the French, Danish, Italian, and English inscriptions on the buildings. They were international banks, American liquor trading companies, British tobacco groups, and Danish telegraph firms. Several companies hung the Star of David on the wall. He smiled, remembering that people on the ocean liner said that Jews had arrived in Shanghai to make a fortune as early as in 1843, after Britain defeated the Chinese Qing dynasty during the first Opium War. When the Bolshevik Revolution broke out in Russia, many Russian Jews, fearing persecution, had fled to Shanghai as well.

The fact that his fellow men had found successes in Shanghai gave him great confidence. Surely, he would make a living here. Admittedly, there were obstacles: he couldn't understand the language, didn't know anyone in Shanghai, and had no expertise in banking, engineering, baking, or trade. He loved photography and piano, but photography was a hobby and he had given up on piano a few years ago. But he was nineteen, and he was willing to do anything to survive.

He decided to try his luck at a barbershop behind the building with the Greek god; it had Russian words on the door and a faded poster of Rosh Hashanah on the window—his people, after all. He walked in. The shop had five empty chairs, and a middle-aged barber with a mustache, holding a broom like an ax, frowned at him. Before Ernest could ask, the barber shouted, "Get out of my shop."

Stunned, Ernest backed out, a faint murmur chasing him. "Refugees. Rats!"

He had been called many things; this was new. He shrugged and continued his search down the street. He walked into one shop after another, offering his services as a clerk to a Russian hardware store owner, a hauling jockey to a French businessman in a leather and fur shop, then a dishwasher, a gear polisher, a fish fryer, or anything. No one would hire him. He left the stores, his head hanging low. He had been driven out of his home for being a Jew; now, after crossing the oceans to an alien land, he was driven out again for being a refugee.

4

AIYI

On the way to my club, watching the red-brick buildings and red-tiled villas passing outside the window, I thought of the blue-eyed foreigner. He seemed different from the attackers. I could guess he was arrested because he was with me—the Sikh policeman must have realized I was a victim, but he had to put up a show to appease my attackers. Arresting the young man was unfair. Yet this was what Shanghai had become, a city so far from justice, so close to jail.

Who was he? Why would he bother to help me? Didn't he know the rules in Shanghai?

Shanghai, my home, my city, was no longer mine after a plague of wars; it belonged to the foreigners from many countries. The British, having defeated us a century ago, controlled the rich and prosperous Settlement with the Americans, and the French built their villas in the Concession. The Japanese, armed with terrifying fighter planes and rifles, were the newly minted victors. They had established their own domain for many years in the Hongkou district, north of the Huangpu River, where they played baseball in the park and staffed hospitals with their women and soldiers from Japan, and now they marched on our streets and slept in the homes they'd seized. We Shanghainese, the conquered, were powerless. Many lost their homes in the Old City, south of the Settlement; only a few lucky ones, like my family, got to keep their ancestral homes, and many others crowded under the shadows of the art deco buildings or scattered around the rice paddies and mosquito-infested fields in the north and west.

Segregation was not a law, but prejudice was rampant like disease. We all stayed away from one another. We Chinese tended our sick at home and the foreigners cared for theirs in their hospitals. We dined in our courtyards, the Europeans drank in their coffeehouses, and the Japanese ate in their restaurants lined with tatami.

Out of business necessity, I kept friends like Sassoon and socialized with them; often we drank brandy mixed with new interest and old resentment. I was aware of the risk of mingling with them. Getting assaulted was not a surprise, but it was a surprise to be aided by a white man, a complete stranger.

My Nash turned on Bubbling Well Road and stopped on a street lined with plain trees with bare branches. I stepped out of my car, pulled my mink coat tighter to fight against the wintry chill, and walked to a stately three-story art deco building with a sleek circular overhang in white stones. The air was vibrating with jazz tunes; the evening session had started. In the dimness that was swallowing the city, One Hundred Joys Nightclub, crowned with a crystal glass dome topped by a stylish flagpole, glowed brilliantly in red neon lights. A vision of beauty and opulence, it was the first luxury nightclub in Shanghai and had earned the envy of Sassoon at its opening.

And it was mine.

ళ్ళ

I entered the building. In the high-ceilinged atrium, a chorus of voices rose to greet me. I nodded at the bellboys and restaurant owners who rented the spaces on the first level, crossed the tessellated floor, and went up the marble staircase to the ballroom on the second level. On the landing, one of the bouncers opened the thick wooden doors of my club, and I went inside. Instantly, the sound of music and voices of customers rushed to my ears, and familiar gauzelike vapor rich with imported cigarettes, expensive fragrances, and sharp aroma of alcohol enveloped me. As a habit, I studied everything: the brilliant eighteen thousand light bulbs meticulously embedded in the vaulted golden ceiling—a sight that never failed to make a first-timer gasp in awe—the round teak sprung dance floor aglow with pebbles of light, the band on the curtained stage, the customers in the corners, and the curved wrought iron staircase leading to the third floor.

No one was complaining about liquor, fortunately.

I gave my fur to the coat man, walked down the circular path around the dance floor, and headed to the bar. On the stage, the band started to play the music. The sound of double bass dribbled first, a trickle of dark molasses; the drumbeats pulsated, playful like a lover's tease. Then with a bolt of pure energy, the trumpet blared. Shadowy figures leaped up in the darkness and rushed to the dance floor. Spinning, swaying, they kicked up their feet, black suits and glittery gowns whirling in a sea of jade green, wine red, and ginger yellow. The ballroom had everything the merriment seekers wanted: all music, all lulling voices, and all joys—loose, dark, as intimate as hot breath.

My customers were Chinese, and I knew many of them: the young men in pressed suits and pants, the modern girls in leather shoes and fitted dresses, the thick-bellied businessmen who recently doubled their wealth by some dubious means, the Western-universities-educated architects with glasses, and even Mr. Zhang, a gangster, who had a habit of spinning a folded pocketknife in his hand. There were also Nationalist turncoats, toadies to the Japanese, nameless assassins, and Communist spies.

They all came for their own reasons, but I would like to think they craved jazz, the foreign music of love and yearning that puritans criticized as erotic and dirty, and the waltz and tango that the traditional stoic men derided as immoral and indecent. And most importantly, they all had money. For entertainment in my ballroom was not cheap: an hour's rate cost more than a meal for many families and a drink more than a week's wage for many laborers. But with a fallen Shanghai, many shuttered businesses, rampant diseases, beheadings, assassinations, and daily shootings on the street, what else could you do to feel alive other than dancing and singing some songs from your heart?

I tapped my leather shoes against the teak floor and swung my hips and arms, just slightly so no one would notice. I loved jazz and loved to dance, but as the owner of the nightclub, I had learned to show great restraint of my passion or some unwanted hands would find me. So I never sang, or hummed, or swayed on my own dance floor.

Customers were calling me: "Good evening, Miss Shao."

"You look lovely, Miss Shao. Where is my favorite whiskey you promised?"

"Have you gotten my brandy yet, Miss Shao?"

I struck a pose, a nice, appealing silhouette that worked well at attracting eyeballs and helping customers spend more money. Being a young female business owner in a man's world had taught me how to keep a balance between attracting customers' attention and driving them away. I was good at creating an impression of affability without encouraging their approach. "Don't you trust me? Of course, I'll get all the drinks. Soon, very soon."

Then nodding to a group here and waving to the dancers there, I sat at the bar. By the shimmering lights, I counted the bottles on the shelves. Sixteen. All I had. Including the cheap local rice wine, some soda, and leftover gin. They would last for three days, five at most. Then I would be out of stock, and the market had run out of soda, sorghum wine, beer, gin, and all kinds of whiskey months ago.

My business had started to decline last year, and I had been hoping to sustain it with the sale of alcohol. Now I didn't know what to do. I had never imagined having to deal with this kind of problem. Three years ago, before the war, I was the wealthiest heiress in Shanghai with the inheritance Mother had left me, and I had never thought to manage a jazz club—working wasn't meant for someone like me. But the Japanese bombed the city, and the coward Nationalist armies failed to protect us. Victorious, the greedy Japanese took over the city, froze my bank account, and confiscated my family's fortune. I was poor—I was stunned. I never thought I would need to work, but to survive, I had to learn how to make money.

Desperate, I ended my college plans and asked for help from a cousin, a former shareholder of this jazz club that had gone bankrupt. I sold my jewelry, bought the business at a bargain, and donned a long, fitted dress with a slit near the thigh. I learned to multiply double digits in my head. I carried a peony-hued ledger in my purse to keep track of the daily expenses. When I came across lascivious men and their outstretched claws, I seldom screamed; instead, I trained myself to be an excellent drinker and invented a drinking game to encourage their spending on alcohol. This club, this business, was my life.

The band finished their song, and the crowd swayed off the dance floor, rushing toward the bar, toward me. A wave of groans rose. "What? No brandy? Let's go to Ciro's."

Ciro's, Sassoon's nightclub, also catered to the locals. It was one of the many competitors I faced, among them a number of dance clubs in the French Concession that lured customers with exotic Russian dancing girls, and a dozen small local clubs with cheap admission fees.

I took a glass from the counter. "Who wants to play a drinking game?"

"Sorry, Miss Shao. We need good whiskey and brandy," Mr. Zhang, the gangster knife spinner, said.

"I have brandy."

"You've been out of the good stuff for a month."

He headed to the entrance with his men. Several customers, shaking their heads, followed. The band looked at me, their violins and trumpets in their laps.

"Let's hear some Duke Ellington." I waved, touching my tender forehead. I had two choices left. Either let my business continue to languish or go visit Sassoon again.

5

ERNEST

The lobby in the Embankment Building was dimly lit by a lamp in the corner, the globe of light shedding a sheen of yellow on the steel bunk beds spreading from wall to wall, some plaid cloth hung between them as curtains. The radiator grille buzzed somewhere; the air was rank and humid, but Ernest grew used to it. Quietly, he made his way through the bunk beds, taking care not to step on coats and hats strewn on the floor. In the hallway, people were piled on the stacks of suitcases; it was hard to tell one from the other. Twice he stumbled over an elbow until he finally reached the dim ballroom, where his bunk was.

Miriam was asleep on the top bunk, their suitcase at her feet. He lay down, listening to all sorts of noises: the phlegmy coughs, the stressful sighs, the muffled sobs, and the grumpy voice of a woman speaking German—"How can we survive in this strange city?" He could feel the dreadful weight of stress from all the people around him. At least one thousand Jews, he was told, had crammed into the ground floor of the building. Some of them were German, most Austrian, arriving at Shanghai via ocean liners. Germany had attacked Poland when Ernest left Berlin for Italy to board the ocean liner, which he and Miriam had waited six months for. Now rumor said Germany had conquered

Poland, and France and Britain had declared war against Germany. It was devastating, but he couldn't confirm it without reading a newspaper or hearing the radio.

The voyage from Italy to Shanghai had taken nearly one month, stopping at Port Said, navigating through the Gulf of Suez and the Gulf of Aden, veering eastward, and finally reaching Shanghai. The time on the ocean liner had been a time of luxury and hope. Yes. He could do this; he would start a new life in Shanghai, protect Miriam, and wait for his parents left behind. But when he arrived, he'd had to take a moment. Shanghai was under Japanese occupation, he had learned, but he had not imagined the city in such a sorry state. The Huangpu River, where many banana-shaped ships, skiffs, trawlers, and sailing boats docked, was a turgid yellow sluice filled with glistening oil and lumps of trash. Across the river, behind the high-rises and art deco buildings, were the bomb-gutted houses; dark, burrow-like alleys; and low windowless shanties. The entire city was boiling with an overpowering stench and a cacophony of automobiles' honks and the sharp squeaks of rickshaws' wooden wheels; on the street bicycles, wagons, automobiles, and carriages weaved among emaciated rickshaw pullers, amputee beggars, and coughing Chinese refugees with sickly sallow skin and dead eyes.

But this was the most beautiful city in the world. It had no sickening swastika flags, no damned Nazi uniforms, no Germans threatening to arrest him. Occupied Shanghai was the only open port for Jews, the only city that accepted him without an entry visa. This city was his dream; Berlin a nightmare. He would not go back until Hitler was gone.

"Ernest! Where have you been?" Miriam stuck her head out from the top bunk, chewing on the chin strap of her trapper hat. The beige shearling hat was a souvenir she'd picked up on the ocean liner. It was for boys, but she loved it.

"I thought you were asleep. I went to look for a job."

"Did you find one?" Miriam's large eyes were filled with hope. "I'm hungry. I could eat a dozen *Pfannkuchen*."

"Not yet. But don't worry, I'll find a job." And when he did, he would treat her to anything she wanted. She was twelve years old, a reserved girl. He had played the dreidel with her when she was a toddler and trudged in knee-high snow to buy *Pfannkuchen*, her favorite breakfast, for her. After Leah, he swore he would take good care of Miriam.

"Ernest, the Komor Committee was looking for you," Miriam said, her innocent voice filled with fear that had begun to creep in since their departure from Berlin. "They said our bunk beds would be reassigned to the incoming refugees. We need to move out. We have five days."

The committee, a volunteer charity group organized by local Jews, had picked them up at the wharf and transported them to this building, a reception place. He had been told their stay would be temporary. But five days . . .

He turned onto his side and rested his head on his hand. Suddenly, exhaustion enveloped him, and all the courage and optimism that he had forged on the ocean liner evaporated. He closed his eyes. He was just tired. He just needed a good night's sleep.

The next morning, he felt worse. His head ached, his legs were sore, and listening to the endless din and complaints around him, he became pessimistic—he would never find a job in this city. Eventually he got up and rummaged in the suitcase for a toothbrush and a stub of toothpaste saved from the ocean liner, his hands brushing his entire assets inside: his precious Leica, a Montblanc pen, a stack of music sheets he had salvaged from under the Hitler Youth's boots, Miriam's clothes, his clothes, and a pair of gloves his mother had packed.

The line to the lavatory was long. Many people held canteens and tin boxes to refill with water, their faces grim. By the reflection on the windowpanes, Ernest saw his own face ringed with stubble, desperate, just like everyone else. He looked away, wishing the line would move faster, for his bladder was full. But to cut ahead of the line was unthinkable. So for one long hour, he stood rigidly, holding his breath as his bladder expanded, growing heavier and then painful. Who knew after escaping the war in Europe he would face such a human misery? And what he would have done for a stall to relieve himself! When he was certain he was going to have an exploding bladder and die an undignified death, finally came his turn to use a stall.

By God, he swore, it was the most blissful moment of his life, to let himself go, to release every drop that had caused him so much pain. When he was done, standing at a sink to wash his hands, it was as if he were reborn—a new man, unburdened, invincible. He hummed.

"Ah. Chopin in a latrine," an old man wearing a felt hat mumbled beside him.

Ernest grinned. "Did I come across you on the ocean liner, sir? I'm Ernest Reismann."

"Carl Schmidt. Are you ready to get out of here? It's so crowded."

"As soon as I find a job." Ernest squeezed out some toothpaste and began to brush his teeth. He'd have liked to chat more, but people behind him were waiting for his sink.

"What do you do? Are you a pianist?"

"Oh no." He had kept his scores, still remembered how to play Chopin's C-sharp minor nocturne from memory, but he had given up piano years ago. Now Mr. Schmidt made him think. Surely people in Shanghai listened to music?

"May I borrow your toothbrush, Ernest? I'll give it back. Mine was stolen. Yes, my toothbrush! Don't trust anyone here. People are desperate," the old man said.

Ernest gave his teeth a quick scrub and handed the old man his only toothbrush. "Here, Mr. Schmidt. Wish me luck. I am a pianist, in fact."

6

AIYI

At the revolving door, I paused cautiously, studying the lobby I had fled a few days ago. The memory of the attack and the blue-eyed man's arrest came into my mind, making me flinch. Then I saw the Briton holding his silver-crusted cane, limping, making a beeline for me.

Sir Victor Sassoon was a tall man with black eyes, thick graying eyebrows, a carefully trimmed mustache, and a long face. Dressed impeccably in a black suit with tails, a white carnation on the lapel, and a black silk top hat, he appeared severe like an iron rod, plain like rice, and way too withered to be my friend. But what did it matter? He was the wealthiest man in Asia, a billionaire, in all likelihood, and the owner of more than eighteen thousand properties in Shanghai, including this hotel, nightclubs, high-rise apartments, a racecourse, and transportation companies.

He was fifty-nine, still single, living by his own rules, deaf to the salt-and-sugar warning. He ignored his associates' frowns and openly invited me to many of his perfume-filled parties and silk-swirling balls, even though he couldn't dance. A womanizer, I believed, he changed his female companions more often than I changed my dresses—an Indian princess wearing a bejeweled head wrap, an American movie star with the face of a doll, and scores of scantily clad Russian dancers with voluptuous bodies. He was proud, showing them off in the hotel.

I put my hand on my waist, relieved. No one would assault me in his presence. People respected him, even the Japanese. When shrapnel had scraped the corner of the hotel's awning during the bombing a little over two years ago, a Japanese officer had bowed deeply from the waist to Sassoon, apologizing for the misfire.

"Good evening, darling. A momentous occasion to see you. I was going to phone. How do you do?" His British English was impeccable; his voice was warm, confident, but as always, arrogant. I was used to that.

We'd rarely had business dealings, but I knew him well from staying in this hotel as a guest with my best friend, Eileen. Those teenage mornings of breakfast in bed, days spent viewing trendy magazines, afternoon teas sampling towers of golden pastries, and evenings filled with private jazz entertainment—how I missed them. Sassoon was sometimes generous, occasionally acerbic, and thoroughly arrogant, but I liked him well enough. He was different from the Chinese I knew. Though always complaining of the pain in his leg, he held the door for me before I entered, pulled the chair before I sat, and filled up my cup with coffee. I found the behavior intriguing. Cheng—my fiancé—and all of my relatives would not deign to fill their own cups; they had servants to do that.

I had no doubt Sassoon would help me out—he had many cases of gin and whiskey to spare since the Japanese restriction on alcohol only applied to the Chinese. But seeing his face reminded me of his perverse passion for nude photos. "I'm well, Sir Sassoon. About our meeting the other day. My apologies. But I assume you've heard what happened?"

"The incident. Utterly appalling. You'll allow me to make it up to you, darling?" His cane clicking against the marble floor, he led me to the Jazz Bar. His entourage followed, a blond lady in a blue evening gown and his bodyguards.

"How would you make it up to me?" I entered the bar. The gramophone was playing Shanghai jazz, a blend of American jazz and Chinese folk music popular with the locals, not American jazz. The bar must have encountered some problems. The stage, where an American band usually played, was empty; the fallboard of the piano was closed. And the bar was smoky and noisy; many people crowded around octagonal tables. All foreigners. A thought occurred to me. The man who'd rescued me might be a guest of the hotel. If I saw him again, I should at least express my gratitude.

"Darling, I'll be happy to give you a discount on any suite of your choice. Remind me, when was the last time you came here? Last year? You should come more often." Sassoon sat at the table closest to the entrance—he disliked walking—so I sat across from him where I could look, in envy, at all the shining bottles of brandy, scotch, absinthe, and gin on the shelves.

Even in his effort to compensate, he still intended to make money. That was what Sassoon and I had in common: we were businesspeople, with an instinct for profit. "I'll be glad to consider it. You know how much I love the suites. And your alcohol. Look at those bottles!"

"Ah. You can have anything you like, darling. What may I treat you to? Martini? Or my drink?"

"I can never say no to your famous cocktail." He made the best drink, called the Cobra's Kiss.

"Good choice, darling." He signaled for his entourage; two sprinted to the shelves behind the counter. "I shall have the Jacobean suite reserved for you tomorrow, if you wish. Remember, the door of my hotel is always open to you."

"But the world has changed, hasn't it? I can't believe it's no longer safe."

"Darling, my hotel is the safest place in Shanghai. And you're my most distinguished guest. You're an extraordinary woman, shrewd and beautiful. I confess, if you were Jewish, I would marry you."

He always talked about that—Jewish and Gentile. I didn't know the difference; to me, they were all foreigners. But marriage with the wealthiest man in Asia? I would be more than happy to accept the proposal if it were genuine and realistic. After all, a marriage might be too hot or too cold, but it was essential, like porridge.

But a union with Sassoon would never happen. For I knew well of this: a marriage between a Chinese and a foreigner would be a cautionary lesson, not a fairy tale. "Sir Sassoon, are you seducing me?"

"Is it successful?"

"I don't know, but I'm serious. If you were Chinese, I would marry you."

He chuckled. Rejections were rare for him, thus intriguing. "How disappointing, darling. I do hope you'll change your mind." He took a bottle of absinthe from his entourage member's hand, poured the green liquid in a mixer, and shook it expertly.

I eyed the bottles of brandy, curaçao, cream, and green absinthe on the table; the strong scent of alcohol was intoxicatingly heady. "Between you and me, Sir Sassoon, I'm having a difficult time filling my customers' orders. There is no alcohol for my club. I'm sure you know the reason why."

Out of the corner of my eye, I caught sight of several men in suits. The Japanese, whom I could identify with one glance, raised their heads toward me. I quickly looked away.

Sassoon leaned over me and said in a low voice, "Those militants. They've been ingratiating themselves at the council. I loathe them."

For that, I would overlook all his flaws. "What's their business at the council?"

Sassoon, a powerful man, had the ear of the chairman of the Shanghai Municipal Council, the governing body of the Settlement, which consisted of British, American, Japanese, and Chinese members but was largely controlled by the Britons and Americans. When the Japanese conquered Shanghai, they had left the Settlement untouched, and the council was still firmly controlled by the same members. Sassoon poured some green mixture into two stemmed glasses and placed one in front of me. "Some very annoying business. But they won't dare to do anything foolish."

"Of course they won't." I picked up my glass. The first sip gave a sharp sting to my tongue. Strong brandy. I hadn't tasted anything like this for months. It would sell well in my club. "I have a favor to ask. Would you sell me some of your alcohol stock? Say, some gin and whiskey? Ten cases each. Or any amount you're willing to part with."

He leaned closer, the shoulder pad of his fine suit licking my shoulder. "Darling, I shall be happy to help you. But what do you say you come visit my studio first?"

I pulled back. He hadn't forgotten.

"Well, darling." He poured himself some more of the Cobra's Kiss. "May I remind you again. You have a perfect figure, and you're young and beautiful. Why not show it off now? Nude photography is art."

It was awkward. Nude photography, no matter how tasteful he claimed it was, for me, was just another name for pornography. I would never agree to it, not for hundreds of dollars, and definitely not for some gin. I also had a feeling that it was more than my photographs Sassoon was after, womanizer that he was. But I was a woman with good morals. While I would be glad to tango with him in a ballroom, I would not tumble with him in the bedroom.

However, if I refused him outright, displeased him, I might as well forget about the alcohol.

"Well?" His black eyes were close, too close.

I smiled. "Let me see, Sir Sassoon. You're Asia's richest man—of course, you always get what you want."

"I do."

So did I. "Sadly, I'm a businesswoman, not a model."

He groaned, slapping his hands on the silver-crusted cane, his mustache sagging. He would be grumpy and morose for a while, and I would give him some grace, some time to think, mollify him, and then negotiate the alcohol. I stretched out my legs and turned my head to the side, and that was when I saw, through the hazy air, punctuated by wafts of pale smoke and pearls of light, a man at the entrance of the bar who raised a gloved hand and waved at me.

7

ERNEST

It was the girl he had helped the other day. She looked up at him, her wide black eyes dancing with surprise, her face glistening with light. She had one elbow on the table, her body turning slightly, showing off a slim and curvy figure wrapped in a long green dress embroidered with bamboos, a slit near her thigh revealing a sliver of her pearly skin.

He snapped upright and strode toward her. Such a pleasure to see a familiar face. His job hunting had been a disaster. Who would have known the music halls, theaters, and cabarets were closed? Several cinemas and dance clubs were open, but as soon as people saw him, the doors were shut.

He had learned that there were about eight thousand Britons, two thousand Americans, and another few thousand Russians and other Europeans in Shanghai, and now the city was overrun with thousands of Jewish refugees. Each day, Ernest walked past grim-faced European refugees spreading their valuables on the street, shawl-wrapped German hausfraus selling their fur scarves or necklaces to middle-aged Russian women who seemed to have established themselves in this city, and desperate Austrian men peddling sausages and knocking on people's doors. It dawned on him: war-torn Shanghai, with a flood of Jews and thousands of displaced Chinese refugees, simply didn't have jobs left for a newcomer like him.

This was the fifth day of his job search and he was feeling discouraged again. But then he heard the distinct swinging rhythm of music coming from the green-pyramid building, Sassoon's hotel. It was similar to American jazz, with the orderly chorus of a trumpet and piano, but imbued with a smooth rhythm, sung by a sweet feminine voice. Exhilarated, he sprinted up to the landing and strode through the revolving door he had left a few days ago. Following the music, he passed a brightly lit Rolex store, the Jasmine Lounge, a café, and found the source—the gramophone in the Jazz Bar. And right next to the gramophone was that lovely face of hers.

"Hello! We meet again," he said in English, reaching her table.

A smile appeared on her face. "You got out!"

"I got away." She was still beautiful, still sophisticated, with a reserved look, almost distant. But she remembered him.

"Good for you."

"Are you okay? No one bothers you, I hope?"

"No. And I'm glad. Can you imagine? Getting attacked not once but twice?"

Her voice had a gentle feminine lilt, like the jazz singer he'd just heard. Ernest smiled, unable to take his eyes off her, her red lips, her smooth face, her bright eyes.

She continued, "I was hoping to see you again so I could thank you. There are not many foreigners like you. I'm grateful for your help. What brings you here? Are you a guest of the hotel?"

In fact, her voice sounded more melodic than the jazz singer's. "Oh no. I heard music." It had stopped. A man in a suit was bending over the gramophone on the counter; someone shouted in the corner of the bar. Ernest turned to look and froze, a thrill running through him. In the dark bar filled with cigarette smoke and absinthe and men's shadowy figures, the instrument dearest to him was sitting near a stage—a piano.

"Do you know him, darling?" said the old man across from her. He had a fresh white carnation pinned on his suit; a walking stick, like a royal scepter, rested near his hand. He looked to be in a bad mood, his glance mirthless, almost hostile.

"Sir Sassoon, when I was attacked in your hotel the other day, this man helped me. He was arrested for his gallantry," she said.

The charitable man, the third Baronet of Bombay, a Baghdadi Jew—Sir Sassoon—was sitting right in front of him. His luck was turning. Ernest smiled. "I'm Ernest Reismann, sir. It's an honor to meet you. I hope this is not too rude of me, but do you need a pianist? You have such a fine Steinway. I just arrived in Shanghai, and I'm looking for a job."

The old man poured some green liquid into a glass in front of him. "I'm glad you helped Miss Shao, young man. She's a good friend of mine. But everybody asks me for a job. There are so many of you, and you keep coming. Refugees! I'm done with charity. I've given you my Embankment Building, donated a $150,000 grant to small business owners, and supported people like you for five years, before Anschluss! Now you need to make a living on your own. Ancient Chinese, they were very wise. They said, 'Don't give a man fish; teach the man how to fish.' Young man, learn how to fish."

The words drenched Ernest like cold water; all his giddiness vanished. He felt the dead weight of his feet, the soreness of his legs, and the empty stomach that had growled and now mercifully stopped. For days he had heard brusque refusals, degrading curses hurled from strangers. Now this. "Of course, sir. Sorry to bother you."

"Well." Her voice came again. "Don't go yet. Perhaps you'd like to have a drink?" She lifted a cocktail glass.

He felt a lump in his throat. With all her attractiveness, this was the true beauty of hers—treating him with dignity. Yes, he would like to have a drink, a strong drink to quench all the disappointments, a strong drink to collect his thoughts so he could stand straight again. But he didn't have a single penny.

"Sure. What are you drinking?" he said.

"The Cobra's Kiss, Sir Sassoon's treat."

He turned to the old man; he had nothing to lose anyway. "Would you mind if I have a sample of your cocktail, sir?"

"You can certainly take a sip, young man, but how would you pay for that?" Sassoon's voice was all annoyance.

Ernest picked up a glass in front of him and drained it before he regretted it. The cocktail, a hot, murderous fire, burned his throat—just what he wanted. "I'll pay you with a piece of music, sir. May I have your permission to play?"

Sassoon's eyes narrowed—the man didn't like him, he got it—and there came her voice again. "I love the piano, Sir Sassoon. I'd love to hear that."

"Go on then, if it pleases the lady," Sassoon grumbled.

Ernest tipped his head and strode toward the piano. His recklessness had earned him a chance to play for her; that was all that mattered. And he wanted to play well; he wanted her to remember his piano, remember him before he left this bar. For he was tired down to his bones, and he was unsure how much more he could take.

He reached the piano, sat on the bench, took off his glove, and lifted the mahogany fallboard. His naked fingers touched the cold keyboard; a shiver raced down his arm and the familiar feelings of fear and resentment, mixed with anger, sprouted in his chest. It had been almost four years since he last touched a keyboard, since his piano was seized. His arms that used to strike out powerful arpeggios and silky legatos were soft from lack of practice. Before him was the nightmare again: the hand he was afraid to show in public, the grooves on his skin, and the crooked pinkie where the bones had been shattered and healed wrong.

All he could hear was the near silence in the bar, the huffs and puffs of the drinkers. He couldn't see her, but she was listening, watching.

A new sensation—a fiery burst of tenderness mixed with a familiar ache—powered through him. He inhaled deeply, let his shoulders drop, and gazed down at the keyboard. Notes of Beethoven, Debussy, and Chopin, bouncing, tingling, streamed through his mind. He could no longer hear the crowd, or smell the cigarettes, or see the silver dots printed on the fallboard. He was in a bar, but he might as well be standing on a peak of the Harz mountains or in the center of the Leipziger Platz.

His heart full, he lifted his hands.

This song was for her.

8

AIYI

Notes swept the air, a trickle as delicate as spring mist; then gradually, they grew to be a wave of gentle legatos. The air bubbled in a fountain of sounds, soothing, putting me at ease, and then suddenly they leaped, the rhythms exploding in a passionate deluge of fire, and staccatos, accents, and arpeggios boiled one after another. The air grew incandescent; the bar roared with booming chords. A battle raged in my head; my body grew hot, bound by an infectious cord of excitement unknown to me before. It was a joy to stay there, to be held captive, to ride to the peak, and to be torn apart. But the music was kind; it sought no destruction, only comfort, as its magnificent cascade slowed and eased and dipped, gently like a rock falling into the embrace of a river, to a tender drip. When the notes murmured and finally faded in the air, a pocket of silence descended.

I let out the breath I'd been holding. I had heard different types of music: the energetic jazz that sent the dancers in my club into a frenzy and the melancholy folk music played by the street musicians using three-string violins. But not the classical music played on the piano, the Western music usually only available on gramophones. The foreigner who'd rescued me was full of surprises. A refugee. A bold man bargaining a free drink from Sassoon, and a pianist.

People were clapping. I itched to go up to talk to the pianist, but I had already thanked him. It didn't make sense to socialize with a foreigner if there were no financial benefits.

"Well, darling, here's your Chopin. Perhaps he'll leave us alone now." Sassoon frowned, still grumpy.

"Just one moment. Would you mind?" I said without thinking, then, weaving between the octagonal tables and smoking men, I walked to the pianist, his fingers still gliding over the keys in a wave of fluid motion.

"You played well. That was worth a cocktail. Thank you. I rather enjoyed it."

"I'm glad. What else can I play for you?" He did a crossover on a higher octave. His scarred hand seemed to distract him, his crooked pinkie marring the purity of the arpeggios. But the wonder of the piano. There was nothing like that.

"You played it for me?"

"Of course. The most beautiful girl I've ever seen. I'll play anything for you."

"Anything?" I teased him. People flirted with me all the time, and I had gone along unfazed. This felt different.

"Absolutely."

"I like jazz."

"The American music? I love it too. What's your favorite song?"

No one had ever asked me about my favorite song before, not the band I hired, not Cheng or my brothers, who believed jazz would corrupt my soul. *Good girls listen to Mother; bad girls listen to jazz,* Sinmay, my brother, had said. I couldn't contain myself. "'The Last Rose of Shanghai.' It's Shanghai jazz, a blend of American jazz and Chinese folk song. The gramophone was playing that. You want to hear it? It goes like this." I hummed, swinging to the beat. "'There is a kind of love that strikes like a thunderbolt; it blinds you, yet opens your eyes to see the world anew.' There, there. That's my favorite line."

"Like this?"

His shoulders swayed; his fingers danced over the keys. The syncopation, the energy, and the flowing appassionato. He understood my favorite song; he understood how it made me feel. I forgot myself, tapping along, swinging my hips, humming, roped by the rhythm. And all the while I saw his eyes on me, his indulgence, his undiluted affection. My heart raced and my cheeks warmed. I had never felt like this: giddy, silly, like a young teenager.

"Ernest, right? I'm Shao Aiyi. Call me Aiyi." Most people called me Miss Shao; only my family had the right to call me by my given name, but I didn't care.

"Ayi?"

"No. It's Ai-*yee*, down tone and then up tone. It means love and perseverance. It's okay if you can't pronounce it. I also answer to Ali, Haylee, Mali, and Darling."

He laughed, but then he repeated my name with concentration and determination that made me stare at him with happiness. And he was playing something else—George Gershwin's "Summertime." But the technique Ernest used!

"You know the stride piano?"

The new jazz. I had heard it at this exact spot, performed by an American band, before the war. It was incredibly rhythmic, richly provocative, with the pianist's left hand playing a four-beat pulse while the band played the melody.

"I'm a pianist, Aiyi."

"Ah." I wished I had a pianist like him in my club. I had always wanted to introduce the stride piano to my customers, which I believed would be immensely popular. But the war had ruined everything. The few Chinese pianists had fled the city, and pianos were seized by the

Japanese along with many homes. I couldn't even find one on the market for my club.

Sassoon was saying something; Ernest glanced up. Quietly, he closed up the fallboard and stood. "Thank you, Aiyi. Thank you, sir. It has been a pleasure."

I watched him put on his glove and leave the bar. All the light of passion, the effervescence, dimmed on his face, and it struck me—the depth of his disappointment. As a foreign refugee, he had no place in this city, where many people, including the locals, struggled to make a living.

When I sat at Sassoon's table again, I asked him if he would reconsider hiring Ernest. Sassoon shook his head adamantly, saying his American band, taking a vacation for the moment, was popular in the bar. But he agreed to sell me twenty cases of gin and whiskey, and again, he reminded me to reserve the suite.

I raised my glass to toast. Twenty cases of alcohol would sustain my business for at least three months—four, if I were creative. This trip had been worth taking after all.

Later in my car, my cheeks hot with absinthe, I looked out the window. My Nash glided through avenues and lanes crosshatched with shadows and lights; the engine hummed and purred. In the distance came the faint music from bars and clubs, the sharp rattle of trains from a railway, and the sporadic gunshots from the Japanese military base in the district up north. It had been hours since I'd heard Ernest's piano playing, but the sound of the music, that face of his, the dancing of his fingers, swirled in my head. I felt different, as though some part of me had been changed and my heart had been turned into a throbbing instrument.

Outside, the wind whispered in a dialect of decadence familiar to me, and the city waltzed in a circuit of winds and shadows. It was as if the city were telling me something wonderful, something most daring: it was mine, all mine—the streets, the wind, the night, the pulsating jazz, and the want, the fresh want of dangerous dreams and delirium.

But this was all wrong. I was engaged, twenty years old, a businesswoman, and I should never feel this way about a foreigner. I must have had too much of the Cobra's Kiss. Tomorrow when I awoke I would feel different, and I wouldn't even remember who Ernest Reismann was. And with Shanghai being so vast, we would perhaps never cross paths again.

But I would like to see him again.

I could hire him, now that Sassoon had declined him. And I could find him easily. The location of Sassoon's Embankment Building, where Ernest stayed, was near my family printing press before it was forced to relocate. But Ernest was a foreigner, that in and of itself should be an important warning to stay away. I would be asking for trouble, for it was unconventional for a Chinese woman to keep foreigners as staff, and the patrons of my club, the locals, had a tendency of viewing the foreigners as enemies.

But I wanted to hire him. Ernest—the best pianist I had ever met—could play the stride piano, which my instinct told me would be a sensation in my club and revitalize my business. If Ernest caused trouble, if it didn't work out, I would let him go. It was business, after all.

Would I dare hire him?

I lowered the window, loosened my dress's spiral knots at my neck, and let my carefully curled hair unfurl like a bedsheet. Just for a moment.

9

ERNEST

In the dark, he lay on his bunk. *Aiyi, Aiyi, Aiyi,* he mouthed, first down then up, *Aiyi, Aiyi.* It sounded like he was climbing on a strange scale of tones, but it grew on him, lingering on his tongue with a warm echo, a shape, a strength that fitted his mouth perfectly. It was the name of beauty, the name of love, and each time he repeated it, the vision of her face bloomed in his mind like a hot summer sun. But this was silly. He had just arrived at this alien land; he was jobless, penniless, and homeless. The last thing he wanted was to fall in love.

He closed his eyes. In his sleep, he was on the train's platform, and his parents' anxious faces appeared, their voices drumming in his ears. "Ernest, take good care of your sister," said his father in his earth-colored coat, and, "Ernest, have a good life and marry a good Jewish girl," said his mother, eyes swollen from crying, face mapped with fear and anguish.

He woke up, his face wet with tears. They'd had only two exit visas for the four of them, so the decision had been easily made. And now he listened to the breathing of Miriam from the top bunk, his youngest and now only sister.

The committee had sent him a final notice; he was to leave the shelter the next morning. Yet to his despair, he hadn't found an apartment—or a job.

At the first light of dawn he squeezed through the crowd in the hallway, one hand holding the suitcase, the other grasping Miriam's arm. Nodding at the fellow refugees, he asked how to get in touch with them. Mr. Schmidt shook his head; the others sighed.

"Then may peace be with you," he said, giving them all the cheer he could muster. When he came to the lobby, it was more crowded than ever. A wave of new refugees had arrived, all carrying suitcases, hair unkempt, faces grim. They were fleeing for their lives, they said, for Jews in Berlin were sent to camps and Jews in Austria were deported to Poland.

Stunned, Ernest didn't know how he made it to the sidewalk outside. His parents. Did they receive exit visas yet? Were they sent to camps? And next to him, Miriam rubbed her eyes, yawning. "Where are we going? It's so early."

The cold morning air clawed at his face; he shivered. His parents were stuck in a war zone, and he didn't know where to find a safe shelter for Miriam. He didn't know where to go.

Two rickshaws passed him, loaded with refugees; behind them, Mr. Schmidt, seeking shelter in a church, climbed into a truck. A brown car pulled up and stopped near Ernest. He heard a shout but couldn't make it out. Then from the car stepped a Chinese man in a black jacket and a black cap, who waved frantically at him. Ernest stared, unable to comprehend a word.

Then he heard a name. Her name. Shao Aiyi.

He dashed toward the car and peered through the window just as it rolled down, and staring at him was that lovely face of hers.

"Hello, stranger. I'm glad I found you before you left. I was wondering if you'd like to play the stride piano in my club?"

"What?" He didn't know she owned a club. Had she mentioned it yesterday? The chauffeur stuffed something in his hand. A postcard with a band on a stage flashing neon lights. At the bottom of the postcard was an address in Chinese and four English words: One Hundred Joys Nightclub. "Oh yes. Of course. I'd love it."

A beautiful smile bloomed on her face, and she glanced behind him at his sister and their suitcase. "Then come in. I'll take you both to your dorm."

The so-called dorm was an apartment located on the west side of the Settlement, south of the Suzhou Creek, a few blocks from the nightclub. Aiyi said she provided her employees a wage and lodging, since finding a place to sleep was always a challenge with the flood of refugees fleeing from the north. All her Chinese employees, the band and the ballroom dancers, lived in the Old City, which was unsuitable for him because he was a foreigner. So she had taken ahold of her best friend's uncle and rented his apartment.

"And don't worry, I'll deduct the rent from your wage," she said.

It didn't seem important how much his wage was—he had a shelter for Miriam! The room measured about twelve feet by twelve feet, with no heater, no fireplace. But it had a bamboo bed, a wall calendar, a wooden stool, and a chipped cabinet with twelve lidless square drawers. The shared kitchen was at the end of the hallway, the communal toilet near the staircase. Many Chinese lived inside the building, but some rooms were boarded up.

Aiyi had her chauffeur walk into the apartment with him and Miriam; Aiyi didn't come in. It would cause some gossip if she, a Chinese woman, were seen with him inside the building, she said. But she would like him to start to work in three days since she needed time to find a piano.

"She's pretty, Ernest, but I don't think she likes me," Miriam said, after the chauffeur left.

"Of course she likes you."

"She's cold."

"Aloof, maybe, not cold. But she's very kind once you get to know her. How do you like this, Miriam?" He went to the window and shook the latch. It was stuck. Still, it was a room with a roof.

Miriam's wide eyes looked desperate. "There's only one bed."

"So?"

Her face turned pink. Miriam was tall, like him, with long legs and broad shoulders. "I can't share the bed with you, Ernest. I'm almost thirteen."

The age of growing up, and he would be glad to give her some privacy, but they were not in Berlin anymore. "Then you better not kick me in my ribs. You want *Pfannkuchen*?"

"You have money, Ernest?" She pressed down her trapper hat. She looked happier.

"Let me see." He picked up the suitcase and dug through their valuables, a Montblanc pen and the Leica he treasured. He took out the pen.

He sold the pen for ten Chinese *fabi* on the sidewalk, and then they searched for *Pfannkuchen*. But there were no bakeries nearby, only makeshift stalls selling bolts of silk, posters, and albums, and shops selling knitted handbags. Finally, Miriam settled for some soup in a shop.

Four cents bought them two bowls of buckwheat noodles, the best meal Ernest had had since his arrival. He drained the rich brown broth flavored with ginger, garlic, scallion, and flakes of fish. Watching

Miriam's lips shining with soup fat, he felt his heart was bursting with happiness.

He loved the city, the smell of fried peanut oil, the constant squeaks and honks, the quiet alleys, and the luxurious, bright hotels. He had a job and an apartment now. One day, he would buy forks and spoons, scissors and shaving blades, coats and vests; he would get Miriam snacks and shoes, pancakes and noodles. He would survive.

He would play the piano in her club. Aiyi, first down then up. He wanted to know more about her, her joys, her fears, her hobbies, her favorite food, her favorite drink, her favorite color.

There is a kind of love that strikes like a thunderbolt; it blinds you, yet opens your eyes to see the world anew. Within its light, a pathway was illuminated.

10

FALL 1980

THE PEACE HOTEL

Two women walk to my table, one Chinese, the other a foreigner. The Chinese, my niece, wears a pair of round sunglasses that shields her face with its burn scars; the other, I can see, is the documentarian. She appears to be in her thirties, tall, wearing a large cowgirl hat, a brown leather jacket with a long fringe on the sleeves, a brown handbag with similar fringe—even the hem of her vest peeping from under the jacket is decked with a thick border of fringe.

"Aunt." Phoenix—my niece but also my attorney, my counselor, and my private investigator—taps my shoulder. "This is Ms. Scarlet Sorebi, the documentarian. She just flew in from Los Angeles yesterday."

Close up, the documentarian's face has a nice softness, but her bright eyes hit me like headlights in fog. I'm nervous again, but I shouldn't be. After all, it's unlikely she'll refuse my offer. "It's a pleasure meeting you, Ms. Sorebi," I say.

"The pleasure is mine, ma'am." She takes off her hat and sits down on a chair across from me; the fringe of her handbag sweeps the air, narrowly missing my face, but she doesn't notice. She's polite, expressing her gratitude for the paid airfare and the stay in the hotel and her excitement about this meeting. She doesn't ask, but she must wonder why I flew her all the way from the US.

I squeeze out a smile. Maybe I've been surrounded by too many soft-speaking business associates, or maybe I'm too set in my ways and not accustomed to talking to strangers anymore, but I have a hard time catching up with her. Her cowgirl attire is undoubtedly a distraction, for in my opinion, people who wear this sort of costume have yet to grow up. And her voice is crisp, a pitch too high, as if she has a habit of talking over others; her accent is tinged with the dreadful Southern drawl I'd hoped never to hear again.

A wave of sadness, unbidden, engulfs me. I blink away the tears on the verge of rolling out—Ms. Sorebi is staring at me.

I hurry to speak. "My apologies. I didn't catch your words."

"Oh, ma'am, I was just saying I did some research about you before the flight. I hear you're the owner of an international hospitality company that has a portfolio of many hotels around the world. You're a Canadian citizen, aren't you? People in the US have yet to know you. There's not a single article or a photo of you. You're perhaps the most reclusive billionaire in the world."

She's making an effort to befriend me. "I'm old now. I don't care for fame as I used to. But, Ms. Sorebi, you must be wondering why I asked to meet you in person. Allow me to explain. When my niece told me about the exhibit you showcased in LA, I was impressed. It's remarkable that you've conducted the interviews about the Jews who survived in Shanghai during World War II and featured the stories of so many people. One of them is very precious to me. I would like to offer you an opportunity to make a documentary about that special person, since Phoenix said you're a trained documentarian."

"That would be lovely. Who is that special person?"

"Ernest Reismann. I hear you dedicated a section to him."

She nods. "Mr. Reismann. Of course. He was one of the highlights of the exhibit. He was a hero, a legend in Shanghai in the 1940s. Many people I interviewed were grateful to him. They said he was selfless and had a heart of gold."

I smile, but I control myself beyond that. "I hear you found more than a dozen photos of him."

"I did. I found a treasure trove of photos about Shanghai in the 1940s. They were very interesting, but I didn't show all of them in the exhibit. I brought some with me. I can show them to you if you'd like to see."

Somehow the word *photos* is stuck in my head. "I'd like to see them. If you don't mind, I'd like to see what you've showed in the exhibit as well. I didn't have a chance to see it while it was open."

"I actually brought a lot of documents with me. Let me see." She takes out a manila folder from her fringed handbag, pulls out a notebook from inside, and flips open to a page.

I hold my breath. I shouldn't be nervous. There can't be anything she found that I don't already know.

"Mr. Reismann, right? Here's the background about him. According to my research, the Jews in Berlin faced inhumane pogroms after the Kristallnacht. They were ordered to get out of Germany or risk being sent to concentration camps, but many countries were reluctant to accept them. With the world closed to them, about eighteen thousand Jews found their way to Shanghai. Mr. Reismann was one of those refugees. He was nineteen years old."

Phoenix presses her fist to her lips; I want to close my eyes. It has been so long since I've heard someone talk about Ernest. "Right. He was one year younger than me."

The fringe of Ms. Sorebi's sleeves sways as she continues, "Mr. Reismann grew up in a two-bedroom apartment in the district of Mitte in central Berlin and spent most of his time in a music conservatory until he was expelled for being a Jew. He was a bright, optimistic youth.

At school, he was always the first one to class and the last to leave. When he made extra money at a cabaret, he treated his friends to beer. Until all the cabarets refused to hire him. His parents lost their jobs in the university. His two uncles, in despair, had committed suicide among the rising hostility in Berlin. His older sister, a promising painter who had displayed her works in a famous gallery, stole a can of olives in hunger and was caught. She was beaten to death by a group of Hitler Youth. Her body was left inside a dumpster while the whole family searched for days."

I'd heard of this straight from him, but still a shiver runs down my spine. "Go on."

"In Shanghai, life was different for him and his sister. Let me see. Miriam Reismann. Am I right? They came to Shanghai together. They were very close, and he cared for her deeply."

My heart stops for a moment.

"Mr. Reismann also found a job in Sir Victor Sassoon's nightclub."

"My nightclub. The One Hundred Joys."

"Your nightclub? Gosh. Is it true? That was what I said in the exhibit. Did I get it wrong? How would a woman own a nightclub in Shanghai in the 1940s? I thought many Chinese women had bound feet."

It's naive of her to make assumptions about me. "You're right. Many did, but not me. I wasn't an average Chinese woman in the 1940s."

Ms. Sorebi massages her temple, and her voice is softer when she speaks. "I'm sorry. I do apologize if I made a mistake. I only recorded what I was told."

"I was not in the exhibit, which is understandable. But did your interviewees mention me? A Chinese girl who got involved with Ernest?" I ask.

She hesitates. "I'll need to think about it, Ms. Shao."

But by the look in her eyes, I can tell she doesn't need to. "Do you believe what they said?"

Something in me has not changed after forty years. I still care about people's opinions of me.

"Well . . ."

I take a deep breath. I should have presented my donation earlier, and now it looks like a bribe. "Ms. Sorebi, I forgot to mention that if you agree to make a documentary about Mr. Reismann, I shall donate the Peace Hotel to you."

Her jaw drops. "This hotel?"

I see she understands the value. The Peace Hotel, opened in 1929, was originally named the Cathay Hotel. It had guest rooms from floors four to nine inside the towering Sassoon House. Described by many as the Waldorf Astoria of the East, it's a valuable asset culturally, historically, and financially. In the course of the fifty years since it opened, the hotel has had different owners: Sir Victor Sassoon, the Nationalist government, and the pro-Japanese Wang Jingwei government, and now it's my property. I have had it privately evaluated, and it is said to be worth at least ten million dollars.

"But I have a request. You must listen to my story."

"I'd love to, Ms. Shao." She turns to her fringed bag and tries to dig something out but stops. Her hands are shaking. My offer has taken her by surprise, and she obviously doesn't know how to react yet. "I'm honored to make this documentary about Mr. Reismann, but I must make it clear, and I don't mean to be rude, Ms. Shao, but as a documentarian, I'm not allowed to twist the truth or distort the history."

"Of course. So you must hear my story."

"But why donate this hotel? You know the value of it. It can make thousands of documentaries."

"I've told you Mr. Reismann is precious to me, and I'm an old woman with one foot, as you can see. I only wish to have no regret before I go to my grave."

She cocks her head, looking skeptical.

"I shall put this into writing, if you still have doubts. And one more thing, Ms. Sorebi. Please do me a favor and don't call me ma'am."

"Why, of course, Ms. Shao." She's smiling to placate me, or perhaps to try to forget the unfavorable description of my association with Ernest that she has heard.

I lean back in my wheelchair. "The first thing you need to know, young lady, is the truth: in Shanghai, if you're a woman and a business owner, you cannot climb through a tunnel of spiders without catching some cobwebs in your hair."

I was the seventh and youngest child of the Shaos, one of the wealthiest families in Shanghai, and people called me a jade leaf growing on a gold branch, *Jin Zhi Yu Ye*. My illustrious grandfather, whose name was on many lips, had modernized the mud town Shanghai and founded many enterprises in the late 1800s—a railway company, a telegraph firm, a large iron-and-steel joint venture, and a university still prominent today. He was a prime minister of the collapsed Qing dynasty. When he died, his funeral procession was attended by officials and ambassadors from Russia, Britain, Germany, the United States, and even Japan. It extended from the west end of Nanjing Road to the Huangpu River. He had left my family the great fortune we relied on as well as a legacy of patriarchy my brothers seemed all too happy to carry on.

My father, who had lived like a typical dandy, was an intrepid mayor of Shanghai for years before his opium addiction. I had few memories of him; all were unpleasant, including his bouts of anger. Maybe he felt threatened by Mother, the oldest child of a powerful warlord. A woman with bound feet but an excellent skier who took trips to the Alps, she was known for her shrewdness and clever maneuver of finance. Thanks to her, in the throes of my father's opium addiction the bulk of my family's wealth was squirreled away.

As a child, I grew up in an enclosed compound, educated by an aging tutor who lectured on obedience and family honor, pampered by an army of servants, and screened from the vileness and violence of the world. As a young woman, I was materialistic, in love with dresses and purses, lipsticks and limelight. But I knew my future as soon as I could understand things: I would marry Cheng, my cousin, and after marriage, I would become a mother and produce as many children as possible. As a child, I hadn't known better and had gone along with this plan, since this was what Mother had arranged for me—but it would become the biggest sorrow of my life.

I think my story would have been different if I had never heard jazz at my best friend Eileen's house. Once I heard it, I became an ardent fan. There was no popular music in Shanghai, in the sense of music as you know now. Recorded music didn't exist in our culture when I was born. I begged Mother to send me to the high school where Eileen was enrolled, St. Mary's Hall, a private girls' school run by American missionaries, so I could hear more of the music. Mother doted on me, so even though everyone else in the family objected, I was enrolled.

At school, I feigned sickness during Elizabeth Barrett Browning and Emily Dickinson and hid in a spacious red-brick auditorium, listening to Louis Armstrong and Duke Ellington, marveling at their sensational record sales. I decided what to do with my life: become an entrepreneur like Elizabeth Arden or Coco Chanel. So it was apt to say that literature taught me Western tradition, but American jazz inspired me to become a businesswoman.

While still in school, I made my first investment, a secret investment, in a record company run by a cousin, with my sizable allowance. The company failed, and I lost all my money.

Then tragedy struck: Mother died in an accident, a heavy blow after the death of my father the previous year. After her funeral, I wept as my siblings, one by one, left my life. My second brother joined Chiang Kai-shek's Nationalist army to hide in the heartland; my third brother severed the family bond to become a Buddhist monk; my fourth brother died of fever; and my only sister ran away with a tycoon selling porcelain toilets in Hong Kong. When the nightmare of war started, Eileen fled to Hong Kong, the maids who pampered me were relocated, and I was left with two brothers, a fiancé, and no bank account.

I purchased the jazz nightclub with the help of my cousin, the same cousin whose record company I had invested in, and began to work. I had been struggling, managing it for two years, when I met Ernest. My life was changed forever.

11

AIYI

All was going well.

After many phone calls and inquiries on the day I hired Ernest, I finally heard that one of Cheng's cousins kept a piano for his second wife's daughter, so I borrowed it from him and had it swiftly transferred to my club.

Sassoon, to my delight, delivered the alcohol to my club three days later. Gordon's Distilled London Dry Gin. Gilbey's. And Old Taylor from America. Their fragrance perfumed the air as my managers carried them to the storage room and displayed them on the shelves at the bar. Holding a highball glass filled with gin adulterated with water to save the alcohol, I examined the piano—a small instrument in oak, not a Steinway like the one in Sassoon's Jazz Bar—and toured around the empty tables that I hoped would soon be filled up with eager customers. Ernest's stride piano and Sassoon's imported gin and whiskey. This could be the turn of my business.

I gave a few more instructions to my managers and went to my office at the end of the hallway. Holding a small mirror, I reapplied red lipstick and powder and carefully arranged my bangs—I had the trendy hairstyle some calendar-girl models copied. I looked fashionable, with my gold leaf earrings and gold necklace, the essential jewelry that signaled I was still richer than most people. But I had a second thought. Unbuttoning the fitted pomegranate-red dress, I put on a Western bra saved in the drawer in my dressing room, the type with padding, and tucked in it a ball of tissue sprayed with perfume so the scent wouldn't be overpowering.

Today was Ernest's first day.

⥈

"Good afternoon, Miss Shao." Swinging music burst through my office door as Ernest entered, dressed in his same double-breasted coat with creased lapels. A cloud of stubble traced his jaw; there was thoughtfulness in his movements, as if he were holding something precious but afraid to lose it. But his eyes. They were radiating energy, fondness, and warmth, a powerful tune that made my heart bubble with happiness. Just like that, I wanted to smile with him and talk about music.

But I composed myself. He was, after all, a pianist I'd hired. "I'm glad you came. Today is your first day. Let's talk about your work. Sit, sit."

"Thank you for the opportunity, Ms. Shao." He took off his glove and extended his hand.

He was well mannered and respectful, but I had to say, "Ernest, may I remind you? This is a Chinese club. It might be good for you to know some etiquette. It's rather inappropriate to shake a woman's hand."

"I didn't know. Why?"

"Chinese people consider touching between men and women an intimate action."

"Even for business?"

I nodded.

"Hugs?"

52

A newcomer, he was truly unaware of how people in Shanghai viewed the outrageous nature of that Western custom. Most Chinese were practically hug averse. "That's for friends, very close friends."

"Kissing on the cheek then? In Europe, the custom is to kiss three times on the cheek."

I coughed. Such intimacy was unthinkable in Shanghai; even married couples refrained from publicly demonstrating intimacy. Certainly not between a Chinese and a foreigner.

"So what is the proper social etiquette in Shanghai?" He looked baffled, staring straight at me, another bit of etiquette he needed to learn—we showed respect by lowering our gaze.

"In greeting, we bow or do this." I folded my hands together and gave him a deep nod.

"I sincerely hope I didn't offend you, Miss Shao. I only wish to express my respect and gratitude for the employment."

I had no doubt about that, and I actually quite missed the way he'd repeated my given name in his guttural accent. "Ah. You'll repay me by playing the stride piano. I'm counting on your music to make my club more competitive. I've made a plan to introduce you and publicize your appearance. So people will know how unique your music is. Today, you'll get acclimated. Sounds good?"

"Of course."

"Now, let's talk about your wage. We use three currencies in this city. Usually, foreign employees are paid in American dollars in foreign companies. Some local businesses here are switching to the currency the Japanese issued, but we still use our Nationalist government's *fabi* since our employees need that to purchase food. Would you accept that?"

"I'm fine with *fabi*."

"You'll be paid ten Chinese *fabi* every evening. That's after the rent. The workday starts at four o'clock in the afternoon and ends when customers leave, generally around three in the morning. Do you have any questions?"

He looked pensive. "You said this is a Chinese club. Do you have any foreign employees? Do any of your people speak German or English?"

"No. All employees and customers are Chinese. And I'm sorry, my four managers speak some pidgin English, but most people only speak Shanghai dialect." He would be a foreigner, alone, surrounded by the opinionated locals, a stranger unable to understand our language. "Come, Ernest. I'll show you the piano."

In the ballroom, the evening session had just started. The band was playing "Summertime," and as I had hoped, there were already some customers; Mr. Zhang, the knife spinner, had come with his buddies, and they had ordered a bottle of Gilbey's. They didn't pay attention to Ernest as we walked to the piano in the left corner of the stage, for which I was glad. I absolutely didn't want to have unnecessary exchanges with that gangster.

The bandleader, the trumpeter, Mr. Li, came to me near the piano. Glancing at Ernest, who had put on his glove and fluttered his fingers on the keyboard, Mr. Li frowned, not surprisingly, his eyes filled with hostility. He had worked at Lianhua, the film studio, before the war, and now did some moonlighting at weddings and funerals. His band had worked for me for four months. Usually bands didn't stay long; they came and went. Sickness, better payments, or death.

"Mr. Li, meet your new band member," I said in Shanghai dialect. I was not an amiable employer; I believed in distance, for Mother had said men's egos prevented them from taking a woman's order, so I gave orders with few explanations, which, surprisingly, produced respect.

"Miss Shao, my people work very well together as a band."

"Now you'll work with a pianist."

"Can he speak Chinese?"

"No."

Mr. Li stood apart from Ernest as though his new band member would bite him.

"If you don't mind, I'd like to tune the piano. Do you happen to have tools?" Ernest said.

"The manager will find something for you." People were turning their heads to me and Ernest. Manager Wang, who was at the bar, rushed over. Always blunt, he looked like he was going to start a brawl with me, and I knew he'd lecture me about the heinous crimes the foreigners committed. So I walked away.

What concerned me was not the objection of my employees—they could get used to my decision or quit—but rather the customers' reaction. Mr. Zhang, who was talking to my dancers, was glaring at Ernest. Several patrons, who had just entered the club, caught sight of Ernest's tall figure and stood perfectly still.

Did Ernest turn them off? Would they refuse to step into my club because of him? They didn't know what they would hear yet—the breathtaking, toe-tapping stride piano. Besides, I had twenty cases of imported gin and whiskey!

Mr. Wang took the new arrivals to their seats, and Mr. Li started to play on the stage. I let out my breath, gave one more look at Ernest tuning the piano, and went back to my office.

I was calculating on my abacus when a howl, full of pain, roared in the ballroom. The music had stopped.

I rushed out. Under the eighteen thousand glittering lights, a crowd had gathered, peering at a figure on the floor—Ernest. He writhed, holding his right hand, still gloved, a knife piercing through it.

12

ERNEST

The pocketknife was completely embedded in his hand, his scarred hand. Was this an irony or a curse, he wondered. He had kept it gloved to help repress the memory of being mutilated, the fear, the despair, and the hatred, and now again it was a target. Blood gushed out; a trail of deep red splashed across the keyboard. God. He would never play the piano again.

He staggered back, his ears filled with a storm of strange words, gasps, and shouts. The man who'd plunged the knife into his hand was flinging his arm, and the dancers and the band watched with curiosity and something like excitement.

It had happened so fast, so confusingly. When Ernest had entered the building, he was dazzled by the grandeur of Aiyi's club, the sophistication, the decor, the lights, and the dance floor, all reminding him of the imposing music halls in Berlin. Seeing her face, her aplomb, and her poise steadied him. She was now his boss, a privilege, but he could sense, too, the distaste of the people glancing at him. Never a stranger to hostility, he worked on the piano with the tools a manager gave him as quietly as he could, as quickly as he could. He just wanted to play his music.

But his tuning, or perhaps his presence, must have distracted the customers, because the man holding a knife had come to kick him. Ernest raised his hand, giving an apology, but the man seemed irritated, unleashing a torrent of Chinese. Ernest raised his hand again, and before he knew it he was thrown against the piano and a knife stabbed his hand.

The floor was now slick with his blood and he slipped, falling on his back. When he opened his eyes, Aiyi's face appeared above him; she said something rapidly in Chinese, and then he was helped to his feet and out of the ballroom to the atrium. "It's not that bad." He slid into her car. The blade felt chilly in his flesh, his fingers numb, and the blood had pooled and dripped out. It was hard for him to focus. "Sorry I gave you trouble."

She sighed. "I should apologize. I was worried about this. That man is a gangster, Ernest. I'm sorry he picked on you."

"Because I'm Jewish?"

"Because you're a foreigner."

It felt silly, but that was the most comforting thing he had heard. "I didn't know this would be a problem." This must be Shanghai.

"You'll have to get used to it, Ernest. Foreigners and the locals are not best friends. We live separate lives. You'll learn. You've lost lots of blood. Try not to talk."

His teeth were chattering. He closed his eyes for a moment. Fresh fear pierced him again—he had been forced to give up the piano after his hand was scarred, and now it looked like he would never be able to play the piano again. What could he do? He had a sister to care for.

When he opened his eyes again, the chauffeur was telling him to get out. He managed to stand; in front of him was a red-brick building, Hôpital Sainte Marie. He almost collapsed when a Catholic nun wearing a cross rushed to support him. Rapid French rang in his ears; arms supported him as he entered the hospital. All was a blur: the pungent alcohol smell, the calmness induced by morphine, and the confusing

French spoken by the Catholic nuns. When the knife was extracted, his cries sounded like ramblings of a madman. But no bones were broken, no nerves were severed, fortunately. He swallowed a handful of pills he couldn't identify, gulped down a lot of strong liquids, and slept.

When he left the building, dawn was breaking, and a few rickshaws squeaked past. Aiyi's car was still there.

He opened the door gently. Aiyi was sleeping, leaning against the back seat; her chauffeur was also dozing off in the driver's seat. She could have left after she dropped him off, or told him to take care of himself after being stabbed, or not hired him at all, a stranger, a foreigner. But she had treated him with dignity, given him a refuge when he was homeless, taken him to a hospital when he was wounded. Had anyone else cared for him like she did? Had he dreamed of anyone like her, a woman of another country, of another race?

She stirred and opened her eyes. "Ernest? You're back. How's your hand?"

"Good as new," he said, holding up his bandaged hand. "Those Catholic nuns were the best nurses I've ever seen. They gave me seven stitches. Once I heal, I can play the piano again."

"That's good to know. I was worried about that."

Her voice had a soothing rhythm; he wanted to hear her speak forever. "Thank you for bringing me here, Aiyi."

"I'm your employer. I have no choice. I'm a terrible caregiver, just so you know. You won't want to be in my care again, or you'll lose more than a hand."

But she did have a choice.

"Let me take you to your apartment." She told the chauffeur to start the car. "How long did the doctor say it'll take your hand to heal?"

He looked at his bandaged hand, devastated. "To completely heal, it'll take four months."

"Four months." She sighed.

There was no reason she should keep him for four months if he couldn't play the piano. "I can play with my left hand."

"I'd rather you not do that. That's not the stride piano. My plan is for you to be the band's melody, not accompaniment. Now, usually I wouldn't offer this, but I'll make an exception. You'll have a paid leave for a week, so you can recover and let your hand heal. How's that?"

If he stayed out of the club for a week, would he be allowed to return? The car's engine droned, an endless run of moans and groans, like life's sickening spasms, relentless. But he would make it, with a damaged hand or not. "I'll see you tomorrow, Aiyi."

13

AIYI

His insistence. Was he going to get even with Mr. Zhang? I glanced at his hand.

"I just want to work," he said.

His face was paler than dawn, but he had no rancor, no hint of revenge, not even a wrinkle of anger in his eyes. Here was someone who was nonviolent and insisted on working to receive pay. I wanted to know more about him. So even though I was tired, I asked him about where he was from, what his parents did for a living, how he was trained, and why he'd come to Shanghai.

He told me all. He was from Berlin. His parents were professors in a university. He'd come here because of the war, and he'd started to play the piano at a young age because his mother insisted.

"What did you play?" I asked.

"Classical music, mostly," he said.

I nodded, still remembering his music in Sassoon's hotel. "I like jazz better. You know why? We have lost the war to the Japanese. People die every day like flies; everyone is scared. Jazz makes us feel alive; it helps us forget about reality. Classical music is different; it's about remembering."

"I can't put it in better words." He smiled; in his blue eyes shone the same light, the same indulgence that I had seen when he played in Sassoon's hotel.

My heart raced. I felt my cheeks grow warmer. I turned my head to the window.

"I'm also interested in photography, as a hobby," he said.

A popular hobby among the foreigners—Sassoon, for one—but it was expensive since cameras and film were imported. "What else do you like?" I asked.

"Movies."

The things we had in common. He adored Marlene Dietrich, the German actress, he said, and I loved Katharine Hepburn. I also enjoyed reading movie magazines, which were hard to get, but manager Wang had a knack for finding them for me.

"And skiing," he said. A coincidence, for Mother, a woman with bound feet, had been an avid skier. "And you."

"Oh, stop." I flicked my hand to dismiss him, but I must have been crazy, for I kept thinking about his blue eyes even after he left, the jewels of light that could change and reflect his moods like a magical movie.

The next day, when I was ready to go to work, Cheng, my fiancé, came to my home. He offered to take me to the club. He did this frequently, saying it was to ensure my safety, but I knew it was his excuse to watch me.

A fashionable man, he was dressed meticulously in a purple tweed suit, a black silk tie, black trousers, and black-and-white leather oxford wing tips. "What are you wearing, Aiyi? That thing is so tight it shows your ribs," he said, standing by his black Buick as I got in.

He was a controlling man. It was his nature to tell me what not to do, who not to talk to, and what not to wear. This always irked me, for

Cheng, a man with an excellent taste in men's fashion, preferred me to cover up from head to toe. It displeased him that I'd wear a sleeveless dress that showed my shoulders or a short dress revealing my calves.

I was wearing a fitted long dress printed with red peonies; it showed my curves and my bare arms, which were currently covered by a short wool jacket.

"If you need new dresses, I'll send you my seamstresses." Cheng sat beside me as the car started to drive. He was the scion of a shipping magnate. His family's fortune was dwindling, like mine had, but he was still rich and well connected through his six sisters' marriages. With his wealth and good looks—a chiseled face, wide shoulders, and strong muscles from years of horseback riding—he attracted many women. My family had believed I had made an enviable match. They were right; Cheng was a catch.

But I had only felt a cousinly connection with Cheng. When I told Mother about that, she had said that was enough, for marriage was a business that would run smoothly without romantic love. I believed her, so I rarely thought to question my eventual marriage. I liked Ernest, a foreigner whom I had never imagined befriending, and I was attracted to him in some ways I shouldn't be, but I would never risk anything to ruin my future with Cheng.

"I'll wear a different one tomorrow." Cheng also had an explosive temper. I'd rather not provoke him.

"And a bra, Aiyi."

He meant the traditional bra, a triangle piece of cloth that flattened my breasts. He knew I hated it, but arguing with him only aggravated him. "Fine."

He took out a packet of cigarettes. "So what did I miss? A knife incident? Why did you hire a foreigner?"

He must have heard this from my managers, and he must be irritated because I hired Ernest without first consulting him. As my fiancé, Cheng felt entitled to my business. "He can play the stride piano; I was going to tell you. He's very good at it. It will help my business thrive and make more money."

"It looks like your customers didn't like him."

The apathy in his tone. "They will, once they hear his music."

Cheng looked offended; he was always like that, getting angry when contradicted. "This isn't over. There will be more trouble if he sticks around."

I was quiet the rest of the way to my club, for Cheng had made me nervous. What if he was right? The last thing I needed was to see more bloodshed, which would drive away the modern girls, the fashionable young people, and other customers. Sassoon's alcohol wouldn't help.

When I stepped into the ballroom with Cheng, I froze. Ernest was already there, and he was doing something he shouldn't.

14

ERNEST

He could still make himself useful. Helping customers to their seats, delivering their drinks—if he'd understood them, he would have taken their orders too. When the customers went to the dance floor, he took a broom and swept away the peanut shells, the sunflower seeds, the ash, and the cigarette stubs.

He asked to deliver drinks to the man who had stabbed him, Mr. Zhang—he was seated with two men with their shirts unbuttoned. Manager Wang looked stunned, but Ernest nodded, assuring him there would be no trouble. Reaching the round table where the men sat, Ernest bowed, remembering Aiyi's instruction of the Chinese custom, offered the tray of glasses and a bottle of gin they'd ordered, and poured for him.

Mr. Zhang muttered, *"Guizi."*

A slur, Ernest could tell, but he didn't feel threatened. "Good evening. My name is Ernest Reismann. I'm at your service. If there's anything I can do for you, please let me know."

He could tell Mr. Zhang didn't understand his English, but all the same, Ernest stood there, pouring his drinks. The man looked rather surprised and then pleased. In fact, all the customers looked surprised and pleased.

Mr. Zhang had another folding knife visible, but he didn't use it.

"Ernest, are you sure you want to do this?" Aiyi asked him backstage. She looked shocked, standing next to a well-dressed, handsome man with thick black eyebrows, a fine jawline, and fierce black eyes. Her companion was frowning at him.

"Is there a problem?" Ernest said.

"No. It's just the foreigners usually do not serve the Chinese food or drinks. It's, you know, beneath them."

He shrugged. "What does it matter. People are strange. Some think they're superior to others because of their wealth, their pride, the history of their country, their religion, or their looks. I'm just a man from Berlin, a guest of this city. I do my best to look decent, and I hope, if possible, to be a friend of this city. I'm more than happy to serve the customers in your club until my hand heals."

She tilted her head, looking incredulous. "Of course. You're welcome to help out."

She looked like she was going to say something else, but the well-dressed man took her arm and they walked away.

So Ernest worked as a server, a bartender, and a busboy. Mr. Zhang didn't bother him anymore, and the other customers and the staff in the club seemed friendlier, often asking him about his hand. "Good as new." He raised it like a flag, a flag of peace.

While keeping busy, he listened to the conversations of the customers and mouthed their words, tuning to the rising and falling tones, like her name. But of course, nothing was as special and endearing as her name. Whenever he saw her, his gaze followed her. It would perhaps do him good to keep his feelings under wraps if he wanted to keep the job, but it was hopeless. He felt like he was a different man. He laughed as loudly as he wanted; he could jump off a cliff on a dare.

He counted the days until he could play the piano again. When the band played, he listened with great focus and memorized every song. "The Entertainer," "On the Sunny Side of the Street," "Memories of You." Swing, ragtime, jazz, all the popular American music he had heard of but was not familiar with. He noted the pentatonic scale, the main melody, and the free improvisation of the clarinetist, the trumpeter, and the violinist. The fiery beats made his heart pound; he tapped the floor with his feet, and his good left hand struck invisible keys in the air. His mind roared with the outpouring of energy and the thrilling chorus of the instruments.

His passion for jazz swelled. He learned the music had arrived in Shanghai during the late 1920s when many American musicians came there during the Great Depression. Aiyi's favorite song, "The Last Rose of Shanghai," was composed during that time, by Buck Clayton and Li Jinhui, a Chinese composer. After the musicians left, their songs were recorded, copied, and fused into traditional Chinese ditties. Inspired by jazz, the music industry in Shanghai, once almost nonexistent, flourished in the 1930s. Songs blending the notes of jazz and folk tunes were broadcast on the radio and composed for films, a new breed of female singers rose to fame, and companies were founded to produce gramophone recordings.

Ten days had passed when one evening he noticed something. "Why does your band never play your favorite song, Aiyi?"

She put a finger on her lips.

No one in the club knew what her favorite song was.

One day, Ernest finished his work near dawn. On the way to his apartment, he bought a block of tofu and some bits of coal from a peddler in order to boil some water since the tap water in the kitchen was unsanitary. Ten *fabi* a night was still his payment, thanks to Aiyi's kindness, but he was barely scraping by, feeding Miriam and himself.

The other day he had bought a cup of rice. When they were ready to eat, Miriam had found ticks and two squirmy mealworms in her bowl. He dared her, and she swallowed the invaders, giggling. Life was hard, but as long as they were together, they could glean small jewels of joy from a bowl of rice with mealworms.

He was humming when Miriam, in her beige shearling trapper hat, opened the door. She was barefoot, holding a fly swatter. He lifted his hands. "Look what I got."

"Tofu? I told you I don't like it. It tastes like dirt."

Miriam was moody. Since they moved to the apartment, he had told her to stay inside for safety. It might be out of his fear or him being overprotective, but after Leah, he was not going to take any chances. Miriam had agreed, especially seeing him wounded, but the confinement was taking a toll on her.

He placed the coal bits and food in the cabinet. "Look, I have a job now. When I get paid more, I'll get you better food."

"Can we talk, Ernest?"

"Later, maybe? I'm tired. It's been a long night." He took off his shoes and coat and dropped on the bed with a groan. He was spent, unable to keep his eyes open. After all these days, he still couldn't get used to staying up all night. "Wake me up at noon, will you?"

"I don't have a watch."

"Fine. I'll get up myself. Do you want to go back to sleep, too, Miriam? It's still early."

"I can't. Too many rats and cockroaches. Do you know how many cockroaches I squashed? Thirty-four!"

To cheer Miriam up, he had started a human-against-pest game.

"That's good. Keep it up, second lieutenant." He yawned and closed his eyes.

"Ernest? Ernest! Don't go to sleep. Talk to me. I have no one to talk to. I have nothing to read. I can't understand what people are saying.

This is so boring. I don't like this life. How long are we going to stay here?"

Miriam was a typical bookworm. At five, she'd read about the well-behaved bunnies Hans and Grete in *Die Häschenschule* and entertained herself with the stories of mischievous Max and Moritz in *Eine Bubengeschichte in sieben Streichen*. By ten, she became an avid fan of Franz Kafka's *Die Verwandlung*. Since schools refused to admit Jewish kids in Berlin, she had read and reread Kafka. Ernest had wrenched the book from her, tired of hearing her scream in her sleep. Kafka was not for kids.

Miriam was lonely. If he were not so exhausted, he would spend some time with her, talk to her, or play a game, but his limbs slackened, and sleepiness crept over him. "I don't know. But Mother and Father will come soon. Remember that."

"Can I go to the club with you?"

"It's not for a twelve-year-old girl."

"I just turned thirteen."

He had forgotten her birthday. "It's not for a thirteen-year-old either."

"But I want to do something. Get a job, like you. Can I get a job? Wake up, Ernest!"

He yawned. "Who will hire a thirteen-year-old? Actually, you should go to school. But I hear the Japanese had shut down Chinese schools, and they are still not allowed to open. Schools owned by the Americans and British might be open, but I doubt there is a Jewish school." He was about to fall asleep when he felt Miriam's hand shaking him, and he caught something she said. "What did you say? Opium den?"

"I didn't know it was an opium den. It was dark inside. Many Chinese were smoking on cots. I thought they were sleeping, but they were holding long pipes. The place smelled so good! Like a flower shop. They almost caught me."

Ernest sat up. Exhaustion, lack of sleep, and fear pounded in his head. "Did you wander to the Chinese area? I told you not to go out. The streets are not safe for girls. What if, what if—"

"It's fascinating, the Old City, so different from Berlin. The buildings had curved eaves perched with dragons, like an emperor's palace in the history books I read. The streets were dirty, and there were many weird things going on. There was a stage for executions or something. I saw a man hanged! Near the temple, some girls were—"

His sleepiness vanished. "Miriam, it's dangerous. You need to stay inside."

"I can't stay here and talk to the cockroaches all day, Ernest."

"What happens if you get lost on the street? Or . . . or . . . God! I have to get some sleep so I can go to work tonight. But you stay in this apartment. Can you promise me, Miriam?"

He heard nothing for a long moment; relieved, he was falling asleep again when he heard a grunt. "You don't care about me."

15

AIYI

Two weeks and five days. That was how long Ernest served the customers. I supposed I should have been pleased, for his humble attitude had appeased everyone—Mr. Zhang and even Mr. Li and manager Wang. But each time I scanned the dancing customers, the drinking men, I was bothered. All my competitors had something to attract customers: Sassoon's Ciro's had the fanciest brandy, Del Monte had the exotic Russian girls, and those small dance clubs had cheap admission fees. My club had no signature feature. Stride piano was my plan to raise my club's competitive edge. But four months would be a long wait.

But I couldn't force Ernest out; I had promised.

I closed the clothbound ledger in my office. I wondered what had happened to me, this indecisiveness.

My Nash stopped in front of a massive walled building guarded by two gray stone lions with carved manes. From inside the high wall, my old butler called that he was coming and pulled open the double wooden gates painted in vermilion.

This was my home, but it belonged to my oldest brother, Sinmay. Our grandfather had built this fifty-eight-room compound in the late 1800s in a prime location inside the Old City, hoping to house many generations of the Shao family. The compound, encircled by high walls mounted with stone dragons, had four wings in four directions, a central reception hall, and a fashionable swimming pool Sinmay had installed. Sinmay's residence, the east wing, included a study, a music room, and a salon where he showed off his poetry collection to his literary friends; my room, an individual building near a koi pond, was located at the west wing near the back. The compound was the last legacy my grandfather had left, poorly maintained and in need of a thorough cleaning, but still a jewel in Shanghai's landscape and an indicator of my family's standing and past opulence.

It was before dusk, the air a swath of gray, the sky pale like rinsed silk, and the century-old ginkgo trees, pines, and oaks—blackened and leafless after the bombing—looked forlorn with their bent limbs. Near the fountain in the courtyard, in a spot reserved for Cheng, was his black Buick. Next to his car was Sinmay's black Nash—so he had returned from his trip out of town. It occurred to me that Cheng must have filled Sinmay in on the goings-on at my club. It made me nervous.

As the oldest of my siblings, Sinmay was the patriarch of the family. If he grew angry at me for hiring Ernest, he might find it a good excuse to drive me out of this house. He'd been looking for an opportunity to kick me out since our inheritance fight. Our clash had started when Mother wrote me into her will, entitling me to a share of the family's fortune equal to my brothers'. Sinmay argued that since women traditionally were not eligible to receive an inheritance, he, the firstborn son, had the right to execute the will his way. I sued him by the law under the new Republic of China, an unthinkable step for many people who regarded lawsuits as scandalous. But I won, and the money was returned to me, and Sinmay never forgave me for shaming him publicly.

Neither of us could have foreseen that we would lose all our inheritance to the ruthless Japanese.

I had thought to move out and live in an apartment, but I simply couldn't do it. It would be a declaration to sever my relationship with my family. Besides, only divorced women, widows, and prostitutes lived away from their families. And now the war had emboldened rogues and gangsters who made a living kidnapping and robbing women like me. I must be accompanied by my chauffeur, who was also my bodyguard, to and from my club. I couldn't go shopping alone or go to the Sincere, my favorite department store. Radio was a memory because it was banned by the Japanese, playing music on a gramophone was a dream because it was restricted by Sinmay, and parties and festivals were forgotten fancies because of food shortages.

The truth was I wouldn't dare to live alone. I was raised to value my family, and family was in my blood. So million-dollar-business owner that I was, I still lived in fear of my older brother, who, at his whim, might make me homeless. This, of course, would never have happened had Mother been alive.

I missed her. Life was not the same without her. Each day I got out of bed, thinking of this hard truth: a family without a mother was like a pearl necklace without a string.

I ducked out of my car, my high heels hitting the ground overlaid with stones in shapes of diamonds and circles. I could hear the clashing of mah-jongg tiles coming from the reception room near the fountain. My siblings, Cheng, and my sister-in-law all held the fervent belief that passing the days by playing the game of mah-jongg would kill the indignity of occupation and possibly heal all wounds of pain.

"Aiyi? Is that you? Come here." The voice of Peiyu, my sister-in-law, came from the reception room.

I had no choice but to turn around and thread down a pebble path, passing the osmanthus evergreen bushes and yellow dahlias that bloomed each spring. On a bench near the gardenia garden, my nephews and nieces were playing under the watch of Peiyu's nanny; behind them, my family cook fetched a live carp from a wooden basin, smacked its head, and began to scale it.

"Who won?" I asked in Shanghai dialect, crossing the high threshold of the reception room.

At a round table, Sinmay was sitting at the east; Peiyu the west; my youngest brother, Ying, the south; and Cheng, the north. No electricity again, so the curtains were rolled up to let the natural light in. Around them, two house servants, all we had left of the twenty we used to have, walked around with small clay jars of stewed chicken bits, milky porridge cooked with red dates and ginseng, bite-sized thousand-layer cakes, and sugar-coated rice crackers. A shabby party before the war, but a decent one in these days.

"We don't know yet. Aiyi, look. Cheng's mother and I finally found an auspicious date for your wedding. It'll be spring next year, a good time. We've started planning. We'll hire a traditional band, put a deposit on a restaurant, and send out invitations," Peiyu said.

She was the matriarch of the family, replacing Mother, now in charge of my wedding. She wore a purple tunic with golden braided frogs. Her stomach was protruding, pregnant with a sixth child, due any day. Peiyu had bound feet and rarely left the compound, but she was a capable woman, negotiating the ever-changing land tax with the rogues working for the Japanese, running the household, and gathering gossip from relatives.

"The traditional band playing *souna*? It's so old-fashioned. I prefer a jazz band, sister-in-law." Planning my wedding was not my favorite topic; it was Peiyu's.

"No jazz band, little sister. Cheng's mother wants a traditional band. What took you so long to get home? Was there another shooting on the street?"

This was all I could do about my own wedding. Tell them my preference, then be overridden by the wishes of Cheng's mother or Peiyu. "Two. It's good you stay at home."

"Aiyi, guess what? Sinmay has questions about the foreigner you hired," Cheng said in a chiding tone. He was always like this, treating me like a child when he grew unhappy with me.

Sinmay glanced my way. He was thirty-four, fourteen years my senior, and in his black eyes was his usual bitterness that had appeared since my lawsuit. Sinmay was a publishing tycoon, the owner of several literary imprints and a newspaper called *Analects*, and also a poet in his own right. He was Cambridge educated, yet he embodied tradition, always garbed in a long gray robe; all he needed was a long pigtail to complete the picture of an old-fashioned scholar from the dead dynasty. "Is that true? I heard there was some kind of brawl in your club," he said finally. His voice, slow and raspy, sounded like a series of scratchy rhythms coming out of an old gramophone.

In front of him, all my womanly craft of feigning and smiling was of no use. I had to be submissive to make him believe he was in charge. "That was a few weeks ago."

"Why did you hire him?"

"Older brother, he's good at the piano, and he's different from other foreigners. He's not biased."

"All foreigners are biased. They don't care about us. The Japanese dropped their bombs on Shanghai, but they all sat in their cafés, admiring the technology of the fighters flying by."

"He's just a pianist." I kept my voice even—Cheng was watching me.

"I didn't know your club had a piano."

"I borrowed one."

"Now, this is most perplexing to me. That someone as shrewd as what people say you are would take such extraordinary steps to jeopardize your own business. I assume you know what you're doing."

I smiled eagerly. "I do. I have a plan. He's going to play a new type of jazz, called the stride piano. It'll be very popular, and the whole of Shanghai will flock to my dance hall."

"That type of music only plays in the Jazz Bar."

"Precisely. Now I'll bring it to everyone." One of the maids handed me a bowl of bird's nest soup on a saucer.

"Eat it. It's delicious," Peiyu said without taking her gaze off the mah-jongg tiles.

Just the distraction I needed. "I'll eat it in my room." I turned around with the bowl.

"Why in such a hurry? I warn you, Aiyi. Let him go. People will gossip. You know how we feel about the foreigners. This will turn into a scandal, a threat to our family's reputation. Aren't you at least concerned?" Sinmay said. "This is a dangerous time for our country. The Nationalists have lost Shanghai and Nanjing, and we are the lamb on the butcher's table. And the Japanese are insatiable! They want to conquer the entirety of China. I hear they will soon bomb the Nationalists' new capital in the heartland."

The Nationalists had been retreating for years; Chongqing was their new capital. "They already bombed it," Ying, my youngest brother, at the south, said.

"Those animals!" Sinmay cursed. "Did you know that dog Yamazaki was promoted? He confiscated our family's fortune, and now he'll lead a division that'll deal with people in the Settlement. Aiyi, if you're also involved with foreigners, you'll get his attention, and you'll lose everything—your customers, your club." He tossed out a tile of nine dots. Peiyu groaned. It was a tile she needed, but with her west position, she couldn't take it.

The name Yamazaki made me tremble. I still remembered the mole under his eye, his repugnant malice. The head of a cavalry unit confiscating the locals' property, he had burst into my home and declared that all my family's possessions were now the property of his emperor. He ordered us to fill out the forms that contained our bank accounts and our shares in a steel company, a railway company, and a silk trading firm, or we'd earn death. He would have confiscated our home, too, if it had not been for my grandfather, who I learned later was friends with the head of the Imperial Kwantung Army before it became a slaughter machine.

I held the bowl. "My club produces lucrative tax for his government. And when people dance, they don't think of revolt. Yamazaki knows it."

"Aiyi, you should think about starting a family. We're good families, and girls from good families don't work to make a living. You are not young anymore." Peiyu's game was not going well. She was grumpy. A traditional woman who believed a woman's role was to be a wife and mother, she disliked that I worked—in an immoral nightclub, no less! She always said I was old, since she believed girls with my upbringing must be engaged at ten, married at fourteen, and give birth to a first child at sixteen. Like her. But I wondered if she wanted me to have children so I could lose my good figure. After five children, soon six, Peiyu had trouble finding her waist.

"When will Emily come for a visit?" I said.

That silenced them all, including Peiyu. Emily Hahn, an American journalist who had moved to Shanghai five years ago, was Sinmay's mistress, which was hardly shameful for Sinmay, since many Chinese men kept concubines. Emily Hahn, to Peiyu, was just like a concubine, but Emily was American, which irked Peiyu.

"Why did you ask that?" Sinmay's gramophone voice sounded stuck.

He had broken the "salt and sugar must not mix" rule. And he had paid for it, shunned by some of his artist friends and business associates. Emily Hahn likely suffered similar punishment, but I didn't really know her very well. I felt a certain camaraderie with her since we both worked, defying the traditional role of women.

"Never mind. I'm tired. I'm going to my room."

"You want to play? I'm winning." Ying winked at me. He was kind to me because I was his lender; he borrowed money from me without any intention of paying it back, but I still couldn't refuse him. Of all my brothers, he was the closest to me, even though he was like a walking firecracker filled with the dangerous gunpowder of youth. He had gotten into trouble fighting, was jailed once, and recently he was seen attending an underground Communist meeting, according to some customers in my club.

"Well—"

"We're not done yet." Sinmay gave me a long look, a warning that he'd had enough. "The pianist. Are you going to let him go?"

"I forgot to mention it. His hand is wounded."

"So he can't even play the piano."

I rubbed my forehead. I preferred not to fight Sinmay, the brother who could decide my fate, but he reminded me that my business was always the priority. There was no reason to pay a sweeper at the rate of a pianist.

"I'll be happy to tell the foreigner to leave, Aiyi," Cheng said, looking rather smug. It was no secret that he, too, resented my running the nightclub. *What kind of man would let his wife flirt with other men?* he had asked when I'd acquired the club. But it was agreed between us that I would manage it before our marriage, and after our marriage I would give it to him and stay home. With this agreement, he had a say in every decision about the club.

I took a deep breath. "No. I'll tell him."

16

ERNEST

He was working backstage when manager Wang called him to the bar and whispered something in pidgin English. Ernest couldn't understand what he said, but manager Wang's worried look concerned him.

Aiyi was sitting at the bar, and Cheng, the well-dressed, handsome man, who Ernest had heard was her fiancé, was smoking a cigarette by her side. An imposing figure with wide shoulders, Cheng wore fine suits and a golden watch. Ernest had seen him a few times and was intimidated by his presence, his wealth, his cultivated finesse, and even his good sense of fashion. It also gave him mixed feelings to see Cheng walk in and out of the ballroom with Aiyi. They seemed a finely matched couple, both with good looks and expensive jewelry. But he noticed the awkwardness on Aiyi's face and the possessiveness of Cheng—his hand was always clasped on her arm as if to stop her from fleeing.

"Ernest, I owe you an explanation," she said, holding a highball glass filled with light-colored liquid, her eyes twinkling in the dim light, her face strained.

His heart sank.

"As you might know, my club has been going through a difficult time for a while, and I was hoping your stride piano could revitalize my business. But you were attacked. It's not your fault, of course. But I don't know how long your recovery will take, and this club is important to me. Many people's livelihoods rely on it . . ."

If he lost this job, he wouldn't have tofu or a bowl of rice with mealworms for Miriam. "It won't take that long. One more week is all I need."

Cheng blew out a streak of smoke, looking as though he rather enjoyed the situation. "You have to go now, foreigner."

Ernest ignored him. "Do you still wish to show customers the stride piano, Miss Shao?"

"Of course I do . . ." She glanced at Cheng.

"One performance," Ernest said. "One chance. If I ruin it, I'll leave."

"But your hand."

"I'll deal with it."

"One week, you say . . ."

"Aiyi." Cheng was frowning.

"Actually, I can play now," he said.

She rubbed her forehead.

"Aiyi." Cheng's voice was louder.

She looked troubled but smiled. "One performance, Ernest. I'll give you that. But not tonight. I must introduce you properly. How about the day after tomorrow? I'll put an advertisement outside the building to make sure people will notice."

Cheng grabbed a highball glass on the counter, gulped the drink down, and slammed it on the bar top. Then he stormed away. Ernest looked at Aiyi. She put a finger on her lips.

Happiness coursed through him—she had sided with him over her fiancé. Maybe she didn't care for Cheng at all. "But may I make a request, Aiyi?" he said in a low voice, hoping the music was loud enough so no one else would hear him. Everything about her was fascinating: the way she rubbed her forehead when she was thinking, the way she talked, the way she walked.

"What?"

"If my performance is successful, will you go to the movie theater with me?" Through the haze of smoke and lights at the bar he could see the curve of her slim body. He was in love with her, and he could hardly control himself. He longed to be a drink in her hand, to enter her, to be inseparable from her.

"Are you taking advantage of my kindness?"

"That's my master plan."

The veil of aloofness slipped off, and a smile rippled across her face. She was the girl listening to his piano in the Jazz Bar again. He wished he could kiss her. Just a kiss.

She stood. "Good luck, Ernest. If your performance goes wrong, I'm afraid you'll need another master plan. Want a drink?"

"Sure." He took the highball glass from her hand and gulped down the liquid. "Good wine."

Her jaw dropped, and she started laughing. And all of a sudden he heard the people at the bar laugh, too. He licked his lips. It was not wine, only cold water.

✦

He listened more attentively to the band that evening than he used to. Jazz was about forgetting, she had said. It was more than that. Jazz was the music of joy, of youth, of personality; it was the music of sweat and tears, of heart and soul. Jazz was freedom.

He itched to play.

✦

On the evening of his performance, Ernest checked his face on the cymbal to make sure it was clean. He had donned his best suit and a black oxford shirt, which he had washed and hung to dry on the headboard in his apartment the previous evening. His shoes were also mud free.

He stepped onto the stage with the band. Through the smoke, he could see Cheng standing on the edge of the round dance floor, smoking, carrying the superior air of a man accustomed to wealth. Even though it was too dim to see the expression on his face, Ernest could feel the sting in Cheng's eyes. Aiyi was sitting at the bar, browsing a clothbound ledger. Then she turned to the round tables around the dance floor and frowned.

He followed her gaze. Only a few heads bobbed in the dark; several men crossed their legs and leaned back in boredom. Her club was indeed having trouble. Would his piano really revitalize her business?

As the band settled in their seats, Ernest sat at the piano and stared at his bandaged hand. He had not worn his glove since the stabbing. He probably wouldn't wear it again; he had no use for it. He was not going to let the scars ruin his future. That was all he cared about, his and Miriam's future. He flexed his fingers. The scar tissue tore at his wound, the dressing crammed between his fingers, and a sharp pain shot through the nerves straight down his arm. But his fingers were still flexible, and it was wonderful to touch the keys. He took a deep breath, let his shoulders drop, and listened to Mr. Li count, waiting for his chance, the rhythm of freedom, the metronome of life.

17

AIYI

I tucked the ledger into my purse and looked around the ballroom. I wore my usual steely expression to give myself authority, but I was so nervous I could hardly sit. Ernest's hand was not completely healed. Forcing him to exert himself might backfire. If he failed, he would need to leave, which would be a sad blow to me, for I would never admit to Cheng or anyone, or even myself, that I had grown attached to Ernest—his humble ways, his boldness.

Someone called my name. I searched among the faces moving in the dark, smoky air. Many customers wore Western suits and trousers; a few adhering to traditional Chinese ideas had on long robes or boxy jackets with mandarin collars. I knew their faces, the regulars. They must have seen the advertisement I put out and decided to give Ernest's stride piano a chance. Mr. Zhang had not visited the club for a few days. I hoped he was gone now.

I turned to my taxi dancers, all trained in popular ballroom dances such as foxtrot, Charleston, waltz, tango, and swing. They yawned in their section near the stage, sunflower seed shells scattered at their feet. Lanyu, the most popular dancer on the customers' demand list, was cracking a handful of seeds between her teeth, shells dropping from her mouth like dust. She had complained she was not making much money the other day.

She was a tall, curvy twenty-three-year-old, the sort of girl who made me self-conscious, the best dancer I'd cultivated. She was flirtatious, and unfortunately, well aware of her worth. If she quit, the other dancers would follow; it would pose a huge problem.

Running a business during the occupation was a constant challenge. There were too many bills and not enough profit. Routinely I haggled with lighting crews, cleaning staff, food providers, and rental contractors. I also supplied my dancers with nice clothes and shoes and paid them to be trained in the latest dance moves. I had yet to pay back the loan to the plaster company that had repaired the roof when the Japanese dropped a bomb on Bubbling Well Road. Then there was a hefty weekly business "tax" paid to the rogues of the enemy government. So many bills to pay.

Ernest's stride piano, with its spectacular sound and novel appeal, would bring more customers to my club and greatly improve my finances—if he succeeded in delivering the magnificent music with that wounded hand of his.

"This is not going to end well. Don't say I didn't warn you," Cheng said, suddenly beside me.

If his warnings could be counted as raindrops, there would be a flood. But what if he was right?

Three gangly boys staggered toward me; they were young, fifteen or sixteen. I had no doubt they received allowances from their grandparents, but I welcomed all kinds of customers.

I slipped off the bar stool and smoothed my dress. With a pearl hairpin, gold leaf earrings, and a gold necklace, I looked sophisticated enough to manage the club but still young enough to be manipulated. A risk I was willing to take; I adored fine clothing and jewelry. "Welcome to my club, young men!"

"Miss Shao, so glad to see you. I saw the advertisement. I hear it's the pianist's first show, so I had to give it a chance. But why did you hire a white man?" one asked, his face covered with red pimples like lanterns.

"Everyone says he is a German sausage. Is he any good?" The second one was cross-eyed.

The third with a loud voice echoed, "German sausage? I thought you said you were a vegetarian, Miss Shao."

I raised my eyebrows. These boys should be ashamed of talking to me like this.

"Fuck off." Cheng, who had turned around, rolled up his sleeves.

The trio stumbled back, recognizing the tailored suit and fine leather shoes. But I didn't want them to be scared away. "Cheng, would you rather go to the office?"

"I'm not going anywhere."

The band was about to start. I walked away, only to face a burly man with a thick gold necklace, who shook his head at me. "Miss Shao, Miss Shao, you shouldn't have. If you fancy meat, Chinese horses are the best, and an old horse outlasts a young stallion. You know the saying: an old horse knows the way. White men—"

"I'm sorry, but I think they're going to start now." I walked to the other side of the dance floor, where I could see Ernest's face. He looked pale, his hands trembling.

Oh no. I should have given him more time. This would be a disaster.

Mr. Li began to count. Then out rang the song "Let's Do It (Let's Fall in Love)."

Ernest cocked his head, listening. Suddenly, as if he had waited long enough, his fingers struck the keys in a quick, infectious succession, and the rich, luxurious, crystallized piano notes poured out. The band seemed surprised; chagrin appeared on Mr. Li's face, but he took down his trumpet a notch and Ernest seized the moment, pounding out ascending arpeggios that seemed like they would never end. The air vibrated, explosive with unstoppable scales. A tantalizing sensation erupted, flooding the dance floor with an effervescence of light and dynamics. People whistled, shouting in surprise; Lanyu and my dancers flowed to the dance floor, arm in arm with their partners.

A stream of euphoria coursed through me. This was real jazz. Ernest had done it.

From near the dance floor, the gangly trio was shouting—"Oh, Miss Shao, this is fantastic."

Then came the yapping of the burly man with the gold chain, pointing at his lap: "This is phenomenal. Look! Miss Shao. It's big, and it's so hard. You must come sit on it. It's not my chair."

Where was Cheng when I needed him? But I was so happy. Ernest was perfect, and the band knew it. Together they played "Summertime," then "What Is This Thing Called Love?" with Ernest taking the lead, the band accompanying, all in seamless harmony, and people swung and laughed on the dance floor.

At dawn the music finally wound down. It was the longest session ever. All gin from Sassoon was sold out. Ernest's piano, as I had hoped, was a huge success. I smiled, and smiled more. And it took me great control to not jump into his arms. So silly I was.

Word of Ernest's spectacular performance quickly spread on the streets. Many people who had rarely entered my club came to hear for themselves. Once they did, they told their friends and relatives. Within one month, a crowd formed outside the building every night, waiting to be admitted.

To maximize the profit, I mixed the rest of Sassoon's whiskey with water and raised the price by a notch. It was hard to believe but nobody seemed to care. The drinks were in high demand, and the dancers took few breaks. Very soon Sassoon's whiskey ran out, too, but fortunately, I found some alcohol on the black market, so I was able to fill every customer's orders. Everyone was happy, my dancers were making money, and profits piled up.

And Ernest was tireless each evening, his face shining in the glow of eighteen thousand lights. His hand was fine, and he knew not to exert himself, he said. He was the maker of joys, his music the golden sunlight on gloomy faces. With the passing of each evening, he grew more famous, his name on customers' lips, his music smoothing the folds on their foreheads.

Even Sassoon phoned to congratulate me after two months. "The stride piano has been quite sensational. I'm rather surprised. You possess admirable business acumen, darling."

I was very pleased with myself. This was the phenomenon I had been dreaming of, and very soon, my club would reclaim the recognition of the most popular nightspot in Shanghai. Then its value would multiply, opening the door for more business opportunities. I could even sell shares of the nightclub and cash out.

I was right all along—Ernest and I made the perfect winning pair; we were meant to be. When he played, I couldn't take my eyes off him, drinking in his music, his smile, his rapt face.

When I arrived home late one night, my old butler told me Sinmay wanted to see me in his study.

"What do you think you're doing, Aiyi?" Sinmay said, sitting at a giant redwood desk strewn with scrolls and four of his study treasures: a black ink stone, a brush, sheets of thin calligraphy papers, and his personal seal. "You said you'd let the pianist go, but why did I hear that all of Shanghai is talking about him?"

"You've heard of it?" I walked to inspect the bust of Sappho in a glass frame, his most prized possession. He had thrown away fifty thousand silver, a small fortune, for that bust. Calling her a goddess, he had composed three poems lauding her beauty and peerless inspiration. But I thought this was his most laughable folly of all, all that money for a plain Greek poetess with blank eyes.

"I do own a few magazines."

"I was going to let him go, older brother. But many people come to listen to his stride piano, so it would be foolish to fire him. He's good for the business—"

"He's bad for our family's reputation."

Sinmay wouldn't listen to me. I was tempted to lie to get out of this. "Who told you?"

"None of your concern."

Did Cheng tell him? Or his poet friends? Emily Hahn? Then it occurred to me Emily would have been the last person who would care about my family's reputation. In fact, Emily could help me. A journalist, she held the great weight of swaying the pendulum of reputation with her words. If she wrote a feature on my club and put out a good word for me, then Sinmay would stop pressuring me. As an additional benefit, her article would help promote Ernest and his status, create buzz, and further increase my club's value.

There was only one problem: Emily, fifteen years my senior, a well-known reporter, could be quite condescending. And frankly, until now, I had not felt inclined to befriend her, a foreigner, out of my concern for Peiyu's reaction.

"Is Emily coming here soon?"

"How am I supposed to know?" Sinmay said grumpily, holding a black calligraphy brush made with wolf fur. "She does whatever she wants. I told her to stop drinking with Sassoon, but she drinks anyway, says she loves whiskey. What's wrong with the sorghum wine? It has more than one thousand years of history!"

He was jealous. Emily had been Sassoon's lover before she was Sinmay's.

It seemed I needed to make a trip to meet up with Emily, and I must talk her into helping me.

18

ERNEST

After months of playing the piano, he could no longer ignore the pain in his hand. The wound that had healed was growing tender again; the muscles in his arm contracted, his fingers were stiff, and it was difficult to find the keys. Ernest went to the Hôpital Sainte Marie for more morphine and chatted with the elderly Catholic nuns, asking them how to stay in touch with people in Europe since he would like to know when his parents would arrive. There was a German post office in the Settlement, the nun with gray hair said.

He thanked them. He would need to find the post office later.

With morphine, the pain in his arm eased and he was able to play the piano again. Each morning he crashed in his apartment with jazz in his ears, and each afternoon before dusk he returned to play, basking in the smiles of the crowd. People treated him with cigarettes—Garricks, Red Peony, Front Gate, the local brands made of coarse tobacco, often soggy from the incessant summer rain. He was no longer called *guizi*, the ghost, but *laowai*, the old foreigner, a friendlier nickname; he loved it.

He was living in a dream where money, adoration, and friends surrounded him, where he was loved, valued, and accepted for being a jazz pianist. Aiyi raised his wage to forty *fabi* a day, and he was beginning to have savings.

With the money he made, he purchased a pair of shoes for Miriam. She had grown withdrawn and irritable since they'd talked months ago; she even stopped asking to go out, which he thought was a good change.

Then one day in June, when he returned, the room was empty.

"Miriam?" He spun around in their apartment. "Miriam!"

He raked his hands through his hair, feeling sick at heart. He should have understood it was too much to ask a teenager to stay inside an apartment all day. Miriam was lonely and bored, and she had run away. If anything happened to her, he would never forgive himself.

Alley by alley, street by street, he searched, shouting at the top of his lungs, "Miriam!"

It was just after dawn; the streets were empty and shops were not yet open. He asked the coal sellers, the noodle peddlers, the night-bucket collectors, the rickshaw pullers, the shoppers, and even the sanitary truck drivers collecting abandoned bodies. They couldn't understand him.

No one would help. Chinese police were nonexistent; Japanese soldiers couldn't care less. He rushed down the streets to the Settlement; near the barbed wire gate, he begged for the help of two enormous Sikh policemen in black turbans. One grabbed him. "I let you go and now you're back!"

It took Ernest a moment to realize this was the Sikh who'd arrested him at the hotel. "You're a good policeman," he said, begging. "Please help me. Please find my sister—a girl with a beige shearling trapper hat." The Sikh policeman turned his back on him.

Ernest staggered to his apartment, his eyes sore from lack of sleep, his right arm throbbing with pain from playing for almost twelve hours straight. It occurred to him how terribly he had ignored Miriam. With the warm weather, she wouldn't be wearing her trapper hat. But he had not even noticed. She had wanted to talk to him, but he had refused. He didn't pay attention to her; he was uncaring; he was not a good brother.

The smell of burning peanut oil made him nauseated, and his head ached. It was afternoon. Soon he would need to go work in the club, but he couldn't play the piano while Miriam was missing. He slumped on a rock in front of his apartment building and dropped his head between his legs.

The image of Leah, bloody, unresponsive, appeared in his mind, and tears poured out of him. He had never told Miriam how Leah died, and in silence, in tears, he had grieved with his parents. He was determined to keep Miriam from the eyes of evil in this world, because Miriam, his innocent, quiet, bookworm sister, should have a life of joy and fairness. But what had he done? If something happened to Miriam, if she were beaten, or abducted or raped or murdered, like Leah, he would never forgive himself.

"Ernest."

He raised his head sharply. There. Miriam, like a dream, stood in front of him, hugging her shoulders, topless. She didn't have on her skirt or shoes, only her underwear. Blood trickled down her nose.

"Miriam! Thank God! You're here! Where were you? What happened?" He ran to her.

Her large eyes were filled with tears. "A thug took my stuff, Ernest. He had a knife."

"Good God." He enfolded her in his arms. "Oh, God. I thought I lost you. I thought . . . I was so worried. I told you not to go out. I told you."

"I'm sorry." Miriam sobbed, her head on his shoulder. "I wanted to get a job like you. Why can't I be like you? But no one wanted me. People aren't nice to me. I tried. I tried so hard. I'm so scared. I don't know what to do."

"It's fine now. I'm here, Miriam. I'm here for you. I'll figure something out for you so you'll have things to do, okay? I'll find a school for you."

Her eyes widened. "There's a Jewish school, Ernest. I passed it. Will you enroll me?"

He took off his shirt and wrapped it around her. He held her close to his heart so he would never forget how precious she was to him. Gratitude and relief made him tearful again. "I will. I'll do anything for you."

The next day after work, he took Miriam to Shanghai Jewish Youth Association School. Founded by Sir Horace Kadoorie, a wealthy Jew in Shanghai, the school was located on the far west end of Bubbling Well Road, miles away from where he lived. It was a one-story building with a courtyard surrounded by a high brick wall. The school taught first grade to eighth, with courses in religion, music, Chinese, and English. Miriam's English was not proficient enough, so she would be put in the sixth grade. But this was the end of the spring semester; she would need to wait to enroll and attend classes in the fall. Enrollment included the registration fee, a monthly fee of five American dollars, and a fee to a host family the school arranged—it was too dangerous for children to commute. A sum of twenty American dollars. Given the accelerating inflation and fluctuating exchange rate between the Nationalist currency and American dollars, he estimated it would be the equivalent of six hundred Chinese *fabi*.

He was in luck, for after all these months of work he had saved just about six hundred Chinese *fabi*.

19

AIYI

I went to Sassoon's hotel a few weeks after speaking to my brother. In the bright lobby, I encountered no hostile foreigners this time, to my relief.

It was easy to spot Emily Hahn, slouching on a burgundy chesterfield near the Jazz Bar, scribbling something on a notepad, her lipstick dark, her eyebrows two dramatic arcs.

Emily, a reporter originally from St. Louis, had published many essays about Chinese people in the *New Yorker*, shedding light on China, an unfamiliar country to many Americans. The only female foreign journalist I knew, she managed to establish her literary reputation among the privileged—and opinionated—Chinese scholars like Sinmay and became the go-to essayist for many foreign publications by writing insightful articles as an American in Shanghai. She had been reporting in Nanjing about the massacre there and also writing a book about the Soong sisters.

Referred to as Big Bottom by Peiyu, Emily was not beautiful to traditional Chinese eyes: her face was too full, her profile too sharp, and she was too tall and fleshy. She didn't have the coyness that Shanghai girls were trained to learn. Her wantonness, as many remarked, was legendary—first Sassoon, then Sinmay. And if I was old to Peiyu at twenty, Emily was ancient at thirty-five.

But I didn't mind what they said about Emily. I had hoped she could be my ally, or a friend—I'd have liked to have a friend, for since Eileen left for Hong Kong, I had been very lonely. When I saw Emily at Sinmay's literary salon six months ago, I had attempted to befriend her by introducing my seamstress to her. But Emily, talking about writing a biography about Madam Soong and her sisters, looked irritated. She blew out a stream of smoke in my face, mocked me, calling me a brainless and boring girl, and shooed me away.

I was not quite ready to forgive her, so I stopped at a good distance from the chesterfield, waiting for a right moment. Then suddenly, she threw down the pen. Her shoulders quavered; a sob escaped her.

Writers, they were like babies. They needed long hours of creative slumber and whined and threw tantrums constantly, but they also needed to be held once in a while.

I dug out a handkerchief from my purse and handed it to her.

She raised her head. Her dark eyes were large and watery, her complexion ghastly pale, like Sinmay's. They were both addicts. "What are you doing here, little girl?" She took the handkerchief, folded it over her nose, and blew into it like a trumpet.

That was how different we were: American women blew their noses like opera, while Shanghai girls like me were taught to play it down to an unnoticeable diminuendo. And being called *little girl* in that unflattering tone was rather humiliating. But I needed her help. "Is something wrong?" I asked.

"What do you care?"

The same old arrogant, whiny Emily, but I knew she could also be perceptive, from all her articles I'd read. I had to put up with her. "Well, if you have time, I'd like to tell you something newsworthy. I hired a pianist. A European pianist. He's the newest sensation in Shanghai. You might want to interview him."

She sniffled. "You come here to tell me that? After you got attacked by the foreigners?"

So she had heard. "They were drunk. They wouldn't be that violent if they were sober."

"Clearly you're going to get yourself killed someday."

I said, a bit nervously, "There's no law prohibiting Chinese hiring foreigners. I'm a business owner; I know. He's brilliant, and customers love him. Besides, I can see you and my brother are mixed very well."

"You have no idea what I'm going through. Your brother ruined everything for me. Now Sassoon doesn't take me to his parties; my friends refuse to answer my phone calls. I'm no longer invited to their salons. I'm ostracized because of your brother."

"But Sinmay said you are still friends with Sassoon."

"Do you see him anywhere? He says he's too busy and won't come down from his penthouse. That jealous goat. He gets his hands on everything, and I find closed doors everywhere I turn."

"Come on, it can't be that bad."

She sniffled and sat up. On her wrist was an emerald jade bangle, a gift from Sinmay, which used to belong to my mother. "I have to go. I have an assignment."

"What do you think about the article? And my pianist? It's newsworthy, you know it. He's changing the way Chinese listen to music."

She wavered through the revolving door and disappeared.

I thought to follow her and talk her into it, but a woman like Emily made her own decisions. I picked up her notebook from the chesterfield. The pages were as clean as snow.

෴

It was raining, an early August shower, damp and chilly, and the drenched roof tiles, neat like nails, lay smooth and shining. Inside my club, it was still hot summer—the heat hugged dancers' naked faces and bare shoulders, and white light brushed at red lips and half-closed eyes. When the sound of the piano streamed out and the trumpets blared, a flood of beats whizzed through the dark hall, seizing the suited bodies, bare legs, and flying hems with a hot, possessive spell.

I was under a spell too. It was hard to focus on the ledger, calculate weekly business tax and hourly wages. Sometimes I did my best concentrating on my work, sometimes I paused to listen, and sometimes I went to the dance floor, watching Ernest. He had been playing the piano for about seven months now, and thanks to him, my club had been turned around, rising in value as it rose in popularity. I had started to talk to some of my well-connected relatives and see if they would be interested in being shareholders. I would like to cash out and invest in gold—the tax officer working for the Japanese was always a pest.

I wanted to invite Ernest to the glass dome on top of the building for a celebratory dinner. Perhaps I would ask him to dance the foxtrot with me, or perhaps a kiss, just a kiss. Nothing more.

Then I noticed. He had his bandages on, the bandages he had taken off months ago. Had he reinjured himself? The band ended the last note to take a break, and the customers went to their seats. Ernest stood up and popped something into his mouth.

I went to him. "What's that? What's wrong with your hand?"

"That's nothing." He smiled, but his hand was trembling.

"Let me see your hand."

He hesitated, then unwound the bandage. The lights were dimmed during the break, but I could see his hand was swollen, and a trickle of blood was seeping through stitches I had assumed were long removed. It seemed with all these months of playing, his stab wound had never healed properly. Yet he had kept going.

"You'll take tomorrow off," I said and raised my hand to stop him from protesting. "No argument."

"As you wish, Aiyi."

But I wasn't done with him. I pulled him near the curtain where we would stay out of the customers' sight. "You should have told me. You're a pianist. You need this hand. Now you have a stab wound and this—how did you get the star-shaped scar?"

"That's a long story."

"Well, you have plenty of time." I was determined. I needed to know everything about him.

"It was a long time ago." He looked at his hand. "I was leaving a cabaret with my sister Leah. Some Hitler Youths came out of nowhere. Five of them. They attacked me and had me under their boots and carved this on my hand. They reminded me who I was and warned me to never play the piano again."

"Why? Was your country under their occupation?"

"Not like that. Mostly because of my religion."

It was hard to imagine people were tormented because of their beliefs. Buddhism had many sects scattered over Asia, yet Mother often said Buddhists believed in peace and discouraged waging war against one another. But I could see, he, a foreigner, a man of a religion unknown to me, was as much a victim of cruelty as I was, a woman in an occupied city.

"But I still have this hand. My sister Leah . . . she tried to protect me. I was able to get away . . . But she didn't come home that day. People said she stole some olives and was caught by the Hitler Youths, but we couldn't find her. We finally found her . . . found her in a trash bin . . ."

The horror and the grief on his face. It tugged at my heart. I had lost my parents and a brother to diseases and an accident. I knew the hollowness that opened in your heart, but to bear this wound of witnessing a sibling lost to violence and human cruelty was a suffering I couldn't imagine.

His eyes were bright. "But you know this saying—love is stronger than death?"

"Never heard of it." I did something scandalous for girls of my upbringing, something startling to myself—I held his scarred hand and kissed it.

The club felt different without Ernest the next evening. Before the session started, in the quiet ballroom without customers, I sat on the bench, his bench, and I imagined the exact spot where his legs parted. I didn't know what was going on with me. It was only one day, less than twenty-four hours, but I missed him. If he had kissed me, or made a hint, any hint at all, I would have taken my clothes off and lain with him, and I wouldn't have cared if that would ruin me.

When I saw Cheng, I couldn't help comparing him with Ernest. Cheng had a solid, athletic build with hard muscles and a grip like a vise; Ernest was slender and artistic with a gentle glow in his eyes. Cheng was petulant; Ernest was daring. Cheng, a scion, had all the riches in his hands; Ernest, a refugee, must fight for his survival—similar to me, struggling in a man's world.

"Are you sick?" Cheng asked.

"No. Have you thought to learn to play the piano?"

His black eyes pierced me. "You're sick, Aiyi."

20

ERNEST

On the day of his break, Ernest was reminded by Miriam to register at the Jewish school since the fall semester would start soon. So he took her to the school. The weather was gloomy, yet he was content, chatting with Miriam, joking with her. They walked for half an hour to a bus stop, took a tram, and continued walking to the school at the west end of the Settlement. He shouldered through the crowd on the street, holding Miriam's hand even though she protested. Now and then he patted the envelope filled with the twenty American dollars in his coat pocket to make sure it was not stolen.

When they arrived at the school's courtyard, he finally let Miriam go in order to meet the headmaster, a man wearing a black apron, who gave him the enrollment form and explained the fees. Ernest paid them all; afterward, he and Miriam went to meet the host family. He was no longer in a joking mood—Miriam would stay with the host family for the semester, and he was having second thoughts. They were strangers, and Miriam was only thirteen, no longer a child but not yet a woman.

They were Americans. Mr. Blackstone, a middle-aged man with a baritone voice, was dressed in a brown flannel jacket, and his wife in a black coat and a black wool skirt. They were Protestants, childless.

It was agreed that the Blackstones would provide lodging and food for Miriam, and Mr. Blackstone, who worked near the school, would drive her in the morning and pick her up in the afternoon.

When it was time for Miriam to leave, she looked at him with an expression that pained Ernest. Since the robbery, Miriam had lost weight, her shoulders now thin and her eyes timid. It seemed all the fire that burned inside her had been extinguished and she was scared about what to do with her new life. "Will you come to see me at school?"

Ernest teared up. Miriam was not the affectionate type. This was perhaps the closest she would come to expressing her love. "Of course I will."

"The headmaster said Sir Kadoorie, the sponsor of the school, would like to throw me a bat mitzvah. Will you come?"

Bat mitzvah was the ultimate honor for Jewish girls as they were called by God, an important coming-of-age ceremony, a recognition for the child becoming an adult. Had they been in Berlin, their parents would have organized an extravagant party, inviting all their friends and relatives to celebrate the occasion.

"Of course. I won't miss it for the world. I didn't know they had bat mitzvah for girls here."

"I didn't know either. Headmaster said Sir Kadoorie was following the practice in America and he didn't want me to be left out. Isn't that nice? You had your bar mitzvah."

"I see. Now you'll need to learn how to read the Torah."

Miriam smiled. "I'm going to learn everything, Ernest. Everything. So you'll come? You'll be my only family at my service."

He held her shoulders and gave her a firm squeeze. "Believe me, Miriam. I won't miss it for the world. If Mother and Father were here, they would come too. They would be so proud of you."

Miriam's smile broadened, and she climbed into Mr. Blackstone's gray Packard. Ernest watched her and waved as she turned to him from inside the car, waved when the automobile began to drive away, and waved until its red taillights were replaced by honking Packards and racing rickshaws.

He looked at his hands; he was not used to this, the emptiness of his hands, which had grasped Miriam's since they'd boarded the ocean liner. But he shouldn't worry. Miriam would be happy and safe at school. There was nothing more satisfying than knowing he had taken care of his sister.

He turned around, humming. When he came to the Cathay Cinema with flashing neon lights, he stopped. Sassoon's cinema was advertising *Gone with the Wind*, boasting it had the best picture quality with English subtitles. Aiyi loved to read magazines with movie stars, he remembered. He wanted to get something for her.

He squeezed past the boys selling cigarettes and legless beggars scooting on the ground and reached a glass frame. Inside were magazines in English, French, and Italian, and near them were posters of the beauty Marlene Dietrich in *Shanghai Express* and the American movie stars Clark Gable and Vivien Leigh in *Gone with the Wind*.

Then he saw it. A magazine with a picture of—him! "Shanghai's Newest Sensation: The Pianist of the One Hundred Joys Nightclub," the headline said. Beneath the headline: "The Chinese club overtook Ciro's to become the most popular spot in Shanghai."

He laughed. He had never been featured in a magazine before, and side by side with the glamorous Marlene Dietrich. What more could he ask for? Miriam was in school, and he was featured in a magazine. He had found a stage in this city. All because of the girl with a name of love.

The next day he went to the club early and walked straight into her office. She was alone, sitting on a tufted high-backed chair. Facing her were two ornate black antique chairs, a framed jade carving, and a bust of Buddha in the corner. The office appeared androgynous, with a serious air of the imperial dynasty's flair, but it carried her scent.

"There you are. Have you seen this?" He gave her the magazine he had bought.

"Ah. Emily actually wrote it and took a picture of you." She held the magazine. "I didn't know. But that's her style. She does it her way. Now you're famous, Ernest."

"Will you go to the movies with a famous pianist? I have tickets. *Gone with the Wind.* I see the posters and murals of it everywhere. The star is not Hepburn, it's Vivien Leigh, but I think you'll like her. She's beautiful, like you."

She swept her bangs to the side and smiled.

He loved to see her like this, and he held her gaze, his heart humming. A space filled with infinite happiness seemed to grow between them, transforming into a bridge of delicate, unsung notes.

"But I can't, Ernest."

"Why?"

"My fiancé will kill me."

He shrugged. "It's just a movie."

"I don't know. I haven't seen it. I hear the main character was married more than once. It's quite unusual, isn't it? Chinese movies would never feature a divorcée, or even a widow remarrying. People here like innocent heroines."

This was another lesson on Chinese perception of women and beauty, he supposed. "Who cares. I'd still care for you even if you married a hundred times."

"Don't say that. It's bad luck. I'd be stoned by my brothers if I married twice. Also, I'll be honest with you. We can never go to the movie theater together. It's almost like a taboo."

"That's disappointing." But he didn't want to leave her yet. He picked up a picture frame on her desk; inside was a black-and-white portrait of a woman wearing a tunic. She had a small face, her expression serene. "Who's this?"

"My mother."

"She's beautiful. You're beautiful, like her."

"Are you trying to get a raise?"

He chuckled. "Will she come here? Will I meet her?"

"I lost her a few years ago."

"I'm sorry to hear that."

"I'll meet her again in another form."

"What do you mean?"

"Reincarnation. She was a Buddhist."

"Buddhist. Do you go to church?"

"Temple. They were all destroyed in the bombing. But it doesn't matter. The temple of faith resides in our hearts."

"So you're never going to go to the movies with me." He put the frame on the desk, walked to her side, and, boldly, he took her hand. The air was warm, maddening, like an anticipation, a prelude of something breathtaking. He ran his fingers on her arm and played "The Last Rose of Shanghai." He didn't exert much force, using long fingers to produce quieter and softer notes. He could feel the smooth fabric of her dress, the suppleness of her body, and the tensing and loosening of her muscles.

He tried to remain stoic, to concentrate on playing, but he began to perspire. His fingers slid and lingered; he didn't know whether he was playing legato, or piano, or forte. And he could hear her, too, her sweet thoughts, her breath, her passionate "Yes."

He held her face and kissed her as she parted her lips and invited him in. He was drunk with happiness; it seemed the purpose of his life was fulfilled at that precise moment, with the taste of her on his tongue and the sound of her gentle groan in his ears. She was open, with unstoppable energy, her hands combing through his hair, her breasts rubbing against his chest. Then she hoisted herself up to sit on the desk.

The tightness of her embrace and the longing in her eyes sent an electrifying fire down his spine. He kissed her chin, her neck, her shoulder, and all the way down to her soft breasts, but it was not enough. His skin tingled with an urge to feel her, skin to skin, tongue to tongue. He bent over, lifted her dress to her stomach, and kissed the soft skin of her inner thigh.

Men's voices came from the hallway outside; he froze, unwilling to separate himself from her, but suddenly the voices pounded in his ears.

21

AIYI

I stood up, pulled my dress down, and parted quickly from Ernest, just before the two shadows appeared at the open door: Cheng in an eggshell-white suit and Ying in a walnut-toned jacket with red suspenders. Ernest turned around to leave, and I swept aside my bangs, making a conscious effort to control my breathing.

Cheng watched Ernest as he walked past. Then Cheng looked at me, his gaze drilling deep into my skin. I didn't know what to say. It was only a kiss, except it wasn't just a kiss, because I had wanted more, and I didn't feel ashamed about wanting Ernest, either. But Cheng, my future husband, must never know. I could feel his suspicion, his jealousy, and his rising anger as he struck a match to light a cigarette, each intake of his breath a curled fist to my face.

My throat burned with nervousness. The perfection of Cheng was as thin as fine silk, and years of being babied by his mother, worshipped by his sisters, cousins, nannies, and servants, and groomed by his late chauvinistic father had created a man with a deep sense of privilege equipped with an explosive temper. I knew well of the subtle lift of his smooth eyelids, the pinch of his full lips, and the stiff turn of his body.

"What's the pianist doing here?" Ying asked.

"He's on a magazine cover. Emily wrote an article about him. Everyone in Shanghai knows him now. He's famous. Here, take a look." I was glad Ying asked.

"How did she know about him?"

"She's a journalist. She knows everything. You are here early today. No mah-jongg?"

"Sinmay said the Japanese thugs interrogated him for hours because he published a forbidden article. They set all the journals on fire. Big loss. Sinmay was in a foul mood, wouldn't play. Want to go play poker?" Ying looked at Cheng.

He was looking down at the two movie tickets that I had not had a chance to hide.

"Let's go," Ying said. "Cheng?"

"Aiyi, you come too."

I sat on my tufted high-backed chair, avoiding Cheng's eyes. The way he spoke frightened me. He must have been suspicious, after seeing the movie tickets. "I have things to do."

"Come with us." Cheng put his hands around my shoulders, so I knew this was not up for discussion.

The moment I got in his Buick, I was trapped. Ying had stopped at the club's bar to get a drink before we left, and I was alone with Cheng. He had dismissed his chauffeur.

"You forgot to wear your bra again." He gave a low growl.

"I'll remember to wear it tomorrow." I looked at the window, but I couldn't see anything with the fabric curtain hanging in the way. I could hear the automobiles, the rickshaws, the oxen drivers, the bicycles, and an echo of a gunshot in the distance.

"Come, sit on my lap," he said. This had been our intimacy, me sitting on him and him exploring me. I had been fine with it. But somehow the thought of Cheng's hands on my skin, the skin Ernest had touched, gave me goose bumps.

"I have cramps."

"Come on, you like this." He swung an arm across my shoulder and began to rub my stomach and my breasts with the other hand. Then he parted my legs, his hand going under the folds of my dress near my thighs.

I crossed my legs. "People will see us."

"No one will see us." He uncrossed my legs. His face, dim in the car, was upon me, his breaths driving away all the air in the Buick.

"I don't want to do this, Cheng."

He stopped. "We're going to get married."

"I want to wait."

He straightened and pulled his tie. "Did you let the foreigner touch you?"

"What are you talking about?"

"Let him go. I don't want to see him in the club."

"I can't. Customers love his piano. Business is doing well."

"Find another pianist."

"It's not that easy. Not everyone can play the stride piano."

Cheng was silent, his black eyes glittering. It was that type of silence when he, as a kid, pinched my shoulder when I refused to do hide-and-seek with him, the silence before he smashed the precious porcelain vases and plates because his dog ran away. I felt nervous.

"I want to go home."

He kicked the seat in front of him; the Buick shook. I shuddered. He was twenty, no longer a boy; and the wildness of his strength and the rawness of his emotions were intimidating. If he forced himself on me, I wouldn't be able to fight him off.

But he took me home. In my room, I scooped up water from a small basin and scrubbed, to rid myself of Cheng, rid myself of my own wretchedness. Finally, I flopped onto my bed. I didn't think I would go back to work today.

Cheng and I were cousins, betrothed since we were in diapers when Mother, a cousin of his mother, thought it would be a beautiful thing to unite our families. We were born in the same month, the same year. Mother had believed it was an ideal marriage, matched in all facets of blood, status, and wealth, a marriage for a golden boy and a jade girl. *You can marry a man you don't love, but you can't marry a man who doesn't have money,* she had said countless times. Cheng had money.

Such an early betrothal was like carrying a precious jade ball that required care and attention; with each step, the weight increased. I was not allowed to glance at other men, not allowed to play mah-jongg with other boys my age. Shopping was done with Cheng's supervision, parties were attended with his accompaniment, and going to the movies required his approval.

It also became clear that Cheng and I were not made for each other. He was overbearing and controlling, often hanging around the racecourse and gambling tables, and I was, as he described, spoiled, selfish, and unable to stay away from the gramophone, jazz, and movie theaters. At least he was fastidious about clothes, so in all our finery we stood together like two carefully pruned trees in a garden, side by side but never intertwined.

As a child, I had adored Cheng, a playmate with whom I fought to ride wooden horses, did tugs-of-war, and played mah-jongg for five pennies. But my adoration of Cheng wore off in St. Mary's Hall. By the time I invested in the nightclub, the connection between us had become tenuous. He made a sport of criticizing me, and I criticized him for doubting me. We only kissed a few times, a chore. When he demanded, I also sat on his lap, and my young body responded with fear and pleasure while he explored. But we had never shared a bed.

I supposed a marriage to him was like the expensive bird's nest soup, the opaque netlike thing that had the texture of jellyfish and was sweetened with hard rock sugar, a delicacy, overpriced, but I had accepted it because Mother had chosen it for me. And never in my dreams did I think I would doubt this marriage because of another man, a foreigner.

22

ERNEST

Out of her office, into the hallway, and onto the stage, he felt dazed, his heart pounding with the sensation of holding her, his mind throbbing with the light of utter bliss. She was the magnet to his thunderbolt, the starburst to his gloominess, and the music to his silence, and unthinkable as it was, the converse was also true.

Only when he heard the voices of the customers did he realize the trap he had spread under Aiyi's feet. She would need to explain to Cheng. It was not his intention to cause a rift between her and Cheng, but all the same Ernest wouldn't mind having her, and he wouldn't mind getting in a fight for her.

He began to play her favorite song, "The Last Rose of Shanghai," ignoring the surprised looks of Mr. Li and the band. This was his confession. His pledge—he was hers.

༄

The next day, in his apartment, Ernest wrote a letter to his parents and enclosed in the envelope a bill of two American dollars, which he had exchanged in a bank near the waterfront. He underlined his address in

Shanghai and asked when they would arrive before sealing the envelope. He had finally located the German post office, so he would send out the letter today.

He missed them. His father, Tevye Reismann, was a man of earth. His face and hands, having been baked in the sun for years, were the shade of dirt; his jackets and trousers were an earthen brown, and when he took off his coat in the parlor, he freed legions of clods of earth. He smelled of earth, even after five cigarettes. An archaeologist, he devoted all his attention to the digs, excavating relics and uncovering runes and often taking months-long trips overseas. He was a taciturn man, rarely wore a tallit except on the Sabbath, and was more attracted to graves and stones than politics and religion. *All men are made of earth: kings and pharaohs, rabbis and priests*, he often said.

His mother, well, she was something else. Her face was a theater of cosmetics with yellow and blue eye shadows, red rouge, and purple or black lipstick, her clothes a whirlwind of colors—emerald green, sea blue, acorn brown, or royal purple. A daughter of a jeweler, she taught theater and was fluent in German, Yiddish, French, and Italian. An extrovert, she could talk up a storm with strangers while shopping for gefilte fish. On High Holidays, she ordered his siblings to the synagogue to sit through hour-long services, but only on High Holidays, for she was too busy with her social commitments. She was like her name: Chava. Life.

A strict mother, she interrogated him about whom he socialized with and ordered him to practice the piano daily. She held high hopes for him. One day, he would win international prizes and become a world-renowned pianist, she believed.

That was before the Kristallnacht, before his father's arrest. At their last Passover, a day after his father had been released from three months' incarceration, looking anxious and haggard, she had observed with one piece of matzah and a deep, reflective reading of the Haggadah. Her usual dramatic voice was stretched tight with tension, and her long black hair, which she often styled in a French braid, was messy. Her head was hung low, her back stiff, her eyes an ocean of sadness.

When she arrived in Shanghai, she would be her extrovert self again. She would without a doubt tell him what to do, too. He wondered if he had said too much about Aiyi in his letter. His mother would definitely discourage him from socializing with her—he could imagine her shock: "A Gentile! A Chinese! Why would you see someone like that?" "You can do better than that, Ernest." "For the love of God, Ernest, can you stop seeing her?" On and on.

But he was not a religious man. He preferred pilsner over schnapps and believed shaving was more hygienic than growing facial hair. He ate chicken that was not kosher and always thought nonkosher food tasted better. He became a bar mitzvah, but after the party he kept the money and forgot both baruchas of the Torah. He didn't care that Aiyi was not Jewish. She wore a dress of finery and aloofness, but she was truer than any woman he had ever met.

23

AIYI

The next morning after kissing Ernest, I finally put on loose trousers and a long tunic and went to the reception hall to talk to Peiyu. My eyes were swollen from crying, my hair messy; in the calmest voice I could muster, I told her about Cheng in the car.

Peiyu was eating sweetened lotus seed soup with dried chrysanthemum blossoms. She had given birth to a baby girl in the spring. For several months, she had stayed in bed, and today was the first day she succeeded in making the longest march from her bedroom to the reception hall.

"I see. Cheng must be angry. What did you do wrong?"

"I didn't do anything!"

She spooned some soup into her mouth. Each time after she gave birth she had the lotus seed soup for six months and then complained about her waist. "So he stopped when you told him. What's the matter? He didn't force himself on you. Nothing happened. He's a young man, and young men have urges, they have needs; they're different from women. Besides, your wedding is next spring. I've had the invitations printed. They're in the drawer. Would you include a note and your personal seal with each? Have you tried this soup?"

I was speechless. Had I overreacted?

Another spoonful of soup. "He's waited long enough."

I couldn't argue with that. We would have wedded years ago had it not been for the sudden deaths of my parents, the sudden war, the sudden occupation, the not-so-sudden dwindling wealth of my family, and the must-not-be-so-sudden process of finding an auspicious date for marriage, which included considerations of our birth dates and our animals and the signs of the Heavenly Stems and Earthly Branches.

"I'm leaking again. Where's the baby? I shouldn't have let the wet nurse go. Don't forget to mail the wedding invitations with your notes and personal seal, Aiyi." She waddled away on her tiny, bound feet.

I took out the stack of invitations and placed them next to the lotus seed soup. It was my marriage, my future, except it felt like a time bomb.

"What's wrong?" Emily Hahn stood in front of me. Her voice was husky, like smoke, and slow, like Sinmay's. But she looked sober, her eyes discerning. She wore a navy-blue cotton shirt with sailor front and wide-legged black trousers with a sash, the style of my favorite movie star, Hepburn.

"Nothing." I gathered the invitations. She didn't come here often.

"You won't thank me for the article?" She went to sit on a rosewood chair, a gift from the late empress of the bygone dynasty.

Emily had done a lot for my family. When the Japanese won the war, they had tried to confiscate Sinmay's printing press imported from Germany, which had the world's most sophisticated technology. Without it, his publishing business would collapse. Emily went to great lengths to save it. She produced a marriage certificate with Sinmay, sealed by the American consulate, and argued that the printing press belonged to her, an American citizen, so it couldn't be confiscated. And she succeeded. She relocated the press to a warehouse in the Concession, essentially saving Sinmay's publishing business.

"I suppose so, but was it a favor?"

She lit a cigarette. "You're right. It wasn't. I wrote that because it was newsworthy, like you said. So thank you for the lead, little girl. Frankly, I was rather surprised. An aristocratic Chinese woman who had the audacity to hire a Jewish refugee, who somehow won over the motley crew of locals. I didn't expect that. It was a good article. You're a businesswoman, a woman with brains. You've grown up."

A surprise to hear that from her, and gratifying. Perhaps Emily would be my friend now. I longed to have a friend again—to go shopping, get a drink in a bar, or go to tea. "So will you not call me *little girl*?"

"It's a term of endearment, but fine, Aiyi."

Her Chinese was impressive. She even got the tones of my name right. "So you saw my pianist. He's brilliant, could you tell? A brilliant pianist. I've never met anyone like him."

Emily gave me a look. In that instant I knew why she could make a living as a journalist.

"A warning, Aiyi. Falling in love is like teetering on the edge of a precipice blindfolded. It's wonderful, but it might cause life-threatening injuries."

"I don't know what you're talking about." Fortunately, Peiyu was not around.

"You don't like me talking about your secret? I'll tell you mine."

"You're pregnant."

She nearly choked on the smoke. "What made you say that?"

"You rarely come here. It must be something important."

"So you assume I'm pregnant? Why do you Chinese like children so much? Sinmay wants me to get pregnant. He said Chinese people love children."

"Not me." I disliked those infinitely annoying brats. Once my nephew had set off a firecracker in my bedroom, and another nephew had added rat droppings to my tea. Not to mention all the candies they stole from my drawer. "I'll never have children."

She shrugged. "I came here because I'm miserable. I don't like Shanghai anymore. I used to be loved by poets and plutocrats, female friends and male friends. Look at me now, ostracized, lonely, and poor." She was the woman on the chesterfield again, distant and irascible.

"Come on. It's not that bad. You still have your job."

She sniffled, and her husky voice was drenched with sadness. "Actually, I just lost it."

I didn't know what to say.

"I guess the saying is true: salt and sugar should not mix. Remember that." She laughed, her mouth open, pink tongue visible, and her voice, untrammeled, all sadness.

Sinmay walked in, his long robe swaying. "There you are, my love. You look like you need a good smoke. Shall we?"

"I can't live like this anymore. I want to leave. You must go to Hong Kong with me, Sinmay. I beg you. If you don't go with me, I'll die." Her short hair bounced around her ears, her lipstick flat like a scar.

Sinmay whispered in her ear. There was agony in his eyes, I believed. As selfish a brother as he was to me, he loved Emily—but he was the father of six children, the firstborn son of the Shao family.

It dawned on me—they were trapped. Emily was miserable in Shanghai, and Sinmay was miserable for her. *Is this what happens when you choose someone who's not your kind?* I took the invitations and left.

In my bedroom, I started a fire in Mother's incense burner and threw them all into the flames.

24

ERNEST

A few days later, Ernest finished his work and stepped down onto the tessellated floor in the empty atrium. He was ready to head out when someone called him from behind. Cheng descended the marble staircase, his black-and-white leather wing tips smacking against the stairs like an out-of-tune song.

"You're fired," Cheng said.

Ernest thought he must have heard wrong. The business was doing well, and Aiyi was pleased. "I don't understand."

"You're fired. Understand now? Do not come here again."

Ernest was worried. He needed this job to support Miriam, and he didn't want to leave Aiyi either. Cheng, who disliked him, must be suspicious, and Ernest had no love for his boss's fiancé, either, a petulant and possessive man. He wished he could ask Aiyi, but she was said to be under the weather and hadn't come to work since their kiss. "Does Aiyi know this?"

"If you see her again, I'll kill you."

Cheng rolled up his sleeves.

He was acting like a spoiled schoolboy. If they must fight, so be it. Ernest took a step forward. "If I win, I'll stay."

Cheng's blow was quick and heavy; Ernest shook it off. A kick from Cheng struck his stomach, making him groan. But he got even when he thrust his leg under Cheng and tripped him. Cheng fell flat on his back, cursing.

Grinning, Ernest extended his hand. "Peace?"

Cheng's eyes were murderous, but he took his hand, the bandaged hand, and instead of getting up, he pulled Ernest down and slammed on it with his elbow.

Ernest screamed, rolling on the floor, blinded by the excruciating pain. Through his fogged vision, Cheng's handsome face appeared above him. "Fuck off, foreigner."

Ernest got up and staggered out on the street. It was a cold morning; the predawn air flew around him like dark water. He had lost the fight and lost the job, the job that supported Miriam. And the apartment. Would he be evicted? He had no savings left.

And Aiyi. He had not had a chance to see her since he kissed her.

꧁

He was stumbling down the street when he heard a gentle voice say, "Tough day?"

He looked up; the Sikh policeman who had arrested him was smoking by the tram stop.

"Good morning, sir," he replied warily. "Everything all right?"

"Couldn't be better. Don't worry. I'm not here to arrest you. They have the best samosas on this street. Cigarette?" He glanced at Ernest's bandaged hand. Blood had drenched the gray dressing, staining his sleeves.

"Thanks." Ernest shivered. The pain in his right hand was unbearable, and his fingers were numb. He tucked his hand close to his stomach and took the cigarette with his left hand.

The Sikh lit it for him with a fancy silver lighter. "Wipe your face. You've got blood all over it."

The Sikh might be the bulkiest man in Shanghai, but he had the gentlest voice. A good policeman, despite all that had happened between them.

"I'm Ernest Reismann, sir."

"Jyotiraditya Mirchandani. Call me Jyo."

"Jyo." Ernest smoked, staring at the street where one-wheelers, bikers, and tofu vendors began to emerge. Coming toward him was a truck loaded with Japanese soldiers in khaki uniforms, holding their rifles with bayonets. "I lost my job today."

"Tough day."

The truck passed; several soldiers fixed their gazes on his face and bloody bandages.

Jyo pulled his arm. "Turn around and keep walking, Ernest."

"What's going on?"

"Nothing to be alarmed about. There was a skirmish between the Japanese soldiers and the members from the council last night. Luckily we were there, but a fellow officer shot a soldier. The Japanese are investigating. It has nothing to do with you, but it's better to stay out of their sight. Avoid them if you can."

Ernest nodded. They were now in an alley. "Don't go. Let's finish this cigarette."

In his apartment, it occurred to him that the next day was Miriam's bat mitzvah. So he got up early in the morning, washed up, and put on his last good oxford shirt, taking great care with his right hand—it was swollen and painful. He feared another trip to the hospital was needed.

When he went to the school, Miriam shuffled toward him wearing his other oxford shirt, the only decent shirt he'd given her, and black pants. She looked miserable.

"Are you ready?" When he found a job again, he would buy her decent girls' clothes.

"You're too late, Ernest."

"What time is the ceremony? You said it was in the morning, wasn't it?"

"It was. But the ceremony was yesterday. Yesterday!"

He wanted to kick himself. He had forgotten Miriam's bat mitzvah. And she had gone through the most important ritual in her life alone. "I'm so sorry, Miriam. I've been—"

"You don't care about me. Nobody cares about me. The service was horrible. It wasn't like a boy's bar mitzvah. They didn't have a full aliyah to the Torah, they had all of us crowded together, and they wouldn't let me read the Torah." She sobbed.

"But it's still—"

"This place hates me; everyone hates me."

Poor Miriam. She had wanted to get a job but was robbed, then wanted to have a proper bat mitzvah but had her heart broken. No reading of the Torah, no attendance of her family.

He apologized, over and over, but Miriam just sobbed and sobbed. When she finally calmed down, he asked her about school. She replied in her listless voice that she studied prayers, music, and the English language, and she'd just started to play the violin. She wanted to take the Oxford and Cambridge overseas examinations before her graduation, because Mr. Blackstone said once she passed them, she could go to Vassar College in America. Mr. Blackstone even let her borrow his Webster dictionary, and she had been reading it before bed every night.

"America?" That was where Mr. Blackstone was from, but it was far.

"That's what Mr. Blackstone said."

"Well, he's a good man. You should be grateful to him. I'm grateful to him." Ernest made a point of telling her, even though he didn't know much about the man with a baritone voice. "How's Mrs. Blackstone?"

She had migraines, disliked noise, and lay in bed all day. But they ate well, had peas occasionally, a glass of milk every day, and meat loaf every Sunday, Miriam said, her voice monotonous.

When it was time for her to leave, Ernest tried to give her a hug, but she turned away, gave him a cold stare, and left.

Near dusk, Ernest went to the nightclub. He wanted to see Aiyi and explain why he wasn't in the club. Perhaps he could get his job back. He needed money desperately to pay the school's monthly fee, the examinations Miriam mentioned, his hospital visit, and of course, the rent. But most importantly, he wanted to see Aiyi.

When he arrived in front of the building, manager Wang greeted him, his eyebrows two squiggles of apology. Ernest was probably the only foreign friend he would have, he said, but he couldn't allow Ernest to enter the club. Cheng had given his order.

"Is Miss Shao feeling better?" Ernest asked.

Manager Wang shrugged.

25

AIYI

Two days later, I returned to work. But Ernest was gone. I was furious. For the first time in my life, I argued with Cheng. "Why did you let him go? Didn't you see how successful he's made my club?"

"The club will be fine without him," Cheng said in his low but fuming voice.

"You shouldn't have done that. This is my club."

"I'm your fiancé."

"I'm going to hire him back!"

Cheng pulled his purple tie and glared at me with a look like an animal that was ready to bite but was holding back. "Then I'll fire him again."

I took my purse, ran down the staircase, and got in my Nash. I told my chauffeur to drive to Ernest's apartment as fast as possible. As the car wove through the narrow lanes, veered around the red-brick buildings, and rushed by the plane trees, each squeak of the rickshaws, each honk of the trolleys, and each creak of the ox carts pierced me with fear that I would never see Ernest again.

I found his apartment—he was still there! "Come," I said, beckoning him.

"Aiyi! I was fired, did you know?"

He looked pale but happy, his eyes clear like fine blue glaze on a porcelain vase. "I just heard. This is upsetting. But would you come with your former employer?"

"Where are we going?"

"To the cinema."

But when the Nash arrived at the Cathay Cinema with its movie posters, I told my chauffeur to keep driving.

It was a small inn, a one-story building hidden among rows of residential homes in an alley, a place for secret rendezvous, a temporary shelter for poor out-of-towners before they got on their feet—nothing like a luxury hotel.

With steady steps, I walked in and asked for a room from the proprietor, a short woman with a bun, who kept glancing at Ernest beside me. Once we entered the room, I bolted the door, kicked off my high heels, and kissed him with the recklessness girls of my upbringing were lectured against, the boldness that seemed to be part of him, the keenness that was unfamiliar to me. I was happy, grateful, and I never wanted him to leave again.

"I love you," he said, his body a powerful instrument inside me.

Throbs of happiness, relief, and gratitude flowed in my veins. A virgin I had been, but no more. I was glad. This was what I wanted, his face, his voice, his arms, his embrace, all of him. I kissed him, leaning against his shoulders, close to his heart, to his skin.

"From now on, I'll go where you go, I'll lie where you lie, I'll love what you love." His voice was the most beautiful music to my ears, and I ran my hands over his bandaged hand, his arms, his hard muscles, his pale shoulder. I laughed.

"But I don't want you to go anywhere. You'll stay in the apartment I rented, won't you? If you move to another place without telling me,

I won't be able to find you. Besides, it'll be a waste of money. I already paid for another year."

"I'm not moving anywhere, but I'd like to work. I'll find another job."

"You can't. Not yet. Let your hand heal first. Take two months off, or as long as you need. I'm serious. It doesn't look good," I said. "And you'll do as I say, because once your boss, always your boss."

He chuckled. "Marry me, Aiyi."

Now I could see Mother's photo and Cheng's angry face. Since I was little I'd been told that I, a woman, belonged to my parents before marriage and would belong to Cheng after marriage. To Cheng, I had committed an unforgivable sin. "I can't."

In my club, I went about my routine. When guests asked about Ernest, I said he was taking a break, assured them of his return, and encouraged them to buy more drinks. The customers were disappointed, but my promise was enough to make them keep coming, and the dance floor was full each night. I had also secured more alcohol from the black market.

It was difficult to face Cheng. Out of guilt, I listened to him with great patience and even put on the Chinese bra to please him. Cheng's gaze, as usual, was critical, but his reticent nature spared me from many moments of awkwardness. I might be wrong, but I didn't think he suspected me of deceiving him.

In my office, looking down at the Japanese military jeeps racing on the street, I swung my hips, humming jazz tunes. My club was enjoying a gratifying revival of popularity, and I had found myself a new obsession in Ernest. It was unconscionable, and it was possible that potentially serious consequences awaited me. But who would say it was wrong to indulge in a song from your heart during the winter days of your life?

26

ERNEST

On a humid November morning, he walked toward the waterfront, the wind tousling his long hair behind his ears. He glanced at a restaurant's glass window. A man with shoulder-length curly hair and a beard glanced back. He rubbed his chin. He had not shaved for two months; he looked clean at least, older and distinguished, like a man in his thirties. Not bad for a pianist.

Since he'd gone with Aiyi to the inn, he had seen her again several times. Each time after their meeting, he dreamed of her: her supple body, her smooth porcelain face, and her teasing smiles. She had insisted he take a break from work, providing him with financial support so he could heal his hand completely. Following her advice, he had gone to the hospital again. The Catholic nuns had taken a liking to him. They taught him French, told him about good French restaurants in the area, and sent him away with extra bandages, aspirin, and even laudanum. His hand was healing like a miracle. The muscle contraction subsided, the trembling stopped, and the stiffness faded away.

Miriam was still at school. When the winter break started next month, she would come to stay with him in the apartment, which was pest free thanks to his good care and diligence. With all the time he had, it became a habit to walk to the wharf where the ocean liners docked, where he would meet his parents when they arrived. He didn't know when they would arrive because he'd never received a reply from them. Still, each day he waited with eagerness, with hope. To pass time, he brought his Leica with him. Unwilling to waste his last film, he took few pictures, only exploring the city through the viewfinder, where the images of Packards and Buicks and the flow of the people calmed him.

He had been in Shanghai for close to a year, and he would turn twenty in a month. He liked this city, clothed in gray smoke mixed with odors of peanut oil, engine fumes, and women's perfume, and noisy with human voices, rickshaw squeaks, and trams' thunderous clunks. How strange the world was. In Berlin, he'd been forbidden to play the piano; here he was known as a pianist. In Berlin, he'd been haunted by nightmares and pain; here he was free to dream, free to love. He had thought to return to Germany eventually when he first arrived in Shanghai; now he would not leave. This city was his home now—she was his home.

He could speak some Shanghai dialect, some simple Chinese phrases, and even some expletives. Chinese was a challenging language, with erratic tones and messy grammar, but he supposed German was equally exhausting to a foreigner. Strangely, to him, English—which he had learned from his father—was sensible, with a reasonable degree of bewilderment.

When he arrived at the pier, a horn from an ocean liner sounded. His heart racing faster, he dashed to the edge of the pier, watching intently. The river hadn't changed since his arrival, still a roiling yellow sluice, a parking lot for banana-shaped skiffs with cages of chicken, coal-stained sampans loaded with barrels of petroleum, and commercial boats. On the distant wharf across the river, where an ocean liner docked, a stream of refugees carrying suitcases walked down the gangway.

He caught sight of a yellow dress and cried out in elation. "Mother! Mother! Chava!" That sunflower-yellow dress was her favorite; she had been wearing it on the train platform when she saw them off.

"Chava!" He cupped his hands around his mouth, shouting. Happiness chugged inside him like an engine. She had received his letter and arrived. He couldn't wait to embrace her, to dance a hora. But the figure didn't turn in his direction and disappeared among a group of men in black coats and hats, just as he caught a glimpse of a cadaverous face. She was not his mother.

His heart sank. Where was she? And his father? Had they received exit visas? Had they left Germany yet? They must leave as soon as possible.

But maybe they had left for another country; maybe they were still on the way to Shanghai. They had received his letters, they knew his address, and they would find him.

He turned around, facing the Japanese warship *Izumo* docked nearby, a massive gray superstructure with gun towers and three immense funnels spilling columns of black smoke. He had seen the warship with the rising sun flag and had rarely paid attention. But now he could see rows of marines in white robes wielding swords in a slow and solemn ceremony, their shouts, strange and piercing, hovering over the turgid river like a cloud.

Izumo was not the only warship on the river. Downstream, far away from the Japanese warship, behind sailboats, sampans, and other ships, were two cruisers: the American USS *Wake* and the British HMS *Peterel*. Three gunboats, each belonging to a different country, docked on a river that belonged to none of them.

27

FEBRUARY 1941

AIYI

One evening when I passed the coatroom, I heard some passionate groans coming from inside it. Which only meant one thing.

Dancers: they were always trouble. They were the beacon of my business in good times and the shipwreck in bad. When I'd bought the club, ballroom dancing was already popular, but the business wasn't stellar as the guests needed to bring their own partners. My hired taxi dancers solved the partner problem and brought in extra revenue. In effect, I created the first professional ballroom dancers in Shanghai, who then became independent breadwinners.

I stood at the counter of the coatroom and coughed. I had a strict rule that my dancers must not act improperly with customers. My club was not a brothel.

The groans ceased, and a figure appeared from inside. Lanyu, the most popular dancer, buttoned the knots at her neck. "Oh, Miss Shao. I was changing my dress."

I could fire her for this. But she had lost her mother and two siblings during the bombing, and she was supporting her father with her wage.

"Next time, change your dress alone." I let her go on with her work.

She skidded away, giving me a look of gratitude. I hoped she would make things easier for me from now on.

I was near the bar when I glimpsed a man in a bold chalk stripe suit standing on the edge of the dance floor, facing the stage. The light shifted, shining on his face. A sharp countenance with a sharp jaw, a black mole under the right eye. The enemy of my family, the enemy of my country.

"Miss Shao." In a few strides, Yamazaki stood in front of me. He looked courteous, and his voice was placid, mild, but fear surged through me.

He was a maniacal Spirit Warrior but pretended to be a Bushido-biding samurai. He gave perfect forty-five-degree bows, cleaned his hands with a fresh cloth before meals, and used a hand, never a finger, to indicate the direction. He never blew his nose in public or raised his voice. But I knew courtesy was only his garment. He was a dangerous man.

Yamazaki was from Osaka, Sinmay had said. Son of an impoverished rice farmer, he grew up in Japan's victorious afterglow over their defeat of the Russian Baltic fleet in 1905. At school, he learned about land mines, explosives, and machine guns in science, battle games in PE, military matters in arithmetic, and the principles of bravery in combat and absolute loyalty to his emperor in ethics. At eighteen, Yamazaki joined the Kwantung Army, part of the merciless Imperial Japanese Army, to obliterate China and Korea in his country's bloody quest to expand their territory. He rose from a delivery messenger to eventually a cavalry officer who confiscated my family's fortune. Now Yamazaki, Sinmay had said, was involved in supervising foreign businesses in the Settlement.

I had prayed to never see him again. The muscles in my face grew tight, and for a moment I was too petrified to speak.

"Why are you playing this rubbish jazz?" His Chinese was too good for a Japanese.

"Ah. It's American music," I replied.

It felt surreal to be in the proximity of a mad dog that would bite any second. But I knew why Yamazaki was patient with me. A typical Spirit Warrior, he believed in hierarchy. His emperor was the highest, followed by the aristocracy, the army, and the peasants, and then at the bottom, the untouchables such as the butchers and the undertakers. Aware of my family's reputation and my social standing, he had decided to give me, an aristocratic woman from the country his army had conquered, a share of his patience, but not respect.

I wished I had the right to kick him out, but instead I was forced to stay calm for my clients' sake. They obviously hadn't realized yet that Yamazaki in his business suit was Japanese, or they would have panicked. With daily shootings and beheadings on the street, the last thing they wanted was to see a Japanese officer in the ballroom.

"Lowlife people's music." Yamazaki frowned, scanning the dance floor.

I couldn't figure out why he would deign to come here. He still remembered me, so he must know he had confiscated my inheritance, and he must know this was my business, too, since I paid a hefty business tax each week to the local tax office. "If you don't mind, I'll go tell them to play a different song."

"You'll stay right here and tell me, Miss Shao." He looked directly at me, his cold eyes level with mine—he was quite short, but his clear contempt made my blood boil. "Where's the white man?"

"I don't quite understand what you mean."

"Chinese are all whores and liars, but I think better of you, Miss Shao. Don't make me draw my gun." He turned up a corner of his suit, revealing the round barrel of his black Mauser in the holster.

My brain froze.

"The man who was on a magazine. I hear he works here. There is a warrant for his arrest."

Arrest? Ernest? "The pianist? He worked here. He was very popular, following all rules. The tax officers know about him." Hiring him was not breaking the law, I wanted to add. "Is there some kind of mistake?"

I was distracted. People around me had noticed the gun; they gasped and slipped away. On the dance floor the dancers skittered off; meanwhile the band played frantically. This was a disaster. Everyone had realized a Japanese, with a gun, was talking to me. It wouldn't take long before they all fled.

"I don't make mistakes, Miss Shao. A few months ago we had a dispute with the Towelhead policemen, and one of our soldiers was killed. The murderer was wounded and escaped. We don't know who he was. We only know he was a white man with blue eyes, recruited by those policemen. We've been looking for him. After months of investigation, we have a witness saying that the morning after the murder, your pianist was seen with a Towelhead on the street. The pianist's face was bloody, his hand wounded. He has blue eyes. The descriptions match."

This sounded so farfetched, but Yamazaki wouldn't need to lie to me. Still I couldn't believe it. Ernest was not a violent man, and he wouldn't shoot anyone.

"Where is he?" Yamazaki demanded.

"He left." Ernest's hand had healed slowly, but each time I brought up the topic of hiring him back with Cheng, Cheng refused. I was going to risk Cheng's wrath and rehire Ernest since some customers had stopped patronizing my club.

"Why did he leave?"

"I don't really know. He wanted more money, maybe."

"What's his name?"

I bit my lip. He already knew if he had read the article. Emily had stated Ernest's name. But Yamazaki wanted the affirmation from me.

If I told him, Ernest would be in danger. But if I refused, I would be dead. "Ernest Reismann."

"Liceman, Liceman," he murmured in his heavy Japanese accent. "Where's he from? America? England?"

I lied. "I don't know where he's from . . ."

He pulled back his hand and covered the Mauser with his suit jacket. "He will be punished for his crime. Bring him to me."

"I don't know where he is."

"You'll find him. Then you'll bring him to me, or I'll confiscate your club. Is that clear?"

His voice was low pitched, and his tone wasn't threatening, just casual, but it was the casualness of a man watching a fish caught in the pond of his own garden. He strode out of the ballroom.

I went to the bar and poured myself a glass of adulterated sorghum wine and emptied it. The alcohol ran down my throat; a hot streak burned my stomach. I put my hand on my chest and gasped. I was still alive.

When I raised my head again, the laughter, jazz music, and dancing had ceased. The dark figures at the tables had vanished, and the bright light from the vaulted ceiling showered on the empty dance floor like flakes of pale skin.

My body was so stiff I felt a great pain in my neck. *Bring him to me, or I'll confiscate your club.*

Cheng, Ying, and I argued about what to do in my office.

"Give him the foreigner," Cheng said, a cigarette between his fingers.

I sat on my high-backed chair. "I don't know where he is," I lied. "You fired him."

"If you don't give him the pianist, you'll lose your club."

"You think I don't know that?" The band was playing "Summertime" in the ballroom, each beat giving me a pounding headache. Should I tell Yamazaki where Ernest lived? If I refused, he would take my club, but if I gave Ernest to Yamazaki, he would kill him.

"I'll take care of Yamazaki," Ying said, his hand on a bulge in his jacket pocket. He made me more nervous than ever. The Japanese had fighter jets and guns, and we had nothing. Confronting Yamazaki would get us all killed. Fighting was not a solution. Giving him Ernest was not a solution. Letting him seize my club was not a solution. There was no solution.

I went to Ernest's apartment the next morning. I trusted him. Busy playing in my club all night, he wouldn't have had time to conspire with the policemen. But it was necessary to get to the bottom of this.

It was an overcast day, the air pale like smoke. In the alleyway of Ernest's apartment, I waited long enough to be aware of the stares of tattered beggars. He was not in his apartment. I finally left. The next evening, I went there again and found him. I asked my chauffeur to leave so Ernest and I could be alone in the car. A loyal man whom I trusted with my life, my chauffeur nodded and waited outside on the street.

"Were you involved with a Sikh policeman?" I asked Ernest.

"Jyo? He's a good man. We came across each other a while ago. Why do you ask?"

I told him about Yamazaki's visit to my club, his claim, and his threat.

"Murder a Japanese soldier? I don't know what he's talking about."

Yamazaki had the wrong man, just as I had thought. "You must be careful," I warned Ernest.

He nodded, but he looked worried. "What about your club?"

I didn't want to think about that. I cupped his face in my hands and kissed him instead. I never considered myself a loose woman, but I couldn't keep my hands off him. I sat on him, lost in his kisses, hungry for his touch. I made love to him with my shoes on.

Four days passed since Yamazaki's visit. In the dark, cigarette-scented ballroom, the band slumped beside their instruments and the managers whispered in a corner. On the dance floor, dots of lights glittered like lost silver; along the walls, empty tables cast shadowy figures like land mines. I walked across the teak floor, my high heels leaving a trail of dull, hollow beats of sound.

Yamazaki's visit had spooked the customers. This empty ballroom would be a painful sight for months, and the loss of business would haunt me. It would take a while for people to overcome the fear and return.

But even this bleak ballroom was a luxury. As days went by, Yamazaki would no doubt lose patience, return, and seize my business if I couldn't give Ernest to him.

That evening, I went up to the building's rooftop with a glass of brandy mixed with soda.

The streets were dark, the night pregnant with silence. With the shifting lights from windows, I could see the faint contours of houses and villas, the palisades of shops, and the foggy domes of plane trees. There was no rustling of night creatures or rumbling of machine guns or clunks from railroads—a rare moment of quiet, peace, filling my heart with the wonder of the otherworldly dawn of what-ifs. What if I didn't have to choose? What if there were no Japanese in Shanghai?

28

ERNEST

Ernest walked up to the landing of Sassoon's hotel, the same landing he had stepped on last year, and slid through the revolving door. The lobby looked just as he had remembered: golden, elegant, sparkling with marble and glittering with expensive decor. Once again, he came here looking for a job. His hand had healed completely, and he was anxious to play the piano. But when they were in the car, Aiyi had said, for his safety, it would be best if he worked in another place.

There, just a few paces from him, the old man, clad in his usual top hat and tails, holding the walking stick, limped across the lobby. Sassoon had a camera hanging around his neck and was followed by an assistant hauling a tripod.

"Good afternoon, Sir Sassoon," Ernest said with an easy smile. However brusquely Sassoon had treated him, he bore the man no ill wishes or rancor.

The man stopped. "Young man, I've met you before. You look familiar."

"Yes, indeed, sir. I asked to play in your Jazz Bar last year. I'm a pianist." His eyes were on Sassoon's camera. It was an old-version Leica. His own camera was superior.

"Do you need a job? Wait. Aren't you working for Miss Shao?"

"Not anymore, sir. And yes, I'm looking for a new job."

Sassoon smiled. There appeared, perhaps only an illusion, a leap of friendliness in his sharp eyes. "I'm glad you came here. Ciro's could use a pianist like you, but my American band just left Shanghai. Perhaps you'd be interested in playing in the bar? Classical music or jazz, whatever you like. The stage is yours. Five American dollars a week. You'll need to find your own lodging, sadly, since my Embankment Building is no longer a dorm. How does that sound?"

That was much more than what he'd received in Aiyi's club. It must be because he was now a famous pianist. And with the soaring inflation and the exchange rate now favoring American dollars, one dollar could fetch one hundred Chinese *fabi*. Ernest grinned. "When do I start?"

It was just as Sassoon had promised. The Jazz Bar was his stage, where he played anything he liked. Reading the scores he found in the piano bench, he played Schumann's *Kinderszenen*, Mozart's C-minor fantasia, and then Chopin's nocturne in E-flat major. Chopin's fine tune opened a window on his memories: his last recital in a music hall, playing this piece, his head pelted by beer bottles and insults, but his hands never missing a note. He was thirteen then. After that he was never allowed to play in music halls again.

The crowd in the bar was different from that in Aiyi's nightclub. Many were British or American, who listened with the rapt expression of an audience who appreciated classical music. During the breaks, Ernest mingled with them, asking them about the war in Europe. When he had worked in Aiyi's club, he hadn't heard anything about the war, and English and German publications were difficult to obtain. Countries were crumbling under Hitler's assault, they said. France had signed an armistice and surrendered last year, and London was bombed for months. Britain, in desperate need of manpower, had ordered the Seaforth Highlanders in Shanghai to sail to Singapore, and from there they'd leave to join the fleets in the Mediterranean.

Ernest was shocked. If the Seaforth Highlanders withdrew, British citizens in Shanghai would be left without protection, and the military power of the Settlement, bolstered by the British force and the American Fourth Marines, would be greatly weakened.

The ripples from the war in Europe, it seemed, had reached the shores of Shanghai.

Sassoon often came to listen to the music with a gaggle of Russian showgirls dressed in scanty, shimmering costumes. They were stunning, their glances sensual heat, their limbs dazzling sweeps; men in the bar gulped and stared. Sassoon showered the women with lavish gifts: perfume bottles, fur coats, leather bags, and chocolate. At midnight, the group squeezed in the elevator while people sighed and whispered about Sassoon's studio with its darkroom and the photos he took.

"What kind of photos do you take, sir?" Ernest asked him when he came to the bar again. He was beyond excited. Sassoon, a fellow photographer.

Sassoon looked guarded. "Nudes. Do you have a problem with that, young man?"

This was not the type of photos Ernest would take, but it was not his business to judge. "Which style do you explore? New Vision? Formalistic? Surrealist?"

"I hate Brassaï! The man is a butcher. You know about photography?"

"Only as an amateur. I brought my Leica, the best kind. I was hoping to show you. Would you like to see it?" He went to his bag near the bench, where he kept his camera. "I bought it in 1935."

"Leica. Good camera, good company. I've always admired Leitz, an audacious man. Let me see." Sassoon dug out a monocle from his pocket, put it on, and fondled the camera with apparent envy. "Finest thirty-five-millimeter camera. Viewfinder, range finder, and adjustable slow shutter speeds. There aren't many cameras like this in Shanghai. I bought a few via mail order but never received them. With this camera, you can take the best pictures, Ernest."

Ernest grinned. The fact that they had the same hobby somehow made him feel Sassoon was like a friend.

29

AIYI

Sassoon phoned me in the office. "Darling, I haven't seen you for ages. How do you do?"

It was good to hear his voice. He had called me a few times since my club grew popular; each time we spoke, I flinched at the possibility that he would mention nude photos again.

Sinmay had told some interesting stories about Sassoon lately. A Japanese officer from the Greater East Asia Co-prosperity Sphere, a new organization the Japanese government formed in an attempt to establish their vast economic power, had proposed a joint business venture with Sassoon, but he refused. Not only that, but Sassoon, who disliked the conquerors of my city, delivered scathing remarks about them. That drew rebuke from his fellow businessmen who believed a friendly relationship with the Japanese would benefit the Settlement. He didn't back down and continued his blistering attack, annoying the Japanese, who had arrested two of his trusted men.

I said, "How wonderful to hear from you, Sir Sassoon. Indeed, it has been ages. Thank the gods of favorable winds for the phone. I hope you don't miss me terribly. I would have called, you know, if I hadn't been so busy with the club."

His cultured voice carried a smile. "Darling, you're so busy, you're taking clients from Ciro's. Are you aware? Your stride piano has been a sensation for months. How long will it last?"

"I'm afraid it's already ended. Didn't you hear? My pianist doesn't work here anymore." I longed to see Ernest again, to be lost in the bliss of his arms and forget about Yamazaki.

"Well, you must tell me all about it. Maybe you'd like to have some wine and a dinner in the Cathay Room?" He added that he had caviar, foie gras from Périgord, Persian figs, and California peaches.

I didn't believe him. We all suffered a shortage of many goods and fresh fruit recently since the Japanese had banned many imported goods from entering the port. "This is a kind invitation, Sir Sassoon. I would love to have a treat. I shall be glad to phone you with a date."

"You promise?"

"Have I ever lied?"

"Darling, as always, I have absolute faith in you. Now, I hear there's trouble in your club with a Japanese official. I don't know the details, but it's appalling that those Japanese would threaten to seize your business. Are you rather distraught, I presume? But I'm confident you know how to deal with it."

Word traveled fast. "To be honest, Sir Sassoon, I haven't figured out what to do yet."

"I have an easy solution for you. Marry me."

This couldn't have come at a worse time. "I'm sorry, Sir Sassoon. I'm not in the mood for a tease. I hope you'll understand."

"This is not a tease, darling. You marry me, you'll have my protection, and your nightclub will be a British and Chinese joint enterprise, protected by the SMC's law. The Japanese can't touch you."

Sassoon was right, but he didn't know about Ernest. "I'm afraid it's not that simple."

"Let the Japanese have your club then. You walk away. It's not worth dying for. If you marry me you'll have my properties in Shanghai, all my assets: the hotel, the apartments, the transportation company, the cinemas, the racecourse. Everything."

The solemnity in his voice. He was serious about the proposal, but it couldn't be possible. Sassoon, a womanizer, would not propose to me. Blood rushed to my head. "As I mentioned, Sir Sassoon, you might want to tell me your joke another time."

He sighed. "Have I given you the impression that I'm a frivolous man, darling? Lately, I've been thinking about this. I'm sixty years old. When you get to this age, few things matter. I'd like to marry you."

He really wanted me for his wife, and he would share with me his wealth, his half of Shanghai. This wouldn't have happened in my wildest dreams. My hands trembled.

"Darling?"

"I'm engaged. You've heard of my fiancé."

"You don't care about him. There's no legal responsibility between you. You won't get sued if you change your mind. Besides, once you marry me, you can go to any city you wish. New York. San Francisco. If you want to avoid him, I shall guarantee that."

It felt hard to breathe. I covered my mouth, too shocked to speak. Finally I said, "But . . . but I don't understand. Why me? Why now?"

"I've long admired you, darling; you're aware of that. You have superb business acumen. You need a bigger platform, and my properties provide you that. Who knows, perhaps you'll even build me another empire. And you're young and beautiful. I enjoy your company. What do you say, darling?"

"I . . . I have to think about this. I promise I shall call you soon," I stammered. I felt dizzy. This was an easy path, a tempting path that was worth risking Cheng's and my family's wrath. I would never reach Sassoon's level of wealth on my own, not in this lifetime. And from what he said, he was glad to give me the reins of his empire, and all his assets would be within my reach.

He was arrogant, a womanizer, a foreigner, but he was generous and an honorable competitor. Not a lover. But if you could be as rich as Sassoon and own half of Shanghai, what did it matter to marry a man who was not a lover?

However, Sassoon was wrong about one thing. This was not a solution to Yamazaki's threat; it was an escape. For me. Not for Ernest. He would still be wanted by Yamazaki.

Perhaps this was not an escape, either; it was a complication. For marrying Sassoon meant I would need to let Ernest go.

But the proposal. The wealth. The idea—the richest woman in Asia.

30

ERNEST

After two hours of walking, he finally arrived at Miriam's school. He had missed her. He hadn't visited her since she returned to school for the spring semester. But the school was quiet, and the property, which was usually filled with children, was empty.

"Where is everyone?" he asked a sweeper in the school's courtyard.

The children had been given a day off at the zoo in honor of Sir Kadoorie, where they would have an open concert and a picnic before returning later that day, the man said in pidgin English.

Ernest waited for an hour and finally left. Miriam was with her friends; she was in good hands.

Ernest had just arrived at the bar when he saw a Japanese officer and two Japanese soldiers in khaki uniforms march into the main lobby. He wondered what was going on. When he had a chance, he left the piano and went to the lobby. Sir Sassoon, surrounded by his bodyguards and hotel staff, was hitting his walking stick against the floor, facing the officer. There seemed to be a moment of stalemate until the officer finally bowed and left with the soldiers.

"Ernest." Sassoon had caught sight of him. "Come. Take a seat. Everyone, go to work. Leave us alone. Come, sit. You must be absolutely honest with me, Ernest. Have you seen that Japanese officer before?"

"No, sir." He glanced outside, but the men had already left.

"Well, he was asking about you. He knows your name, says you're from America, and believes you're a murder suspect he's looking for. I told him you're German and he had the wrong guy. He wasn't convinced."

Ernest frowned. "Is his name Yamazaki by any chance?"

"So you've heard of him."

Ernest took a deep breath and told him what he had learned from Aiyi. "I'm innocent. I didn't shoot anyone."

"I see." Sassoon sighed. "I'm sorry you were involved. I owe you an explanation. This is about the security of the Settlement. You must tell no one, understand?" When he nodded, Sassoon continued, "This is quite a long story. Where should I start? Anyway, since England declared war against Germany, I've received some threats from the Japanese. They covet my business and bully me. Yes. Me! So I decided to take some measures to strengthen the police force and ordered the Sikh policemen to recruit men to safeguard the Settlement. Well, that was last year. Things didn't work out the way it should have. There were some conflicts and a Japanese soldier was shot. The Japanese have been investigating it for months. Now for some reason, Yamazaki believes it was you who shot the soldier."

Ernest laughed nervously. He had become a fall guy, and how on earth was he supposed to protect himself if Yamazaki persisted in hunting him? His life was going well so far—Miriam was at school, he had a job, and he could see Aiyi regularly. "Maybe he'll give up."

"They never give up." Sassoon shook his head. "No one understands them, but I know the Japanese people are a mystery, not a paradox."

The old man was wary. He owned many hotels, apartments, and trading companies in the Settlement, but with the Seaforth Highlanders' withdrawal, Ernest could tell he was vulnerable. "Of course."

"The fellows at the council are foolish. They said the Japanese were polite and not a menace. All they worry about is Europe. But the Japanese are up to no good." Two lines cut deep in the folds on Sassoon's forehead.

It almost sounded as though the old man was worried about a possible attack from the Japanese. But Ernest wondered if he was overly apprehensive. The Settlement was within the jurisdiction of Britain and the US. An assault on the Settlement would mean an assault on those two countries. It was unimaginable to see a small country like Japan take on these giants.

A few days later, on his way out of the bar, Ernest saw an English magazine on a table. The magazine was dog-eared, water stained, and dated December of last year, but Ernest read it hungrily. Inside was a black-and-white photo of three figures: a German official in a uniform with a swastika, an Italian official wearing a cap with an eagle clenching a fasces, and a Japanese official with a military cap emblazoned with the rising sun. Their hands joined to grasp tightly, their eyes dark with ambition.

The three evil Axis powers had signed the Tripartite Pact! He was disgusted. But he realized now why Sassoon was agitated. His fear of the Japanese attacks wasn't entirely baseless, for with the Japanese being the allies of Germany, all the Britons in Shanghai became the enemies of the Japanese.

Ernest's heart sank. If war broke out in the Settlement, then his job, Miriam's school, and all the security he had built, even their lives, would be in danger.

31

AIYI

For days, Sassoon's proposal kept me up. So I went to see Emily, the only person I felt I could trust, to whom I could speak freely.

Emily lived in an apartment in the Concession. Her cook led me to her bedroom. As soon as the door opened, a wave of smoke, filled with a sickeningly sweet flowery odor, hit me. My limbs grew soft, even as anxiety gripped me. Unbelievable. She was smoking the "great smoke."

"Emily? Why are you smoking? Is everything all right?" In the dim room, a vague figure lay on the bed. "Emily?"

"I can hear you, Aiyi." She struggled to rise, her hair spilling around her face like a dark cloud.

I sat on a couch across from the bed. Part of me wanted to lecture her about the danger of falling into the morass of addiction; part of me understood nothing I said would make a difference. My father, an addict, had showed me every ugly aspect of addiction. "I thought you'd quit. Why are you smoking again?"

"He doesn't love me anymore."

"Sinmay? Of course he loves you."

A sob reverberated in the dimness. "But he won't leave Shanghai with me. I'm done. My life is over. I want to find another job, but I can't write a single word. I'm dry, I'm spent, I'm stuck."

"It's temporary. All writers have writer's block, Sinmay said once. You need to get some fresh air. You're throwing your life away by smoking. Would you like to go to Kiessling's Café with me? We can have tea. We can talk."

She was quiet. Her voice was still husky when she said, "No one asks me for tea anymore; no one comes to visit."

"So you want to go?"

She got out of bed, turned on the light, and sat next to me. The robe was loose on her, exposing her shoulders and breasts, full and drooping slightly; her large eyes looked sad and tired, her face pale. Emily, Emily. A woman with many talents, many lovers, many faces, and many moods, yet utterly alone. "Is that Sassoon's hotel's robe?"

"It's a robe."

"Look, Emily. I have something very important I need to ask you. I wonder if you can help me. You know I'm in love with my pianist, and now I don't know what to do." I told her everything: Yamazaki's threat, my relationship with Ernest, and Sassoon's proposal.

"Sassoon proposed to you? That goat. He never asked me to marry him. If you marry him, you'll get his money and protection for your club."

"It's not that simple, Emily. I'm going to open the windows, do you mind?"

She shrugged. "I see. That pianist. You're in love with him. But you also don't mind marrying Sassoon and sleeping with him because he's rich and he can protect you."

I supposed I could get used to her style, but had I not seen the roomful of ribbons of toxin, I wouldn't have believed she'd been smoking. Her mind was sharp and perceptive. I leaned against the window. "I didn't sleep with Sassoon."

"Come on. You love money."

"Everyone loves money."

"Maybe not more than everything else. I left Sassoon for your brother."

I looked out the window. "All I can tell you is, Emily, I would do anything I can to protect Ernest."

"You really do care about him, I see. What about your cousin-fiancé? Never mind. It's an arranged marriage, and you should not be bound by it. But now you have to choose. Which one can't you live without? You can't have both love and money."

"Why can't I have both?"

She shrugged again. "Fine. You sleep with Sassoon and then Ernest. One on Monday, the other on Tuesday."

"Emily," I called out indignantly. I was not a promiscuous woman; I was a woman with morals.

She took off her robe, and naked, she walked to the wardrobe near me. I had to avert my eyes—most Chinese women were too modest to bare themselves. Emily didn't seem to be embarrassed, however, opening the drawer and taking out some clothes. "Or you marry Sassoon and leave Ernest."

"If I wanted to, I would have accepted Sassoon's proposal, and I wouldn't have come here."

"But you don't want to. Listen to yourself, Aiyi."

I sighed. Unwilling as I was to give up Sassoon's money, I saw I had no choice. "But I'm desperate for Sassoon's protection. What should I do when Yamazaki returns? I have to turn Ernest in, or Yamazaki will seize my business."

She picked up a velvet dress and peered at herself in the mirror. "Now you're making sense, Aiyi. You need to figure out a plan to protect your business and your man. Maybe you can make a counterproposal asking for Sassoon's protection of your business."

That was a good idea. If he became a shareholder of my club, my business would be a joint venture protected by the SMC law, and

Yamazaki couldn't do anything about it. "But there's no way Sassoon will help me if I reject him. He'll be so angry. He'll never talk to me again."

"No doubt about that. He's vengeful. He ostracized me after I left him. He'll do the same to you, unless you give him what he wants."

What he wants. "He wants nude photos."

"He has mine."

"You're kidding!"

"Why not? It's my body."

What a woman—free, open, independent, the owner of her body and soul. Could I ever be like her?

"He's quite a photographer, Aiyi. I'm not ashamed of it. It's not pornography. It's only pornography in the eyes of a dirty man. And I was beautiful in those photos; you should see them. I was young, attractive, and charming. Now look at me." She dropped the dress, cupped her drooping breasts, and her voice was veiled with sadness again. "This tired flesh, this decaying mind, this soulless body of an old woman."

"The great smoke did this to you, Emily." I seized the opportunity.

She didn't look pleased, like all the addicts who refused to hear the truth. "Our conversation is over, Aiyi. Do whatever you like. Leave me alone now."

I went to the door. "I know you won't like it when I say this, but you must stop smoking, Emily. You're an extraordinary woman. Don't let opium take control of your mind. Think about it. I'll give you the contact information of the physician who treated my father. I'll leave it in the kitchen."

She stared at me. Those dark eyes, perceptive.

I went back and gave her a hug, which I had rarely done to a foreigner. Emily didn't respond at first, and then slowly, her arms held mine and she pulled me closer.

In my courtyard, I had just gotten out of my Nash when I heard Peiyu call me into the reception room. She was holding the baby, sitting on a rosewood chair.

"Come, come, Aiyi. I need to ask you something. Let me get her settled. My breasts are like rocks and she won't latch on." Peiyu, the puritan who buttoned her clothes up to her chin, flipped open her tunic and presented two giant breasts. For someone who had six children, Peiyu had impressive assets, perfectly round, much larger than mine. How weird. For my entire life I saw women cover themselves to their necks, and in one day two women revealed themselves before me. "Did you post the invitations?"

"What invitations? Oh, yes. I posted them." I had completely forgotten about them.

"Then I don't understand. The concubines' families said they didn't receive them. I'd rather they not come, such pests as they are, but it seems not a single relative has an invitation. It has been more than six months. They should have received them by now."

"It's the Japanese. They suspended the mail." Sinmay had entered the room.

"What are we going to do, husband?"

"Send another batch." He stopped beside me and sniffed. "Were you smoking?"

"What? No. I went to see Emily. She was smoking."

He frowned. "Why did you go see her? Leave her alone."

"Will you order your factory to print new invitations, husband?" Peiyu lifted the satiated baby off her chest; her previously perfect, giant breast had become a distant memory.

"After I pay the workers' wages." Then he went to my Nash and pulled up his long robe to get in. His own car had run out of gasoline, so he needed to borrow mine, he said.

"The wedding is coming up in two months, husband!"

"It looks like we need to postpone it," I said, and hurried to my room.

32

ERNEST

Two weeks later, Ernest was walking down the sidewalk at the water-front when he heard the drone of a plane overhead. It was a Japanese fighter with the red rising sun logo. The aircraft turned above the river and circled over the majestic Shanghai Club building with its twin Baroque-style domes, where the municipal council members and other powerful businessmen held their meetings. Before he figured out what was going on, the streets around him seemed to convulse. The cars swerved on the street, horns blasting; people ran amok, screaming.

In front of the building, a group of Japanese soldiers were shout-ing, their bayonets pointed at several policemen kneeling on the pave-ment. Jyo was among them, his arms behind his back in surrender. From the building stomped more Japanese soldiers accompanying dozens of businessmen in suits. Ernest spotted Sir Sassoon, his walk-ing stick stabbing the ground, hobbling at such a fast pace that he almost tripped.

Ernest's heart chilled. The Shanghai Municipal Council functioned as an administrative government, rectified laws, drafted trading permits, and even issued identity cards to refugees like him. Now all the British and American members were being driven out at gunpoint.

Later that evening, the bar boiled with men's curses. Sassoon slumped at a table, surrounded by his bodyguards and his cousins who managed the hotel. His face livid under the light, Sassoon gulped down a drink and smashed the empty glass on the ground. He rarely left his hotel, only going to the Shanghai Club for meetings; now he was kicked out.

"The Japanese cut off the legs of the pool tables in the club because they were too tall," someone said.

"The Japanese have organized their own police," someone else said.

"They're asking for war," another said.

All quieted, their heads down.

Ernest looked at one wary face after another. Sassoon's plan to protect the Settlement had failed, their Seaforth Highlanders had left Shanghai, and Britain was fighting for its life in Europe. All Britons in the Settlement were on their own.

The next day, the bar was unusually quiet. Only three customers came, eating peanuts and drinking red martinis. Colonel William Ashurst arrived late, ate his favorite spaghetti, and left in a hurry. Ernest hoped quiet evenings like this wouldn't become a pattern. If no one came to the bar, then there was no need for a pianist.

When he left the bar after midnight, Ernest put his Leica around his neck and went to the pier where the Japanese cruiser was docked.

Through the lens of his camera, he could see the marines patrolling on the deck. At dawn, just after the bell on the Customs House struck five, a motorboat, loaded with German beer and boxes of frozen steak, reached the cruiser.

He pressed his camera shutter.

33

AIYI

By the light through the window, I wiped off the powder and lipstick and took off the pearl hairpin, the gold necklace, and the gold leaf earrings. I stared at myself in the mirror. I rarely frowned to keep crow's feet from creeping up around my eyes, never did laundry or scaled fish to avoid roughening my hands, and only drank warm rice milk to keep my skin free of black spots. For I had learned, even though I had the business acumen that Sassoon praised, my looks were valued most by my customers.

I took off the skintight dress and stood in front of the mirror. My figure was lean, lithe; my waist was slim; and my breasts were small but pointed. My body was not plump and voluptuous like Emily's, my breasts not dramatic like Peiyu's, but I was youthful and beautiful.

Growing up, I was told that revealing part of my body and, God forbid, showing cleavage was shameful. So even though I'd learned the Western ways in St. Mary's Hall and seen nude paintings in magazines, I considered nude photos scandalous. If I had nude photos taken and Cheng or Sinmay got wind of it, they would skin me. My family's reputation in the city, and my own, would be destroyed. I was not free like Emily, and my body could never be a form of art.

I opened my rosewood wardrobe to find something to wear. Inside were the one hundred silk dresses I had collected. Each was meticulously tailored and lovingly folded. They gleamed in colors of sea turquoise, metallic gold, peony red, milk white, and bamboo green, with various fasteners such as braided frogs, spiral knots, round medallion closures, classic buttons, and woven loops. Dresses were of utmost importance to me, like Mother's jewelry, which I kept in drawers with the perfume bottles. They were the reminder of the life I used to have.

In one of the drawers, I had a hidden latch that stored five hundred American dollars. No one knew this, but I also hid cash in a drawer in my office. *Always save money for a rainy day,* Mother had said.

I picked out a turquoise silk robe from the wardrobe and put it on. Pulling aside the flaps of the silk tent over my four-poster bed, I climbed in. Tomorrow I would go see Ernest.

In my car, parked in a dark alley, Ernest said he had found a job in the Jazz Bar, which he greatly enjoyed, but trouble was brewing in the Settlement. The Japanese had taken control of the SMC and ordered the disbandment of the Sikh police. All the British were frightened.

I frowned. "This is disturbing. Did Yamazaki come to your bar?"

"He came to the hotel."

Of course Yamazaki was still after him.

"Has he visited your club again, Aiyi? How's your business?"

"Not good. But I'll take care of it. You stay safe."

Ernest had a smile on his face, his eyes the shade of blue that had become my favorite color, and his hand had healed completely, the stab wound a straight line in the center of his old scars. Just like that, I made up my mind.

Later I entered my office and closed the door. I took Mother's photo and put her beside Buddha's head. I knelt and prayed. Mother had said Buddha blessed the room wherever his statue rested, but kneeling in front of them, I asked not for their blessing, but their forgiveness. Then I picked up the phone near the calendar on the desk and dialed.

His impeccable British accent came through once I gave my name to his secretary. "Darling, I could hardly believe it's you. Such a pleasure to hear your voice."

"I promised to call you back, didn't I?"

"Ah, I'm delighted. Would you like to have a tiffin or a supper at your leisure? Say, tomorrow?"

"A supper would be lovely."

"Marvelous. Where would you like to meet?"

"How about in the Cathay Room?"

The next day, I arrived at the Cathay Room, embellished with a golden coffered ceiling and walls of intricate carvings, which many believed was the most luxurious restaurant in Shanghai.

Sassoon ordered a twelve-course meal. He chatted about his charity balls and fundraising parties, bemoaned the lack of beautiful-women attendees, and then boasted about a famous singer who shared his bed.

"What about the Japanese customers in your hotel? Have they bothered you?" I asked.

He dabbed his mouth with a black napkin and shook his head.

When the eighth dish, curry chicken, arrived on the table, I decided to talk about business. "I've been thinking about your proposal, Sir Sassoon. Your affection honors me so much. This is a dream for all girls in Shanghai, and you have made me the luckiest girl. I have no words for it."

"A *yes* will be sufficient."

154

I smiled. "I wonder, Sir Sassoon, if you would ever consider another type of partnership with me. A business partnership. I'll sell you forty percent of the ownership of my club for one hundred thousand American dollars. It's a fair price."

He put down a bottle of chilled Bass pale ale and frowned.

I said, before he grew sour and unleashed a barrage of questions regarding my refusal of his proposal, "To express my gratitude for the partnership, I shall also be glad to consider a photo shoot, if you're still interested."

He picked up his ale, the frown loosening. "A photo shoot."

"You're still interested, aren't you? This is to show my goodwill, and I shall ask for your goodwill, too, to pledge the photos will never appear in front of other people's eyes."

"Of course people will see them. I put my photos up for display. It's art."

I nearly dropped my fork. Imagine. Nude photos of me hung on a wall for everyone to see.

Sassoon sighed. "Fine, darling, if you insist. I shall honor your wish. Your photos will be private. I shall be glad to be your business partner even though you break my heart. You'll still consider being my marriage partner in the future?"

I nodded. "Of course I will. When will you consider drafting the contract?"

"I shall have it drafted in a few days. And you know my penthouse is the safest place in China. No one could enter it without my permission."

That I believed.

He extended his hand, and I shook it. "I'll see you when the contract is ready."

I had just let go of the chance to become Asia's wealthiest woman, yet I had no regret. With the contract, I would be able to protect my business and Ernest. If Yamazaki threatened me to turn in Ernest, I could refuse.

34

ERNEST

On a late afternoon, he was about to enter the hotel when he saw Jyo's familiar giant figure on the sidewalk, his hand on his Webley, watching two Japanese soldiers hopping onto a motorcycle. Before Ernest could call out, Jyo turned around and disappeared.

The Sikh police had been ordered to disband, Ernest was aware, and he wondered how his friend still possessed his gun. At least Jyo was safe.

Ernest slipped through the revolving door and headed toward the Jazz Bar at the end of the lobby. He stopped midway, catching that lovely face of hers standing in front of the elevator wearing the black mink coat with tuxedo collar, her hair styled in neat ringlets around her face, her lips—the lips he had longingly kissed—the color of a red rose. Her quiet beauty was catching light, attracting the gaze of the guests, but her most avid admirer, it appeared, was Sassoon, who took her arm, his mustache flying wide like wings, and ushered her inside the elevator. Ernest faintly heard the murmur of *studio* across the lobby.

He wouldn't have given it a second thought had it not been for Aiyi's nervous smile, the unusual jittery movement of her hands, and the triumphant look on Sassoon's face, like the one he often had when he marched toward the elevator with those scantily clad Russian dancers. The thought jumped into Ernest's head, blinding him, like a camera's flash.

Suddenly he disliked the Briton, his fine black suit; his long, thick eyebrows; his suaveness and confidence; and even his friendliness. Ernest skidded toward the elevator just as it started to close, just as she raised her head and caught sight of him. *No! Come back.*

As if hearing his thoughts, Aiyi took a step forward inside the elevator, but the door clicked shut.

35

AIYI

I was glad the door was shut, glad Ernest couldn't stop the elevator. And the look in his eyes, as if he knew. For a moment I thought to confess my plan to him. Yet that would be a disaster. What man would like to imagine his lover naked in front of another man?

"He saw us," I said.

"Ernest? He plays good piano but also has a sharp mind. One day he'll be a great businessman," Sassoon said.

"Did you tell him anything?" I asked.

"Of course not. You must trust me, darling. I am a man of my word."

The elevator stopped at the eleventh floor, and Sassoon, in his usual intriguing manner, held the door open with one hand. "Shall we?"

I stepped into his penthouse, the safest place in Shanghai.

The studio's door swung open. There was a comfortable dimness and strong scents of fresh carnations, cigar smoke, musk, and lavender. The air was warm, soft like silk. No music, only a low hum from a machine somewhere. Sassoon moved ahead of me, his walking stick stabbing the lush Persian carpet.

I could still back out, excuse myself, renege on the contract, and bolt.

The door clanked closed.

The light was turned on. I faced a bunch of white, fat carnations planted in a glazed blue vase; near it was a small table, a leopard fur blanket on a chesterfield, and a tripod like a spider. It was just Sassoon and me. No one else.

A League of Nations of women gazed at me from the wall. They were all naked, in various poses, with various eyes, and with various lengths of thighs. Some were bold, some coy. My head spun.

"You look nervous." Sassoon limped to the tripod.

What an understatement. I cleared my throat. "I don't understand, Sir Sassoon. Why do you like nude photos?"

"Darling, you must not consider me a rotten man."

"Absolutely not. Only a man of rotten taste."

He laughed in a roguish way. "You don't understand men; you don't understand me. No one does, and I don't care. You may sit on the lounge."

I sat as he suggested, but I was not ready to take off my clothes yet; my throat felt raw.

"Here's the contract." He handed me a manila folder. Inside was a sheet with the hotel's letterhead and his signature. He was now a partner of my club, and the funds, one hundred thousand dollars, would soon be transferred to my account.

I tucked the contract inside my purse. My head swam.

"Do you need my assistance with your coat, darling?"

"I'm fine."

"I'd be more than happy to help, darling."

"Partner, let me be clear: I shall show myself in front of the camera, not between the sheets."

He sighed. "I do hope you'll change your mind."

"Will you promise me again no one else will see these photos?"

"Even if this building burns down, darling."

The light, the heat, the camera. I perspired. Disrobing in front of Sassoon was a vastly different matter from getting naked in front of Ernest. What to tell Ernest?

I slipped off my mink coat, unfastened the frogs of my dress, and peeled it off. Then I took off my silk underwear and lace stockings and climbed on the chesterfield. I had one leg flat against the cold leather, one leg up, upon which I rested my shaky arm. My head was tilted away from the camera, my gaze fixed on the carnations leaning in the vase. I had an urge to raise my hand, to shield my face and my body—this nakedness, this exposure.

There was a suck of breath from Sassoon, and I shuddered, afraid he would pounce on me. He didn't, only wobbled into the white light to adjust something in front of the camera. Then he turned in my direction, those dark eyes looking not amused but rather thoughtful, reminding me of his overwhelming power and the backlash if anything went wrong.

"Ready?"

No. The camera flashed; a sea of carnations swelled, the petals pale as skin. In the following darkness, I was sure a piece of my soul was snatched. *What have I done?*

Coming out of the elevator, I heard piano from the Jazz Bar, thundering, as if the sky were raining glass shards. Standing near a pillar, I watched Ernest from a distance: a sharp profile, his eyes mad, each note an accusation.

I turned and left as fast as I could.

In my office, I stared at the contract. I would send a copy to the tax office so they would know from now on my club was a joint venture protected by the Settlement law. Yamazaki would be notified. He wouldn't have the power to confiscate my club, and Ernest would be safe.

Yet I felt sick. I took out a bottle of whiskey I'd saved and drank. I drank until the chairs, the statue of Buddha, and Mother's photo began to float. I could see the sharp profile of Ernest and my nude photographs rain down on the streets as people looked at them, laughing.

36

ERNEST

People were laughing, drinking, and shouting, but he heard nothing. With great force, he pounded on the piano. His hands leaped from keys to keys, faster and faster, his shoulders shook, and his entire body bounced to the furious rhythm, unleashing a march of fury against Sassoon, against his greed, against his perverse hobby. Nude photography was immoral, and he should have condemned it when he had a chance! He was angry at Aiyi, too, for turning herself into a showgirl, a toy, a fool. He was wrong about her; she loved money more than anything, more than herself. Did she love him at all?

Gulps of air writhed in his chest, sweat burst from his forehead, and a savage fire sizzled in his stomach. His hands raced along on their own, his notes a raging storm. He saw nothing, heard nothing, thought nothing; he was overrun, kidnapped by the very sound he created.

Finally, he stopped and released the captive air in his chest. For a moment he sat, staring at the scars on his hand, the fire dying in his stomach. Tears welled in his eyes.

Someone was calling him. When the light in front of him coalesced, Sassoon's figure appeared. He looked to be in a good mood, his mustache two happy wings. He asked him to play Mozart. He said he was not a fan of Chopin.

Ernest shook his head. If Sassoon fired him, so be it.

Sassoon put his hands on the silver-crusted cane. "I had a good day, a very good day, young man. Something I've wanted for years finally happened. I could show you the photos, but I promised to keep them private. They are the best of my work, I shall vouch."

He wanted to strangle Sassoon.

"You're sulking, young man. Does this have anything to do with Miss Shao? Let me ask you, how long have you been in Shanghai, Ernest?"

"Over a year."

"I've been in Shanghai for almost fifteen years. Life in Shanghai is not easy for a rich bachelor."

Ernest snorted.

"I'm the richest bachelor in Asia, but also the loneliest man on this planet. Good women from honorable families do not sail across the ocean to find a husband, and those who do sail across the ocean want anything but a husband."

So Sassoon was the prey of predatory women; didn't that make him pitiful. But what was wrong with the world? Were there any decent women?

"Miss Shao is young, beautiful, shrewd, and a sensible business-woman. There are not many like her. She's not Jewish—a pity—but she deserves all my respect, and yours, rightly. I'm an old man, Ernest. She makes me feel young, and I believe I could love again."

Ernest felt nauseated.

"I almost married a woman when I studied in Cambridge. But her family rejected me because I was a Jew. That's ancient history now." Sassoon sighed, as if he were capable of feeling anything. "The business world is tiresome, harsh, and precarious. It's only through the lens I find beauty and joy. You're a photographer. You understand what I'm talking about."

No. He could never understand perversity, and he was wrong. Sassoon, a rich man collecting his trophies, could never be his friend. Ernest played on, seeking the note of veracity and companionship in music. Chopin, always his favorite, and Schumann. When he looked up from the keyboard again, Sassoon had left.

He shouldn't blame her. She was only twenty-one, a girl still, but a businesswoman in this wolfish world run by men, in this precarious city ruled by the Japanese. She had done so much for him, helping him get on his feet, providing him a place to stay, showering him with support and protection when he least expected it.

A love that couldn't accept a lover's flaws was a selfish love. He wouldn't be selfish. He would love her, all of her, her beauty, her smiles, her secrets, her mistakes, and her faults.

He began to play again, a tender tap, a loving stroke, and a lingering press, and using long fingers, he let his fingertips kiss the keys like his lips would fall on her. Gently, longingly, he began to play Debussy's *Clair de Lune*.

Around midnight, he left the bar. The art deco buildings near the waterfront were tented in blackness, and the streets were illuminated only by lights coming from closed banks. Leica around his neck, he walked to the Japanese warship by the Garden Bridge. A movement caught his eyes.

A flashlight split the dead of the night. It came from a warship on the river, where a uniformed Japanese officer was climbing into a motorized boat near it. Then with engines growling, the boat cruised by, following a red beam sent from the bridge house.

He had a gut feeling. The Japanese were up to no good.

The boat reached a makeshift pier near the bridge house; the officer climbed out and raised the flashlight. At that signal, another gunboat with a wide hull and a gun turret slid close; from inside a group of eight Japanese servicemen leaped onto the pier. They bowed to the officer, jumped onto his smaller boat, and ducked under a canvas tent that covered a good portion of it.

Ernest held his camera and ran silently closer. He had just found a good spot behind a telegraph pole when the servicemen left the boat and jumped onto the pier, each carrying a bale of heavy machine guns. In a careful and disciplined manner, they transferred the machine guns from the motorized boat to the gunboat with gun turret.

Were the Japanese arming their forces in secret to prepare for an assault? His heart pounding, Ernest held up the camera. He was close enough to take pictures, but he had to turn on the flash, which would expose him. But he couldn't let the moment slip. Jyo must see this; the Settlement must be prepared. He raised the camera, aiming at the group, and pressed the shutter.

The white light lit up the officer's face, a mole visible under his eye. Rapidly Ernest took more photos as his ears filled with surprised shouts in Japanese.

A gunshot.

"Shit!" He turned around and ran.

Another gunshot.

The street before him seemed so dark and distant. It was a while later when he finally passed a row of art deco buildings and dove into an alley. Something was trickling down his arm.

In his apartment, he dropped on the bed. An excruciating pain raked his body. A bullet had grazed him; blood dripped from his shoulder to his arm to his scarred hand, and the taupe jacket and oxford shirt clung to his chest like a wet bathing suit. With sheer willpower, he peeled off his jacket and shirt and grabbed a small bottle of brandy he had received as a gift from a guest. He gulped down the alcohol and, gritting his teeth, poured the liquid on his arm. He screamed. Panting, he tied up the arm with a tie to stanch the blood. The entire process was like rubbing his flesh against a blade. In the morning, he would go see the Catholic nuns again. But this must be a curse: his right hand had been stabbed, and now his right arm was shot.

He lay flat on the bed. The Japanese were plotting something dangerous.

37

FALL 1980

THE PEACE HOTEL

Memory is a forest; it turns with the seasons. It swells in summer, dries up in fall, dies in winter, and sprouts furiously again in spring. Now, talking to the American about Ernest, about my past, I see the forest of my memory grow lush again.

But how did I let slip my old secret of the nude photos to a woman I barely know? I wish I had kept my mouth shut. So I change the subject. "Shanghai was a mess in the 1940s. It was called a solitary island, abandoned by the rest of the world."

"I've heard of that, Ms. Shao. The solitary island. But . . . you declined Sir Sassoon's offer? How did you come to own this hotel?"

"I bought this. Four years ago. The hotel was poorly run under the Gang of Four and on the verge of going bankrupt."

"I see. May I say, Ms. Shao, your entrepreneur spirit is quite ahead of your time, and your relationship with Mr. Reismann sounds incredible."

I ask carefully, "Do you mean you'll cover the nudes in the documentary?"

"It was art, Ms. Shao. Of course I'll cover that."

"But I'd rather you not."

Ms. Sorebi digs her hand into her hair. "I'm open to discuss this, if you're not comfortable with them. One thing I can promise you is that I shall not sensationalize them. I understand it'll be awkward to deal with scandals at your age."

I study her, her eyes, her nose, and her lips. A flush of pink, a tinge of excitement, has emerged on her cheeks, and her hand digs in her hair frequently. She's nervous. "You have a nice hat."

"Thanks. I love this hat. Let me assure you, Ms. Shao, the nudes are not something you should be concerned about. As far as I can tell, there aren't any nudes in Sassoon's collection."

My heart skips. "Sassoon's collection?"

"Southern Methodist University in Dallas, Texas, has a collection of Sassoon's diaries, letters, and photographs. I also found a copy of the magazine that featured Mr. Reismann. It was called *Good Friend*. It says he was the most popular jazz pianist in Shanghai. I'm intrigued. How did a pianist rise to become a man of wealth and then save many refugees' lives?"

I turn my wheelchair away from her. "I'm rather tired, Ms. Sorebi. Would you be so kind as to meet me tomorrow?"

She looks at me and then Phoenix.

"I think tomorrow will be lovely, Ms. Sorebi," Phoenix says to help me.

"Terrific. I'll take a walk and visit the Embankment Building since I have plenty of time. It'll be good for research." She picks up her notebook.

"How long have you been a documentarian, Ms. Sorebi?" I ask.

"Five years. I have two partners. We're a small documentary firm; we haven't yet won an Oscar. Making documentaries isn't profitable, but I enjoy doing the research."

"Why did you decide to do the exhibit about the Jews in Shanghai?"

"I've always been interested in Shanghai. I came here before."

"For the exhibit?"

"No, not for the exhibit. When I worked on the research in 1977, I was told China didn't yet welcome foreigners to the city. So I conducted all interviews by phone and met many survivors in person in the US. Many Shanghai Jews came to the US and became prominent professors or lawyers, and it was easy to find them."

"So when did you come to Shanghai?"

"In the late 1950s as a tourist. I was almost arrested."

"Arrested?"

She puts on her hat. "Well, I was a silly teenager. I didn't know much about this country. I just arrived and saw a sign in the hotel's elevator that said, 'The People's Party, Special Passes Needed,' so I thought it might be a fun evening. It was only two floors above my room, so I took the staircase up. When I got there, there was no music, and everyone stared at me. Two guards in uniforms pinned me to the wall. They thought I was a spy."

I laugh. Only young Americans could easily confuse the Communist party with a regular party. "You didn't have to worry. The government won't arrest you in a hotel."

"Why not?"

Americans hear all kinds of news about China on TV, but few understand what it's like to live here. Shanghai today is probably the safest city in the world, where a young single woman can wander at midnight without being harassed. Most people are friendly, hospitable, and full of humility.

Phoenix is clearing her throat. So I say, "I'll see you tomorrow at the Cathay Room at eleven for lunch. Will that be fine with you?"

"Of course; I'll be there. And I'll bring some photos to show you. But forgive me. I have to ask you something that's stuck in my mind. You know well the value of the hotel. It's worth millions. Why would you propose to donate it to me?"

I've expected that question. "You don't wish to accept it?"

"Oh, gosh. Yes, of course, I'd love to. It's just, you know, this is so difficult to believe."

An interesting habit of hers, making exclamations. "You've spent three years on a project that involves the man dearest to me, and you're the first one who looked into the plight of the Jews in Shanghai. I think you deserve the reward. And don't forget, you still need to make a documentary and show it to the world."

"It'll be my pleasure. I believe Mr. Reismann's survival in Shanghai and his relationship with you will touch many people's hearts today. But may I ask you, Ms. Shao, why you wish to make a documentary about him?"

I take a deep breath. "Because, Ms. Sorebi, I did something most unforgivable."

38

AUGUST 1941

ERNEST

For many days after he discovered the Japanese secretively transferring guns, Ernest, the camera around his neck, had spent any time not at work searching for his giant friend in order to warn him. But Ernest was disappointed. Jyo was nowhere to be found.

Sassoon could use the film and alert the Settlement if necessary, but Ernest was still angry at him. After much consideration, though, Ernest decided to put aside his personal feelings for the good of the Settlement. Finally, one day in August, Ernest asked the front desk to see the old man, but he was declined—Sassoon was busy.

Suddenly the British people from India and England seemed to vanish from the streets and inside the hotel. When he looked up from his piano, Ernest could see the Americans were drinking and glaring at the Japanese, who had crowded the entire bar. With a mysterious look, the Japanese men stared at him. He flinched at a twinge of pain from the wound on his arm the nuns had stitched.

❧

Fall arrived. After everyone left the bar one night, Ernest packed up. Outside the bar, the lobby was almost empty. The unlit sconces sat on the wall like black spiders. It was past midnight; there were few guests ambling about, the only sound the tap of his shoes and the soft hum from the radiator grilles. It gave him an eerie feeling, as if he were treading in a forest where all living things were holding their breath.

"Have you seen Sir Sassoon?" he asked the bellboy, a skinny youngster with long arms at the revolving door.

He shook his head. "He's resting, sir."

"Have a good night."

Ernest waved at Miriam as she appeared in the courtyard, which was crowded with refugee children shivering in thin black jackets. It had been drizzling all morning, and the air was chilly. He had walked for an hour and changed five buses—two had dead engines on the road—to see her.

He had counted the money he'd saved—almost one hundred American dollars. Not bad after paying for Miriam's summer school, fall semester, host family, clothes, and one year's rent for his apartment. Today, he had brought a coat and a canvas bag for Miriam.

"What are you doing here, Ernest?" Miriam stood, clad in a black blazer over a white necktie blouse and a black skirt—from Mrs. Blackstone, he figured. She looked prim, graceful. He was amazed, unprepared. Since when had his little sister turned into a proper woman? But the indifference on Miriam's face pierced him.

"I bought this coat for you." He was suddenly awkward. He'd only managed to see her briefly the past few months, since she stayed at the Blackstones' home over the summer. "I need to tell you something important. Want to have a treat? Let's go. I've talked to your school, so we can spend some time together." He walked her out of school and crossed the street to a shop selling *baozi, youtiao*, and fried cakes with green onions.

Miriam picked two *youtiao*, fried flour strips. "What's in your bag?"

"It's for you. Look, I want to warn you. Shanghai will be at war and—"

"I know that."

"How did you know?"

She shrugged. "Mr. Blackstone told me. He said his colleagues were leaving Shanghai. He's thinking about it too. He said Germans were winning the war in Europe and bombed aircraft factories and radar stations in London. What's his name—Churchill, right? Churchill has withdrawn the navy from China to Singapore, and what else . . . I don't remember."

Mr. Blackstone must have had a radio hidden in the cupboard or something.

"And we have new refugee children from Europe pour into school every day. One hundred arrived yesterday. The school has to stop taking them. Too full."

It was sad to hear, but there was nothing he could do. Sassoon was right—they kept coming, and people in the hotel complained too. *The Jewish communities can't shoulder the burden of refugees anymore. Refugees are the dregs of society in Europe.* The new municipal council, ruled by the Japanese, had added an additional processing fee and demanded to see the refugees' financial proofs before allowing their entrance.

He still hadn't received any replies from his parents, and the ocean liners had stopped docking at the wharf. But he couldn't bring up his concern for them. Miriam would be upset.

"Well, Miriam, we might have to leave Shanghai soon. But I have everything prepared. You don't have to worry."

Miriam stared at the canvas bag. "Mr. Blackstone says the US is neutral. Americans are safe in Shanghai."

"He wouldn't be if war broke out. I'll find another school for you in another city."

"If we leave, how will Mother and Father find us? Mr. Blackstone says international communications have been cut off. Posts can't reach Europe."

Mr. Blackstone this, Mr. Blackstone that. Her tone had a note of trust and deference that made Ernest rather irritated. She had never talked to him in that tone. Ernest took a deep breath. "I hope he's right. But remember, I'm your brother, and I'm here for you."

Miriam shrugged again. "I'm going back now."

"Don't forget the bag and coat."

Miriam took the coat and slung the bag over her shoulders. When he opened his arms to hug her, she sprang back and walked away.

She had grown up, she was a woman now, she was shy, he told himself, watching her tall figure walk away.

He had just reached the high-rise apartment building called Hamilton House, with the US flag and the Union Jack fluttering in the open windows, when a parade came in his direction. Trumpets, horns, and drums were playing "The Stars and Stripes Forever," a familiar tune he had heard the American sailors whistle in the bar.

It was a relief, a boost of confidence, to see the armed forces. So Miriam was right. With the Fourth Marines, the Americans were protected at least. He rushed to the sidewalk, stood behind three businessmen carrying file cases, a girl carrying a violin case, and an old woman walking with a cocker spaniel, and watched.

The leading man in the parade wore an olive officer visor. Ernest recognized him; it was Colonel William Ashurst. He was singing, his face pale and etched with worries. Behind him were the Fourth Marines, all fitted in their jackets with utility pouches tucked snugly around their

174

waists. As they marched, they each pulled the strap aslant across their chests, holding what could be a semiautomatic Garand rifle or maybe a Thompson submachine.

The rhythm of the trumpets, the drums, and the singing lifted Ernest's spirits. He walked along, following the parade, waving at the colonel, who didn't pay him attention. When the regiment reached the wharf at the river, the singing stopped. The colonel saluted and shouted, and the regiment jumped into a large white liner behind the cruiser USS *Wake*.

Someone in the crowd cried out, followed by a string of sobs. Someone else shouted, "God bless you! Goodbye!"

It was a farewell parade. Ernest overheard someone say that the Americans were to sail for the Philippines.

His heart dropped. First the Seaforth Highlanders, and now the Fourth Marines. He glanced at the Japanese warship *Izumo*, the funnels pumping smoke and the deck lined with swordsmen and uniformed soldiers. Downstream under the gloomy sun, the gray American and British vessels, empty without their forces, looked like no more than two paper ships.

He must leave before war broke out. But what about Aiyi? He still wanted her—he would always want her. But would she want him? Would she leave Shanghai with him?

39

AIYI

At dinner, Sinmay was complaining that women had become low, for he had heard from his associates that Sassoon had bragged at a banquet that he snagged a prominent woman in Shanghai to be a model for his nude photography.

I fled the table before he flew into a rage. It seemed unlikely he would know it was me, and Sassoon had promised not to show my photos. But I had forgotten to demand his silence. Did he reveal my name? What had I gotten myself into? I had wanted to save my club and protect Ernest, but I could be drowning in people's spit soon.

The months since I had posed for Sassoon had been an endless slog of torment and tears. When Peiyu wisely notified my relatives that my wedding was suspended due to the mail delivery problem, I could hardly feel any relief. Each day I thought of Ernest and longed to see him and explain; each evening I was tempted to take a detour to the hotel. Yet his furious piano playing burst in my head. He wouldn't forgive me; he would lash out at me, like Cheng, like any Chinese man who owned a woman's body. It was over between us. I didn't sleep well or eat well. I cried myself to sleep.

At the club, I covered myself up with long tunics and a coat and did my best to run the business, which had declined since Yamazaki's visit. I had put out some promotions, which had attracted desperado customers looking for cheap entertainment, but many chose to stay away. I withheld the news of the partnership with Sassoon from the public, waiting for his payment. But his bank account was under Japanese inspection, I heard, which meant it was frozen. I had a terrible premonition that my plan had gone awry.

Then I got a phone call from Emily, who told me to meet her at the wharf.

"I want to say goodbye before I leave," she said, a leather suitcase near her feet. Around us, throngs of porters, their backs bent low with suitcases, yelped and teetered, and passengers in black coats rushed to the gangplank of a two-story steamer to Hong Kong.

The sky was gray, and so were the clouds. Even the steamer, belching with noises, was masked in gray. But the water was bright muddy yellow, on top of which floated wreaths of black trash and sodden paper lanterns poor families tossed in to guide the souls of their deceased family members.

My eyes moistened. I had so much to tell her: my photos, my torment—I hadn't seen Ernest for months, and I felt I was dying. I wanted to ask for her advice about what I should do with Ernest. She was the only person who would understand me, the only friend I could have. "Why leave, Emily?"

"You gave me the physician's address." But I never meant she should leave Shanghai. "It's time for me to go." She looked different, wearing a white silk blouse with ruffles at the collar, a deep-red wool jacket, and wide-legged black trousers. On her head was a stylish red velvet bicorn hat with a bow. She was not sniffling, her lethargic gaze replaced by the discerning calm I loved to see. "The treatments were horrible. I still curse you."

"Does Sinmay know you're leaving?"

She pulled the hat lower. "No."

Love was a conundrum. Emily loved Sinmay, yet she decided to leave him; I wanted to see Ernest, yet I had to stay away.

Tears were threatening, so I gave Emily a red-cloth pouch from my purse; inside was a jade leaf, custom made by the best jeweler in Shanghai, a symbol of me, a jade leaf grown on a gold branch.

"Is that your name on the leaf? How precious. I shall cherish this. You know, I have one regret. I wish I had written an article about you, the first woman entrepreneur in China. You've done extraordinary things, hiring women and foreigners. Are you still in love with the pianist?"

Still? As if love were a glass of wine that you should empty easily.

"I don't remember what I told you, Aiyi. I hope I didn't tell you anything disastrous. You know this better than me: You two won't work. You'll end up alone. Like me. Kicked out of Shanghai. Rejected by two sides." Her voice was sad, hollow.

"But . . ."

"It's for your own good. Chinese have these suffocating customs and traditions. You're better off without him. You're still young. You'll get over it." There came a blast of the horn and a shout in Cantonese. The gangplank would be drawn up and the steamer would cast off. Emily picked up her suitcase.

"Emily . . ."

"I've grown rather fond of you, Aiyi. I wish we had bonded years ago. You're a friend I'd love to keep. But don't cry. I came to Shanghai with a broken heart. I don't want to leave with tears in my eyes." She walked up the gangplank and boarded the ship. A moment later, she appeared at the railing at the bow, where she turned to face the city and raised her hand to brush something on her cheek.

The horn blasted and the steamer belched, a cloud of smoke ascending. Then it chugged away from the wharf.

It dawned on me that in the river of life, people came and went like boats. Full of steam and noise, they docked, and all would be blown by a wind that you couldn't predict. The boat of Emily had sailed away. We never had the tea at Kiessling's after all, and we might never see each other again. Would Ernest, like Emily, depart from my life as well?

It began to rain, a quiet sprinkle, a mist of whispers, the street slick like peanut oil. The Nash was too slow as it left the wharf—too many rickshaws, too many people in robes and suits. Two more blocks to the intersection, three turns to him.

I went straight to the Jazz Bar. There he was, playing the piano in an empty bar. He had grown stubble, and his hair was longer, reaching his shoulders. The curls bounced around his cheeks as he played. His music was a quiet musing, a hopeful tune, as if he was contemplating embarking on a new journey of his dream.

I held my purse, swept my damp bangs, and sat at a table by the stage. My face was wet, and my heart raced in a joyous rhythm. I had the urge to run to the stage and kiss him like a young schoolgirl. I would confess to him, promise him anything, if I could take back his love.

40

ERNEST

He felt her before he saw her, sitting nearby, wearing a peach-hued dress, beaming so beautifully. He jumped off the stage and strode to her table. All these months without seeing her. How he had missed her. He still loved her, perhaps even more than before. Nothing she had done would change that.

"So you're not going to play now?" she said. In her hand was a silver purse with studs like diamonds; those gold leaf earrings swung like wind chimes.

"What would you like to hear?"

"I feel like classical music."

"Do you? Once someone told me she likes jazz."

"People change."

He sat next to her. "I'm glad to see you, Aiyi. I have something I need to tell you. There will be a war, Aiyi. War in the Settlement. No one will be safe." He told her about the machine guns, the departure of the Fourth Marines, and the declining business of the hotel.

She covered her mouth. "I can't believe it. I only heard the British have left and that there's been some trouble in the banks."

He held her hand. "Will you leave Shanghai with me?"

A pearl of rain flowed down her cheek. "I was born and grew up here. My family has been here for generations. This city is my ancestors' home, my home, Ernest. And I have my club."

"But when the Japanese attack, you'll be in danger."

"We say, *Luo Ye Gui Gen*, fallen leaves long for the roots, Ernest. We always remember our roots, remember our home."

He remembered Berlin, too, but Berlin was not his home anymore. His parents, however, were always on his mind, and he would find a home for them, too, once he reunited with them. If he left Shanghai, would they be able to reunite someday? That was his major concern. But he had to leave to protect Miriam. "I want to be with you, Aiyi. We can start fresh in a new city. No one will know who we are. I have savings, and I can find another job. I will protect you, take care of you. We'll have a new life and leave all the mistakes behind."

The color on her face changed from pale to pink. She knew what he was talking about.

"I love you, Aiyi. I haven't changed. Nothing has changed. Come with me."

She laughed, but he couldn't tell if she was touched or if she thought he was ridiculous. "I want to tell you something, Ernest. I just saw off a friend at the pier, and I just learned something important. I don't care about anything else. I want to be with you. Yes, I'll go with you."

He lifted her and spun. She was in his arms, but he could feel the world in his embrace.

⚛

They risked getting a room at the end of the fifth floor in the hotel and slipped upstairs without attracting the attention of Sassoon. Once the door locked behind them, they messed up the clean bed. Later, with sheets wrapped around them, they discussed where to go. She wanted to go to Hong Kong, where her friends were. Hong Kong it was, then.

They planned out the next steps. He would inform the hotel of his departure from the bar, pack, purchase the tickets for the boat, and meet her on the street outside her club, while she would go ahead and stop at her club for some cash—she insisted on it—and then they would fetch Miriam, go to the wharf, and sail to Hong Kong.

༄

After Aiyi left, Ernest went downstairs to the bar. He stacked the music sheets, returned them to the storage bench, and closed up the fallboard. Carrying the bag where he had carefully kept his Leica, he was ready to go to the front desk to resign but hesitated. Once the Japanese attacked, Sassoon's business empire and even his life would be in peril.

In the lobby, Ernest asked one of Sassoon's bodyguards to speak to the old man because he had something important to show him. He was told to go up to the penthouse. A surprise. The penthouse was an exclusive place for Sassoon's close relatives and female friends.

Ernest stepped inside the elevator decorated with redwood panels and inhaled the scents of expensive cigar and perfume. The operator, in his beige uniform, pressed the button for the eleventh floor. When the elevator stopped, he passed two masculine Chinese men in hotel uniforms rolling on the wine-colored carpet with a brand-new vacuum cleaner, a noisy round machine attached to a broomstick.

At the penthouse's door, the bodyguards in black suits let him in. The first thing he saw was a mahogany Steinway with redwood panels, near a burgundy chesterfield and lush golden curtains. It was warm in the room, with a blast of air humming from a massive radiator grille. The penthouse was spacious; it must take up the entire floor.

Sassoon was seated near a cabinet with shelves of whiskey bottles, clothed in a blue-gray British uniform, a brown Webley in the holster. A man with a mustache, his doctor it seemed, was massaging his leg.

"Good afternoon, sir. Thank you for receiving me. Is that a pilot's uniform?" Sassoon's uniform imbued him with a grave expression of authority.

"Of course it is. I was a pilot. I volunteered for the British Royal Flying Corps during the first war. My plane crashed and smashed my leg. That's why I need this cane for the rest of my life. But I would fight for England if I could walk again."

"Of course you would." Sassoon, threatened by the Japanese, must have decided to arm himself.

"Once a pilot, always a pilot. I can still shoot with precision with this Webley. So, Ernest, they said you had something to show me?" The billionaire was eyeing his camera.

Ernest gave him his Leica. "I believe these photos might be important to you."

Sassoon grunted, took it, and limped to his studio. After a while, he limped back, gave him back the camera, and sat. There was disbelief, worry, and mounting anger on his face. "Damn it! Damn the Japanese! Get out! Get out! All of you!"

The doctor went out with his kit, and Ernest took his leave as well.

In the lobby, a gramophone played Beethoven's *Moonlight* Sonata; two guests in gray suits were checking out at the front desk. The burgundy chesterfields were empty, and the scents of withering carnations and roses in unchanged water permeated the air.

Rushing toward his apartment, Ernest heard a shout. Not far from him, a Japanese officer wielded a Mauser at the colossal figure of Jyo, who pointed a Webley at the officer.

"By the authority of the Shanghai Municipal Council, I order you to put down the gun! Put down the gun!" Jyo shouted.

Ernest froze. He'd never had a chance to warn him about the weapons.

A shot was fired.

Screams pierced Ernest's ears; a flood of people swarmed around him. He fought to find his footing, to go to his friend. But more armed men surged to the street. Through the flying coats and hats, he caught a glimpse of his friend sprawled on the ground, his turban soaked.

In his apartment, Ernest took off the camera and stuffed it in a canvas bag he had packed. Then he waded through the crowded streets to the wharf. The earliest departure was in three days; he bought three boat tickets. Without a delay, he headed to Aiyi's club.

41

AIYI

I only needed one thing: the five hundred American dollars in my desk's bottom drawer, the profit I'd saved. But maybe some banknotes as well. Maybe some dresses from home too. I couldn't start my new life without my favorite dresses. I would also warn Sinmay about the attack, so he would take actions to protect Peiyu and the children. And Cheng and Ying.

Eloping with Ernest would work. In Hong Kong, I would not be haunted by the nude photos and I could forget about haggling for the price of apples or watching out for loose dancers. In Hong Kong, I would have Ernest, and we would go to the movies.

But as my Nash turned on Bubbling Well Road, the thrill of seeing Ernest began to cool. My club. It was my life; I couldn't just abandon it. And Cheng. I didn't know what to say to him. Then all my thoughts evaporated when I arrived at my club—in front of the building was a military jeep with the rising sun flag.

Yamazaki had returned. After all these months. My legs trembling, I stepped out of my car. It was about five o'clock in the afternoon, a good hour in the ballroom. Yet no sound of jazz.

The doors to the ballroom were open, no guards or bouncers. Thick smoke, mixed with the smell of alcohol, floated inside the club. On the stage, the drummer hit the crash cymbal and out came the broken notes of "Summertime"; all the dancers, including Lanyu, were hunched at the edge of the dance floor. Under the glittering eighteen thousand lights paced Yamazaki in his damned uniform, his eyes glazed and face red like roasted meat.

He had brought a soldier.

The three gangly teenage boys near the ballroom's entrance, caps askew, stumbled toward me. "He's going to kill us all!" the pimple-faced one said.

"I told you we shouldn't come here again," the cross-eyed boy added.

The one with a loud voice said, "Miss Shao, he came for you. You better run. He's going to kill you."

My legs weakened; my breath stuck in my throat. But this was my club; if I ran away, my customers, my dancers, my workers would be the scapegoats.

"Where's the bitch? Is she hiding? Tell her to come out!" Yamazaki was shouting. Then he saw me. "There! There! I see you! Don't move! Where is the foreigner?"

He was drunk, all his cultivated courtesy slipped off, and his voice that used to be placid was high pitched and full of menace.

I took out a cigarette from my purse. Cold lights of red, green, and blue sliced the faces around me; in the calmest voice that I could summon, I said, "He's gone. I can't find him. Look, I have important news about my club that I'm dying to tell you. Cigarette? This is from my new partner, Sassoon. He sends his regards."

Yamazaki's mole glistened in the light. "The British billionaire?"

"He owns Ciro's and now nearly half of my club." I blew out some smoke, nervous, but I saw my managers, busboys, dancers, and food servers gathered around me to form a protective human wall. Even the gangly boys, who would have fled for safety, joined.

"Is he here?"

"Sassoon doesn't like to walk. He's in his hotel. Maybe he'll come tomorrow."

"A partner, you said?"

"He offered a deal I couldn't refuse. The contract is in my office. I'd be much obliged to show it to you. It's so quiet here. How about some music?"

To my relief, Mr. Li blew his trumpet, and Lanyu, reading the message in my eyes, grabbed her partner and glided to the dance floor. Yamazaki, looking surprised, staggered to the soldier he brought. The two conversed in their language, groaned, and burst out laughing.

Fear crawled on my skin.

Laughing as though he had heard a joke, Yamazaki stumbled toward me again. "I don't care what contract you have. The Briton can't protect you. Soon he will fall onto his knees to our emperor, Hirohito! Japan, the mightiest empire, will conquer all Asia!"

I perspired. My dress, soaked with sweat, stuck to my back, and my high heels pinched deep into my ankles. Before I could speak, he seized my hair, pulled, and thrust my head lower to force me to kneel. It felt as if my face were lacerated by a knife.

"Honorable guest, would you like to dance?" I heard Lanyu's voice.

"How dare you speak to me, bitch."

I was thrown to the floor. When I scrambled up, the madman was rummaging for the pistol in his holster. Hiccupping, he missed, then gripped it and raised the Mauser at Lanyu.

A sound exploded.

A shocking silence descended. Like a skillful rumba dancer rapt in her dance, Lanyu leaned back gracefully. But no one was there to catch her, and she thudded to the floor.

A crash came from somewhere. The ballroom dimmed, and a wave of screams shot up to the ceiling. A drop of scotch fell on my lips. I tried to stand straight, tried to push aside the jostling arms and feet, tried to reach Lanyu lying in a puddle of darkness. *Someone save her!*

A voice called out for me; in a shadowy blur I saw Cheng and Ying burst into the ballroom. Ying raised something in his hand. Another explosive sound. Glass shattered, wine bottles exploded, chairs crashed, windows shattered. Damage that would cost a fortune to repair.

In a cloud of spilled-alcohol spray and the pungent odor of sulfur, I came face to face with a Mauser. It was close, too close. But this couldn't be happening. I didn't do anything wrong. I only wanted to protect Ernest and my club. I couldn't be shot. I was too young. I didn't want to die.

A pop. It sounded like it came across from me, or from the ceiling, or through it. It rang in my ears, piercing, but I barely jumped or screamed.

42

ERNEST

She was gone. The club was closed. No neon lights, no men smoking cigarettes, no idlers loitering around, all the music and life were sucked out. For hours Ernest sat on the empty staircase outside the building; he asked everyone passing by.

There were gunshots, people said. Someone was killed. *Who?* No one knew.

He went back to Sassoon's hotel and borrowed the phone from the bar, using the privilege as a former employee, and dialed Aiyi's home number, which he had memorized. A man with a British accent answered. The Cambridge-educated brother, he supposed. He hung up when he heard Ernest introduce himself.

Ernest clutched the black canvas bag, heavy like a carcass. Aiyi was alive; she had to be.

Ernest was heading toward the revolving door when the bellman said Sassoon had asked to see him. He nodded, slung the bag across his shoulder, and took the elevator up. Sassoon, still in his blue-gray uniform, was chatting with a woman on the chesterfield near the piano; he waved at Ernest to enter as he spoke to her. "I wish you the best with your work. But have you lived through war before, Laura?"

"God laughs when man plans, but I'm going to plan anyway. Now, who's this young man?" The woman stood up, winding a red wool scarf around her neck. She looked to be in her thirties, with short hair and a plump face, wearing a black coat and a pair of sneakers. No makeup. She had a matronly demeanor that reminded Ernest of the mother of a strict conductor he used to know in Berlin.

Ernest smiled, surprised at the frank way she stared at him.

Sassoon chuckled. "Laura Margolis, meet Ernest Reismann, a pianist and a photographer. Ernest, Laura is a social worker, a representative of the Jewish Distribution Center in New York."

Ernest shook her hand. It was rough, calloused. "Pleased to meet you, Miss Margolis." He had never heard of the distribution center in New York.

"Who did this to you, Ernest?" She was looking at his hand.

"Hitler Youth. A long time ago."

She nodded. "Are you married, Ernest?"

"No."

"Wonderful. How old are you? Twenty-eight?"

"Twenty."

"You look much older than that. Or is that my wishful thinking? If you were twenty years older, I would insist you be my husband."

Ernest grinned. She was outspoken; he rather liked her.

"I'm serious. It's a cruel world. I fly all over the world, first Cuba and now Shanghai, looking for a husband. Now I see good material, but you're too young. Are you a refugee, too, Ernest?" She dusted his sleeve as if he were her son.

"I've settled in."

"Good to know. We're doing our best to help the most recent arrivals here, eight thousand of them, all in dire need of help. Many are old, have no skills. Some are in poor health. They can't find jobs, and they're crowded in the *Heime* with deplorable sanitary conditions."

He had heard of the *Heime* in the Hongkou district, which had the lowest rent. "I see fewer refugees coming from Europe these days," he said.

"That, I'm afraid, is bad news. I hear the Nazis are implementing more abominable plans against the Jews and many Jews are teetering on the brink of death. Do you have family in Germany?"

Her eyes, brimming with sympathy, tugged at Ernest's heart. "My parents were waiting for visas when I left."

"I'm sure they got the visas and escaped. But the situation in Shanghai is quite concerning, and we don't know how things will work out. Right now, the JDC can still wire us the kitchen funding for the refugees, but if war breaks out, communication to New York will be cut off."

"If there's anything I can do, Miss Margolis, I'd like to help."

"You are a mensch. I'll remember that." She tucked the red scarf under her black coat. "I better get going. I really appreciate your contribution to the loan, Sir Sassoon. Half a million dollars! I get nervous just thinking about it and can barely get any sleep."

"I'll walk you out. Ernest, would you wait here?" Sassoon took his cane. "This way. Laura, it was my pleasure. But I warn you, make a contingency plan. It's best you depart Shanghai and return to New York as well."

"I can't leave Shanghai while people are hungry." The two went out to the hallway.

Ernest stood. *The Nazis are implementing more abominable plans against the Jews.* Did his parents escape on time? He was still thinking about that when he heard Sassoon's voice.

"A dauntless woman, Miss Margolis. I quite like her. Sit, Ernest. Sit." Sassoon limped to the coffee table where a tray with a decanter was set. "Cigar?"

Ernest took it. His fingers were trembling, and he couldn't focus, worried about his parents.

"Ernest, I'm flying out tomorrow to attend a meeting in New York. But I'm not deserting Shanghai, if that's what you're wondering. I've given up India for Shanghai. I shall not give up Shanghai for anything."

Ernest cleared his throat. "I'm planning on leaving, too. When will you return, sir?"

"In a month. When do you leave, Ernest?"

He hesitated. "In three days. To Hong Kong."

"So soon? I was going to ask you a favor."

"What favor?"

Sassoon's shrewd eyes locked on him. "You know my hobby. The photos in my studio are a treasure to me. I developed them in the darkroom myself. In usual circumstances, I wouldn't worry about leaving the city for a month, but with the Japanese and the talk of war, I fear the security won't be as tight as it should be. So, Ernest, I was hoping you'd keep an eye on my collection for me."

Her photos. Fury balled in his stomach. "You shouldn't have taken them in the first place. You put all the women's lives and their reputations at risk."

"Do not judge me. I never thought of this day. This is my penthouse, my building, my Shanghai."

Ernest wanted to smack him. If war broke out, no place would be safe. Even this penthouse.

"I have an obligation to keep these photos safe. When I return, I'd like to see them again. I could take them with me, but transferring all the albums to the plane will put them in the hands of crass movers. I'd rather not risk it."

Ernest took a drag of his cigar. No matter how angry he was at Sassoon, he still cared for Aiyi and her reputation. "Even if I'd like to, I don't know how to keep them safe, sir."

Sassoon smiled, limped across the sitting area, and disappeared behind the cabinet with shelves of whiskey bottles. When he returned, he held out a key. "This is the key to my studio. Come to check the penthouse once in a while if you decide to stay in Shanghai. I'll give you the permission to access the penthouse. You don't need to open the studio unless it's necessary. Make sure not a single photo is damaged. If one is damaged or missing, I'll hold you responsible. Agree?"

Ernest stubbed the cigar in the ash tray and took the key. It was golden, cold, like a frozen fish. "I can't promise anything, but I'll do my best."

"That's good enough." Sassoon picked up a decanter on the side table and poured some whiskey into two glasses. "I hear you were using the hotel's phone to call Miss Shao."

"There was a shooting incident in her club."

"There was a shooting in Ciro's too. Two men were shot by the Japanese. Unbelievable. I would never have imagined the Japanese attacking my property years ago. But the Japanese want control of the Settlement, and I fear there's nothing we can do. Your photos are disturbing. My fellow businessmen have vowed to do all they can to protect the Settlement. Maybe it's not too late. How's she doing?" The Briton had the steady gaze he must have had when seated among the members of the Shanghai Club, though something in his sharp black eyes betrayed him for a fleeting moment.

The thought of telling Sassoon of their elopement crossed Ernest's mind. "I don't know."

"I shall call her. Perhaps she would fly to New York with me."

Ernest looked up. "She won't do that."

Sassoon handed him a glass of whiskey. "You seem to have strong feelings for her, Ernest. I'm not surprised. She's an attractive woman. But I have a plan. A good plan."

It was irritating to hear the confidence in the old man's voice. Ernest drained the whiskey in one gulp. "God laughs when man plans, sir."

43

AIYI

I felt sick on my bed. The bullet hadn't penetrated me and barely touched my skin, but it seemed it had left a hole in my soul. In my twenty-one years of life, I had witnessed plenty of deaths, driven by the bloody execution stage, stepped over littered bodies, wept at the funerals of my parents and my brother, and heard stories of deaths at dinner. But I had never thought I would die.

I heard Ying's voice, close by yet distant. He had saved me just before Yamazaki fired and brought me home. Ying was still talking about the shooting. He sounded proud, bragging about his skill, regretting that he'd only killed the soldier and missed Yamazaki.

So Yamazaki was still alive. Would he be enraged now, seeking revenge, or perhaps become more reasonable, letting Ernest and me go?

"Sassoon called. He said it was urgent. Since when did you become friends with that foreigner?" Ying said, opening my wardrobe, searching for cash, mumbling that he would pay me back once he won a poker game.

"Take my purse." I buried my face in the soft silk quilt. Sassoon was the last thing on my mind. "Can you stay with me?" Never in my life had I been so frightened. My body ached, and I felt chilled.

"Can't." Ying emptied my purse and slipped out.

After a while, Sinmay came in. "You have brought this on yourself. You are reckless, thoughtless. I warned you not to get involved with the foreigner!"

I was almost shot, and that was all he could say.

"Why did you visit Emily and send her for the treatment? Now she's clean and left Shanghai! You should have had the decency to tell me what you were doing behind my back." He stormed out.

Peiyu, on her small lotus feet, waddled in with her handkerchief, her face strained with fear. This was bad luck, she said. The calendar had said we needed to avoid leaving home that day, and she should have told me. She must plan something festive to drive away bad luck. The wedding must happen as soon as possible. Finally, she toddled out.

None of them asked how I was doing.

Insomnia. A plague. For hours I lay in bed, thoughts of whys, hows, and what-ifs swinging in my head like crazy legs in the ballroom. I heard groans vibrating in the ceiling, caught shadows lurking behind the wardrobes, and glimpsed shapes of people: Lanyu, Yamazaki, the three gangly boys, Cheng, and even Ernest. They were bleeding, covered with blood, yet they all danced to the sound of gunfire while the windows, the lights, and the broken glass cascaded in a waterfall of shards. Lanyu was digging at my eyes. "Save me, save me!"

And the music. It was so loud. Disjointed. Raging. It wouldn't stop. *Make it stop.*

Silence was a noise with teeth; it gnawed on my skin and left deep marks. Silence was a noise with arms and legs; it crawled across the rafters and spread its spawns of spells. Silence was a noise with a face, a face of dust and doom, a face of motes and moans.

I was in a cold sweat; I couldn't sleep. I was not as strong as I thought I was.

After two days, I got out of bed and stood in front of the mirror. What a mess I was. My face was pallid, eyelids swollen; my hair was tangled, on my cheek a black blossom of bloodstain. I washed up, put on a clean dress, and went to my club. It would be heartbreaking to see the damage, but I could still revive the business if I worked hard, and many people's livelihoods depended on me. And Ernest. He must be anxious.

The three-story building looked haunted under the gray sky. People walked by it without a second glance. By now all of Shanghai had learned of the shooting; few would patronize the club at the risk of facing a Mauser.

In the atrium, my managers, the band, several dancers, the accountant, the busboys, the bellboys, and even the cleaning staff greeted me with relieved faces.

"The ballroom has been swept clean, Miss Shao."

"And Lanyu. We gave her a decent burial."

"Would you consider hiring more dancers?"

And the accountant murmured, holding a stack of bills: power bills, utility bills, payments for the band, rent, food, and drinks.

I did my best to stay calm. I would take care of my employees. They needed work and needed to be paid. But the moment I stepped inside the dark ballroom—the Japanese had cut off the electricity—I shivered, the image of the shooting clear in my mind.

I rushed out to the landing, where I froze. Two Japanese soldiers climbed up the stairs; they roughly pushed me aside and plastered two long strips of paper on the gilded doors of my club, making a huge X, under which, in red ink, was written the Japanese kanji ENTRY FORBIDDEN, UNDER INVESTIGATION.

They wouldn't confiscate my club, a joint venture, but they had ordered my business to cease operations.

I held on to the stair banister, feeling dizzy. The drawer of my desk stored the contract I had bargained with Sassoon, the cash, and a few banknotes I'd saved. My club, which I had worked so hard to manage, my livelihood, was only a few steps ahead of me, but it might as well have been thousands of miles away.

༄

In the atrium, I passed my employees, went out to the street, and got in my car. My legs were weak, but I held all my emotions tight inside, trying hard to stay strong.

"Aiyi, Aiyi!"

I rolled down the window of my Nash.

On the street stood Ernest, carrying a canvas bag, his fedora askew, his face flushed with joy. "You're safe. Thank God. I've been waiting for you. I was so worried about you. Are you all right?"

Something in me fell apart. "They sealed up my club, Ernest. My business is gone."

"You have me." He looked at me. It was the same look he had when he said something like *Love is stronger than death*, when he said he'd care for me even if I were married a thousand times.

"But . . ." What would I do without my club? My business. It was my life.

"Let's go, Aiyi. The boat will leave tomorrow."

I felt a sting in my eyes. He had helped rebuild my business; he was a partner I had trusted, a man I loved, the man for whom I'd turned down enormous wealth. But an innocent woman had died, I was almost shot, and my club was seized—all because of my obsession with him. I should never have gone this far with Ernest. This distraction, this whim, this dangerous confusion had cost me my business.

I pulled tight my mink coat; my leather shoes felt freezing against my ankles. "I can't leave with you, Ernest. I'm going home."

His jaw dropped.

I told my chauffeur to drive.

44

ERNEST

He was freezing. He put on two shirts, a vest, and two jackets over his taupe suit; still a chill balled in his stomach. He spent a sleepless night. Then staring at the rice porridge, his daily breakfast for the past two years, he had no appetite. He stood up, went out to the street, and bought a bowl of soy milk at a stall.

The drink was opaque, bits of yellow soybean shells floating on the top. It tasted bland, no sugar or salt, with a distinct odor of soy, and it was gritty, like a flood of sand over his tongue. He could get used to this taste and texture, get used to her change of mind, too, but what he couldn't get used to was a future without her. Anxiously, he held the tickets to Hong Kong as the hour of departure ticked closer. He prayed she would change her mind and come to meet him before the tickets would expire. She didn't.

The ship sailed without them. The shots rang on the street; more and more desperate Europeans crowded at the pier to get out of Shanghai. The cold wind blowing on his face, Ernest bought another two tickets, overpriced, to Hong Kong. He must leave Shanghai to keep Miriam safe.

At the pier where he often stood, he gazed at the river. There were no cruise ships, no gangplanks, no crowds of refugees carrying suitcases, no signs of his parents.

What had happened to them? For almost two years he had been writing to them, but they'd never replied. *The Nazis are implementing more abominable plans against the Jews.* And Miss Margolis's sympathetic look. A chill shot through Ernest's brain and ran down his spine. He doubled over and sobbed.

Growing up, he had locked horns with his father, who was more enthusiastic about mummies and bones than him, who loved Leah and Miriam more than him. A book person like Ernest's sisters, his father didn't care for his son's hobbies of photography or movies. So Ernest had avoided him. When they went to their favorite resort in Czechoslovakia for vacation, his father went skiing, Ernest stayed behind and drank pilsner; when his father drank schnapps, Ernest went skiing.

His mother, despite all his love for her, was a critical woman. He still remembered her criticisms: *Your Schumann is so loud you could wake up a dead man in a grave. Your Beethoven is so stiff you might as well play the drum in a marching band. Who is the young woman you talked to outside the school? Didn't you know she isn't Jewish?* When he was a child, he had placed more importance on pleasing her than himself. But in adolescence, rebellion began to sprout. It became difficult to balance the piano and her control of him. He fought her. He ate nonkosher foods like shrimp and ham and hung out with non-Jewish friends; he stayed out for beer on Shabbat night.

His battle had been so inconsequential and childish, he could see that now. If he could see his mother again, he would tell her how he survived in Shanghai as a pianist. If he could see his father again, he would ask him to drink schnapps and go skiing together.

❧

Later, he went to fetch Miriam, whom he had visited a few times since he bought tickets for the three of them. When Aiyi declined to leave with him, he had told Miriam to get ready for the new departure date. When he arrived at the school's courtyard, Miriam was sitting on a bench, holding a small brown leather suitcase. She had her hair in a French braid, his mother's favorite hairstyle; Miriam looked healthy, her cheeks filled out, her eyes flashing intelligently. What a beautiful woman she had become. His parents would be so proud. Ernest choked up.

"Ernest, I've been waiting for you," Miriam said.

"I'm glad you're ready, Miriam," he said. Mr. Blackstone, dressed in a brown flannel jacket, was next to her. Ernest shook hands with him. "It's very kind of you to see us off. I'm indebted to you. Thank you for looking after my sister."

"Your sister has brought us immense joy, Mr. Reismann." Mr. Blackstone's impressive baritone voice rang out. "I'd like to tell you an important decision my wife and I made. It's no longer safe in Shanghai. The school has decided to close earlier, so we're leaving for America."

Ernest nodded. Still he was grateful that Mr. Blackstone had taken Miriam in, fed her, and let her borrow his Webster dictionary. "Safe travels. I hope our paths will cross again."

"Ernest." Miriam stared at her feet. "I meant to tell you that Mr. Blackstone and his wife wish to adopt me and take me with them. They have a farmhouse with horses in America."

"What? Adopt you?" He must have heard it wrong.

"So we'll make it legal, and she can leave with us," Mr. Blackstone said.

Miriam was staring at her feet, but Ernest could see it in her eyes: some fear and a sliver of excitement.

This couldn't be happening. He had just realized the fate of his parents, and now Miriam wanted to leave him. "You can't be serious, Miriam. We're going to Hong Kong. I've told you. Adoption? That's crazy. You don't need to be adopted. Besides, the processes must be very complicated."

"No need to worry, Mr. Reismann. My wife and I already have the paperwork prepared. All we need is your consent."

He wished the man would leave them alone. "Miriam?" He held her shoulders. She was so young; she was confused. She didn't understand the consequences of being adopted. "Look, can we talk at home? I'm . . . I'm very surprised. This is rather unexpected. It's a serious decision, can't you see? Can you talk to me?"

Miriam looked away. Ernest trembled. It was true. She didn't want him, her brother, her blood; she wanted Mr. Blackstone, a passerby in her life.

"Mr. Reismann, regrettably, we won't have much time. I promise you, my wife and I will treat her well. My wife loves her. She helped her pack. You like the suitcase, don't you, Miriam? The canvas bag was too small."

Never in his life had Ernest hated a baritone voice more. He should never have sent her to live with the Americans. Who was this Mr. Blackstone anyway? Did he play that silly football game? Did he go to church every day like a fanatic? Did he even like jazz? The school had said he was engaged in an import and export business of stockings and garments. But for all he could tell, Mr. Blackstone might be a drunkard, or even a criminal—ordinary, decent Americans wouldn't travel overseas to Shanghai.

"Ernest?"

Miriam's pleading eyes. His thoughts scattered. What had he done wrong? How could he have lost her love, her trust, when he did his best to support her and protect her? "You want to leave with him, Miriam? Is this what you'll choose?"

She looked down at her feet again. "I don't like Shanghai. I don't want to stay here. I don't want to swat flies all day."

"We're going to Hong Kong, Miriam. You won't swat flies. Things will get better."

"Mr. Reismann, if we adopt her, she'd be an American citizen," Mr. Blackstone said.

And she would have a Webster dictionary to read and peas and meat loaf to eat every Sunday. This was a good life, the best life he could dream of for her, but he was unwilling to let her go. He had promised his parents to look after her, and he loved her.

"If you leave, Miriam, I'll never see you again . . ."

Tears welled in her eyes. She loved him after all. Maybe she remembered how he protected her, how much he cared for her. But she wiped off her tears. "You don't care about me, Ernest. You never did. You didn't remember my birthday, and you forgot my bat mitzvah."

He felt a pang in his stomach. She was right—he had not done enough. "Well, if this is what you want, I'll let you go. I wish you all the best. I wish you a bright and happy future in America."

Miriam gazed at him with happiness, relief, and what he thought might be an apology. "I want to go to Vassar College, Ernest."

He could barely nod when Mr. Blackstone gave him a form from a manila folder; he signed at the bottom and gave it back. He stood straight as Miriam picked up her suitcase, stood straight as Mr. Blackstone steered her out of the courtyard. His back grew stiff, his hands chilled, his face numb. He couldn't protect her anymore. She was on her own. She would become a professor like his father or grow up like a cowgirl, learn to ride horses, and meet eccentric people, but he would never know.

Miriam paused at the courtyard's door and turned to him. She looked . . . like his mother at their last Passover. Then Miriam turned around and disappeared through the door. He covered his face. He had lost his other sister, his parents, his lover. If he lost Miriam, too, he would be utterly alone.

He picked up his canvas bag, stumbled out of the courtyard, and grabbed Miriam's hand just as Mr. Blackstone opened the car's door. "I changed my mind. You can't go. Please, Miriam. Please stay with me. I love you. I love you very much."

"Ernest. Have you lost your mind?"

"I'm sorry. You must stay with me, Miriam. I'm sorry, Mr. Blackstone. She can't go with you. I won't allow it. I will not give you my consent. Please give me back the form."

Mr. Blackstone let out a heavy sigh, handed him the form, and ducked into the car. Miriam screamed, trying to get in, but Ernest pulled her back. He held her tight as Mr. Blackstone's Packard growled and staggered forward, as the red taillights disappeared among the rickshaws at the end of the street.

"Get off me; get off." Miriam shook him off. "I hate you. I hate you!"

He closed his eyes. Relief, sadness, and guilt washed over him.

45

AIYI

When I came home, Peiyu was studying a pile of red envelopes on the round mah-jongg table. New wedding invitations, she said. She and Cheng's mother had picked out another auspicious date for the wedding, and she had made a deposit at the best restaurant in Shanghai, the same restaurant where the generalissimo and his wife, Soong Meiling, were wed. She also made a reduced list of two hundred people. Many were my spoiled aristocratic relatives with lost fortunes. Some of the concubines' families were strategically left out.

"The new date is the last day of February next year, in about three months," she said. "Cheng's mother agrees that this wedding will drive away bad luck, and we'll have fortune, happiness, and prosperity. Are you sick? You look terrible, Aiyi."

"I don't think a wedding is going to change anything."

Sinmay came in, hands folded behind his back, his long robe casting a long shadow. He looked angry, gloomy, trapped in a garden of thoughts, mumbling that Emily had not replied to his letters.

"Well, a wedding is all we need. Right, husband?"

I looked at Sinmay, the ultimate authority in the house. We were different. He was the cherished firstborn son who'd received a baby elephant for his fifth birthday; I was the insignificant girl who received instructions of obedience. He, a Cambridge graduate; I, a local college dropout. He loved poetry; I loved money. He donned traditional Chinese scholar's robes; I wore figure-showing dresses. He had an American mistress; I was to wed my cousin.

And the inheritance fight had separated us like a wall; there was nothing I could do to repair our relationship.

Sinmay coughed. His slow gramophone voice rang out. "Don't be stubborn, little sister. Your wedding is our family's business."

"You're nervous, Aiyi. Every girl gets nervous before the wedding. That's normal. Your mother made a good betrothal. You and Cheng are meant for each other. It's a marriage well matched from the door to the roof," Peiyu said, quoting a proverb.

"They sealed up my club," I said.

A red envelope dropped out of Peiyu's hands. She gaped at me and then Sinmay.

"What a disaster," Sinmay said. "Did you tell Cheng?"

"I haven't."

"Maybe you shouldn't tell him."

I didn't understand.

Peiyu scanned the envelopes on the table. "We just agreed on the date. And you've lost your business . . . They won't cancel the wedding, will they?"

Sinmay didn't say anything, and I thought, for the first time in my life, he felt sorry for me.

Until now, it had not occurred to me that with the freezing of my business, my marriage to Cheng was no longer matched from the door to the roof.

❧

Silence again. Its cold feet crawled, teeth gnawing noiselessly. My skin prickled; I shivered.

I was poor. I'd lost my club, my business, and now I had nothing.

You must have money and own things, so you won't be a ball people kick around, Mother had said to me when my addict father sold the mountain in the outskirts of Shanghai, her dowry, for some pipe money. His addiction would grow worse, his temperament would change, and he would beat her when she refused to give him money. He would grow ill and die eventually, and months later, toddling on her three-inch golden lotus feet, Mother packed up for a ski trip in Switzerland. She loved the feeling of being airborne, she had said, and she had hoped this would be a trip to start her life of freedom, but she knocked her head against a rock. I would learn she had surreptitiously changed her will before the trip, adding my name and entitling me to a share of my family's vast fortune, against the tradition that women couldn't inherit properties.

And she had arranged my marriage with Cheng for the same reason—so I wouldn't be poor, so I would always be looked after.

What had I done?

It would never work out with Ernest—a foreigner, a pianist, a poor man. He wouldn't be able to give me a decent home, decent social standing, or decent food. We would always live in scorn, in hostility, in danger.

What should I do now?

I went to the moon-shaped bamboo shelf and took out the small brass brazier and the porcelain pot that stored aloeswood chips, a gift from my third brother before he left behind his share of inheritance to live a life of solitude in the Jing'an Temple. My third brother and Mother were both Buddhists and often meditated with the aloeswood chips.

I scooped out some chips from the pot and added them to the brazier engraved with coiling dragons. Sitting in lotus position, I lit the match and tossed it into the brazier. A blue seed of flame flickered from beneath the chips; a stem of pale smoke sprouted, grew plumper like a fruit, filled to the brim of the brazier, and then bloomed into the air. A smoky gown enveloped me.

I sat still, transfixed by the drifting smoke, the veins of air. I thought of my childhood days, happy days, the sound of runes Mother had mouthed, and the circle of life she believed in as the pale plume swiveled, growing, shifting, transforming into a grand dance hall filled with animated figures, and then it lengthened to form the mah-jongg tiles, the silk ties, the familiar world of courtyards, a world without ghosts, doubts, or fears.

Really, the best life was the safest.

I felt a lightness on my shoulders, like long hair had been snipped off. I got up, washed my face, picked out a blue dress, and went to Cheng's home.

He lived in a compound similar to mine, with high walls and a wide wooden gate. Inside the compound were willows, pines, and some dwarf bushes I couldn't name. Nature, flowers, and plants were not a fancy of mine, and birds and animals were a great pleasure of Cheng's. Another difference between us.

I wondered what he would say. He hadn't asked me to sit on his lap since I'd refused, and we hadn't talked that much since then. Would he back out of the wedding?

He was in his game room decorated with horses and roosters. The room was cold, but he wore a burgundy velvet smoking robe with a wide black collar that barely covered him, exposing his muscular arms and chest. He held a stick, feeding a rosefinch in a bamboo cage. The cigarette smoke wafted from his fingers to the bird as it shambled from one bamboo slat to another like a drunkard.

"It doesn't seem that he likes the smoke," I said.

"He'll be fine." He sat on a bamboo lounge covered with a plum silk pongee cushion and propped up one leg. He had big feet, which his mother praised as a good sign since he would be sure-footed, but it also meant he had to have all his brogues custom made.

He had many admirers, or mistresses as I would call them. One was a general's daughter, another a popular singer and actress; some were much older than him. He never told me about any of his female admirers, but I had my ways with Ying, whose mouth became loose when he wanted to borrow money from me. Women loved Cheng, Ying had said with apparent envy.

Cheng studied my dress.

I had deliberately put on the Chinese bra. No more criticism should come.

"Shouldn't you wear another layer?"

I grimaced. "They sealed up my club." I stared at a tuft of rose-hued feathers on the bird's head. The sentence felt like a blade; each time I said it, it carved deeper into my skin.

"You brought this on yourself. I've warned you."

"I thought you should know in case you have second thoughts about the wedding."

He smoked. A speck of ash fell on his velvet trousers. "What are you talking about? It's our wedding."

"Maybe you want to tell your mother about this."

He cocked his head; the arrogant side of him seemed to say it was his decision, but he was always his mother's boy. He threw the cigarette, stamped on it, and called a servant.

Her arms held by two maidservants, his mother, my aunt, came over, wobbling on her tiny feet. I'd never liked her, and she'd never liked me. She was the type of woman who believed her boy deserved a wife who was no less than a saint. A critical woman, she tended to see other people's flaws and said many negative things about me. I suspected she had regretted the lopsided nature of the marriage deal since the loss of my family's fortune. Now she would have the perfect excuse.

I bowed. "Good afternoon, Aunt."

"Aiyi, Peiyu said you hired a white pianist. Is it true? You should have told me. What are you doing here? What's going on with your club? What else is wrong?"

Cheng cleared his throat. "Ma, Aiyi's club was sealed. It's not a big deal, I say. I was just telling her about our wedding."

"Sealed! Wa, wa, wa. How horrific! Why didn't you tell me sooner? I just sent out the invitations."

"Ma," Cheng said.

She sighed. "You're so young and naive, my son. We're a family of honor and esteem. We keep our word. But the world has changed. No one has decency anymore. Awful weather, just awful! Nothing is going well these days." She turned around and left.

In silence, I sat on a wicker chair next to Cheng. My face burned with humiliation—my aunt always knew how to have the upper hand. Yet I would learn to tolerate her, and I could imagine my life with Cheng as we wedded and bedded, smooth and placid, like a cold winter pond. It was perhaps life's greatest happiness, for there was safety with Cheng, which I could never have with Ernest.

46

ERNEST

Two days passed since he refused the adoption. Miriam had been sulky. She slunk away to the street during the day; by nightfall she came back and slept on a pile of coats in a corner. When he tried to talk to her, she screamed, "You ruined my life. Leave me alone!"

Guilt hammered his heart. He itched to do something to make it up to her. He went to search for bookstores that sold English books and finally found one. With five American dollars, he purchased a Webster dictionary and left it on the pile of coats where she slept. When Miriam saw it, she took it, held it, and turned her back on him.

He could do more. He set out to scour for a bakery. Near a church in the Settlement, he found one, owned by Mr. Kauser, a stout American, and his wife. The bakery was crowded with European refugees who wore double-breasted coats and hats he knew well. It was such a joy to see them, even though they were from different countries. Beaming, Ernest asked Mr. Kauser if he could make some *Pfannkuchen*.

Mr. Kauser shook his head. "We only make bread and bagels, sir."

So Ernest bought some flour from the bakery, and with another five dollars he bought two eggs and expensive milk—dairy was rare and hard to find. In the dim kitchen in the hallway, he mixed up the ingredients and made *Pfannkuchen* with care as if his life depended on it. And finally, a dozen golden *Pfannkuchen*. He stacked them on a plate and left them in a pot to keep them warm.

When Miriam saw the *Pfannkuchen*, she growled and looked away, but the moment he turned around, she took the pot and devoured all in the hallway.

Ernest sighed in relief. He could never give back the life she had lost, but he would keep doing his best, to apologize for his negligence, to show how much he cared for her, and he would never, ever neglect her again.

↬

It was the first day of December. The day wasn't special, and it normally would have slipped into the muddy river of history like a sodden leaf. But it was the day they would leave for Hong Kong.

In the morning, Ernest reminded Miriam of their departure that afternoon. She growled and left. He scratched his chin, hoping she would be back on time.

There were still hours before the departure, so Ernest went to Mr. Kauser's bakery again. He tried a bagel with peanut butter since jam and butter were scarce. But peanut butter went well with bagels; it was nutty and rich, and the bagel was freshly baked.

Across from him, an old man with a felt hat was peering at a newspaper on the table; suddenly he pushed the paper aside and sobbed.

Ernest recognized Mr. Schmidt, the man who had borrowed his toothbrush in the Embankment Building. "Mr. Schmidt? I'm Ernest Reismann. Remember me? So good to see you. What's wrong?"

"Read it! Germany. Germany has—" The old man choked up and stuffed the *Shanghai Jewish Chronicle* into his hand. People around them gathered to see.

Maybe Germany had utterly destroyed Britain. Or maybe Hitler was dead. Ernest spread the newspaper on the table. Unable to believe what he had just read, he read it again.

It was not about the war; it was about him. The German government had announced that a Jew living abroad could not be a German citizen and all the assets of the Jews would be taken over by the Third Reich. It was official. He, who had been born in Berlin, spoke German, went to German schools, became a bar mitzvah in a fine restaurant in central Berlin, played the piano in music halls and cozy apartments near the Brandenburg Gate, went skiing at the Alpsee-Grünten resort, and bought his Leica in a shop in Berlin, was no longer a citizen of Germany. After all the pogroms, all the suffering, all the anguish, his sister's life, his parents' lives, and Miriam's and his futures, the Nazis still wouldn't leave him alone.

Ernest took out the passport in his pocket and tore up the first page, the second, and then the entire book. He was now a man without a country. Had there been such a thing before? A curiosity, a tragedy, a man without a country.

He laughed, and he couldn't stop laughing even when tears spilled. From now on, he was a wanderer, a drifter, unclaimed, unbound, unidentified.

Mr. Schmidt was moaning, "Oh, Lord," then added a comment that seemed to show how much his time in Shanghai had influenced him: "We are only the lotus flowers in a pond, a shallow bloom. Our shallow roots grasp for water and air, and we drift in the tide of cruelty."

Some people wailed; some dug into their pockets and began to rip their passports too. "Good riddance!" they cried out with tears in their eyes.

Ernest stared at the pile of scraps, his heart wrenched in pain. Without a passport, he was a ghost; without a passport, he couldn't leave Shanghai.

He didn't remember how he left the bakery. Walking toward the apartment where he had stayed for nearly two years, he came across a checkpoint near the Chinese district, where a Japanese sentry was hitting a long-robed Chinese man with a rifle stock. He shivered. A stateless man, he was a target that bullets, bayonets, and bombs could aim at. Even if he bled to death, the killer would claim no responsibility.

The same fate would fall on Miriam. Poor Miriam. Had he known they would be stateless, he would have let her go with Mr. Blackstone. For his selfish reasons, he had kept her and had inadvertently destroyed her future.

In the next few days he rushed from one consulate to another. First the British consulate, which was closed due to lack of staff, then the American consulate inside the towering Development Building. He had never gone there before—America seemed so distant.

The building was crowded with many refugees seeking asylum like him. The staff tossed his application in a large bin overflowing with forms, said their monthly quota of visas was five and good luck, and then shut the window. The office hours were ended early so the staff could attend a Christmas party.

Down the street, the green pyramid of Sassoon's hotel appeared. Something like hope rose in his heart. He would stay in the city, and perhaps he could see her again. He went in the hotel and phoned her.

Her voice, distant, came through the receiver. "Don't call me again, Ernest. I'm getting married."

Ernest walked out of the hotel and wandered on the streets, his ears filled with incessant noise: the ubiquitous drone of jets, the squeaking of rickshaws, the shrieks of thieves beaten by clubs, and the ever-present hawking of street vendors. "Tofu, two cents a block. Tofu, two cents a block . . ."

In his dark room, Ernest sat on his bed, yawning. His fingers fumbled for a button but were unable to find it. He gave up. Everything seemed pointless: finding another job, or getting out of bed, or moving out and finding another apartment. Another endless repetition of life. He didn't feel like doing anything. He was going to stay here until he was evicted. Maybe Aiyi would come to evict him.

A crack came from the glass windowpane, startling him. As he turned to watch, a streak of light appeared. The windows burst; a hot storm roared toward him. He dove to Miriam sleeping behind the cabinet to cover her, all his sleepiness vanishing. When the room was quiet again, he leaned over the broken window and looked out. There was no daylight; it was perhaps around four o'clock.

In the distance, the gray predawn sky of Shanghai was set ablaze by a wheel of violent orange mushrooming above the dark muddy river. By the raging flame, he could see that all the boats—the sampans, the commercial ships—had vanished.

The warship *Izumo*, lit up by stark white light on the deck, its funnels pumping fumes and smoke, sailed downstream toward the American and British cruisers, both in flames. Above the river, three fighters emblazoned with the rising sun fired at something on the street near Sassoon's hotel.

The Japanese had attacked the Settlement.

Her photos.

"Miriam, wake up, wake up." He shook her shockingly still-asleep form. He rubbed his face, didn't know what to do. "Miriam, I'm going out for a minute. You stay inside, stay safe. Don't go anywhere. I'll be right back."

Ernest grabbed the key Sassoon had given him from under his pillow and dashed out. The streets were empty, the air heavy with gasoline and gunpowder, choking him, making his eyes water. Dazzling headlights almost blinded him; straight ahead rolled the armored vehicles with the rising sun flags.

He dove toward an alley, stumbling, fumbling on the wall to make his way to Sassoon House. Somewhere a bomb exploded, the ground rattled, and a wall crashed near him. He covered his head, continuing to run. By the time he reached the pier, dawn was breaking, and from the river came a thunder—a cannon had fired.

To his horror, the side of the American vessel was blasted open; the cruiser quavered. A storm of broken sails, wood, and ammunition shells seesawed in the air, and a few crew onboard, screaming, jumped into the river. A group of Japanese infantry raced to the aft deck, pointing their rifles at several figures crouched in the corner. On the British HMS *Peterel*, a deck-mounted machine gun fired rapidly at a fighter dropping bombs. *Boom.* The vessel was engulfed in flames.

Ernest raced toward the hotel, the street enveloped by a coat of smoke. Then suddenly, just as he came to the hotel's entrance facing the river, he was swallowed by a swarm of screaming people: people in white bathrobes, people carrying suitcases, people trying to get in their Packards.

"Let me through; let me through." He elbowed his way among the throng toward the entrance just as a missile hit the building nearby. A storm of shards, bricks, and flying limbs surged toward him. Ernest covered his head, stumbled past a screaming man rolling on the ground, and, his heart pounding, rushed inside the hotel.

A Japanese soldier was shouting at guests and hotel staff in the main lobby; the emergency alarm blared. Ernest turned to the café and ran toward the elevator—it was crammed with people. He pivoted toward the staircase near the mezzanine, barging through the hotel guests rushing down.

He made it to the eleventh floor. No guards. Sassoon's penthouse was open. He passed the piano and cabinets and found the studio at the left corner. It was locked. He dug out the key from his pocket and jammed it in the keyhole. The door swung open; he turned on the light.

His head swam. Walls of women, walls of photos, all nudes. He cursed Sassoon again for his perverse hobby and searched. No Aiyi.

Footsteps came from the reception room. Heavy footfalls with silver loops clinking on their boots.

His heart pounding, he locked the door. Time was running out. He pulled all the photos off the wall and stuffed them in an empty box for cartridges in a corner. On a desk near the couch, he found rolls of undeveloped film; behind the tripod, inside rosewood cabinets were more film rolls, photos, diaries, and albums.

Voices speaking Japanese came from outside the studio. The door shook. Someone was trying to break in.

If they found him, they would put a bullet in his head. Ernest swept all the undeveloped film, the albums, and the photos into his arms and dumped them into a pile on the floor. Among the pile of chemical bottles, magnifiers, and print papers, he found a matchbox with the hotel's logo.

Not a single photo must be damaged. Sassoon's voice rang in his mind.

Ernest struck a match and threw it in the pile. The flames sputtered, came alive, and grazed the pile. He added in more albums and photos. The fire hissed, licking the carpet and the desk and the couch. It was time for him to get out of there, but there was now laughter and the clinking of glass outside.

Smoke surged. His throat burned. His face felt as if it were on fire; his hair was singed. If he stayed for one more minute, he'd be burned alive. He pressed his back to the wall, holding his nose, staggered past the fire, and reached for the door handle. His arm swept the top of a file cabinet near the door, and something heavy fell to his feet. Sassoon's camera.

He scooped it up, stuffed it inside a leather messenger bag nearby, and swung it across his shoulders. He had destroyed the man's photos; this was the least he could do. Then he opened the door and stumbled out.

The sweet, cold air, scented with cigarette smoke, gin, and whiskey, greeted him. He gasped, sucking it in and raising his arms. But no one yelled at him—the Japanese had left.

Ernest gave one more glance at the flaming studio and ran out into the hallway. He pounded on the button of the elevator. Nothing happened. So he flew down the stairs crowded with panicky guests in velvet gowns and white robes. Reaching the seventh floor, he pressed the elevator button again, and out came two Japanese soldiers, who aimed their rifles at him.

Fear raced through Ernest; he raised his arms. The soldier near him stabbed the messenger bag with the bayonet.

Ernest pointed up. "Fire! Fire!"

They looked up, and he darted toward the stairs and raced down. When he almost reached the landing, he stopped.

Under the brilliant Lalique chandelier, a Japanese soldier directed the crowd on the stairs, and a loudspeaker blasted in English, "All guests gather in the lobby; all guests gather in the lobby. Anyone who refuses to cooperate will be shot; anyone who refuses to cooperate will be shot."

If he proceeded with the crowd to the lobby, he would be trapped. But he couldn't go up to the soldiers with rifles. Frantic, Ernest looked around, tucking the messenger bag behind his back. He had reached the first floor, and on his right, near the staircase, were the windows shattered by the bomb. Elated, he ran across a pile of ammunition shells and debris, leaped on a cushioned couch beneath the windowsill, and dove through the window.

Beneath him were rickshaws, military motorcycles, automobiles, screaming people, carriages, and more Japanese soldiers holding rifles. But he had gotten the floor wrong. This was not the first floor—it was the second.

"No!" He wanted to hold on to the windowsill or the window frame, but his hands caught nothing, and his feet swiped the air.

47

AIYI

Cheng sent a team of seamstresses to make me new tunics. What I wore became his decision, and he had deemed it improper to wear the fitted dresses that showed my curves.

In front of a tall mirror, I stood still as the seamstresses measured my size and cut out the fabric four times larger. There was no tuck at the waist, padding around the chest, or careful trimming on the hemline—all the fastidiousness of a high-quality dress-tailoring technique I was used to. When the tunics were speedily made on a treadle machine, one in black and one in gray, both with an upright mandarin collar that reached my chin, I put one on. With my neck fenced in a high collar, sleeves long enough to cover the tips of my fingers, my body sheathed in a shapeless trunk, I was seamless like a dumpling.

Ernest would not recognize me if he passed by me.

❧

Insomnia. Again.

The night was too quiet. Each scratch on the wall, each scuttle in the garden, each murmur of the wind jolted me like a ghost's breath.

The candlelight slithered on the wall; the shadows curdled behind the wardrobes. The disjointed, harsh music was playing in my ears again. I hugged my shoulders, curling on my bed, fear a cangue on my neck.

Before dawn, I went out to find Ying for some company. But he was not in his room; very odd, especially at this hour. Near the courtyard, I heard a creak come from the front gate. A burglar? The gate, unbelievably, was unlocked. I held the door ajar and looked out. On the street near an alleyway just one block away, Ying was in his shirt with suspenders. Holding a flashlight in one hand, he handed a wad of bills to a short, bald man in a robe. Behind him, two men carried a crate out of the alley. Ying opened the crate with his free hand and picked out a long stick like a broom. A rifle.

I closed the door, furious. All the money I gave him. He was not playing a poker game. He was engaging in an illegal trade of guns. He was going to get killed! I went to the round table in the dining room, waiting for him. But I must have dozed off, because when I woke up, my old butler stood next to me.

"Where is Ying?" It was dawn. The house was still sleeping.

"Youngest master said he had a poker game," he said, swallowing his saliva loudly—his habit. He spread out my breakfast—two tea eggs, a bowl of porridge with green onions, and a bowl of soft tofu—and turned away.

"Can you stay with me?" I said.

"Yes, Miss Shao. Do you need anything else?"

"No. Just stay and say something." I held the warm tea egg. The hard-boiled egg, marinated for hours in tea leaves and anise pods, had a unique, enhanced flavor of tea. It was my favorite. I hit it against the table and began to peel; when the shell came off, I held it—soft, naked, waiting to be eaten. Suddenly, I felt sad. I had no business, no love, no future. I felt like a peeled egg, vulnerable.

A thud came in the distance. The ground trembled. "What's that?"

"Miss Shao?"

His hearing was not good. Or maybe I was going insane. I bit into the egg.

Another thud. "Did you hear that?"

I dusted off the flakes of eggshell on my coat and stepped out of the dining hall. It was not my imagination. The ground was indeed shaking. My Nash, parked near the fountain, was rattling; the two red lanterns strung on two ropes across from the courtyard to the central reception room, which Peiyu had installed for good luck to welcome the new year, were swinging. The red tassels swayed, and the golden letters spun, a swirl of confusion. I rushed toward the fountain and opened the gate.

Outside, the dawn air was pungent, sickening with burning oil. I had smelled the air like this before, when the Japanese attacked the city. But the street appeared normal, a rickshaw puller dozing near the alley. Then I saw a bloom of black explode from the direction of the river.

It was happening. The attack on the Settlement, like Ernest said.

His apartment was some distance away from the river. He should be safe, and if he knew better, he would stay away. But what if he was not?

I dashed back inside, almost crashing into my chauffeur, who'd just awoken. "Quick. Let's get in the car. Take me to the Settlement."

"What's going on?" He started the engine.

"Just take me there. Let's go."

We rushed out. The closer we approached the river, the thicker the fumes grew. The street seemed to be rising, slithering with rickshaw pullers, people in long robes, and Europeans in their suits, fleeing in all directions. A tank with the Japanese flag was grinding bikes, rickshaws, and automobiles underneath. Black smoke, rolling with swarms of sparks, billowed; the air, pierced with the shrill alarms of wrecked cars, gunshots, and shrieks, spluttered. The sky, a fiery furnace, exploded.

My car stalled, surrounded by hysterical people and overturned vehicles. It was too dangerous to go farther, and anyway, Ernest had no reason to go near the river. I was just thinking about turning around when something dropped from the sky and slammed against the roof of a black Chevrolet ahead of me. A bone-shattering sound; the car jolted. And I saw on the Chevrolet's roof a face—Ernest's face.

I flung open the door and ran toward him.

"Ernest!" Through the billowy smoke, I saw him roll off the car and onto the ground and disappear among the frantic crowd. I pushed forward, dodging another Chevrolet crashing into a Packard, where a man in flames tumbled out with suitcases.

"Ernest! Ernest!"

He was gone. There was no sight of him. A thunderous explosion set off around me. A coil of metal, hot oil, glass, shards, and severed limbs shot in the air. The ground shuddered; gasoline, smoke, and fire unfurled in the air, rumbling like a black train. A sharp pain stabbed my neck; something wet and sticky was trickling down my dress. My eyes stung, my throat burned, and strangely, I heard no screams or gunshots; a wave of voiceless sound had filled my ears instead, as if I were underwater while the world burned in a silent heap. It was mercifully peaceful.

I stumbled, limped, searched among the running figures. Now and then I grabbed some shoulders to see if they were Ernest. They were not. They were saying something, their mouths open, tears running down their smoke-smudged faces, but I heard no voices. With all my strength I gave a loud yell of Ernest's name, and then magically, the wave in my ears receded and I heard something.

It was pouring generously like wine into a glass, and it smelled pungent and felt warm.

Gasoline.

A Buick screeched beside me. The door swung open; inside sat Cheng. "I've been looking for you. Get in!"

"The gasoline is leaking. I need to find him." I was hot. So hot. My face. My back. My legs and arms. The heat, the awful sound, and the smell. Ernest must leave before it was too late.

"Who?"

The crowd, rushing toward us, banged the hood and kicked the fender, demanding we get out of the way. "Ernest. He jumped out of the window. He's somewhere here . . ."

Cheng reached out, and with his savage strength, grabbed me and thrust me inside the Buick. "Let's go home."

"I can't. I need to find him."

Cheng grasped my shoulders. His face was smudged with sweat and smoke, his fedora askew. "I went to your home. Your butler said you came to the waterfront area. I came as quickly as I could. What were you thinking? You're going to get killed!"

He kept talking, his lips moving, his face pink with anger. He had searched everywhere, everywhere, worried to death about me. "Did you know what you were doing? Why would you come here?" I had never heard him talk so much, so fast, so frantic, and I could hardly understand him, my mind hooked on the image of Ernest as he slammed against the roof of the Chevrolet. I had thought my club was my life, but I was wrong. I had thought it was possible to live a calm, safe life with Cheng. I was wrong again. Ernest wouldn't give me a decent home or decent social standing, but he was the only one I wanted. If he died, I would not be able to live.

"I want him, Cheng." It dawned on me. After all these months.

Cheng's handsome face froze; then he threw his fedora at the window and kicked the seat in front of him. "Fuck. Fuck. Fuck!"

"Listen to me. The gasoline is leaking. I must turn back. I must get Ernest out before it explodes. Turn back!"

The Buick kept going.

48

ERNEST

Gasoline. He heard it, each drop clear like glass shattering, the pungent odor choking him, and he could feel the scorching heat on his skin, the sizzling spark in the air. He opened his eyes yet only saw a blanket of blackness. Heaving, he hit something overhead. A coil of metal. Scalding.

He had rolled under a car after the fall. Groaning and wincing with pain, he crawled out from beneath the car and stood up. The sky had blended into the streets, a sea of smoke. He heard Aiyi's voice but hoped it was his imagination. It was too dangerous for her to be around.

Still he shuffled toward the voice. Somehow, he bumped into a shoulder; his fingers caught some hair. By the shifting smoke, he could see it was a bloody-faced man. He withdrew his hand and stepped back, just as a spinning silver shell sliced through, taking the man's head with it.

Ernest was about to scream when a car near him exploded. A boiling wave of heat swept over him, and he crashed against something hard and lost consciousness.

❧

Sore. Everywhere. His shoulders, his back, his legs, his eyes, his nose, and his lips. He coughed, wincing. He had no idea how long he had passed out or what time it was. His jacket was in tatters, burned off in the blast; his oxford shirt was sleeveless, his right arm swollen, bloody. Across his chest still hung the brown leather messenger bag he had rescued from Sassoon's studio. A miracle, considering the jacket.

An eerie silence had cloaked the street; a rapid session of gunshots came from a distance. He stood up. In front of him, the air was a rag of fumes; on the ground were littered hulks of burning automobiles. A few steps away from him, piles of fire were licking at clothed bodies; some people groaned on the ground, hatless, robes torn to shreds. In front of Sassoon's hotel, a Japanese soldier was shooting upward. The windows cracked, and a brilliant, thunderous waterfall of glass cascaded. A blessing Sassoon was gone, or he would have a heart attack.

Wobbling, Ernest began to walk. He had destroyed the photos and studio; her reputation was unsullied. It was time to go home. On Bubbling Well Road, the throngs seemed to multiply by the minute. The jostling of the crowd propelled him along, squeezing him tightly. Near the racecourse, the Japanese navy flags fluttered on windows and fences; behind the fence, the officers were mounted on game horses, marking it the new headquarters for the Japanese marines.

He came to an intersection and heard a loudspeaker spluttering something. Then he was forced to make room for some gleeful people waving Japanese flags—ahead of him was a parade, a victors' parade.

The uniformed Imperial Japanese Army marched toward him, their leather ammunition pouches bouncing on their chests and grenades hung around their necks. Behind them rolled a dozen green trucks; inside were men in uniforms with the American navy insignia, cowering, their arms on the back of their heads.

Ernest recognized the officer's visor. Colonel William Ashurst, who must have decided to stay for the ship. Helpless, Ernest watched the truck pass by, leaving a trail of leaflets in red, green, and yellow. The leaflets had a caricature of a soldier in a wheelchair named Roosevelt dressed in the Stars and Stripes flag and a big man named Churchill cloaked in a Union Jack shirt; the two embraced each other, watching in terror as two Japanese bombs fell above their heads.

The loudspeaker spluttered again, broadcasting in English. "Citizens of enemy countries—Great Britain, the United States, and the Netherlands—are now the enemy aliens of Japan. They must report to Hamilton House. Anyone who disobeys or flees will be shot. Repeat."

Enemy aliens . . .

He was stateless, no one's enemy. An irony.

A Chinese youth in a bomber jacket next to him was eyeing him and then his messenger bag with the Union Jack flag. "A Briton! Here's a Briton! An enemy alien!"

Ernest shoved the youth, ducked into the crowd, and ran as fast as he could. When he stopped to breathe, he was in front of the towering apartment building of Hamilton House, where a line had formed. There were men in suits, couples holding hands, women wearing velvet pants, and children hugging stuffed animals, all standing in a stoic manner, their faces grave.

Near the line stood a Japanese soldier with a rifle. He raised his hand, and a trickle of people came out from inside the building, each carrying a suitcase, wearing armbands with letters: *A*, *B*, or *N*. Now that he heard the loudspeaker, Ernest understood those letters represented the countries of America, Britain, and the Netherlands.

"To the camp, the camp!" The soldier was shouting in English, herding them toward a truck parked on the street across from him.

It felt surreal. Ernest felt his head swim, taking it all in: the armbands, the rifles, the suitcases, the stunned faces, and the unkempt hair in the cold morning wind. He traced the faces in the truck, then jolted. The last woman climbing on the truck. The red wool scarf. She was seated at the edge of the truck, deep in thought.

The joints of his bones threatening to break, Ernest hobbled after the truck as it advanced through the crowd on the street. He needed to call out to get her attention but doing so would attract the attention to himself. He followed the truck as it passed the Metropole, a luxury hotel famous for Persian rugs and extravagant Jacobean furniture. Unable to catch up, he grew desperate. "Miss Margolis, Miss Margolis. Laura!"

She raised her head, and he swore, even with the growing distance, with all the crowds and cars on the street, she recognized him, and her eyes lit up with joy. Then unbelievably, she unwound the red scarf around her neck, tied it in a single knot, and flung it in the air.

He reached out, but it sailed over his head. The truck turned a corner and disappeared.

Groaning in pain, Ernest searched for the scarf, barging through the throng, and finally found it in the hand of a young man. He snatched it from him, stuffed it inside his messenger bag, and limped away, glad the man didn't attack him. He was exhausted; he would not be able to fight him off.

The street seemed endless ahead of him. He passed an elderly man carrying a bolt of silk on his back, two scrawny youngsters loading crates of guns into a truck, and a uniformed Japanese soldier driving a knife into a man with a burned skin patch. Ernest didn't stop, didn't look into their eyes, and kept shambling. He just wanted to go to his apartment where Miriam slept—and he prayed to God that she'd done as he'd told her.

A motorcycle rammed into a store near him, and a group of men, their faces covered by black cloth, dashed inside a Rolex shop. Inside a trading company selling malt liquor and tobacco, a mob smashed the drawers with hammers; in a bank, the Japanese soldiers were holding a group of businessmen at gunpoint, shouting that all the assets and bank accounts of the enemy aliens were property of the empire.

At last, in a quiet corner, he slid down, unable to muster an ounce of strength to take a single step more.

The clock on the Customs House struck. Five o'clock. From the blustery street came the loudspeaker, announcing a curfew starting at seven Tokyo time, now Shanghai time. Men and women would be shot if caught after the curfew.

Gulping for air heavy with gasoline, blood, and fumes, he thought of the bloody faces of the hostage businessmen in the bank and the foreigners sent to camps. All the Europeans and Americans with wealth and the protection of their countries were now prisoners, and he, a man without a country, without a job, and without a friend, had fallen through the cracks. In a world shooting bullets and bolts, he was alone, stateless, and it was up to him to live, survive, and thrive.

49

AIYI

I turned to the window, my ears filled with Cheng's rant.

"Can you drive faster? Use your horn! Are those people blind? Can't they see my car?" He had refused to turn back, and I had stopped begging. There was no devastating explosion as far as I could hear. Ernest must be safe. I would find him as soon as I got away.

Finally, the giant gray stone lions appeared in the distance, and Cheng locked his viselike hand on my arm as we came to the courtyard. He shouted for Sinmay. A few minutes later, Sinmay showed up on the stone staircase to his study, a building near the reception room, his long gray robe crawling with shining worms of sunlight falling through the oak. "What's going on?"

Half of Shanghai was bombed and burned, but he appeared unperturbed as if watching the fire lit up in a stove. The foreigners in the Settlement didn't care about us, Sinmay had said bitterly when his reporters described that the Europeans and Americans, drinking their beverages in the coffeehouses, had praised the sophisticated weaponry of the Japanese as they bombarded the Chinese area. And now the Settlement was on fire, and he sat in his study with his legs up. How strange we humans were. We built a barbed wire fence between ourselves and turned away from the suffering of others, but we forgot the immunity to pain was delusional. For though salt and sugar we might be, we all had blood in the veins and a heart in the chest, and we all died when hit by a bomb.

"I'm going to my room." I tried to shake off Cheng.

His grip tightened. "We need to talk, Sinmay."

"Come in." Sinmay frowned.

I had an inkling of what he wanted to talk about. Cheng, a proud man, would not forgive me for what I had told him in the car. Perhaps he wanted to revoke our engagement, which must be approved by Sinmay, the authority of the house. Relief washed over me. This would be the most ideal solution. Cheng's dignity would be saved, and I would be free.

Elated, I stepped inside my brother's dim study, stuffy without the flow of air; the sunlight made an attempt to squeeze through the intricate lattices of the door but was not able to pierce through. Inside, Peiyu sat on a redwood chair beside a black table, a teacup in hand. Behind her, a nanny was carrying the baby bundled in thick layers of coats.

"You're bleeding, Aiyi." Peiyu put down the teacup. "And your dress!"

"It's not my blood."

"What's going on?" Sinmay went to sit behind a cedar desk covered with scrolls.

"You won't believe it. Aiyi went to see the pianist and almost got herself killed." Cheng let me stand like a criminal. The gears of his fiery temper yanked into motion, each tooth sharpened, rolling on twenty-one years of practice.

"The foreigner on the magazine?"

"You should hear what she said in the car! Never mind, older brother. May I have your permission to have her live with me? It's for her safety."

I was shocked. "I can't live in your home, Cheng. Actually, I've long waited to tell you this: I would like to call off our wedding."

The soft cooing of the nanny rocking the baby ceased; the footfalls of Cheng's pacing vanished.

"Call off the wedding? But we already sent the invitations!" Peiyu's voice was incredulous.

Sinmay shot to his feet, sending the rosewood chair flying across the room. "Are you out of your mind?"

I cringed. His disapproval was to be expected, but I had not imagined this spectacle.

"You are engaged. Everyone in Shanghai knows."

"I want to rethink my future."

"Your family makes decisions for your future."

I turned to Cheng. "Would you talk to me, in private?"

Cheng struck the desk with his fist. "You want to leave me for a foreigner? Is that it? Did you fuck him? Did you?"

"Do not talk to me like this—"

Sinmay yanked me. "You slept with a foreigner?"

Cheng grabbed me to face him. "I knew you lied to me. I knew. You lied to me."

Sinmay yanked me again. "You better explain this, or I'll never forgive you."

Dizzy, I backed away from them, my back hitting a swinging door. Cheng's face was the face of a bully and Sinmay's was that of a furious superior. I, a woman of twenty-one, was a person of no importance, a trifle.

Cheng laughed. A terrible sound. "Have you thought of me? How does this make me look? People will laugh at me! You can't do this to me!"

"We won't face this shame. We will not mention this to your mother. The wedding will go on as scheduled," Sinmay said, his face pink with rage. "It's not up to you, Aiyi. You'll marry him. As the oldest brother, I order you. Oldest brother acts like Father," he said, quoting a proverb.

I hugged my chest, but I wouldn't look away.

"If you won't listen to me, you should leave. And never come back," Sinmay blustered, pointing at the courtyard.

Outside, the courtyard was cloaked in a pale gloom, the sunlight banished, the ground laid in shapes of diamonds and circles wet with yesterday's rain. If I left, I would never be allowed to step inside again, and my place in the family would be erased. I might as well never have existed. This was what happened to my disgraced sister who became a concubine to a tycoon in Hong Kong.

I refused to be banished. "Emily was right to leave you. She's better off without you."

His arm swung; my head was thrown back. The slap, crisp and loud, tore at my ear.

I had never been slapped before, not even pinched by a rough hand. I held my face, the door of childhood memory flung open like a storm. All those years I watched and shivered as my addict father grew mad, throwing tantrums, cursing, and beating Mother when she hid money from him. I never thought I would be a victim of violence, hit by my own brother.

"Sinmay!" Peiyu's voice.

"She disobeys me!"

Somehow Cheng stood in front of me. His black eyes furious, he looked wild as a raging feline. "You don't deserve this. I would never hurt you. But I hate you. I hate you so much. I'll never forgive you."

He walked out. In the courtyard, the engine roared, let out a loud wail, and then faded.

Sinmay was raging. "Go to your room!"

In a daze, I went obediently; my head ached and my eyes burned. There was a voice in my head telling me this was the right thing to do, but the other voice, calm and aloof, said I had made a terrible mistake and thrown my life away. Both voices agreed that my life was now like a decorated paper lantern adrift in the wind.

"Do you need a handkerchief? Or some cream for the swelling, little sister? Here, take my handkerchief." Peiyu's voice was sympathetic. She meant well. She had watched, unable to help.

"I want to lie down," I said.

And I slept. For the first time since the loss of my business, I saw no shadows, heard no ghost murmurs. I dreamed of Mother, a vivid vision behind the incense smoke. I saw myself, too, a seventeen-year-old wearing a mourning hemp cloak beside her coffin. So young I was; the depth of her death hadn't hit me yet, and I only felt the unaccustomed emptiness, like a precious jade bangle that I had worn for years but had slipped off.

When I awoke, the burning sensation on my face was gone. I leaped from my bed and pulled at the door.

It wouldn't budge—locked from outside. I shouted; my butler, who always napped in the garden, answered, his voice blurred from constantly swallowing his saliva.

Sinmay hadn't thrown me out; he had locked me in.

50

ERNEST

When he finally made it to his apartment, it was empty. He would need to search for Miriam later. He sat down on the bed, groaning in pain. All his bones seemed to crack, and if he lay down, he would be unable to get up. He looked down at the red scarf in his lap and tried to untie it with his shaky fingers. Maybe there was a message from Miss Margolis. His fingers were too weak. It took him a while to loosen the knot and unfurl it.

A piece of paper. With two signatures at the bottom. Actually, it was a power of attorney regarding the execution of a relief loan, valued at half a million dollars, between Miss Margolis and some attorney called K. Bitker. Ernest sat up. Why would Miss Margolis toss him this important paper? Did she wish him to keep it? What was he supposed to do with it?

Too exhausted, he put the paper aside, picked up the messenger bag, and took out the camera he'd saved. A miracle—after all the falls and crashes, it remained intact. He was going to put the bag away when an album fell out. It was thick and wide, dated 1940; the cover showed two naked women sunbathing on a yacht's deck. He grew nervous. Was Aiyi inside? If he saw her, would that violate her will? She had been adamant about keeping the secret from him. And would he be calm, his eyes on her naked skin?

He walked out of the room with the album. In the communal kitchen, he started a fire in a coal stove. When the flame leaped, he threw the album in the fire. He would never know if her nude photos were inside the album.

When he returned to his room, Ernest checked the bag again. Something else was inside. It was a thick envelope with the hotel's logo, addressed to him; tied to the envelope with an elastic band was a note, written on the hotel's stationery, with the signature *V. E. Sassoon*.

Dear Ernest, if you find this note, then all my fears are confirmed. Curse the Japanese! Take the envelope. It was meant to pay you for the film you showed me. One day I'll teach you how to do business with this money.

His film. Now that he thought of it, Sassoon owed his survival to him. Had he stayed in Shanghai, he would have been sent to a camp too. Ernest took off the elastic band around the envelope, dipped his hand inside, and took out a stack of bills. His hands trembled.

In all his twenty years of life, he had never seen this. A sheaf of American dollars. All in hundreds. Ten thousand dollars.

The door opened. Miriam entered, dressed in a hooded black jacket he had never seen before. She tossed the Leica on the cabinet, muttering it was not her fault that it was broken.

He could hardly scold her. "Miriam!" He waved the bills in his hand. "Look!"

He was rich—they were rich. He would give Miriam anything she wanted, buy her a warm coat, or two coats, or cigarettes, or milk, or meat. He could give Miriam a comfortable life; they would own things: another Leica, a watch, an apartment, a house, or an automobile. Or maybe he wouldn't spend it all; maybe he would become a businessman, like Sassoon. But one thing was for sure: he would make a name for himself.

51

FALL 1980

THE PEACE HOTEL

Looking at the wood panels inside the elevator, I can't help thinking that years ago, I, wearing my favorite mink coat, stood next to Sir Sassoon in the same elevator to his penthouse. He has been dead for almost twenty years but still owes me one hundred thousand dollars. Sassoon, I've heard, tried to wrangle back this hotel and his thousands of properties from the Nationalists that returned to power after 1945. I don't know what he managed to salvage, but the hotel slipped from his control forever. He must have been disappointed, living in the Bahamas under the care of a nurse whom he eventually married. So many memories I can't forget, so many I'd rather forget.

The elevator stops at the ninth floor, and I wheel out. Ms. Sorebi is already there, sitting on a chair near the window, a few diners around her. I like people to be punctual—Ernest was always punctual. "Thank you for meeting me again, Ms. Sorebi. Do you like this restaurant? Cathay Room has a rich hedonistic history. Emily Hahn, the reporter, used to come here."

Today Ms. Sorebi wears black jeans and the same leather jacket. She pushes her chair away from the table, leans back, and scans the walls, the ceiling, and then the balcony. A silver bird I haven't noticed before, tethered on a necklace, flits across her chest—a cross.

"Emily Hahn? I remember seeing some of her photos."

"She was a friend." I haven't talked to her for almost forty years, and I don't know if she's dead or alive. A wave of sadness laps toward me that even my medications can't help. Maybe this is too much for me to handle—the memories, the documentary, and the documentarian.

"My niece can't make it today. It'll be just you and me," I say, trying to smile. "Have you tried any Chinese food here? It's rather good."

"We have Chinese food in LA. But I'm sure the food is different here." She hesitates.

"Are you all right? How did you sleep? You must be exhausted after the flight."

"To be honest, I didn't sleep well. Our meeting, the donation, and the documentary. It was a lot to think about. I meant to ask you yesterday, but I didn't want to be rude. What did you do that was most unforgivable?"

"I'll tell you all today." I take the menu from the waiter's hands. The sheet looks like a canvas covered with ants. I put on my glasses, squint, and hold the menu at arm's length. What I need is my magnifier, but I've forgotten to bring it. Finally, I give up and, with the help of my memory, order eight dishes. "The Chinese dishes here are modified to suit Westerners' taste. But if you want something authentic, you can ask to see the Chinese menu. Do you speak Chinese?"

She laughs. "I'm sorry to disappoint you, Ms. Shao."

"I didn't mean to test you. But did you learn a bit of Chinese while working on the exhibit?" I give the menu to the waiter and see manager Yang waiting smartly near the bar. He's curious about the American, her hair, and her eyes.

"I can say *fan dian*, hotel."

"It also means restaurant."

"Really."

"The Chinese language is an ambiguous language. The same word can mean two different things. Like *jiao tang*. It means church, but also synagogue. The word *ai ren* means wife and lover."

"Thanks for telling me that. What a big difference, wife and lover! What else should I know?"

"Chinese has many words for wife, such as *qizi, furen, taitai, airen, laopo,* and *neiren*. There might be more, but I can't think of them now."

"My goodness! This is fun!"

I think I'm growing used to her way of exclaiming.

"Ms. Shao, you must think I'm such a pest, but the most unforgivable thing you mentioned . . . Would you tell me what it is?"

The room is cold. I wind the cashmere scarf tighter around my neck. "I think there are a few answers to that. Before I tell you, I'd like to hear what your interviewees told you about me."

"They said an uncommon relationship developed between you and Mr. Reismann, which put some refugees in danger. That was during the Japanese occupation, I was reminded. They also mentioned an unfortunate tragedy that you were involved in. And Mr. Reismann was never the same again. But no one seemed to have a clear memory of how the tragedy happened. So my assumption is there might be a misunderstanding."

I control myself. I want her to like me, I really do. "Misunderstanding? Or do you believe it was all my fault, just like what they told you?"

I regret instantly my sharp tone. People say old age tames us and dulls our tempers, but old age for me is like a key to a Cadillac that permits me to wreak havoc.

She runs her hand through her hair. "When I was documenting for the exhibit, I rarely thought of accusing anyone, Ms. Shao. My only intention was to show the refugees' suffering. Mr. Reismann suffered;

we all understand that. Believe me, I have as much respect for you as for my other interviewees."

But they all love him, only him, and I was in the shadows, the other, the one they shunned, despised. It has been like this for years, and nothing has changed. "Do you know why some people in China only drink tea, not coffee?"

"Why? Everyone in the US drinks coffee."

"People here say coffee will cause cancer, that's why. You know what happens when people believe something? They believe they're absolutely right and nothing will change it."

She rubs her temple. She's struggling. She wants to trust me so she can receive the donation of the hotel, but she has heard too many inconsistent stories about me. "I'm confused, Ms. Shao, my apologies. I understand the past is traumatic for you to reflect on, but would you help me? Mr. Reismann's documentary must be important to you. What can I do for you?"

This is what I want—to have her ears, to place the story of Ernest's struggle into her hands, to free myself from the past, but I don't know why I nearly lost myself. I can't blame the refugees who didn't know me; the truth is I've been blaming myself for all these years. I feel the prick behind my eyes. "I suppose we're both responsible, Ernest and me. Had it not been for him, none of the tragedies could have happened. I would not regret what I have done for all my life, and I would not be sitting here talking to you."

52

JANUARY 1942

AIYI

The Chinese New Year came at the end of the month. It was the Year of the Horse, with the element of water. An unlucky year, as water indicated tears. For the past seven weeks I had been locked inside, I shouted, screamed, and pounded on the doors, but no one listened. Food and water were delivered at the door, which was chained and left only wide enough for me to reach out. I had nothing to do. I slept day and night, and I paced from the purple-tented bed to the rosewood chair.

To keep sane, I played jazz in my head: "Summertime," "They Can't Take That Away from Me," "Crawl Charleston," and my favorite, "The Last Rose of Shanghai." I laughed and cried, remembering how Ernest used to play that for me, and me humming those notes of joy, swaying my hips, stomping the floor. Music, once my livelihood, my passion, now the hymn of freedom, my medication.

Each week, my pragmatic sister-in-law, Peiyu, reminded me of my wedding at the end of February. Sitting on a chair outside my room, sipping her soup, she tried to talk sense into me. "You understand, you can't find a better husband than Cheng. He's the only heir of his family.

Once his mother passes, you'll be the matriarch; you'll be entitled to all his wealth, his family's shipping business."

"If you like his money so much, you should marry him."

"Don't be silly." A slurp of soup. "Would you like to have some sweet rice ball soup with red dates? We ran out of dried *longyan*. Everything is so expensive. The inflation is killing us. The same fish costs five cents in the morning, fifty in the afternoon!"

Finally, she sighed and left, her small lotus feet padding across the stone ground, the squeaky toddler trailing behind her. She was two, or three, not that I cared.

Ying's voice came one afternoon. "So what did I miss? You cheated on Cheng with that pianist. Is it true?"

I pressed to the door. "I'm going crazy, Ying. Can you let me out? Do you have the key?"

"Fuck." He sighed. "Look, he shouldn't have hit you, but this is about your future. You know well we don't decide whom to marry. We owe our lives to our parents. You and a foreigner. What the hell were you thinking? When is your wedding again?"

"I want to get out. Let me out, Ying."

"It's not up to me. By the way, your lover came to see you."

"Ernest? He came here?"

"No. I was talking about Cheng."

He had come once, giving me a resolute statement that there would be no annulment, and his mother would not be told of my request. The wedding was still on. In two weeks.

I threw a pillow at the door, and Ying said, "Grow up, little sister. You have no idea what a good life you have. The world is turning upside down. Shanghai is a living hell. The Japanese soldiers are patrolling everywhere. People are hiding behind doors, and the foreigners in Shanghai are collected for slaughter."

"I don't believe you."

"Your lover is probably dead by now. Or sent to a camp."

"What camp?"

He was chewing an apple; I could hear the crunch. He went on to say that Japanese carriers, Mitsubishi Zero fighters, bombers, and destroyers had descended on Pearl Harbor and attacked the United States of America on the same day they attacked the Settlement. The Americans finally declared war against Japan. But the Japanese had launched a full assault. They invaded Hong Kong, their naval and air force killing thousands on the island. They flew over South Asia and sunk two British battleships, one named the *Prince of Wales* and the other *Repulse*. They captured Malaya, bombed Manila, and attacked the Dutch East Indies. The British had surrendered Hong Kong and retreated to Singapore, and the Americans had given up Manila and fled to the Bataan Peninsula. "They are helpless. They can barely cover their own asses."

"What camp were you talking about, Ying?"

"The world is on fire, little sister. Forget about your pianist. No one is safe; no country is safe. If you want to stay alive, stay in your room."

"Let me out!" It was quiet outside. I kicked the door in frustration.

Three weeks into February, Ying delivered me more grave news of war. The Japanese had poured into Singapore, and the mighty British troops fell apart under the onslaught. Singapore surrendered in seven days, and thousands of British, Indian, and Australian troops were captured and sent to internment camps. "I hear a Japanese submarine even shelled an oil refinery near California! The Americans want to retaliate, but what can they do? They have navy aircraft carriers in Hawaii, but they don't have long-range bombers to fly across to Tokyo and return to Hawaii."

Very soon, Ying said, the Japanese would take over all of Asia. Just like Yamazaki had boasted.

I wondered how he received such detailed news, but I couldn't care less what territory the Japanese had conquered.

"Ying," I said. "If you're not going to let me out, at least let me talk to my chauffeur."

"What for?"

"So I can tell whether you were lying."

He obliged, and when my chauffeur came, he confirmed some of what Ying had said. The foreigners were indeed rounded up and sent to camps. I could hardly believe it, but my chauffeur was most loyal, driving me around since I was six. I often gave him a fat envelope at the Chinese New Year as a token of my gratitude.

"Listen," I said, my lips near the gap of the doors. "Go to his apartment and see if you can find him. You know where his apartment is. Find him, make sure he's safe, and tell him I want to see him."

When my chauffeur left, I paced in my room, anxious.

Seven days before my wedding.

53

ERNEST

The wailing of a Klaxon awoke him. The dawn's pale fingers hadn't reached the windows, and the room was yawning with night's shadows. He sat up, thinking of her, and with some jealousy, he hoped that Cheng would make her happy.

Ernest put on his dark-taupe coat and went to the bakery that sold bagels for breakfast. Miriam followed behind in her black hood. She was still grumpy, but the windfall had cheered her up somewhat. She would go wherever he asked her, and sometimes he caught her eyeing the messenger bag hung behind the headboard.

Outside, the February sky was a waxy sprawl; the air a mournful, chilly pall; and the streets bleak and desolate, drenched in sheets of cold rain. The broad avenue Bubbling Well Road, which had always bustled with people and automobiles, was empty. He encountered not a single pedestrian. There was no music from clubs, no squeaking of rickshaws, no honking of automobiles; as far as he could see, all the fur shops, porcelain boutiques, calendar stalls, nightclubs, and opium dens in the hidden alleys that had been part of the city's landscape were closed. The other day, when he'd gone to the French hospital for more morphine, he had found out it was closed, too, and the nuns had disappeared.

Ernest passed a block where a stray dog was attacking a beggar's still body, turned a corner, and finally reached the bakery. It was about six o'clock, but the clock tower, which had switched to Tokyo time, said it was seven.

"Good morning." He took off his fedora and greeted the people inside. He loved this bakery and cherished seeing his fellow people, like Mr. Schmidt, here. They gave him hope that he was with a community, not alone in this dreadful world. This was also the only place where he could find decent food since all the restaurants and stalls were closed, and hotels like Sassoon's only accepted Japanese and their European ally, the Germans. It was temporary, he hoped; soon, life would become normal and peddlers would appear on the street again.

No one greeted him back; a heavy, depressive air hung in the bakery. Mr. Schmidt, hunched in a corner, was weeping, and Mrs. Kauser, the stout woman in a flour-speckled apron, bawled near the counter. The Japanese had rounded up her husband, an American, and taken him to an internment camp. She, German by birth, had been spared; for the sake of their children, she must flee Shanghai as well.

"Ernest, are you going to help?" Miriam was talking into his ear.

"What?"

"Didn't you hear? Mrs. Kauser is fleeing Shanghai. She's going to close the bakery."

"Well, I'm not sure what I can do." He was sad to see the bakery, the only place he could go for breakfast, would close. With the imprisonment of the wealthy British and Americans, refugees like him were truly on their own.

"Think of something! You're rich now."

He looked at the sad faces, the small round tables covered with red-and-white checked cloth, the aluminum utensils, and the brick-built oven beyond the counter. Miriam was right. "Mrs. Kauser, what do you say I purchase the bakery from you? You can have some cash in your pocket when you leave, and we'll keep this place open."

Mrs. Kauser wiped her face and stared at him in surprise. Ernest glanced at Miriam; she was smiling. A trickle of warmth coursed through him. It struck him—this was the purpose of his life now: Miriam's happiness. He would do anything for her. So five minutes later, Ernest became the owner of Mrs. Kauser's bakery. He took the offer from her without negotiations—110 American dollars, a decent deal even before the war, and Mrs. Kauser, grateful, hugged him and kissed him on his cheeks. She gave him all the flour sacks in storage and the names of her soy milk suppliers.

A business owner now, Ernest was pleased, but he had never run a business before, and he was no baker. He turned to Mr. Schmidt, who stared at him incredulously. "Will you help me?"

"Of course, Ernest, it'll be my pleasure. But how on earth did you manage to get that much money?"

He smiled. "It's a long story. I'll be happy to tell you when we have time. Miriam, what do you say, would you work for me?"

"I can't." She sat in a corner, her head shrouded in the hood like a priestess. But her voice, he thought, had lost the edge of bitterness.

Ernest set to work with Mr. Schmidt, now the manager, and they let the word out that they were hiring people. By the end of the day, he'd hired ten people, all stateless refugees like him. Some came from Austria, some from Berlin. Some had baking experience; some didn't, like Golda Bernsdorff, an actress in her late twenties. She had just arrived in Shanghai via Japan.

It was wonderful to see people bustle around the bakery, talking in Yiddish and English, their faces smiling in the warm glow of the oven. But outside on the street, trucks raced by loaded with foreigners carrying their suitcases—Americans and Britons wearing armbands. What would the Japanese do with him, Miriam, and all his friends in the bakery, all stateless? Ernest looked away, forcing himself not to think about that.

What he didn't expect was that Mrs. Kauser would introduce him to a Canadian national who worked in an accounting firm for rice rationing. Spooked by the Japanese invasion of the Settlement, the Canadian had put his apartment and businesses on fire sale to flee Shanghai. He asked if Ernest was interested in his apartment. A deal was struck; Ernest bought it for five thousand dollars.

It was a nice apartment with two bedrooms and a balcony. Ernest wondered if he should move out of the apartment Aiyi had rented and live here instead. It would be more comfortable for Miriam. But the apartment, located in the area where many foreigners lived, was a target of Japanese soldiers' constant roundups. It was not as safe. Besides, if he moved, he might lose his last connection to Aiyi, and she would never be able to find him.

But that deal led to another. Three days later, he took out 4,390 dollars from the messenger bag and became the owner of another apartment located in the busy commercial street of the Huaihai Road.

Investing in real estate was risky during the occupation, he was aware. Buildings could be pulverized; money would turn into dust. But he would rather see his money in shapes of apartments than have it tied to the back of the headboard. Besides, he soon found out, inflation was rising rapidly, and American currency was devalued overnight. His remaining five hundred American dollars, that once had fetched five hundred thousand Chinese *fabi*, now only were worth five thousand.

However, soon after his purchases, more apartments and villas were put up for sale as more foreigners fled to escape the Japanese's arrest. With many apartments and villas on the market and fewer buyers, the value of his two apartments plunged.

That night in his room, he thumbed the last few bills left in the leather bag and rubbed his chin ruefully. He had bought too early.

At noon, while the bakery was not as busy, Ernest went to the One Hundred Joys Nightclub, hoping to come across her somehow. The club remained closed; the windows boarded up. He made a bold phone call from a post office to her home—as a friend, a former employee. Again the man with a British accent answered.

"Are you that pianist? Aiyi refused to get married because of you. Would you please stop calling?"

Ernest put down the phone and laughed.

When he returned to his apartment that evening, he stopped short in the alley. In front of the building stood a familiar stocky figure of a Chinese man with a cap. Aiyi's chauffeur.

54

AIYI

Two days before my wedding, my chauffeur came to me with good news. Ernest was safe, unscathed, not arrested or imprisoned in a camp. And he had set a meeting place, the inn.

I was so happy I cried out. I needed to see him. Now. I couldn't marry Cheng.

I tried various tactics on Ying. Bribery. Reasoning. More bribery. He wouldn't budge. American dollars had depreciated after the war started; one hundred dollars would only buy him a drink. Finally, I threatened him. "I know what you were doing with all the money I gave you, Ying. If you let me out, I'll keep my mouth shut. Otherwise I'll tell Sinmay you turned rogue."

"I'm not turning rogue."

"I saw you near an alley the day the Japanese bombed the Settlement. Don't deny it." He was doing the arms trade for profit, common for reckless people.

"'Life is precious, love is priceless, but compared to freedom, both are worthless.' Have you heard of that?"

"Since when did you become a poet? Maybe I should just tell Sinmay?"

A grunt, then the rattle of the lock. I grabbed a scarf and a hat on the dresser and almost flew out of the door.

"You look terrible," Ying said.

"So do you." Ying, who unlike Cheng, paid little attention to his appearance, was ragged. His hair was messy, vest unbuttoned, a suspender loosened.

"Don't tell Sinmay I let you out. He'll kill me. Wait, where are you going? Isn't your wedding in two days?"

"Who knows." I sprinted down the path to the garden, then to the front central courtyard near the gate. The open air, the long winding path, the rain-drenched osmanthus bushes—everything was freedom. Near my Nash parked by the fountain, I heard the mah-jongg tiles clash and Sinmay's voice from the reception room. I held my breath.

"One hundred forty-two times! Can you believe it? Those bastards bombed the Nationalists' capital one hundred forty-two times for the past three years!"

"That's almost forty-eight times a year, four times a month, and Buddha bless me, once a week!" Peiyu's voice.

"The capital must have been reduced to rubble," Cheng said. "How did they survive?"

"We could win this war if the Nationalists and the Communists unite and attack the Japanese while they are expanding in South Asia." Sinmay's voice.

"That would never happen. They hate each other. Chiang Kai-shek would never forgive his subordinates for conspiring with the Communists to kidnap him."

"He got out alive. Besides, kidnapping wasn't the Communists' fault. Didn't Zhou Enlai negotiate to set him free?"

"Let's not talk about war at the mah-jongg table," Cheng's mother said. "Peiyu, have you confirmed the menu with the restaurant? We must have oranges for my son's wedding. No excuses of orange shortages."

I ducked into the Nash, delighted to see my chauffeur napping inside. I gave him a tap on the shoulder and put my finger on my lips. He looked happy to see me, nodding nonstop—his habit—and started the engine. My Nash had broken a wiper during the bombing, and the engine groaned and shuddered as it lumbered out of the gate. It was excruciatingly slow.

From the reception room came the faint voice of Sinmay asking where my chauffeur was going, but the magic of mah-jongg was most powerful—it bound them all, and no one left in the middle of the game.

Ying had said the streets were flooded with Japanese soldiers; he was not lying. Checkpoints were popping up like bamboo shoots after the spring rain, especially in the streets near the Settlement. When we were one block away from the inn, I got out, tucked the scarf around my face, and passed the patrolling soldiers shouting in Japanese. In the inn, a room was reserved for me, but Ernest hadn't arrived yet.

I took the key and went to the room, previously the inn owner's bedroom. It had bare, drab walls, a bed with a thin white cotton quilt, a low three-foot bamboo nightstand, and a narrow side door open to a walled vegetable garden accessible from the kitchen. Like all private homes of poor people in Shanghai, it had no fireplace, no wallpaper, and no chandeliers, and the bed had no mattress, only a bare wooden board covered with red sheets under the quilt.

I took off my scarf and sat on the edge of the bed. I could hear the shrill berating of a woman outside accusing her neighbor of stealing her socks, the constant chopping in the kitchen, and the vigorous groans of a man and a woman through the wall.

My heart pounding, I waited.

What was taking him so long? I stood up, walked around, and sat. And I stood up again. I remembered once Sinmay had read something like this at his salon about waiting: like riding a boat loaded with barrels of petroleum, there was the calmness of being carried away and the excitement of seeing the light at the end of the journey; yet with each passing minute, each lap of the water set aflame barrels of doubt, suspicion, and anxiety.

I felt only the flame in my heart.

He was not going to come; he had changed his mind.

A tap came on the door. I leaped, unlatched the door, and saw the most beautiful face in my dreams. I jumped on him and threaded my arms around him. Ernest was sobbing, or maybe I was. I cupped his face and wiped off his tears. We laughed, twirled, jumped around, and tumbled on the bed.

I kicked off my high heels, took off yesterday's stockings, and unbuttoned my red dress. I helped him take off his jacket, his shirt, and his trousers until he was naked, until I was naked. I slid back on the bed to make room for him. I opened my arms and parted my legs. I had made love to him before, in the same inn, in the back of my Nash, and in Sassoon's hotel; I was familiar with his body and my desire, yet this felt like it was our first time. I kissed him urgently, greedily, desperately. When he held me, when his body became part of mine, I cried out. From now on, there would be no more secrets, no more hesitation, no more separation, no more him, no more me. Only us.

Later, he kissed my forearm, my knuckles, and my shoulder, his stubble pricking me, a happy ache of a seedling breaking out for the warmth of the sun. Lying on my stomach, I turned to him, my hair damp, my head a roaring engine newly greased.

"I am my beloved, and my beloved is mine." His fingers were playing with my earlobe.

I took his finger and bit it. Just hard enough so he could feel me. "Chinese people don't talk about love."

"Why not?"

"Because we think love is fleeting, fickle, and simply frivolous. Life, however, is a mysterious well of infinity and profundity. So we talk about life and fate. We also believe life is a cycle of chances, karma, and reincarnation." I climbed on top of him, my stomach on his stomach, my palms to his palms, my body taking flight on the rise and fall of his breath. "There's karma between lovers, too; we call it *yuan*. It's like a predestined chance or like a divine coin of happiness for lovers. You earn them by making good choices in this life, and you'd be paid in the next life."

"How do you say that? Yang?"

"No, *yuan*."

"Got it. Yang."

I laughed. "I was so worried about you. I thought you were sent to a camp."

"Everyone is worried about that. I'm hoping for the best. I'm stateless, so maybe the Japanese will leave me alone. You've lost weight. You're so thin. Tell me what you were doing."

I told him all: the fight with Cheng and my family and the lockup in my own room. And he told me of the messenger bag, the album, and the ten thousand American dollars. Him purchasing a bakery and more. He was no longer a penniless refugee. He was a businessman with assets.

I nodded. He had a sharp mind and a poise that seemed to sharpen at moments of distress. Given opportunities, he could build an empire.

"Sassoon took some pictures of me. I wonder if that album has my photos," I said. No more secrets from him. I reached out and cupped his face, watching the blue glaze in his eyes, ready to kiss him and placate him.

A flicker. He would never get over the fact that I took off my clothes in front of Sassoon. But he held my hand. "I burned it. It's gone."

"You did the right thing." I was sore, my legs weak, but I was alive, fresh, and fiery. "Can we do it again?"

55

ERNEST

He loved the smell of her, the shape of her hands, the way she put on her high heels, crossing her legs, her back curved, the arc of grace and seduction. He ran his hands over her taut calf and played on her skin, a sonatina of beauty and harmony. He could live like this, watch her put on her shoes, and make love to her every day for the rest of his life.

It was a punishment to let her out of sight, which he never wanted to happen again, but he had to run the bakery. Still, he made plans with her. He would like to move into the apartment he had bought, but that wouldn't be safe for him. Perhaps she could move into the apartment she had rented for him? She shook her head. She would be a mistress in Chinese people's eyes, and she was reluctant to dishonor her family's name.

So she had no choice but to stay in this inn, where she'd registered with a pseudonym. He came to see her every day but left at night before the curfew. She negotiated a good rate, and he paid it. For three months.

In the bakery, it was a different world.

꧁

Rumors swirled every day, shifty and chilly like gusts of wind through a dark winding alley: The Japanese had placed Mr. Komor, the organizer of the Jewish charity group that helped him get settled upon his arrival, under house arrest. The Embankment Building was shuttered. A Japanese soldier had flipped a refugee into the Huangpu River when he was too slow moving out of the way on the street.

The wistful Mr. Schmidt sang his lament as they rolled the dough. "Moses said, 'I'm a stranger in a strange land.' Indeed. We're all strangers in a strange world!"

A familiar fear that had possessed Ernest in Berlin returned. The muscles in his hand started to contract, and his hand wouldn't stop trembling. He put on gloves, just to be safe, and when people came to his bakery, he offered a seat for them to sit, a warm loaf of bread to eat, a glass of soy milk to drink, and smiles to make them feel better. After all, he was in a better situation than them; he was a lover, a business owner.

Often Ernest thought of his parents, so one day he visited a synagogue, the Ohel Rachel, built by the great-uncle of Sir Sassoon. He didn't know what he wished to see, entering the majestic entryway with rusticated pillars. Passing scores of white-robed yeshiva students, who had arrived from Europe with forged passports last year, Ernest sat by a round window near the ark that held the Torah; in front of him were empty chairs, tables, and candles, solitary, like something left behind. He heard some prayers from the students but couldn't join, unfamiliar with what they were praying. Then he sneezed. Embarrassed, he stood up and left.

He visited the synagogue again a few days later. The sanctuary was walled, windows sealed by tar paper, and dim, yet he felt relaxed this time. He breathed in the air, etched by the plumes of pale daylight running through the door; he could hear the beats of winged small flies, the rush of the breeze, and the faint prayer like a distant voice. The place felt vast, endless, full of unfathomable codes, like a great pensive mind.

He put his hand on the chair in front of him. Its armrest was damp from incessant rain and smoothed by many hands before him and would be smoothed again by many after him. He wondered if this was what his parents felt when they came to temple—to feel the togetherness, to feel the pulse of life, to become part of a tradition that bound generations past and generations to come. He was not a religious man, but he was still a Jew.

He prayed. For Leah and his parents, whose faces, smiles, voices, and frowns would forever stand in the altar of his memories; for Miriam, whom he had disappointed but would always protect; for Aiyi, whom he loved and would always love; and for Mr. Schmidt, the people working in his bakery, and the refugees in Shanghai who were his new family, for whom security and comfort had remained elusive. He wished them the light of peace, the eternal joys, the unbroken spirit for years to come.

One early afternoon when the bakery was just about to close, he was leaving with Golda when he caught a young man sneaking by outside the window. He was shivering, without a coat or a hat, wearing a white sport shoe on one foot and a black oxford on the other. A refugee, an Austrian, Ernest knew instinctively.

"Would you care for some bread?" He invited him in, and Golda went to take out a glass of soy milk and a loaf of bread, a leftover. They sat as the young man gulped it all down.

His name was Sigmund Baum; he was indeed an Austrian, having arrived in Shanghai via an ocean liner, now staying in the *Heime* in the Hongkou district with about eight thousand refugees. They were in trouble, Sigmund said. They were the last group of refugees who had arrived in Shanghai, and for months the JDC had been supporting them, providing food and medical care for them. But since the attack on the Settlement, the eight thousand refugees were left on their own, hadn't received medical care or food, and were crowded in the old unsanitary building, where four hundred people shared two primitive toilets. They had no support from any countries or the wealthy British or Americans, and they had lost touch with Miss Margolis, the representative from the JDC.

Ernest frowned, remembering the power of attorney in the scarf the social worker had thrown to him. "I saw her on a truck when she was sent to a camp."

"A camp? Where? We must find her."

But how? No one knew where the camp was. It could be located in the south of the Settlement, or north of the Hongkou district, or inside the Japanese military base, or even on an island near Japan. "Did she leave contacts in Shanghai?"

"She had an assistant, but he was imprisoned too."

Ernest was sorry to hear that. The power of attorney was about a relief fund for the refugees, he remembered. "Let me see what I can do, Sigmund. By the way, Golda, do you think you need extra help in the kitchen?"

"Ernest, you know I can never say no to you." Golda gave him a wink.

He was getting used to Golda's flirtatiousness. An actress, she didn't mind working with men or on the Sabbath, and her talent in acting helped lighten the mood in the bakery.

He turned back to the boy. Sigmund had large black eyes, skinny arms, and a boyish look. He was about fifteen or sixteen, just a little older than Miriam. "Sigmund, I don't want you to leave yet. Say, would you like to help me in the bakery?"

Sigmund jumped and hugged him. Ernest patted his shoulder; Miriam could use a friend.

On the way to the inn, Ernest thought about how to find Miss Margolis. He must find her and deliver the power of attorney to her. Without the fund, the eight thousand refugees could starve to death.

56

AIYI

"But why?" I said. We were in bed. I had one leg on his stomach, the other brushing his thigh. We had just made love. My veins were still pulsing, a sweet sensation coursing through me like a dream. It was so comfortable I was about to fall asleep.

"She threw me the scarf with the power of attorney that has something to do with a half-million-dollar loan for the refugees. Now she's missing, and the refugees are starving. I need to talk to her."

"You don't have to, Ernest. You don't know where she is. You barely know her." Ernest's kindness was his strength and his flaw. He needed to be more selfish.

"Will you help me?"

"Me? How?"

"You know many people in this city. Someone must have heard of the camp."

"Maybe. But why do you want to help them?" There were many helpless Jewish refugees, that was true, but with the Japanese still bombing our cities every day and trying to conquer all of China, there were thousands of Chinese refugees. Ernest couldn't help everyone. Besides, if the social worker was in a camp, it would be dangerous for Ernest—he could get arrested himself. There was no reason Ernest should risk his life for some refugees he didn't know.

"These people don't have anyone else to help them. They can't speak Chinese, don't have a job, and they're starving."

"Many people are starving."

"Aiyi."

I rubbed myself against him. "Would you listen to me or the refugees?"

It was only a tease, hardly a test, and by no means a trial, but I couldn't explain it. A new sense of possession, like a web, had expanded with our intimacy, and he, like a dress that was tailored for me, had become a prize I was unwilling to share.

"Of course I'll listen to you. I just need to find Miss Margolis."

"Then what? Get her out?"

"I don't know. Help me, Aiyi, please. Help me find out where the camp is. People's lives depend on it."

His eyes glistened brightly. I had seen men lecturing, laughing, boasting, throwing tantrums, and beating women, but I had never seen a man cry for other people's plight. I sighed. "Let me see what I can do."

Honestly, I had some more-pressing matters to think about than finding the camp. I had been living in the inn for about two blissful months, dining on the plain food the innkeeper made, which I never would have touched before, applying the cheap Snow Flake cream bought on the street, and living in the few ready-made changes of clothes Ernest had bought for me. I needed a long-term plan for our future. The day of my wedding with Cheng had passed, and it was time for me to be engaged to Ernest in a proper manner so I wouldn't be a disgrace—an announcement in a newspaper at least. And that would require some reconciliation with Cheng, who must be cursing me, and Sinmay and my family. I couldn't hide from them for the rest of my life. And as for my future with Ernest, we needed a home. I also needed money.

Yet Ernest didn't seem to give it a thought. A brief mention of moving in with him. That was it. And now his preoccupation with the refugees.

Still, I gave my chauffeur a gold necklace and asked if he could help find the location of the camp. It took him a few days. Then he reported that the Japanese had sent the alien enemies to eight internment camps in Shanghai. Two were large camps: one was in the Pudong district near the tobacco factories across from the Huangpu River, and the other in the Longhua area in the southern suburb of Shanghai. As far as he knew, the Americans and Netherlanders were sent to Pudong, the British to Longhua.

Now that I knew the locations of the camps, I was reluctant to tell Ernest. It was dangerous to go to the Pudong island. There were no bridges between Pudong and the Settlement; a ferry was the only way to get across, and some ferry people, I'd heard, were unscrupulous. They might agree to take Ernest across but then leave him on the other side. Besides, the Japanese patrolled the river regularly. If they caught any suspicious people crossing the river, they would shoot the boat and capsize it.

But each day Ernest pestered me. "Did you find it? Did you find it?"

It was easy to lie, but it gave me stress to see him disappointed. So I talked to my chauffeur again, gave him a gold earring, and asked him to find a reliable ferryman. He would arrange everything for me, my chauffeur said, nodding in his nonstop way.

When I told Ernest about the camp and the ferryman, he looked so happy I wanted to change my mind.

57

ERNEST

By the dawn light, he jumped in a small banana boat Aiyi had helped arrange.

The boat wobbled away from the wooden pier, and he turned around to face the island of Pudong where the tobacco factories, cotton mills, and oil factories stood. From the Settlement, it didn't look too far, but the river was wider than he thought. And the water was a cranky, foul monster of a swamp overflowing with rusty hulks of freighters, dunes of fetid fish innards, and piles of black sunken ships and decayed coffin planks with their lamentable owners. The river was a trap.

He held tight to the edge as the boat swayed through the channel of rusty hulls hanging with precarious sails. The wind rattled the sails, brittle and threatening to break any second. The tide was strong; the boat reeled, and heaps of broken engine parts hurtled toward him headlong, almost crashing into him. Then the boat spun sideways and got stuck among mounds of blackened weeds and a drove of bloated bodies. Ernest grabbed a spare oar and stabbed, fighting their way out, his stomach churning.

The Japanese patrol was scouring, its engines rumbling faintly, and now and then the searchlight pierced the dim dawn light. Nervous, he pulled down the straw hat on his head.

When the boat finally reached the jetty on the island, he let out the breath he'd been holding, gestured to the ferryman, and jumped onto the muddy ground. In front of him sprawled a one-story cotton mill with two towering chimneys, next to it three soot-covered oil factories, adjacent to what appeared to be a dog farm and a few shanties with clotheslines in the front yards. Beyond the factories in the far distance were the endless rice fields and a sea of reeds and grass. Several peasants with bare muddy feet walked toward him, eyeing him suspiciously.

Ernest wondered who they thought he was. A businessman? A spy? A camp runaway? For they were staring intently at his eyes and then glancing at his hat, jacket, and shoes. Alarmed, he walked quickly down the dirt road toward the cotton mill. Behind it, right in the shadow of the oil factories was the tobacco factory, a massive square brick building with murals of tobacco, where a sentry in a khaki uniform guarded the front entry. He wondered what he should do. If he walked up to the sentry and asked to visit the prisoners, the man could arrest him as an enemy alien and take him prisoner.

He circled to the back of the building from an oil factory's side. Next to a gasoline barrel, he lay flat and watched the prisoners, all in black-and-white striped shirts, inside a tall barbed wire fence. He heard English. He had come to the right place.

Some voices came from behind him. The barefoot peasants were coming at him, holding hoes. He had yet to get up when two men caught his shoulders. "What do you want? Wait, wait! Stop!"

They took his shoes, his trousers, his hat, and his jacket. Ernest returned to the jetty, humiliated. The ferry Aiyi hired, thank God, was still waiting for him.

He crossed the river again a few days later, holding Miss Margolis's red scarf. Walking along the barbed wire fence in the back, he waved the scarf, hoping to attract the attention of the prisoners who congregated inside. But a Japanese guard shouted. Ernest hid behind an empty gasoline barrel near a muddy track.

Never once did he catch sight of Miss Margolis.

"Maybe she's not in the camp," Aiyi said. She was naked, pacing in the hot, humid room. She had no fresh clothes, she said; the ready-made tunic he'd bought didn't fit. "Will you give up?"

"I can't."

"I won't pay for the ferryman again." She looked irritated.

"What's wrong, Aiyi? You don't mean that, do you? Maybe I should try the camp in Longhua."

"You're on your own then. It's near a graveyard. If the Japanese don't kill you, the ghosts will haunt you."

He hugged her, coaxing her, cheering her up. "I'm a ghost, too, a foreign ghost, remember? I doubt they'll go after me. How about giving me one more chance? Give Pudong one last try?"

58

AIYI

It started to rain. My Nash passed Kiessling's, where Japanese soldiers, who were on every block these days, were drinking beer. Rumor said an entire regiment from Japan had arrived in Shanghai and was preparing to swoop down on the Nationalists and Communists hidden in the central cities in China.

Yamazaki, I'd heard, had been promoted again. His power had grown. A high-ranking official, he now supervised the regiments that patrolled many streets in the Settlement and had control of the entire pro-Japanese government, which was led by the traitor Wang Jingwei. My club was officially out of my hands.

I hid my face in my scarf. Two more streets and I would reach my home. Just one look. I wouldn't enter it. I missed it. I had never been away for so long. I should talk to Cheng and Sinmay since my wedding date had long passed, but I didn't have the courage. Then I saw Ying, holding a black umbrella and hurrying on a lane near the street lined with plane trees. I could always tell when my brother was up to something, in the smoke or in the rain. He stopped in front of a European-style villa with tiles and disappeared through a gate where the board above the entry said MAISON IWAI.

It was a Japanese residence, a home only people like Yamazaki would visit. There was only one reason Ying would go there—he worked for them.

I wanted to cry. I thought I had known my brother well—a big spender, a reckless youth with a tendency to resort to violence. But I was wrong. He was not only a rogue; he was a traitor. The worst kind.

The stone lions of my home stood ahead. I told my chauffeur to drive by. A wave of emotion engulfed me. This was my home, where I had been born, played in summery silk tunics and winter fur vests, rode on the backs of servants as horses, and slept on a bamboo couch with a chorus of cicadas. The home where my parents were wed, quarreled, and fought, where the lengthy vigils were held for my mother after the deadly accident.

My grandfather could never have predicted the paths of our lives, his descendants—one a struggling publishing tycoon, one a traitor, and me, a runaway.

When I returned to the inn, it was late in the afternoon. Ernest wouldn't come tonight, out on his mission to find the American social worker, which had taken all his time. I wondered if he still cared about me.

The weather in May was cool with the light rain, but it grew damp and sticky inside the stuffy inn. A layer of green mold had grown inside my red leather shoes. I left the window ajar, peeled off my dress, and lay on my stomach in my bra and underwear to stay cool.

Someone was knocking on the door. I threw the bedsheet around me and opened the door a crack. But it flew open and Cheng burst into the room.

59

ERNEST

One last try. He went to the back of the building. When he sidled up to the fence near the gasoline barrels, he came face to face with a woman with a plump face and short hair. "Miss Margolis!"

All the hardship, stress, and fear of drowning and robbery in the past weeks went away. He had found her, the woman who held the key to the lives of eight thousand refugees.

"Ernest! You made a big ruckus with my scarf. I thought it was you." She looked ill, her face pallid, and the skin around her eyes was cut with wrinkles.

"How are you doing, Miss Margolis? Do they treat you well?" He grinned.

"Can't complain. Daily fresh weevils in rice porridge. Very nutritious. But no hamburgers, no orange juice, no oatmeal. I advise you not to join me," she said, before a series of coughs stopped her.

"Are you sick? Do they have a medical team to look after you?"

She shook her head. "I'm fine. Just some headaches. But listen. I tossed you the—"

There was a shout coming from the yard. A Japanese soldier entered. Ernest spoke urgently, "Yes, I have your power of attorney. Why did you throw it to me? A refugee from the *Heime* told me they had not received their daily stew for a few weeks. They're starv—"

A gunshot. The fence of barbed wire rattled, and Miss Margolis dropped to the ground.

"Miss—Laura!" He smelled the gunpowder.

The brave woman raised her hand and groaned. "Yes. The power of attorney. I was arrested before I had a chance to give it to Mr. Bitker. I was desperate so I tossed it to you. He doesn't know where I am, and he can't release the money without the power of attorney. I need you to go to him and give him the paper. Go, Ernest!"

"But I don't know where he is." He could see the Japanese soldier raise his rifle behind her, aiming at him. He ducked.

"Two hundred twenty-two Bubbling Well Road. Run, Ernest. Run!"

Another shot.

He dove behind the empty barrels and ran. He didn't stop until he found the boat near the jetty and leaped in.

Mr. Bitker was a man with gray hair, dressed in a gray suit and tie and wearing gray-framed glasses. A Russian, he had been in the legal business for over three decades in Shanghai. His office had a staff of six people, all working in secret to avoid getting arrested by the Japanese. He talked rapidly, as though he were on the run, and carried with him an air of efficiency. He looked relieved, holding the paper with Miss Margolis's signature. He had been trying desperately to get ahold of her but was unable to find her, he said. Now he would be able to move forward to release the relief fund.

"Who would've known, half a million dollars isn't worth that much today, and we have so many problems." Mr. Bitker pushed up his glasses.

"What kind of problems?" Ernest was thirsty from running, but it would be rude to ask for water. Drinking water needed to be boiled these days, and coal was precious.

"We were short of funds, and now we have a scarcity of everything: food, restaurants, manufacturing companies, and people." The British bakeries he had contracted were out of operation with the imprisonment of the owners, the Swiss bakeries had decided to hoard their output, and the fund would likely be burned through in a few months with the rising inflation.

"A few months. It sounds good to me."

Mr. Bitker shook his head. "The war between Japan and the Allies will likely last for a few years. Have you heard the Doolittle pilots tried to bomb Japan last month?"

"What Doolittle pilots?"

"The Americans. People said they attempted to retaliate, but it didn't work out as planned. The planes crash-landed, and no one knows where the pilots went. It looks like the war will go on, Ernest. We must make the money last as long as possible, for a year if we can, and we need bakeries that can produce eight thousand loaves of bread daily at the lowest cost possible. I wouldn't ask you if this weren't such a critical situation, Mr. Reismann. You've already helped so much. But you have a bakery, as you said—perhaps you can help again?"

He wanted to; he couldn't walk away from the helpless refugees, but there was not much he could do. The small oven he had only produced about one hundred loaves of bread per hour. For ten hours of labor, it could only produce one thousand loaves. He would need everyone to work twenty-four hours nonstop in the rising heat of summer, provided that he could have sufficient fuel and ingredients. "I'll do my best. But I'd say my bakery can produce two thousand four hundred loaves a day at most."

"That is better than nothing. We'll ration them; the sick, the elderly, and the children will have priority. It's unfortunate. People have been complaining, since we have been forced to do that for a week."

He didn't realize the situation was so dire.

"You're an angel, Ernest. I hate to impose on you again. But as you know, the American dollars have been depreciated, and the shortage of flour has hit us hard. Would you happen to have any flour in your storage before I secure anything from the Red Cross?"

The flour he had was enough to last his shop for four months, given the current rate of production. If he were to make thousands of loaves a day, it would last for one month at most. But he didn't have the heart to decline Mr. Bitker's request. "I do. I'll get to work now."

60

AIYI

"Here? Here? That fucking pianist can't even get you a decent room?"

Cheng was immaculately fashionable even in the rising heat, wearing white trousers and a white hip-length jacket with four patch pockets, a printed foulard scarf loosely draped around his neck. He made the peeled walls and termite-infested door look like a dungeon, and his eyes flashed with the glint of an executioner.

"How did you find me?" I clutched the sheet. I didn't like it, to be alone with him.

"I saw you drive by and followed you. You didn't see me?"

"I don't want to see you, Cheng. Get out."

He kicked the door shut and bolted it with the latch. "Do you think you'll hide forever? Do you know my mother canceled the wedding? What a joke, to have a wedding without a bride."

"I want you to leave, Cheng."

His handsome face reddened. He kicked the bed in the typical Cheng temper that made my heart tremble. "Our wedding was supposed to be two months ago, and you're fucking another man. Where is he?"

"Please get out."

"Is this all you can say to me? 'Get out'? Not a word of apology? You cheater, adulterer! You should be ashamed of yourself." He stomped closer to me, his eyes raw, savage. I stepped back. The sheet slipped off my hand, exposing me wearing only a pair of silk underwear and a bra. The memory of him in the car appeared in my mind. If he forced himself on me . . .

"Did you know what I went through? All the relatives know you disappeared. I'm a laughingstock! Why did you do this to me? I tried to protect you! For my entire life I've tried to protect you!" He shook my shoulders. "What did I do wrong, Aiyi? Tell me. What did I do wrong?"

There was something unexpected in his voice—it was almost like pleading. I looked at him.

His face looked thinner, which made his eyebrows look darker and thicker. There was a rare haggard look on his face, and his usually smooth hair was loose.

I had to look away.

His scarf slipped onto the floor. "I didn't mean to scream at you like this . . . you are . . . almost naked . . . I lost myself . . . you used to love me. You used to want me . . . I always thought you'd be my wife."

There was something like a sniff. He picked up his scarf, turned on his heels, opened the latch on the door, and walked out.

Sitting on the bed, I hugged my knees. The room was warm, with the smell of cheap Snow Flake facial cream and Cheng's scent. My head was pounding from the exhaustion, the shock, and something else.

It was confusing to see the hurt in his eyes, confusing to hear him pleading. This was not Cheng, the fiancé who constantly criticized me, the boss boy who threw tantrums when things didn't go his way, the spoiled man with no interest in making conversation. It seemed even though we had grown up together, familiar with each other's needs, I had never truly understood him.

He hadn't forced himself on me; he had stayed away. Maybe I was wrong about him.

A cramp rose in my lower abdomen. I massaged it, waiting for the pain to dissipate. Then I stopped, a shiver running through me. I had been careful, but for the entire time I'd been living in this inn, I had not bled.

For the whole evening I agonized, thinking of Mother and how she had protected me. Her toes broken as a toddler, she had refused to break mine, even though my relatives urged it. She was a tiny woman with a small face, her hair always discreetly tied in a knot. She talked in a soft but stern voice of a matriarch, always remaining placid among squabbles of my uncles and aunts.

I remembered hearing her sobs and groans in her bedroom while Father thrashed her. I would have taken a fist for her, protected her, if I could. Once she lay in bed for a month because of a dislocated shoulder, and she said she had fallen off the bed while sleeping.

Even a woman like her dared not to break the wall built by traditions, traditions such as women must never divorce, traditions that women suffering domestic violence must stay quiet.

And what had I done? Her favorite daughter, engaged to one man but impregnated by another, and worse—I carried a child out of wedlock, a child of mixed races, a shame to her family. Mother would never forgive me, and she would have beaten me, had she been alive.

I made love to Ernest with urgency and ferocity I had not thought I was capable of. I wanted him to shatter me; I wanted to leave behind the pit of darkness and fear that threatened to drown me. I had gone too far. *Falling in love is like teetering on the edge of a precipice blindfolded,* Emily had said. She could have warned me about this—the point of no return.

I should never make love again, yet he was all I had. I lay on my stomach, spent.

Ernest was talking about a Russian, some loan, and his decision to help refugees—more of the same stuff he had been saying lately. He would also be busy from now on, and he would like me to meet his people in the bakery.

"Someday," I said, preoccupied by the thought of whether or not to tell him of my pregnancy. I never liked children, and what a disaster it would be to have a child of ours, not Chinese, not European, without a safe home. I knew too well of the fate of those children, despised and denounced. "Do you like children, Ernest? I have many nephews and nieces at home. Those scamps. I don't like them."

His hand smoothed my stomach. "When I can take care of you better, we'll have a family."

I nodded glumly. In fact, nothing he said would lift my spirits. "Yes, let's live somewhere else. I don't want to live here anymore."

Yet there were not many places for us. The Japanese had occupied the Settlement and the Concession. My family home was not welcoming to Ernest or even me. The only option would be the apartment Ernest lived in, but was I ready to see those condemning looks and hear snide remarks?

I held his face close to me. There were his eyes, a lively spring pond. I wanted to smile but also wanted to cry. I was trapped. Now there were three of us.

61

ERNEST

It was tiresome, hard work. For three weeks he labored with his employees in the bakery. They kneaded when the electricity was on, baked when the electricity was cut off, and slept whenever they could. No one complained. When the oven was fired up, the heat was unbearable, and he'd head out the door for some cool air—the early summer rain provided huge relief from the bakery's scorching heat.

Once bread was baked, Ernest packed the loaves in baskets tied on the back of bikes, covered them with oiled newspapers to prevent them from being soaked in the rain, and asked Sigmund and Miriam to deliver them to the *Heime*. As Mr. Bitker predicted, the bread was rationed out, often with many disappointed people complaining. Eventually, some refugees from the *Heime* came to fetch bread themselves, but soon loaves began disappearing mysteriously from the kitchen, and the goal of 2,400 a day was not able to be met.

He hardly had the time to see Aiyi anymore. When he did, he wanted no more than sleep. Remembering how he had neglected Miriam, he did his best to listen to Aiyi, but it was difficult. The anxiety of keeping the bakery running, keeping the refugees fed, gnawed at Ernest. He was running out of flour, yeast, sugar, salt, and even coal.

Mr. Bitker, who had to purchase wheat and flour with the loan, had not paid him, so Ernest had used his own savings to give overtime wages to his employees.

⁓⚬⁓

They were outside the bakery, tying baskets on the back of the bikes, when Ernest saw two uniformed Japanese holding rifles going door-to-door across the street, searching for foreigners, asking to see their passports.

He tensed. Recently he had heard the Japanese had come across German Jews with passports stamped with *J*, and they had not arrested them. It was likely the Japanese wouldn't prosecute them, since they were stateless, but if Miriam and his people were caught without passports, there was a good chance they could still be mistaken as enemy aliens.

"Act normal, no eye contact," he warned Miriam, who was ready to bike to the *Heime* to deliver the bread.

This morning had started out peacefully. He had slept in the bakery for convenience and was planning on going to see Aiyi at noon. He hadn't seen her for three days.

"What would happen if we had eye contact?" Miriam had become his reliable delivery girl. She was thriving in the bakery. She loved to help out, chatted with the workers, sang and danced with Golda as they stamped on the floor and swung the rolling pins, and smiled and joked with Sigmund. Sigmund, who had a habit of making fart jokes, was goofy and helped Miriam relax. The two had become good friends—fortunately not at the level he needed to be alarmed about.

"Then they'll find out we're not Chinese." Ernest took two loaves of bread, tucked them in the basket on the bike, and covered them with an oiled paper. It was raining again, a typical summer day in Shanghai.

"I don't think they'll send us to the camp." She swung onto the bike and beckoned Sigmund, who had just secured the bread on his bike. Across the street, the two soldiers hopped in a jeep and drove away; Ernest was relieved.

"You don't know that. Just don't talk to them, remember?" Someone called him in the bakery, so Ernest hurried to leave. He was at the door when he heard Miriam whisper something to Sigmund. "He's a mensch, your brother," Sigmund replied.

Miriam kicked up the kickstand. "And I'm his keeper."

It was the most affectionate thing Ernest had ever heard from Miriam. His heart was filled with gratitude. He had given his bakery to the refugees, and the bakery had given him back his sister.

Mr. Bitker sent him one hundred sacks of flour and gave him a payment of two hundred dollars for the month's bread, a fraction of the usual price. But Ernest was encouraged. With the flour, he could keep producing as many loaves of bread as possible, and the payment provided relief for the overtime pay he owed. But he had to be careful with the flour, since the Japanese, who'd begun to feel the pressure of food shortage, had started to confiscate flour and rice. Covertly, Ernest bought rice, coal, alcohol, kerosene, oil, and soy milk from the suppliers introduced by Mrs. Kauser and learned how to do business, how to negotiate. Always reasonable and polite, he established sound relationships with several Chinese warehouses with a connection to the black market.

By mid-June, all foreigners with means had fled Shanghai, and those without means were imprisoned or hidden. On the streets roamed the Japanese, the Germans, international criminals, spies, and gangsters. To be safe, Ernest instructed Miriam and his people to put on a tunic that many Chinese wore and warned them not to run into any soldiers.

Then one day Ernest passed Sassoon's hotel and saw a skinny Chinese, the hotel's bellboy, standing by a piano in the alley. "Everyone is taking things from the hotel," he said defensively. "Do you want to buy it or not?"

It was the same piano he had played in the Jazz Bar. Aiyi would love it. Perhaps it was a sign that he should start thinking about their future, since she had mentioned children. It excited him to have a family but frightened him as well, to be a father in a dangerous time. But he was twenty-one, and he didn't want to let her down. "How much do you want for it?"

62

AIYI

I stepped inside the teahouse. In the far corner, Sinmay sat at a table near a window, his back facing the garden, wearing a pair of round sunglasses with black rims; near his feet sat a black umbrella. He would be outraged. Another scandal. His youngest sister impregnated by a foreigner. But he was the only person who could save me.

I sat on a red wicker chair across from him, glad I was not showing. I had asked to meet him at the teahouse near the Winding Bridge in the famous Yu Garden, since teahouses were favorite spots for cultured pundits like Sinmay, who came to gossip and complain about the war since they were too afraid to carry a gun. I had frequented the Yu Garden teahouse as a child—they had my favorite sticky nine-layer chrysanthemum cakes, and I had loved the oddly shaped rocks, the goldfish in the streams, and the architecture of the buildings.

"Good afternoon, older brother," I said.

The teahouse was not busy at this hour; only a few customers sat near the square dark-red tables, the framed lanterns hung from the rafters. An old man in a long robe was counting peanuts in a saucer, a musician was playing a two-string instrument in the corner, and a group of three young men, their heads gathered close, were plotting something at the far end.

"You haven't come home for over three months, little sister. Are you going to come back?" Sinmay took off the black-rimmed sunglasses and placed them near a tea set with blue butterflies.

"So you can lock me up again?" I was ruining my chances, yet I couldn't let him off easily.

The old man was counting. "One . . . two . . . three . . ."

"Longjing or Biluochun?" Sinmay spoke with his usual gramophone voice, but his tone, to my surprise, was without rancor.

A tea aficionado, he could spend hours lecturing on the varied shapes of tea leaves. A Longjing leaf looked like the tongue of a spring swallow, and a Biluochun leaf appeared to be a supple conch from a fertile bank. All that poetic nonsense.

"I don't drink tea. Peiyu loves tea."

"They are the finest of our country. Try them." He reached for a teapot and poured the tea into a cup in front of me.

Sinmay, like Cheng, had never poured tea for anyone, let alone me. I stared at him.

"Don't look surprised. It's tea. The last cup in this teahouse. They don't have any more left. Drink while you can. Hong Kong has fallen, do you know? I received a letter from Emily, dated in December after Hong Kong's fall. It took the letter six months to arrive. But she replied after all. She said the Japanese arrested many American sailors, British soldiers, and their families, and drove them to markets and beheaded them."

A shiver ran through me. "How's Emily?"

"She was arrested, but she showed them our marriage certificate to prove she was a wife of a Chinese citizen. So she was released. Remember the certificate? It was her idea. She wanted to save our printing press from falling into Japanese hands. She carried the certificate with her in Hong Kong, and it saved her life." He handed me a letter.

My dearest Sinmay, my love, my soul mate, she wrote.

"She loves me, little sister. I know love will not turn into ash."

"Is she coming back to Shanghai?" I gave him back the letter.

"She didn't say. She asked about you. She said you were a talented businesswoman. I shouldn't have hit you and locked you up."

Another surprise. Sinmay was too arrogant. Apology was one of the metaphors missing in his poetry. When he'd crossed my name off Mother's will, he had never thought of my rights.

I picked up the teacup, unsure what to make of this change.

He stared at the floating leaves. "I envy you, little sister. I was like you once. Emily and I fell for each other head over heels. We didn't care about what others thought. Your sister-in-law didn't approve of us, my friends didn't approve of us, but they couldn't stop us. Emily was born with a free spirit, and I loved her for that. We wrote our poetry in bed, shared our verses under the moon, composed the rhymes in the sun. We were in love." Scratchiness appeared in his voice. "If you really wish to live with that pianist, I won't stop you. And I shall give you my blessing."

I didn't expect this. A wave of laughter came from the trio at the far end. "You mean it?"

He nodded. "Come home. A good woman cannot live in an inn."

I looked at him. "I'm with child, older brother."

He put down the teacup. "I was worried about that. Come home. You need your family."

Tears of relief, of joy, of gratitude burst in my eyes. "I don't know what to say, but why?"

Sinmay turned to the window, his long aristocratic nose a ridge of sadness reflected by the light drilling through the latticed windows. "These days, I often wonder, who am I? If I'm a poet, why am I flying like a bird who can't see the sky? If I'm a man, why do I feel trapped in my own courtyard? If I'm a husband, why am I miserable with my wife?" He bent to pick up a suitcase, which I had not noticed before. "I don't want to live like this anymore. I'm going to find Emily. I'll get her back."

"Wait . . . Does Peiyu know? Did you tell her? You have a family. You can't just leave."

"If I stay, I'll never forgive myself."

"But what about your publishing business?"

"My publishing business has long been nonexistent. The Japanese burned my magazines. They forbade me to publish my stories, and I refused to publish theirs. The calendar printing was profitable, but it was not enough to sustain the whole enterprise. I've closed them all."

"You didn't tell me. Does Peiyu know?"

"She doesn't. If she needs money she can sell the heirlooms. She runs the house."

"Sell heirlooms! You're broke!"

"I'm a better poet than businessman."

That explained why he asked me to go home. He had lost all, and now he'd decided to run away.

"I can't believe it. You're destitute. You're a terrible person. Irresponsible. What about our family? Did you talk to Ying? Does he know?"

"I couldn't find him."

A mournful tone flowed from the two-string instrument and rippled across the teahouse.

"Can you wait so you can talk to him first?"

"You know Ying. He's never around. Who knows what he's doing. You can let him know when you see him. Our family will be fine. You'll be fine. Your foreigner will take care of you, too."

"But you can't just leave!"

"I have to, Aiyi. Now, now. This is good tea. Let's finish it. I like Longjing better than Biluochun."

I held my head. I was shaking with anger, but tears poured out of me. I couldn't stop crying, couldn't form a coherent thought; I didn't know what was wrong with me.

I saw Sinmay off at the wharf, at the same spot where I bade farewell to Emily. When I left, my thoughts swirled like tea leaves in hot water. Sinmay was broke; I had lost my club. The wealth of my family had declined dramatically. But maybe the situation wasn't that bad. His factory was still there, and our home alone was worth a lot. Peiyu, a formidable woman with a good sense of finance, would know what to do.

And Sinmay had given me his blessing to plan my future with Ernest, the most wonderful outcome. I should tell Ernest of this, tell him of the child I carried. Perhaps he would live in my house, and we would play mah-jongg, drink tea, and listen to music. We would be like Emily and Sinmay, but happier.

It was a rare sunny afternoon, late in the day. The streets were paved with pebbles of sunlight, the sky whirled with white jasmine petals, and the wind surfed on an opaque silky sleeve of smoke.

I went to Ernest's bakery to surprise him.

63

ERNEST

The soldiers were back again, talking to an officer with a mole under his eye. By the window, Ernest watched them with the nagging unease that he was being watched too. When the piano had been unloaded from a rickshaw earlier this morning, one of the soldiers had examined it before giving permission to have it moved inside the bakery.

But perhaps he was overly anxious. He had heard the same story again that the Japanese had left the German Jews alone. Perhaps, he was safe. He walked away from the window, sat on the bench in front of the piano, and ran his right hand, ungloved, completely healed, up and down the keys, reveling in the rushing sound of piano. Aiyi would be so pleased. "The Last Rose of Shanghai" rang in his ears; his heart lifting in happiness, he played. His Chinese, in his opinion, was much improved, but Aiyi always said he got the tones wrong. So he switched to Beethoven.

"This piano must have cost a fortune," Mr. Schmidt said near the counter.

"Fifty American dollars," Sigmund, who had helped move the piano from the hotel to the bakery, replied for him. "Ernest bought it for his girlfriend."

"Did you use up all your savings, Ernest?" Miriam said.

Ernest smiled. He loved it that Miriam looked out for him. "Don't worry. We have enough."

"Will you bring your girlfriend here? Will you let us meet her?" Sigmund asked.

"Of course. She doesn't know about the piano yet. I want to surprise her."

"Is she still cold?" Miriam crossed her arms, a gesture reminding him of his mother.

"I told you, Miriam. She was a bit aloof, but not cold."

"You said she's Chinese." Mr. Schmidt was shaking his head; near him, Golda, tying a plaid apron over her waist, frowned at him as if he were a loaf of overly baked bread.

He knew what was in their minds. They didn't know Chinese people very well; they didn't speak Chinese and had few interactions with the locals. But once they met Aiyi and got to know her, they would like her.

"My friends, I'm going to marry her and start a new life with her. I'm beyond excited."

"This is so fast. Have you discussed it with a rabbi?" Mr. Schmidt looked as though he'd just swallowed a ball.

If he wanted to—if Aiyi wanted to—they could go to the synagogue. Ernest was just about to say that when a man in a khaki uniform and an officer's cap staggered through the door. The pungent scent of alcohol permeated the room.

A sudden silence fell; everyone froze.

Ernest's skin crawled. The Japanese had discovered them. He would demand to see his identification card and arrest them all.

"Nice piano music. Very nice." The officer stumbled to him. His words were slurred; his English had a heavy accent. He attempted to lean against the piano but missed it and nearly slipped to the floor.

"Please excuse me. Today is a good day. A new shipment of sake arrived from Japan and we all had too much. I love Beethoven. Beethoven is the best! Do you agree? The best music! Keep playing."

The man was drunk, his eyes glazed, his face red, the mole shining beneath his eye. He looked familiar, but Ernest couldn't recall where he had seen him. "I'm happy to oblige, sir."

Out of the corner of his eye, Ernest could see Sigmund pull Miriam protectively behind him. Mr. Schmidt looked shorter behind the counter; Golda and the other bakers crouched near the table in front of the counter. Fear penetrated the hot air.

The man gave him a bow. "Thank you. I haven't heard such beautiful music for years. And on such a good day. Have we met before?"

"I don't believe so, sir." Ernest eyed the Mauser in the officer's holster.

"But you look familiar. And your hand. Is it a star?"

He should have kept the glove on.

"Pardon me. I'm Officer Yamazaki. Your name?"

The officer who had been hunting him, the officer who had almost shot Aiyi in her club. Did he still remember him? Ernest's hands trembled. "Ernest Reismann."

"Liceman, Liceman," Yamazaki murmured. "Foreigners are our guests, and I believe they're protected in special places. Why are you here? And these people? What's your nationality?"

His heart raced faster; his fingers shook as he began Beethoven's Fifth Symphony. What he said would determine his fate and the fate of all the people in his bakery. Certainly he couldn't feign being British or American; he couldn't say he was Asian, since even a drunken man could tell his eyes were blue. He could lie and say he was German without a German passport, but Yamazaki would discover he was stateless sooner or later. "I'm Jewish, sir."

Yamazaki hiccupped. "What's that?"

Ernest could feel a wave of nervous heat boiling from his people. Pounding on the piano, he was going to reply when he realized the man had staggered away and yelled at someone at the door. Ernest looked up.

At the entrance stood Aiyi, holding a silver purse with studs like diamonds, gold leaf earrings swinging. Her face was pale, her entire body stiffened with fear.

"Miss Shao?" The officer suddenly whirled around. "I know who you are. You're the pianist from the One Hundred Joys Nightclub!"

Ernest stood. "The bakery is closed, sir. Would you please leave?"

All Yamazaki's friendliness and courtesy vanished. Looking murderous, he pointed angrily. "You killed a soldier. You, a foreigner! Now you're colluding with a Chinese. Colluding with a Chinese deserves death! You! Deserve death. All of you deserve death!"

Ernest could feel the hair rising on his nape. But Aiyi. He signaled her to slide out the door. She took a step.

"Don't move! No one moves!" Yamazaki whipped out the Mauser, aiming at her.

"No!" Ernest lunged at Yamazaki and wrestled for the pistol in his hand.

A gunshot rang out. It was so loud it hurt his eardrums. Ernest stepped back and shouted, warning everyone to duck for cover. But Yamazaki raised his Mauser again. Ernest grabbed a rolling pin from a baker and swung it at Yamazaki. Another gunshot exploded. Somehow Miriam had lost her footing and collapsed in front of him.

"Miriam!" Fear pierced his brain; he smacked the rolling pin harder on Yamazaki's head. He had never assaulted anyone in his life, but he wanted the man to die. The drunkard moaned, flung out his arms, and finally sagged to the floor.

Ernest dropped the rolling pin and held Miriam. "God, God. Oh, God." A bolt of chills shot down his spine. He couldn't see her face very well, and her French braid was wet. "What's going on. What happened. Miriam?"

Something red ran out of her mouth. But she said nothing.

A violent storm of horror slammed him; his entire body spasmed. "Say something, Miriam. Come on. You're all right. Say something. It's going to be fine. Miriam? Miriam?"

But she didn't answer, not even to give him a scoff or a taunt. He held her tight to his chest; he kissed her cheeks, her eyes, her lips, begging her to answer, to say something. "Please, Miriam, please, please. Someone! Please! Help! Help me!"

The bakery was strangely quiet. He could only hear his breathing, his sobs, his voice. Then someone was calling him. He couldn't understand why people called him when they should be saving her. But then came a wail and a wave of sobs. He was drowning, he couldn't breathe, he couldn't stop shivering. He looked down at Miriam's pale face marred with streaks of blood. It hit him: Miriam, his sister, with whom he had sailed across the oceans, whom he had refused to let go, whom he had sworn to protect, was gone.

64

AIYI

She took her last breath in his arms. Still he wouldn't let her go; blood smeared his chest and face and soaked his shirt. He was paralyzed; he couldn't see me or hear me. I stepped aside as people removed Yamazaki and carried him out of the bakery. They needed to get rid of him or they would all be killed if the patrolling soldiers found out they had assaulted an officer. The murderer was unconscious, drunk, but still alive, unfortunately.

I went to Ernest and held his shoulder. His face was ashen, his eyes dead. I wanted to say something, but what could I say? He had protected me from the Japanese, and his sister had protected him. Now she'd been killed, and I was still alive.

I had brought this tragedy to him, to her, to all the people in the room. I felt nauseated, ashamed, standing in the plain Western-style bakery with the pool of blood around me, right next to the people in aprons who knelt, wept, and keened. I could smell the acrid odor of gunpowder and feel the rushing panic, the weakness of my limbs.

"Miss Shao?" said a woman's voice.

She had astonishing moss-green eyes, a pale face with freckles, and jujube-red hair wrapped in a handkerchief. A foreigner, but unlike

Emily, who had black hair and black eyes like me. This woman's mannerisms were different from Emily's too. Whereas Emily acted like an emotional, spoiled writer, this exotic beauty held a sensual, dramatic air. She gave the impression that the bakery, and the world, were simply a stage. Golda, I recognized from Ernest's descriptions of his employees.

I wished she could be my friend. I'd not meant them harm by coming here. I'd only wished to tell Ernest of the news of our beautiful future.

The beauty tucked a stray strand of red hair beneath the head wrapper, a gesture of grace and drama, but her green eyes were sharper than a blade. "Please leave."

Just another person who treated me with hostility. I turned to Ernest, tormented statue that he was, his head bowed, back curved. His body was a crooked shadow, his sobs a trail of sorrow in the air, each a hammer in my heart.

I couldn't leave him like this. "Just a minute."

Her ample bosom swelled, her green eyes flashing. A sob escaped her before she said, "She died because of you. You brought us this disaster. This is your fault."

I fled outside.

It was dark on the street and soon it would be curfew; the area was soundless, save for the sporadic shouts of the patrolling soldiers in the distance. At the end of the alley were two shadowy figures, the old man, Mr. Schmidt, and the boy, Sigmund, illuminated by the faint light from the bakery, propping up Yamazaki against the wall.

There came a long sigh from the old man as they walked toward me. "What are we going to do now? The soldiers might have heard the gunshot."

They stopped in front of me. Sigmund looked as if he were going to punch me, but he wiped his face and walked away. The old man cleared his throat.

"He won't remember anything. He was drunk," I said weakly.

"I certainly hope so. If he does, then we all are going to die."

My face hot, I went back to the bakery, back to the table where no one had wanted me to sit. I wanted a cigarette badly. I dug into my purse, but there were no cigarettes inside. I held the purse tight, my fingers trembling. I must stay; I must tell him why I came here, tell him about the child of our love, the future that belonged to us.

Mr. Schmidt said something in Ernest's ear, and he finally got up. Stiffly, he walked toward me, his lips quaking strangely. Suddenly I was afraid. Ernest, for whom I had fought with my family, for whom I was willing to destroy my future, once nineteen years old, homeless, helpless, and friendless, was no longer the same man I had fallen in love with.

65

ERNEST

Miriam was gone. She'd died to save his life. What should he do now?

It was over. Everything was over.

He could hardly lift his feet, each breath a pin in his throat. The bakery was warm, but he shivered. When he reached Aiyi, he forgot for a moment what he was going to do. He held her hands, pressed them to his face, and closed his eyes. If there were a way to alleviate his pain, to forget about his stupidity, to believe this was only a nightmare, it came from her touch, her breath, and her skin. *Help me, my love, help me,* he cried out in his head.

"I'm sorry. I'm so sorry," she said.

Miriam is gone, my love, he wanted to say but couldn't. If the words were unspoken, then there was a chance what had happened was not true.

He looked up. The ceiling was gray, gloomy; the air lapped toward him like an ocean of vinegar. He heard the wailing of the train's horn, its stuttering chugs, and the rattle of its floor as it slunk away. Outside, his parents were weeping, their eyes full of anguish, and his mother in her favorite sunflower dress doubled over like a wilted sunflower. Their voices, even after two years, sounded so clear. *Ernest, take good care of your sister. Ernest, have a good life and marry a good Jewish girl.*

He had failed to protect the sister he'd loved since she was a baby. He had refused to let her go to America and kept her selfishly. Had he let her go with Mr. Blackstone, she would not have been shot; she would have lived and had a good life.

You understand? She could have lived. She would go to America, she would go to Vassar College.

"Ernest? Ernest? Talk to me."

She died to save my life, Aiyi. He opened his mouth; his chest hurt too much. She, his teenage sister whose life had been destroyed by him, had decided to love him, and gave her life to him. He should have protected her, but he had paid her no attention. Again.

He could never live with this—looking at his lover's face, knowing it had cost his sister's life. "Us. Aiyi. You and me. I can't do this anymore. I can't."

She let out a gasp.

He held her tightly. Oh, Lord, what had he just said? He was breaking her heart; he was a heartless man. He had dreamed of being with her, protecting her since they met, and he would give his life for her. His life. Not Miriam's.

"Don't, Ernest. Please don't. It's not my fault. You can't hurt me. Please don't hurt me. I can't leave you."

She was right. It was not her fault, yet she would bear the blame; it was his stupidity, yet she would suffer. It was not fair; life was not fair. He wanted her, but he couldn't live with her. What had she said about love? Something like divine coins. Something like one love, one eternity. It was rubbish. All was rubbish. Love was not a coin; it was a bullet.

He felt the wetness on his shirt, saw the wetness on her face—her face, a lonely moon across an oceanic sky; he wanted to wipe the tears off, but couldn't raise his hand. Instead he stepped back, closed his eyes, and swallowed the briny air. In his mind's eye, he saw her slim figure waver, diminish, and finally disappear in the maze of tears, bullets, and ashes.

66

AIYI

My body was weightless, a plume of spineless smoke, a shadow of silent sighs. Outside the bakery, I stopped to catch my breath. In and out I breathed. In and out.

From behind me came soft footfalls, the keening, and the voices of Golda and Mr. Schmidt. A man with scraggly hair and a long beard nearly crashed into me, swerved, and went inside the bakery.

Holding my purse, I stumbled to my Nash and climbed in. The car drove into the sickening night. The streets were silent, the bars and restaurants dead like graves. Sometimes I heard the rumbling of vehicles, the patrolling soldiers' yelping; sometimes children's nightmarish screams and people's warped quarrels in the alleys.

In the inn I threw up. I emptied everything inside me, and still the excruciating pain sat like a fire in my stomach. I crawled onto the bed and hugged my shoulders. Everything was unbearable—the clothes Ernest had folded, the dent on the pillow he had left, the scent of him. I buried myself under the quilt. When morning came, I gathered all my things and checked out.

❧

I had nowhere else to go other than home. So my head hung low, I slid through the gates my butler pushed open. Ying wasn't home, and Sinmay had left for Hong Kong. Peiyu watched from the dining room, her eyes piercing. I went to my room as fast as I could. I had left home as a runaway and returned as a disgrace: a used woman, pregnant out of wedlock, and abandoned. If she found out, she would shame me.

I took short walks along the wall near my room. I prayed the life inside me would wilt and melt. I thought of using some herbs or jumping from the wall to eliminate the life that was a burden, the life no one cared for. But I was a Buddhist. It was a crime to destroy a life.

I thought of Ernest, too, of his loss, his grief, for which, even though I refused to admit it aloud, I was responsible. But he was weak. He had abandoned me. I didn't even have a chance to tell him of my pregnancy.

Peiyu would have noticed my condition with her experience, but she had just learned of Sinmay's departure and the closure of his business. When he'd said he was broke, Sinmay had meant it. He was not only penniless but also in debt. She was furious, handing out whatever she'd saved to the creditors, who charged hefty interest. I gave her the cash I'd saved in my wardrobe. But I didn't know how bad inflation was, and in a matter of a few weeks, all my savings were gone, and she still had creditors pounding on the door.

To save the cost of running the house, she dismissed all the servants, including the only nanny for her youngest, and sold my Nash without my knowledge. My chauffeur was dismissed too. I was sad and angry. Although I knew little about my chauffeur, he had been with me for many years, and he was most loyal to me.

Peiyu's temper flared at mealtimes. She frowned and yelled at her children for eating too much, her complaints loud enough for me to hear outside the dining room. Indeed, it was quite unsettling to see how ferociously these children ate. There were so many—six of them. The thirteen-year-old boy lunged toward the pot of rice as soon as it let out steam, followed by the eleven-year-old and the seven-year-old, and each filled their bowl to the rim. They wolfed everything down, licked their lips, and wanted more.

Two months passed. Peiyu began to sell the heirlooms: my grandfather's paintings, his jade pendants bestowed by Empress Dowager Cixi, my mother's favorite Qing dynasty vase, my father's antique snuff bottles. Then more followed: the bulky rosewood furniture, the jade tree, the rare blue porcelain set fired and crafted in Jingdezhen, and the British silverware that was another family heirloom.

Each morning on the first day of the week, Peiyu sat at the round table holding a brush, negotiating with a pawnshop owner, who promised not to disclose her identity to the public to save her reputation and in turn received the objects at a low price. She cursed but agreed.

❧

If I had told Ernest of my pregnancy, would he have changed his mind?

In bed, I asked myself that question again and again. At least he needed to know. Our lives were nothing but drifting leaves in a violent storm, but the seed of our love came from a tree rooted in my heart.

I went to his bakery again on an afternoon in August, dressed in a jacket that failed to cover my bump. The rare beauty Golda greeted me. He had just left, she said, her green eyes, two beams of hostility, fixed on my stomach.

"Would you tell him I'd like to see him?" I asked, and gave her my address.

He never came.

❧

I grew bigger. I put on the voluminous tunics Cheng had made for me before the wedding, but then even those would not conceal the child I carried. With each flutter, each kick of the life inside me, I was pounded with pain and regret and fear. Desperation ballooned as my stomach grew rounder and simple activities such as walking and getting out of bed became a struggle. I wanted the baby to leave my body, to free me, yet I didn't want it to be born either. Whether it was a boy or a girl, it would be the walking proof of my foolishness, the face of my shame.

Then one day I was napping when Peiyu came into my bedroom where my ornate wardrobes were slowly disappearing one by one.

"I didn't believe what my children said, but look at you," she said, her gaze full of contempt.

I turned sideways to sit up, heavy and clumsy like a sow. "I wanted to tell you."

"It's not Cheng's, is it?"

"No."

"He came several times."

I had nothing to say. Our talk at the inn had been the last conversation between us.

She frowned. "Did you tell him?"

"No."

Peiyu sighed. "Who else knows about this?"

"Only Sinmay. Before he left."

"Ying?"

"He doesn't know."

"Cheng's mother?"

"I don't think so."

"You should marry Cheng. You can tell him it's his. He won't know."

"Of course he'll know."

She threw up her hands. "What's wrong with the Shaos? Your brother ran away to an American, and you're pregnant with a foreigner's seed. Don't you have a sense of shame?"

Tears stung my eyes. I looked away.

"What are you going to do with the baby?"

I looked down at my stomach, and I wanted to cry my eyes out. All these months of misery, loneliness, and fear, mulling over jumping from the wall, crying myself to sleep, and watching my slim body turn into an ugly barrel covered with stretch marks and dark spots were not enough. I still needed a plan for a baby whom I didn't care for. "I'll take care of it."

"Yes, you will. Because I can't help you. I have six kids already. Everyone is hungry; the whole household wants to eat. I can't do it all. If you're going to stay here, you'll take care of your own problem. You'll give away the baby."

I jerked. "You can't mean that. Would you abandon your own?"

"You don't get to ask me this question. You were engaged to a wealthy man, but you got pregnant with another man's baby. If your mother were alive, she would have asked you to jump in the well." She left my room.

I had a splitting headache. I didn't want to have anything to do with this new life. But it would be despicable to give away a child of your own. Yet it would be despicable to live with this child, too.

67

ERNEST

He kept Miriam's ashes in a jar near his bed. Each evening before he slept, he read a few words from the Webster dictionary like a prayer. A diligent student, Miriam had underlined many difficult words and made notes within the margins. Tears pouring down his cheeks, he traced the handwriting, thinking of her voice, her broad bony shoulders, her head hidden in the hood, and her lively, happy face in the bakery.

There was nothing else he could do other than work. He rose at four o'clock, ate a piece of bread with peanut butter spread and drank soy milk and cheap watermelon juice, and before dawn, he was supervising the baking, wrapping up loaves of bread, and checking the balance sheet. Work was good for him; it took his mind off Miriam.

But grief was a fat bread dough. You punched it down; it still rose up. When Sigmund talked about Miriam, Ernest teared up. When he saw the bike she rode, he broke down. He grew reticent, incapable of comprehending people's questions, angry at other people's smiles. All he thought of was his negligence that had cost Miriam's life; all he saw was the absence of her.

He should have let her go with Mr. Blackstone.

At seven o'clock, Ernest went to bed, exhausted. Sometimes he slept well; sometimes sleep was hard to come by. Loneliness was a fair punishment, yet he wanted Aiyi—her soft hands, her teasing smile, her flowing voice like a spring stream. He wanted to see her put on her high heels, to touch those soft calves, to run his fingers over her naked body.

He slept less and less. And then he couldn't sleep at all.

He washed his face in a basin, trimmed his stubble, and snipped off his knotty, shoulder-length hair. Then he stuffed all his possessions in his suitcase, locked up the room, and walked away.

In his bakery, he hung up a curtain in a corner near the kitchen and moved a table there. He could afford a large office or move into one of the apartments he'd purchased, but he felt more at home in the bakery; this, after all, had been Miriam's favorite place in Shanghai.

One evening, he felt a hand on his shoulder.

"Ernest. Look at you. Are you sick?" Golda said.

It was quiet in the bakery; it was probably two hours after midnight. The workers were dozing off, catching some sleep. He stood up. "No. What time is it?"

She stood in front of him, wearing a red cotton skirt. Her hand traced his chest. He had not buttoned his oxford shirt to keep cool, and now he could feel her hot fingers and smell her scent. She untied his belt; she kissed him.

"What are you doing, Golda?"

"I want to see you happy."

"It's late."

"I don't mind, Ernest."

He blinked. The warmth, the sleeplessness, muddled his mind.

She took his hand and slipped it under her skirt. She was not wearing stockings or underwear.

He shuddered. He didn't know who he was anymore. A fire burst inside him; a carapace of impossible longing swallowed him. He longed to be lost in an agonizing oblivion, to forget his mistake, to be forgotten. He let his pants drop, pulled her close, and entered her.

❦

A few days later, Ernest was groggy with sleep when he heard someone knocking on the door. Two Japanese soldiers in uniforms stood outside the bakery.

"May I help you?" He snapped awake. How long had it been since Yamazaki's visit? Three months? Four months? But Yamazaki was still alive, he had been told.

The soldiers asked to see his passport and the passports of all the workers in the bakery. Explaining he was a German citizen who had lost his passport, Ernest gave them the only identification card he had, the one issued by the Settlement at the wharf when he arrived. He couldn't make sense of what the soldiers were saying—their English was broken—but it was clear they were investigating the assault of Yamazaki.

They took all of them to a station nearby, where they sat for hours. Ernest was ordered to answer to someone on a phone. Over and over, he heard questions in German with a strong Japanese accent: *"Was ist Ihre Nationalität und wo wurden Sie geboren? Wann sind Sie nach Shanghai gekommen?"*

He tensed. *"Ich bin Deutscher und wurde in Berlin geboren. 1940 kam ich nach Shanghai."*

"Haben Sie einen Offizier angegriffen?"

"Nein, ich habe keinen Offizier angegriffen."

He was detained for two days, and finally, he was told to leave.

❦

Mr. Bitker sent him a hunk of meat as a token of thanks for helping the refugees and in celebration of his release. Ernest shared it with his people in the bakery. Every living day was like a steak, they said.

It was the first steak he'd had for the past three years. He gathered it on his plate, sliced it into strips, then in cubes, and then put a piece in his mouth, and chewed. He tried to enjoy it, savoring every bit—the flavor, the texture. It was true. Every living day was a steak.

He wanted to make more money, both for his own survival and for the refugees who depended on him. When the puppet government led by Wang Jingwei ordered all Nationalist currency off the market and replaced them with its own notes, new *fabi*, at a rate of two to one, the cost of living doubled overnight, and so did the value of the apartments Ernest had acquired. He sold them promptly.

With the cash he had, he bought bags of rice, flour, wheat, dried beans, dried fish, dried sweet potatoes, laces, bolts of silk, straw hats, cotton coats—anything he could get his hands on through his Chinese business associates. He also asked Mr. Bitker to introduce him to the wealthy Chinese merchants who sold coal, seasonings, and kerosene.

It was easy for him to do business, for word spread that he was reliable and generous. With Mr. Bitker's help, Ernest made friends with the Swiss, the Canadians, and the Americans who had escaped from the Japanese dragnet. Through his own connections, he did underground business with the local Shanghai families, textile factories, and packaging companies. The Chinese liked him, and sometimes they even invited him for tea.

Once he let it slip that he had fallen in love with a Chinese girl, and she loved him as well, but he had let her go. The Chinese businessmen nodded. It was wise of him, they said; people from different countries shouldn't marry.

In November, he heard a Japanese battleship was capsized by the USS *Washington* in the Solomon Islands, and Japan, with its assets frozen in the US, ordered the Wang Jingwei puppet government to provide all essential food supplies such as rice, oil, coal, and salt to support their soldiers in Shanghai. A major shortage of essentials haunted the city. Inflation, which had been a plague, worsened. A single grape cost thirty cents in American dollars. Ernest resold the bags of merchandise at skyrocketing prices.

He became a wealthy man.

68

AIYI

On a cold morning in December, I threw myself against the headboard, sweat raining down my face, onto my neck, and down to my naked stomach. After two days of howling and groaning, tormented by waves of contractions, I was utterly spent, my legs sprawled, my bottom stuck to the pool of mucus on a thin sheet. It was such a relief to know I had pushed it out; my body was free.

But I felt no happiness, no peace, only this hollowness, this bottomless grief. I had been a beautiful girl, a desirable woman, a shrewd businesswoman who would have been the wealthiest woman in Asia. Yet here I was, sweating, hemorrhaging, bloating, giving birth to a child I didn't want, a woman forsaken, a helpless thing with no future. How did I let my life get out of my control?

In the air floated a series of strange sounds, vulnerable and heartbreaking, like notes of his piano. A mockery of the jazzy past that had fooled me.

"A worthless girl," Peiyu muttered, swaddled the slippery bundle in a few expert tugs, and put her thumb in the baby's mouth to silence her.

I remembered what she had urged months before. After all these days of self-loathing and regret, I still didn't know what to do with the baby. "Give her to me."

"You shouldn't. Once you hold her, you won't let her go. She's ruined your life. If you keep her, you'll ruin the Shaos' reputation."

I shook my head, yet words failed me. The baby kicked, loosening the cloth that swaddled her, revealing a patch of birthmark on her right ankle. "Please. Just for a moment."

Peiyu stared at the bundle. "What are we women? Only birth tools. Man takes us, puts his penis in us, and then goes on with his life with his other women. We are left to swallow our tears and raise his children. Yet children are no better. They have no gratitude, and they want to be fed and fed, want more and more."

I wished she could say something else, or give me a pat, or tell me I had done well. Or maybe she would leave me alone and let me sleep in quiet. For I was spent, and my body was torn, and my tears wouldn't stop.

There came that faint voice again, like that of a trapped animal. I elbowed up. "What's going on? What are you doing?"

"I'm doing you a favor, little sister. You have no husband, no place of your own, no money. Your mother would have done the same thing if she were alive." She was standing at the door.

"Come back. Let me at least see her. Please, let me see her."

She wouldn't come closer. I pushed, an agonizing pain shooting through my lower body. My arms gave out. "I can't see. Let me see."

Peiyu lowered her arms. I heaved, my damp hair in my mouth, craning my neck. A tuft of down, a pale face with red pimples—the thing gazed at me with Ernest's eyes.

I slept, wept, and slept more. I drank little, ate little. Bound to the room, I was weak, drowsy. I hallucinated. I dreamed of Ernest's eyes.

�⋯

It was a chilly winter. I drifted through the days like the wind sweeping through numbed fingers. The pale morning light doodled at my feet as I rose from bed; the silvery twilight curdled as I padded across the bedroom to the courtyard and to the reception hall. When I gazed at Peiyu's face, it was like seeing through a glass window. *Where is she?*

She wouldn't tell me.

I had lost my daughter because I didn't fight for her, because I didn't love her.

⋯

Cheng's voice came from outside the door. He had brought glutinous rice with chicken, which the entire household had devoured. He asked if I wanted to have some.

"Come in."

In a white suit and a white panama hat, Cheng glided close to my bed, bringing blades of sunlight around him. He looked decorated, strong, and sophisticated as usual, but his voice sounded like he was choked. "What happened to you, Aiyi?"

I leaned on him. I was not asking for anything, not his sympathy or forgiveness, only a shoulder to cry on. It was such a comfort to smell his familiar cigarette scent, to know someone still cared if I wanted rice with chicken. I told him everything.

His fingers touched my cheek. His voice was surprisingly warm, surprisingly firm. "I know things didn't work out with us. You have gone through a lot. I still want to take care of you, Aiyi, even if . . ."

For a man who couldn't bear to see me walk in front of other men without a bra, it meant a lot.

❦

Two days later, I married Cheng.

It was the eighteenth day of January. Life was strange. Since childhood, I was told I would marry Cheng. We had fought, played with crickets in the courtyard, and taken English lessons from our tutor while our parents chatted and drank jasmine tea in the family room. We were the *Qing Mei Zhu Ma*, blue plum and bamboo horse, loving friends from childhood and a destined couple-to-be.

Mother had told me repeatedly of my wedding day since I was little. It would be beautiful and beautifully fitting for a woman of my birth. A jade leaf growing on a gold branch.

I would put on white powder and bright-red lipstick to accentuate my beauty; I would step out of my room, my hair elaborately adorned by a thousand jewels, my neck decorated with at least three thick gold necklaces. A traditional red silk veil would drape over my head, and my fingers, glowing with a dozen gold rings, would lift the hem of a long dress for an easier walk. With each step, the bells, beads, and tassels on the veil would clink and peal, a melody of happiness and fortune. Someone, likely my maid, would give me a hand to guide me down the pebbled path to the central room, the courtyard, and then the fountain near the gate where a red palanquin would await with four lifters whom Mother had hired. As I came close, the musicians would play the lute, cymbals, drums, and French horn, and the fireworks would crack loudly; the throngs of family and relatives, all clad in festive red, would clap their hands, and the gate of my home would swing open, the red lanterns bouncing, and Cheng would take my hand.

But in reality, I was too poor to wear jewelry. I was not beautiful either. My face was swollen, my lips pale, and my waist was soft like a fish belly. None of the dresses fitted me, so in an old gray tunic, I made my way out of the house without furniture, to the empty courtyard without servants. I looked like a woman on the way to buy fish at the market.

Holding a red silk veil, I started to cross the courtyard. It was quiet there, the ground still wet from yesterday's rain. No sight of musicians, or fireworks, or palanquin, or Sinmay, or relatives. Peiyu and her children were still sleeping. Near the fountain was Cheng's Buick.

I stumbled, short of breath, nervous. But I shouldn't be. Cheng would be a good husband. We would have as many children as his mother wanted, and we would live in his vast mansion with horses, birds, and gardens. I could play mah-jongg, rise up late in the afternoon, and scold the servants whenever I was bored.

I put the red veil over my head. The world changed. The air wavered like a red screen, and the puddle near my feet roiled like Sassoon's cocktail. Yet my breath caught in my throat, and my heart thudded. Beyond the fringe of the redness, beyond the fountain, beyond the stone lions stood Ernest, dressed in a traditional red Chinese wedding tunic, a large red bow across his chest. His curly hair was shaped like a precious crown, his smile glistening like sweet honey, his eyes shining like a promise.

No more.

I took Cheng's hand.

69

FALL 1980

THE PEACE HOTEL

Ms. Sorebi holds two pages together like a prayer book and carefully slips her index finger through. She's been silent for a long moment since I finished recounting my story.

I'm ready for her questions, but I'm nervous. The dishes arrive, saving me. Garlic prawns seasoned with pepper. Stewed hen with ginseng and dates. Sauteed broccoli with slices of almonds. Deep-fried fish with red chili sauce. Eight kinds of exotic mushroom cooked in a clay pot. Marinated chicken breast. Shrimp dumplings in translucent tapioca flour. No chicken feet that'll freak her out or whole fish with a head or bones that would have choked her.

Food is a safe topic. I pick up the chopsticks and urge her to eat. "Do you know how to use chopsticks?"

She nods; those headlights in fog avoid me.

I'm worried. "Ms. Sorebi? How old are you?"

"Thirty-five."

"Born in 1945, I see. Do you have children?"

"Yes, I have a son. Ben. He's nine."

"Do you have a picture? May I take a look?"

"I don't want to bore you, Ms. Shao."

"Don't disappoint an old woman, I beg you. I love children. My niece does everything I tell her, except she refuses to get married and have children."

Ms. Sorebi takes out a photo from her wallet. "This was taken last summer in Texas."

Ben is splashing in a kiddie pool, wearing a blue bathing suit printed with sharks. "He's adorable. What's his favorite sport—swimming? Football?" I give the photo back to her.

"Horseback riding."

"It's an unusual sport."

"Not in Texas. He grew up there. But enough about my kid. I don't want to bore you. You've told me so much about your past, and this is precious material to work with."

The moment has come. "So, I've told you that I've given away my daughter. Are you going to put that in the documentary too?"

Actually, I know she will, but I try to ascertain how she might handle it. If she writes as I have confessed, people will understand my pain, but if she is biased against me, then my reputation as a heartless mother is all but sealed.

She puts down her chopsticks; her face blooms with dismay—or is it disgust? "The only thing I can promise is that I won't judge you, Ms. Shao. It's unthinkable to me, yet I hear things like that are rather common in China. It's sad."

It bothers me, the sense of privilege, and the arrogance in her voice—her, America grown. Yet what can I say, being the one who's judged? No donation I gave to the temples for the past decades can wash off my sin.

"I've heard of Miriam's death from the Shanghai Jews, and I confess it was very difficult to understand. Everyone told me a different story. Some said she died of sickness, some said she was shot because she fought, some said you brought the Japanese there. Now I can see how it really happened. This is very helpful, Ms. Shao."

I nod and open my mouth. I need to tell her something extremely important, but I can't bring up my courage.

"Ms. Shao?"

"Yes?" The wall warps. Did I take my medication today?

"Are you okay? Would you like to have some water?"

"Yes, water will be wonderful. Where were we?"

70

FEBRUARY 1943

ERNEST

Mr. Bitker was right. The war went on, and Miss Margolis's loan was spent by October last year. Since then, for four months, Ernest supported the refugees with his own money. He even took one step further, refurbishing the old boiler in the *Heime* with a new one, so the kitchen would be efficient enough to produce much-needed heated water for everyone. Without Miss Margolis's charity, he was the only man in Shanghai who looked after the destitute refugees, and he planned to continue to do so for whatever it took, for as long as possible.

Miriam. What if she had been there? She would have been happy to work in the bakery, happy to see him take care of his people. What if he had allowed her to leave with Mr. Blackstone? She would have been in Vassar College. She would have been alive.

⚜

Ernest put down the jug of pilsner and shook hands with the long-robed Chinese man across from him. The deal was struck. He'd just acquired a fleet of paddle steamers, a coal-burning steamer, a cargo ship, and a second coal-burning steamer with 9,500 dead-weight tonnage.

After months of hard work and his timely investment, he had become a rich man. With the large profit he had made, he had taken steps to diversify his business and expanded to the banking industry with the help of Mr. Bitker's friends. Now with this deal, he became the largest ship owner in Shanghai. His ultimate goal was to purchase large cargo ships, very large crude carriers, and even ultralarge crude carriers to become the leading ship owner along the Chinese coast from Hong Kong to Qingdao. It gave him great confidence that with his growing wealth, he would be able to provide for the refugees in the long run.

He was invited to the parties organized by a small group of wealthy, dauntless foreigners seeking fortune in Shanghai. The parties were quiet—no piano music to avoid attention—but decadent, with cigars, gin, and whiskey; often they were held underground, or in private buildings far from the clubs and hotels. In those ballrooms covered with tar and insulated with sandbags, he smoked cigars and drank whiskey rumored to have been pillaged from Sassoon's private cellar. All the Briton's fortune in Shanghai was lost, his hotel ransacked by Japanese soldiers, his apartments occupied by Germans and his racecourse by Japanese marines.

Occasionally, Ernest's thoughts shifted to the Briton who had changed his life. He would like to shake his hand as a friend if he saw him again, and he would listen to his advice too.

Sometimes, at those parties, Ernest was questioned about why he remained a bachelor. Unwilling to elaborate, he started bringing Golda with him. With her striking beauty and suave actress's charm, Golda walked arm in arm with him, her flaming-red hair rolled in a vibrant curve to frame her pale face. Whatever she asked for, he bought. Jewelry, dresses, fur, shoes, and hats. She loved hats. A cream crochet with a wool ribbon, a velvet pillbox in claret, or a wool pillbox with a black veil. Cloaked in a luxurious fur coat over an ivory blouse with a lace collar, her arms fitted in wine-colored gloves, Golda was the summer rose among withered fall grass.

He didn't sleep with her after the one-time madness, and he gently pushed her away as she sought him out at night. Golda was the banner of his success, not the destination of his happiness.

Despite all the luxury, his growing wealth, and his lush image embellished by Golda, Ernest was unhappy. In the office on Bubbling Well Road, where he had purchased the entire floor of a Gothic twelve-story building designed by the architect László Hudec, he stared at the piano, which he had moved from the bakery. He could still make beautiful music, still remember the songs' lilt and lyrics, but the woman whom he had played for lived in another room of his memory.

He went to the inn where they had met, holding some silly hope that she might be waiting. The proprietor said she had not set foot there since June last year; the room had been vacated.

He called her home. The line was no longer in use.

He thought to visit her at home. Just a glimpse.

The wooden gate was closed. Rain poured down on the massive stone lions with wavy manes, the twisting dragons with long serpentine whiskers, and the thick wall by the street. From behind the wall, the tops of ginkgo trees and elms hovered like a mirage. Her home. It didn't take long to find it.

Holding an umbrella, he watched the compound across from him, waiting for her to come out. But the gate remained closed. Finally, he crossed the street.

A jeep went ahead of him and stopped in front of the compound, splashing water on his trousers. He stepped back and saw the gate yanked wide for the jeep; inside he could see Japanese soldiers wearing black kimonos and white *tabi* near a fountain in the courtyard.

The rain splattered on his umbrella, drenching the back of his silk suit. He went down the street and entered a shop nearby.

"What happened to the Shaos?" he asked.

The family had sold the home to a creditor a month ago, and the creditor had given it to the Japanese, the shopkeeper explained, fiddling with a stack of calendars.

"Where are the Shaos now?"

The shopkeeper shook his head. "Want some calendars?"

He bought ten calendars he had no use for and walked back to his four-door plum-hued Chrysler Imperial. The wiper swished dully; on the back seat, Golda was waiting.

He got in the car and closed his eyes. Had he really lost her, for good?

71

AIYI

Cheng was still the old Cheng I knew. He didn't ask how I felt or what I liked or what I wanted to do. He gave me an apple because he wanted me to have it, ordered new dresses because he believed I needed them. He treated me the same way he treated his bird, feeding it with the hand holding a cigarette, unaware that the smoke might sicken the bird. He was not a man with attention for emotions or tears.

He said nothing when his mother, seated at a round dinner table, hinted at the blank bedsheet; he said nothing when she mentioned grandchildren and nannies. When she questioned him, he cleared his throat, straightened his tie, and reached for my hand under the table.

I knew what I had—a loyal man.

I didn't ask to listen to music on the gramophone, didn't read the magazines that would make him frown, didn't hum, or sway my hips, or dance to the tunes in my head. He wouldn't like all of that.

At night, I waited for him on our marital bed, naked, save for the silk robe he'd given me. He no longer frightened me, and all the wildness of him, his raw energy, his brawny arms, was no longer intimidating. I attached my body to him, ready for him. This was a good life: to eat, to play the game of pleasure, to go to sleep and do it again the next day.

Love would come later, Mother had said. I hoped she was right.

72

ERNEST

When he lost another round of mah-jongg, a game necessary to play for socializing, he asked his Chinese business partners where the home of Aiyi's fiancé, Cheng, was. The men were happy to tell him, but they corrected him. He was no longer the fiancé; he was the husband.

So she was looked after, but he still wanted to see her. The next day, he went to Cheng's house and knocked the ring through a lion's head against the wooden gate. An old servant in a gray tunic opened it. Looking frightened, she screamed and slammed the gate in his face.

But he had found the right place—he'd seen the black Buick.

When he entered his office, Ernest stopped short, his heart skipping a few beats—on a chair by the wall, near the desk where he worked, sat Yamazaki in a full officer's uniform; in his holster was the damned Mauser and a broadsword. It had been about eight months since the man had murdered Miriam. Grief and fury welled up inside him. If he had a gun, Yamazaki would be dead already.

"I'm delighted to meet you again, Mr. Reismann. Allow me to make a proper introduction," the man said, bowing from his waist, his face revealing not a trace of the menace or brutality from the bakery. "I'm officer Koreshige Yamazaki. I've been in Shanghai since the beginning of 1937. I've been involved in a few vital missions for my emperor, and now I'm in charge of foreign business operations in Shanghai."

Ernest held back his balled fists that he longed to ram into the man's stomach. The murderer of his sister, now standing in his office as if nothing had happened, disguised as a man of civility. If he didn't know better, he would think this was a different man. He must be more discerning. Yamazaki was, like Ernest's Chinese partners said, a skillful Noh performer, capable of changing faces.

"Mr. Yamazaki." He gritted his teeth.

Someone in the office cleared his throat, warning him. If he dared lay a finger on Yamazaki, they would all die. Golda. Sigmund. All his business associates, and perhaps even the refugees he helped in the *Heime*. Mr. Schmidt had said, repeatedly, that they were lucky to be released after being arrested.

Then there was a rumor that SS colonel Josef Meisinger from Nazi Germany, Japan's ally, had recently visited the emperor of Japan and urged him to do something about the Jews in Shanghai, who he said were a scourge they'd tried to eliminate in Germany. Meisinger recommended isolating them in rooms sprayed with poisonous gas or using them for vivisection. The Japanese didn't think it necessary to use the Jews for vivisection, as they had endless supplies of the Chinese, but they agreed the poisonous gas was an effective solution to stamp out the nest of rebels among the Chinese and perhaps even wipe out an entire province of troublemakers once and for all. As a result, many tanks of gas had been stashed in a warehouse of a German medical company in Shanghai.

He must be careful, or he would get all his people, unprotected, stateless, killed.

"May I offer you some pilsner?" Ernest walked to a cabinet at the end of the table.

Yamazaki declined.

"Some sake then?" He looked at Mr. Schmidt, who had swiftly laid out two small cups he hadn't known they had.

Yamazaki accepted it. He held the small cup with two hands as if it were a great offering. For a long moment, the well-mannered murderer commented on the cold weather, explained *mono no aware*, described the Japanese art of gardening, and asked Ernest if he had seen the cherry blossoms in Tokyo.

All the bullshit. Ernest was disgusted, but the man wouldn't come here for no reason. And finally, after five cups of sake, Yamazaki spoke with deliberateness.

He came, he said, for a business opportunity. The great empire of Japan was in need of eager partners who would support them in their ambitious expansion in Asia—surely, he had heard of the empire's Greater East Asia Co-prosperity Sphere? He had been informed of Mr. Reissman's growing prowess, and the Japanese government wanted to form a joint business venture with him, specifically regarding the shipping company he'd just acquired. And, would he forgive his ignorance that he didn't know until now that Germany had revoked the citizenship of the refugees like him? It must be of great sorrow to be a ronin.

Ernest felt sick at heart. Never in his wildest dreams did he think of becoming a partner of the Japanese, but Yamazaki's request of a joint venture, masked in casualness, was more threatening than an order. He had to go along with it before he could map out a strategy. "Of course. I shall have a proposal for the partnership paperwork drafted up."

Yamazaki bowed before taking his leave.

Ernest shot to his feet, anger boiling in his chest. The murderer of his sister was right in front of him, yet he couldn't kill him and was forced to consider him to be his business partner.

Mr. Schmidt, in his sleek black suit and tall hat, dressed up like Sassoon, finished the rest of the sake. "The shipping company is important and lucrative. It's not a surprise they want to have a hand in it."

"If they become a partner, they'll eventually take full control of the shipping company, the navigational routes, and the ships."

Mr. Schmidt sighed. "I know. But we don't have a choice, do we? If Yamazaki wants your entire company, we would probably need to hand it over too."

It hit him. Stateless, without protection, he could lose his company and everything he owned. He turned around to look at the clean, spacious room, the solid black furniture, and the piano in the corner. In spite of himself, he went to the piano, removed the fur that covered the fallboard, and opened up the fallboard. His fingers stiff, he hovered above the keys and played Debussy, Chopin, and then Aiyi's song in his mind. He had sworn that he'd never wanted to hear Beethoven again or touch the keyboard again; its music had cost Miriam's life.

He stared at the star-shaped scar on his hand and the stab wound—a thick bar of shiny flesh in the center. With his diligence and fortitude, he had risen to be a prominent businessman and supported the people in need. And now the Japanese wanted to take it all away.

73

AIYI

It was my idea. I wanted to visit Peiyu. Word had come that after my wedding she had sold my family home and moved into a stone-arch-gate building in the Concession to make ends meet. These buildings, meant for poor laborers, prostitutes, and low-income servants when Shanghai had been still a mud town, were notorious for being unsanitary, with a lack of fresh air and sunlight, a hotbed for beriberi and diseases.

I couldn't imagine Peiyu living in such squalor. I planned to invite her to live with me, for Cheng's mansion was large enough to house her and her children. I also hoped she would loosen her tongue and tell me who had taken my daughter, for I had started to think of her.

But Cheng didn't want to go to the stone-arch-gate building. He had rarely set foot in any place paved only with packed dirt, and he worried he'd catch diseases. But when I said I'd go there by myself, he gave in and offered to ride with me in his Buick.

The traffic was light for the afternoon. On the street lined with fur shops and hat boutiques, a Japanese officer in his uniform was walking with his dog, a white terrier.

Cheng's chauffeur slowed down. A precaution. A few days before, a young man had been shot for walking too slowly in front of a soldier; now everyone tried to step out of the way of any Japanese. For the Japanese had lost patience with us Chinese. Fanatically loyal to their emperor, Hirohito, they had believed they could bomb the Nationalists into submission, but instead the war dragged on, and our resistance force had, surprisingly, gathered steam. More and more Chinese turned to the resourceful Communists for help. Some bold Chinese with guns would open fire from the rooftops at the patrolling Japanese or assassinate Japanese soldiers in restaurants. Now the Japanese suspected every civilian was a spy or an assassin.

Rumor also said the Japanese were losing the war against the Americans, who routed them on an island chain called Midway. It was heartwarming to hear of the Americans' victory, but I was also aware that as egotistical as the Japanese were, they would vent all their frustration on innocent people in China.

Cheng was complaining next to me. He would be late. He had just set up a meeting to sell his father's coal-burning steamer. The deal was important for him, for he was struggling with the shipping business without the guidance of his uncle, who had died of pneumonia.

"It won't take long," I said. Then I spotted a familiar face behind a window near a fur shop. "Stop, stop the car."

"What is it?" Cheng leaned over to see better.

It was Emily Hahn. A picture of her, actually, printed on a poster with books behind a window. Had she returned? Had she published another book? I opened the door and leaped out.

Something began yanking the hem of my dress: the officer's dog, arching his back, baring his teeth. Losing my balance, I cried out.

Cheng took my arm. "Told you not to get out of the car. Let's go back."

"Miss Shao." That voice.

I whipped around.

Had I known it was him walking with his dog, I would have stayed inside the car; had I known I would run into him again, I would not have asked to come at all. The nightmares that still kept me up at night flashed before me. Miriam in Ernest's arms. Ernest's tears. Lanyu lying in a pool of blood. People screaming. Glass shattering.

I stepped back and took Cheng's hand. We should run. Yamazaki could kill me.

The hateful man looked at me and then my husband contemptuously. "Last time I saw you, you were with a white man, and now this Chinese? What are you? A whore? You Chinese ought to be grateful. We protect you from violence and crime, we educate your low class, and we promote modernity and prosperity in Shanghai. It's beyond my comprehension why your people sabotage the efforts that are for your own good. Come now, kneel and apologize before you leave."

Cheng came in front of me. "Fuck off."

I grabbed Cheng's arm, holding him back, and desperately I searched in my mind, trying to say something. I could apologize, plead, or simply grab Cheng and run. But one look at Yamazaki and my heart turned into ice. There were no more feigned courtesies, no more pretenses.

A shot. Deafening. Tearing the cloth of the placid sky. The automobiles, the rickshaws, and the streets all seemed to halt. All sounds vanished, all but Yamazaki's hysterical laugh and his dog's maddening barks.

I couldn't move, couldn't speak—all I saw was Cheng, my husband, his fierce eyes, his handsome face.

"You're right. We need to go; we really have to go," I said.

The corner of his lips swept up, as if he agreed to take me home, as if he would promise to protect me with his life, as if he would admonish me again, but he fell back stiffly, pulling me down on to the street. I held him, stroking his handsome face, rocking him. "What did you say? What did you say?"

A trickle of blood sprouted in his mouth and flowed down his chin, wetting his purple silk tie. I screamed. I wished with all my heart that he would talk to me, grasp my hand, and stay with me, but for the first time in his life, he let me go.

⤚

Twenty-four days after my wedding, I became a widow.

My grief was dull, like a cut by a pair of rusted scissors. In the central reception hall where Cheng's mother set up the vigil, I wore a white hat, a white cotton shirt, white pants, white cloth shoes, and a hemp cloak. I sat among the wreaths of crinkled white paper, long strips of white banners, and fluffy white paper flowers; I listened to the drone of the bell and the monotone wooden fish; I tossed into the fire pages of gilt papers shaped like gold nuggets.

Life was a humorless joke. In my childhood, I had sometimes hated Cheng's selfishness, his possessiveness, and his domineering way. In adulthood, I had found nothing in common with him but had found love from Ernest. Yet Ernest had deserted me, and Cheng had forgiven me, taken me back, and given me a life.

For the first time I realized how blind I was. I had known Cheng since infancy, yet I had treated him as no more than a cousin. I had spent less than a month with him as his wife, and I had seen what his love truly was: raw, direct, and veracious. I was grateful for that; I had grown to love him for that. Yet what little time we'd had.

Cheng's mother blamed me. Tears and snot pouring out, she slapped me and spat on me. She wailed and wailed, her grief sharp and pointed like a knife.

Ying, who had disappeared for months, came on the sixth day of the vigil and stood by the coffin; his eyelids were swollen, his face wet, and his lips pinched in a rigid sign of anger. His grief was heavy, dangerous like an ax.

I wanted to lean on his shoulder and weep, yet I wanted to pound on him and tear him into pieces too. For all those months while I wallowed in miserable pregnancy at home, he had paid little attention—he didn't even know about the baby I gave away. He was gone doing his seedy business, a stranger I barely knew, a rogue aiding people like Yamazaki.

I sat and tossed a sheet of gilt paper into the cauldron, evading people's gazes. When they circled in the hallway, I followed them. I was mute, head lowered, and those chants, oh, those monotonous, alien, grave chants, they sounded like a sentence from heaven.

After forty-nine days of mourning, when Cheng's soul left, Cheng's mother sent a servant to my room, asking if I was pregnant.

I wasn't.

She let her words be relayed, heavy and clunky, like a loaded freight train, that given the circumstances, it would be best if I could move out.

Cheng's mother gave me nothing; she kept all that was Cheng's. Our marriage had been swift, and I was not entitled to his inheritance and properties. I couldn't afford to start another legal battle anyway. For the second time in a few months, I packed. I stuffed into my two leather suitcases all my clothes and the jewelry and gifts Cheng had given me. I had no money.

Outside Cheng's mansion, I came to an oak tree. It was early April, the air damp and chilly. I wore my black mink coat; in my hands I carried the suitcases. Alone, I had no chauffeur, nor an automobile, nor a servant. In front of me passed rickshaw pullers, toothless beggars, hunchback street vendors, and a dour-looking Imperial Japanese Army soldier. Cheng's chauffeur, out of pity, stuffed ten *fabi* into my hands so I could use it to take a tram or a rickshaw.

I didn't know what else to do, so I climbed on a bus.

74

ERNEST

Today Yamazaki would come to view the drafted proposal. Ernest sat at a desk by the window. He was ready, the proposal in a manila folder, a pistol in his drawer.

He had purchased the gun on the black market, determined to take matters into his own hands when necessary. But he must be careful. He couldn't afford to make a mistake.

"Shouldn't he be here by now?" Mr. Schmidt asked, taking off his tall hat. He had grown plump and bought an automobile and an apartment near the racecourse. He sat with Golda and several associates in the meeting room; everybody looked worried.

"He's late," Golda said.

"What if he declines the proposal?" Mr. Schmidt asked.

"We'll draft another one." Ernest felt sick at heart thinking about killing Yamazaki. He hadn't told anyone about the pistol. The less they knew, the better.

"I hear there's a rumor that the Japanese had a fallout with Meisinger." Golda was smoking a cigarette on the leather couch covered with a leopard print fur blanket. Her red hair curled delicately, framing her face like an elegant wave, her green eyes alluring. In her boredom, she had been playing different roles: a prim British governess, a jealous Paris courtesan, and today a Chinese singer. She wore a traditional Chinese fitted dress with a slit near her thigh, her skin shining like pearls, but all he could think of was he had seen the same dress on Aiyi. Maybe not the same dress. Maybe not the same color. Maybe not the same style at all. He should go find her at Cheng's house.

"Yamazaki is evil; don't forget that," he said.

"He's evil, but courteous. Isn't that curious? They didn't send us to the internment camp. They let us run our businesses, allow us to purchase apartments," Mr. Schmidt said.

There was a tinge of admiration in Mr. Schmidt's tone that irritated Ernest. Mr. Schmidt was too blind and deaf to know what was happening. The Japanese left them alone because they were busy warring against the Chinese in the hinterlands and the Americans in the Pacific. They didn't forget them, though, or Yamazaki wouldn't come asking for a partnership.

"A courteous tiger is still a tiger." Ernest stood and put his hands in his trousers' pockets. He was dressed in his favorite attire, a gray single-breasted jacket with a tapered waist, a gray tie, and black leather loafers. With all his wealth, he didn't wear any jewelry, only a Rolex watch. He was strong, his body straight and healthy, his face sculpted, his eyes sober.

From the street came a loud screech. He jerked. Two Japanese soldiers jumped off a truck and rushed inside his building. Something was wrong.

"Ernest, they're arresting people." Sigmund raced into the meeting room.

In a few strides, Ernest reached the door, where he nearly crashed into Yamazaki in his uniform. He had to assert great control not to yank the man's collar and spit into his face. "Sir, what seems to be the problem?"

"Mr. Reismann, I regret I didn't have time to inform you properly. I've received an imperial order decreed by my emperor, Hirohito." He gestured, and the soldier beside him took out a set of handcuffs.

Blood rushed to Ernest's head. "What's this? Is it necessary?"

"Ah, you're right. Leave off the handcuffs, please. Mr. Reismann is an honorable man. He won't resist. But I'm afraid it's my duty to take you to the designated area."

He had never heard of such a place. "Pardon me. What's the designated area?"

"I shall be pleased to explain, Mr. Reismann. Recently, we were recommended to take actions to isolate the Jewish refugees in this country, and my emperor has conceived a special plan for people like you." Yamazaki whipped out a piece of paper from his pocket; in his heavily accented English, he read the Proclamation for Stateless Persons, which ordered the restriction of residences and businesses of stateless refugees who came to Shanghai during the war in Europe, the previous German nationals now unclaimed by any country—people including him. All the stateless people must be relocated to a designated area.

They had decided to imprison them after all. A designated area or an internment camp. Same thing. They would be prisoners. But he couldn't leave. His business, his people, and the refugees needed him. "Is there a chance to appeal, sir?"

"I'm afraid any appeal on your part will be denied, due to your special status as the owner of many enterprises. I was ordered to keep you under watch at all times, with specific instruction to look after the large portion of business and finance under your name."

"The paperwork for the joint venture has been drafted."

"Our deal is no longer on the table. Your newly purchased cargo ships, your finances, and all your assets now belong to the Japanese government with this order. Legally."

"Asshole!"

"I have reason to believe that you'll comply with the law for your own safety and those working for you."

All his assets. The immense wealth that he'd accumulated through hard work, the money he used to support his people and the refugees. He laughed.

"You will not comply, Mr. Reismann?"

"I'm afraid I need time to reflect on that." Boldly, he headed back to his desk, ignoring the twinkling anger in Yamazaki's eyes and the soldier's rifle. He opened the drawer and reached for the pistol he had prepared. To hell with the Japanese. Enough of this barbarism. It was time to take the matter into his own hands, to protect himself and his business and avenge Miriam's death.

"Ernest." Mr. Schmidt, his face pale, appeared in front of him. Beside him, Golda, ever dramatic, cursed, wrenching her arms from a soldier. Behind them was Sigmund. His friends, and fellow businessmen. All handcuffed.

It was one thing to kill Yamazaki, another to put his people, the very people he had sworn to protect, in harm's way. He loosened his fingers on the pistol and closed the drawer. With Yamazaki watching his every movement, Ernest put on his coat, his gloves, and his hat and walked out of the office to the truck on the street. He sat between Mr. Schmidt and Golda, who wept, and he put his arm around her shoulder.

Half an hour later, the truck drove down the metal Garden Bridge, the same bridge he had crossed years ago to the Settlement to find a job. The truck passed a pawnshop where a wooden picket said **Bridge Road**, turned onto a muddy track, and stopped in front of a two-story brick building with a rising sun flag. After so many turns of fortune's wheel, he was back in the Hongkou district.

Yamazaki told him to get off.

He dusted off his sleeves and got off, but the truck sped off with his people. "Where are you taking them?"

"The designated area. You'll join them soon. Please follow me."

"What's this place?" Ernest asked, looking at the brick building with a sign in Chinese he couldn't read.

"A place for you to reflect," Yamazaki said.

A uniformed sergeant, wielding a thin, long bamboo-shaped sword, stomped toward him, but it was his armband that caught Ernest's attention. **KEMPEITAI**, it said. Ernest shuddered. Kempeitai were the law enforcers, sadists known for torture, like the notorious German Schutzstaffel.

The sergeant hit him with the hilt of the sword, and he passed out in pain. When he came to his senses, he saw he'd been thrown into a foul-smelling, straw-covered cell, where he received more blows. But that was barely torture compared to what his jail mates suffered. Especially the woman on a bench across from him. She was naked, her face covered with blood and feces, her nipples and her private parts pierced with electric wires. Each time the Japanese soldier turned on the switch of the electric shock board, she jolted and screamed.

A man with a bloody face and bloody fingers sang across from him. The poor soul's fingernails had been pulled out, and he was giddy. Ernest recognized him as an executive from the Jardine Group, who'd often patronized the Jazz Bar.

Near the wall two Japanese held a naked man and poured into his mouth gallons of urine mixed with pungent kerosene. The man groaned, his stomach bloated, but the torture had just begun—they beat him over and over with a steel rod. When they were tired, they kicked the poor man's stomach just for the fun of it.

Ernest shivered. Nausea, pain, and fear writhed inside him.

For days he watched the sickening torture and grew weak from lack of sleep, water, and food. His bones ached from daily blows, and he was running a fever. Finally, Yamazaki showed up in the dark cell. "Mr. Reismann, I hope you're comfortable."

He elbowed up, leaning against the dank wall. "You've already taken my assets; you got what you want. Why take me here?"

"I still have unfinished business with you. I need your signature for a few accounts. But you're right. You're here for a reason. I spent six days in the hospital after you hit me. I never forgot the man who hit me. And I have been watching you. You've amassed great wealth, and you'll give it all to my emperor. You'll confirm all your assets on these forms and write down your bank accounts." Yamazaki took out a stack of paper from a bag he carried.

If he had a rolling pin, anything, he would kill the man there. "How long have I been here?"

"Six days. Pen?"

He closed his eyes. He could refuse and die a rich man. Or go insane like the executive of the Jardine Group. It didn't matter anymore. He had lost Aiyi, lost Miriam. Oh, Miriam, Miriam. She had given her life for him; she had died so he could live. He wanted to weep. "If I do as you say, would you let me go?"

The man gave a bow, a most laughable gesture. "You have my word."

The statements on the forms were clear. All ownership of his newly founded shipping company and his financial services would be transferred to the Japanese government, and there were bank accounts that he needed to fill out. He wrote down the two account numbers he had in a Swiss bank branch. Flipping one page after another, he signed.

He stumbled out of jail, the afternoon sun stinging his eyes. His legs were cramped from sitting on the damp ground, his mind taut and twisted like electric shock wires. Shuffling like a convalescent, he studied the angle of the sun, trying to figure out the time and direction.

The Garden Bridge should be ahead of him. He shuffled down the muddy road, stopped to take a breather, and began to walk again.

A rifle jammed into his chest, choking him. He fought for breath, staring at the chrysanthemum carved in the bolt-action rifle. Shouting, the soldier dragged him and threw him in a truck.

Lying flat, he stared at the muddy sky and didn't want to get up. The truck jolted and bounced, passing a wooden picket that read THE DESIGNATED AREA FOR STATELESS PERSONS.

75

AIYI

I had never thought this wretched life would be mine, to be unloved, to be homeless, to be poor. Without money, I couldn't stay in an inn or rent an apartment. Not knowing where to go, I went to Emily's apartment in the French Concession. If she had indeed returned, I could stay with her.

The streets to the Concession were barricaded; I read the notice plastered on a telegraph pole. It was in Japanese, but I could make out the meaning of kanji. It seemed that the French Vichy government had handed over the Concession to the Japanese, who now had completely dominated the entirety of Shanghai.

A truck rattled past, loaded with foreigners with suitcases. A flyer fell out and dropped to the ground. I picked it up. It said that all stateless people must be relocated to a district in Hongkou. Ernest was stateless, I remembered. Was he in the district now? What a fate for us. He a prisoner, and I homeless.

I avoided the patrolling Japanese soldiers and went into an alley to reach Emily's apartment; it was shut with a lock. No sign of her cook.

In the end I hailed a rickshaw and went to the last place I could seek shelter.

Beneath a high stone arch decorated with European-style carvings was a narrow, dim alley draped with underwear and threadbare rags. Inside the alley, bare-chested men pissed along the wall and old men shot out spit like bullets. The rancid stench of urine and night soil made me gag. Carrying two suitcases like a porter, I ducked and swerved, picking my way through cockroaches and rats and animal feces. Then without a warning, a woman dumped a basin of brown water in front of me, cold liquid splashing on my shin.

I could hear children's screams from behind a low gate at the end of the dank alleyway. I stopped in front of it and called out for Peiyu. The small door opened.

"What are you doing here?" Peiyu was sitting at a charcoal stove in the courtyard, braiding her long hair; near her, two of my nieces, one nicknamed Willow and the other Serenity, were fanning the fire in the stove. The youngest of the six, nicknamed Little Star, was chewing a cricket, a paste of yellow snot and grime on her face.

The courtyard was pitiful, smaller than my bedroom. The walls were covered with mold; the mud ground was slippery and infested with rat droppings. The place had no bathroom, only a night bucket, no electricity wires or water pipes. The only source of water was a communal underground well, heavily contaminated with sewage.

Who knew I would end up here with them. I had wanted to help them, knowing the deplorable living conditions they were in. Had I not told my husband about the trip, Cheng would still be alive, and I could be coming here to help them, not move in with them.

"I hope you'll let me live with you." I told her about Cheng and his mother's decision to force me out.

"That's sad. I didn't know he was gone. Do you have money?"

My face was hot. "I have jewelry."

That night I took out the dresses from my suitcase and spread them on the floor to drive out the chill from the damp muddy ground. The only bed was occupied by Peiyu and the six kids. I listened to their siren-like shrieks as they kicked and complained, barely getting any shut-eye. Around dawn they finally quieted, and I dozed off. When I awoke, no one was in the room. Even the courtyard was empty. I went out to the alleyway.

Behind the unkempt women doing laundry and men pissing in the corner sat a rickshaw. In her small shoes, a knapsack hanging around her neck, Peiyu toddled toward it. She piled quilts and two rattan suitcases on the rickshaw and climbed in. The children clung around her, fighting among themselves.

"Where are you going?" I asked. Peiyu, with bound feet, rarely traveled. The rickshaw was barely large enough to fit her and the quilts, suitcases, and children.

She tucked the knapsack on her lap and slapped at a small hand that tried to hold hers. "To my parents'. You can stay here. Can you leave me alone, kids? I can't live here, taking care of them by myself. Stop fighting! I wrote to my parents a few months ago, and they agreed to take me in. If Sinmay comes back, tell him to find me at my parents' home."

The rickshaw puller, a young man wearing straw sandals, raised the two bamboo poles, and Peiyu and her children leaned back. Wheels squeaking, the rickshaw raced out of the alleyway. It would take them to the railway station in the north, where they would take the train to her parents' house in the Jiangsu province.

I went back to the courtyard and sat by my suitcases. The room was quiet without children's noises, without any footfalls. I was alone.

I had never been truly alone in my life. No matter where I went, I was always surrounded by my brothers, Cheng, Peiyu, my chauffeur, servants, dancers, or the men working in the nightclub. Since my birth, I had been shielded by a glittery screen of awe and wealth. Now I was truly alone. And poor.

For a moment, I was at a loss for what to do. I could remarry—I was only twenty-three—or I could earn a living by becoming a dancer, the profession I created years ago. If I really wanted, I could stop by the home of one of my relatives, ingratiating myself as a guest, and stay there for a few months. Anywhere would be better than this squalid stone-arch shelter. I picked up my suitcases, ready to leave.

A cry startled me. A child's cry. Nearby. I looked around—the room was empty, the bed bare, without quilts and sheets. But the cry continued. I looked underneath the bed.

I couldn't believe my eyes. On the dank floor lay a little bundle flinging its arms. I knelt, took ahold of the arm, and pulled. Little Star, Peiyu's youngest, grabbed a strand of my hair and bellowed.

Maybe Peiyu, busy packing, had unknowingly kicked the toddler under the bed. Deep asleep and bundled thickly with a cotton tunic and a sweater, the toddler had not awakened. And Peiyu, with all the quilts and suitcases and other children demanding her attention, had not noticed Little Star was missing. Such accidents could happen.

Or maybe she had deliberately left the little one behind. While the older kids could help around the house, the toddler was an extra mouth to feed.

I ran into the alleyway and out to the street. The rickshaw was long gone.

⁓⧟⁓

When I came back to the bedroom, the abandoned little thing, garbed in a tunic and sweater that were her entire assets, was still bawling on the floor.

"Stop crying," I said.

The little monster raised the pitch to an ear-splitting howl.

I sat on my suitcases across from her, holding my head. The cries, so loud, hurt my eardrums. I didn't know what to do with her. Little girls were not worth much. All across Shanghai, girls were abandoned, starved, sold, or used; some were as young as five years old. I had seen them, tied with a rope, huddled in the corner near the temple in the Old City as men examined them.

It was sad to be a girl, sad to be born into this world, sad to be left alone. But the little one was not my responsibility. I stood and picked up my suitcases.

76

ERNEST

He leaned against a fallen wall coated with mold. He had never felt this tired. His back ached; his head pounded from dehydration.

All stateless people must establish their residences in the designated area, he was told. So he had gathered his strength and stumbled into a shop near the jail, where he received a registration card printed with a number and a seal. He formally became a resident inside the designated area, where everything required permission.

Permission to sell his jacket, permission to sell his Rolex, permission to buy a bowl of rice. All were granted by a shameless Jew, Goya, who somehow had won the Japanese's trust.

With some luck, Ernest was granted permission to pawn his Rolex for one hundred new *fabi*, issued by the pro-Japanese government, and with the money, he rented a bamboo cot in a corner of a shanty owned by a Chinese man called Old Liang. Mr. Schmidt, Golda, and several of his fellow friends lived nearby on a street called Ward Road. "A courteous tiger is still a tiger," the old man murmured when he saw him, quoting his words as if they meant anything. Golda had huge mood swings, cursing the Japanese, then bursting into tears.

They were truly alone, like all the refugees he had helped for almost a year. Now like them, stateless, he was homeless, helpless.

A black cat shot out from a straw mat in front of him. Under the mat, a hand, all skin and bones, poked out. Feeling dizzy, Ernest staggered back and saw more bodies strewn in the corner, filthy rainwater snaking below their white feet. He barely gave a thought to who these people were—too many these days.

It was late in the afternoon; the April sun gave no warmth. He had been walking, trying to figure out the designated area. From what he could tell, this ghetto for stateless people also had Chinese residents who had lived here before the occupation. Their dwellings were two-story shacks divided by narrow lanes.

The area, a few blocks away from the notoriously unsanitary *Heime*, measured about one square mile. Ernest had walked and walked, first to the east, passing blocks of shacks and abandoned godowns, and reached the muddy bank of the Huangpu River dotted with rusted freighters and half-sunk boats. In the north, he had passed dilapidated cotton mills and dog farms and came to a high wall with a barbed wire fence where armored vehicles, tanks, jeeps, and motorcycles with sidecars were parked. There was even a runway for Zero fighters. It was the Japanese military base.

To the south was the guarded Garden Bridge; to the west was a section unknown to him. It had many two-story cabin-like shacks with cardboard for doors and Chinese shops. A telegraph pole with a wooden board sign read, STATELESS PEOPLE ARE FORBIDDEN TO PASS BEYOND THIS SIGN.

There was no barricade, no sandbags or barbed wire. Only a uniformed Japanese soldier napped in the sidecar of a motorcycle. Ernest could dash away before the soldier fired at him. But what was the point of running away if there was no one to run to?

Sitting on the edge of his bamboo cot, he stared at the leather loafers on his feet, listening to the hacking coughs of other tenants around him. He had arrived at Shanghai penniless with his sister, but he had fought for survival as a refugee, lived as a lover, risen as a popular pianist, and become a businessman, an owner of a shipping company, a wealthy financier. Now, he was once again a refugee, a stateless man, and he had absolutely nothing.

77

AIYI

Her hysterical cries shook me—the loud keening of abandonment, the fierceness of her sadness, and the childish innocence in her voice. I put down my suitcases.

I gave her my sleeve to wipe her nose; she turned her head away. I tried to hold her; she thrashed and screamed more. I told her to calm down, and she screamed louder. It was exhausting, and so hard to believe, too, that such a small imp could release such powerful cries.

Maybe she was hungry. I was hungry too. I found the tin can where Peiyu stored rice. There were only a few grains inside. I threw them all in a pot and set it on the charcoal stove. It occurred to me I needed to start the fire. I had never cooked rice before.

I squatted in front of the stove, threw a match in the furnace, stabbed at some bits of coal, and began to fan the air with my hand. For a long moment the furnace showed no movement. My arms grew sore. But there were still no sparks. I got down on all fours and blew inside the furnace; a blaze shot up and licked my face and hair.

I screamed, and the imp, who was whimpering and hiccupping, began to cry again.

"Stop crying! I told you to stop crying. I'm sick of you." The flame had burned my bangs, but the coal was burning brilliantly in the furnace. I checked the pot. I didn't know how long it would take to cook. My stomach was painful with hunger.

After a while I smelled something burning. I picked up the lid. The rice had turned into a layer of black tar. No one had told me to add water to the pot.

I kicked the stove in frustration. What I would have done for the food I used to have and didn't appreciate: the jelly-like bird nest, the sweet rice ball soup with red dates, the fragrant tea eggs.

It was finally quiet. I looked around. The imp had disappeared. I had forgotten to lock the gate. I searched in the alleyway; she wasn't there. I went to the street. Under the gray sky, a group of jugglers in costumes were playing in front of an apothecary; near them a barber was cutting a man's hair and a cobbler filed a wooden shoe. Then I saw Little Star's sweater in the street among rickshaws and marching Japanese soldiers. She was crying again, and a rickshaw stopped beside her; from inside, a man in a fedora reached out.

"Put her down! Put her down!" I raced across the street and plucked her out of the man's hands. Carrying her in my arms, I rushed back to the alley, into the courtyard, and locked the gate, my heart pounding. Had I been a few minutes later, she would have been gone. I was not a good person, I realized. I was selfish and pampered, and I cared for myself more than others—more than a child.

I put her down and lowered myself to her level. She had Sinmay's nose and chin. Even though her face was smudged with tears and dirt and kerosene, her black eyes twinkled. Then, her lips flattening, she began to cry again. Such a small thing, with so much sadness.

I picked up the pot and scraped its bottom with my nails. When a black, crispy piece came off, I picked it out and gave it to her.

She stuffed it in her mouth and swallowed without chewing, her eyes watering.

"Slowly," I said, and scraped again. Some hard pieces pierced into my nails. I switched to my left hand. "I'm your aunt, Little Star. Do you remember? Your mom will come to get you soon. Until then, I'll take care of you, and you won't run away from me, you promise?"

She stared at me, her eyes calm like precious black jade.

"You promise?"

"Ai."

I bent to wipe off a bit of the burned rice stuck in the corner of her mouth.

We needed food. I took Little Star to the market. I had never shopped for food before—I'd only stepped in the market when I was five with a servant. The market had been a spectacle, with strings of raw meat hanging on ropes, rows of stalls displaying goat heads, buckets of black pig blood, live fish with white bellies, and straw trays with dried squid. But the market near Peiyu's stone-arch-gate room had only two vegetable stalls selling cauliflower and cabbage and only one meat stall. When I tried to get goods with my signature—the Shaos had always signed with a signature and paid at the end of the month—the vendors laughed at me.

Left with no choice, I took a trip to three pawnshops to sell my mink coat and jewelry. I haggled and bartered, using my business-woman's skill, fighting for every penny, only to see thirty new *fabi* in my hands. I managed to use them to buy two cups of rice.

Each day Little Star cried in hunger; each day I heard my stomach growl. I pawned all my jewelry and my dresses to keep her fed. But the prices of food skyrocketed due to the shortages. A carrot cost fifty new *fabi*, for which I had pawned a gold necklace, and a cup of rice was equivalent to a jade vase. The Japanese had rations for salt, rice, coal, and soybeans, and we the locals scrambled for whatever could be found.

I went to look for a job. My nightclub was now owned by a Chinese man who licked the Japanese boots, and Ciro's by a group of gangsters. I went to Ciro's. Inside the smoky lobby, I joined the dancers in tightly fitted red dresses. When I went to see the man in charge, a man with a gold tooth, he glanced at Little Star in my arms. "If you want to work, leave the tyke home. She'll turn off customers."

I couldn't. She would toddle out to the street.

I went to one of my relatives, the snobby Shengs in the French Concession, to ingratiate myself so at least Little Star would have free lodging and food. They were kind and gave us a spot on the floor and meals. But after a month, their generosity was waning, so I hinted at my interest in marriage and asked for their help. They said a proper marriage for a woman of my birth would need to hire a matchmaker, which would cost a great deal. And besides, they glanced at Little Star. She was a burden, and I would need to let her go before any marriage talk.

I held her tight as we went back to the stone-arch-gate home.

The next day, after telling Little Star over and over to be a good girl, I locked her inside and began to steal.

I chose the beautiful villas with wrought iron balconies and shuttered windows behind the towering plane trees, the former residences of the captured or escaped Americans and Europeans. These houses had no central hall, reception room, or covered wells but had a dining room, study, swimming pool, and servant bedrooms. I climbed over the fence near the swimming pool and hit the windows with a rock to get in. From the front entry, I went straight to the food storage, called a pantry, and then to the wine cellar to take whatever I could find.

Which was not that much. For many houses had already been raided and emptied, probably by the families' Chinese servants.

I was doing well with packets of spaghetti, dried soup mix, tomato sauce called ketchup, cookies, and sometimes chocolate, but never rice. Once I found a box of Twinkies among trampled glass and debris. Knowing these were rare desserts that would fetch good money, I carefully ripped those Twinkies, licked out all the crumbs and the cream inside—they tasted like a slice of heaven, even better than the pastries I had enjoyed at the afternoon teas in Sassoon House—and then rewrapped them, sealed them over fire, and traded them on the street. I was able to barter for necessities such as soaps, matches, coal bits, rice, kerosene, and a bowl. It was the most profitable deal I'd ever had.

Little Star was pleased with my loot, and sometimes I took her with me. But life for a woman on the street was dangerous. In my fitted dress that began to show some wear and tear, I was wary of the glances of men. I thought of dressing up as a man, wearing a suit and pants, but I was almost caught stealing the suits at a stall. So when I entered a grand two-story European-style house, I raided the servants' bedroom and found a long black cotton dress with white ruffled cuffs and a high collar, a white apron, a white mobcap, and a leather key holder. I took off the scruffy dress I had worn for months and changed into the maid's dress. I also took the apron, which could be altered into a shirt for Little Star and the leather key holder, which could be used as a toy. Under the bed, I found a pair of worn cloth shoes with rubber soles and put them on too.

From then on, I raided villas in the maid's dress and robbed the houses in daylight. The gangsters left me alone, believing I was a foreigner; so did the soldiers who thought I was a foreigner's servant. I went in and out from the front doors without being harassed.

I grew bolder. When the houses were locked up and emptied out, I crossed the ferry and went as far as the northern district near Hongkou. I saw the sign for the stateless people, but I didn't intend to stay for long. This was not an affluent area, and it was likely I would come home empty-handed.

❧

"Aiyi?"

The voice, so familiar, startled me, and I withdrew my hand that was about to grab a strip of dried yam on a bamboo tray and turned around. I had not imagined it. Across from me, near the sign **THE DESIGNATED AREA FOR STATELESS PERSONS**, stood Ernest.

He looked haggard in the late summer heat, his face wan, his eyes sunken. *What have you done to yourself?* I wanted to ask, but I refused to say it.

"You . . . What happened, Aiyi?"

Irony. We still shared similar thoughts. I could see myself through his eyes. I was no longer fresh, vivid like a painting. I had no mirror, but I had seen my reflection in the water. My skin, which used to shine like a pearl, was lackluster and dull; my face was dotted with smudges I was too tired to wipe off. My eyes, which had reflected the glimmer of a thousand lights, were shifty with hunger; beneath them rippled what I had dreaded. Wrinkles.

"War happened. What else?" I looked straight ahead of me, where a Japanese soldier on a motorcycle was rubbing his hands, humming a tune unfamiliar to me. He hadn't noticed us yet.

Ernest staggered across the sign, his hand reaching out. There were tears, regret, joy, and so much more in his eyes. "I'm so happy. I can't believe it. I thought I'd never see you again."

He was not lying; he still loved me. *But why bother to say that?*

"I looked for you, Aiyi."

He was going to ask me about our daughter, and he was going to lash out at me, at my selfishness. But he had no right. He had let me go, and he had never come to my home. "You said it was over."

346

The soldier swung a rifle on his shoulder to point toward us and shouted at Ernest to stay back. He didn't seem to hear. "I'm sorry."

What did it even mean? Sorry that he had loved me, sorry that he had forsaken me? I had lost my business, fought my family, ruined my life for him. And he kicked me away, pregnant with his child. Now my child was gone, my home was lost, and my life had fallen apart. I wished I never had fallen for him, never had hired him, never had met him.

"Goodbye, Ernest."

78

ERNEST

He watched her leave as the soldier thrust him back to the designated area. He wanted to call out and ask her: What happened? Why was she not with Cheng? And would she forgive him? But he couldn't speak. He had left her when he was wealthy, and now he was destitute and imprisoned; it would be pointless to ask for her hand. Still, he was grateful to see her face, grateful that he had wandered off to the boundary of the district, with no hope and no purpose, when he stared at the maid's dress. There she was. It was almost like a disjointed dream, a vision from a distant sky, a colored picture above a dusty street.

She had changed, but who wouldn't? She hated him, but what else would he expect? He still loved her. He would always love her.

Winter came early.

Holding a chopstick with his freezing fingers, Ernest pressed his thumb down against the taro in his hand and slid the chopstick forward; the black peel slid off easily. Now and then, he stopped to shake off the numbness of his fingers, freezing in the winter chill. When he finished scraping, he placed the taro inside a bamboo basket near his foot. Taro, which looked like a potato but with black skin and fuzzy hair, had flesh pale like a stone. He had never seen a taro until now. It had taken him many tries to become skillful at scraping it with a chopstick. Who would have known a stick like this could be so versatile?

He was paid two sweet potatoes for his scraping job; sweet potatoes were peasant food, but taros, for the Japanese, were more expensive. That was how he survived in the area, the ghetto. It was not so bad; most people had no taros to peel. This penury, this confinement, as he came to reconcile himself to it, wasn't bad either. It was his punishment, his chance to see his failure, an opportunity to atone.

The sound of engines revving resonated in the distance. He looked up. At the end of the street lined with shanties, near the military base, a fleet of Japanese soldiers wearing green winter jackets was riding in armored vehicles. They were leaving the base or maybe engaging in another training in the outskirts. He didn't know what was happening with the war, who'd won or who'd lost. The Japanese were still buying taros; that was all he needed to know.

Old Liang, his landlord and his employer, bent to collect the peeled taros in the basket. He would cut them up later and sell them in the market; the peels would be swept up by Old Liang's wife, cleaned, sorted, and cooked for dinner. Nothing was wasted. "Look, look. Your *qizi* is here." *Your wife is here.*

Ernest looked up. Across the street, Golda, in a red trench coat that was turning black, walked quickly toward him. He was not surprised Old Liang would mistake Golda for his wife. Since his relocation to the ghetto, Golda had sat regularly on his bamboo cot, covered herself with the straw mattress, talked, burst into tears, and talked more. When tired, she wrapped her arms around him, hanging onto him.

He didn't have the heart to untangle her. But when she wanted more, he gently pushed her away. Marriage hardly seemed to make sense. They were prisoners, penniless, without a future.

No. Not *qizi*. Ernest shook his head. He couldn't get the pronunciation right, especially the letter *q*. Aiyi could have corrected him, but Old Liang couldn't speak English; neither did he understand the term for a female friend. But he was kind, and so was his aging wife, who had given birth to thirteen children and lost ten. In fact, most of the Chinese, the original residents in the ghetto who remained in the area, were kind.

"Ernest." Golda was panting. "You have to come. Mr. Schmidt is vomiting."

The old man had suffered an intense toothache and couldn't eat for days. He had fallen sick, either dysentery or typhoid.

"Let's go." Ernest went down the Ward Road, where he heard a whisper of prayers from the shelter for the yeshiva students. He didn't give it a second glance. Once he had stepped inside a synagogue to seek solace; now he had no interest in seeing the students or hearing prayers.

When he reached the two-story wooden building where Mr. Schmidt lived, Ernest ducked his head under the low entryway and went to the old man's cot. The room, filled with about fifty refugees, was cold and dim without a kerosene lamp, noisy with groans and murmurs. In the corner, behind a curtain, a woman was shrieking in labor, some voices asking her to push. Near the curtain, a boy in a tattered shirt recited in a halting voice some verses in Hebrew. Ernest had an impulse to pat the boy's shoulder and tell him to save his energy.

"Mr. Schmidt, do you feel like eating some sweet potatoes today?" Ernest took a good look at the old man. He stank with vomit, and by the light through the doorway, his skin looked yellow like rinsed potatoes.

"Ernest? Oh, Ernest. It's good to see you. I feel like crap." His voice was a wisp.

"What happened to your face?" It had two deep cuts.

"I think a rat bit me. It got a bad deal biting my old bones."

Ernest put his hand on the old man's forehead. It was burning hot. "You need to go to the hospital." He would need Goya's permission. There was a hospital outside the area.

"Five went there yesterday and died there. Why bother? I'd rather stay here."

Golda sobbed, leaning against him. Ernest placed his arm around her.

"Well now, at least you two are getting married. Isn't that marvelous?" Mr. Schmidt said, coughing.

Ernest glanced at Golda and stood. "You'll feel better, Mr. Schmidt. I'll check on you again. I'll take you to the hospital, if you change your mind. Let me know." Then he took Golda's hand and walked toward the door. "We need to take him to the General Hospital. I'll go see Goya."

She stopped him. "I want you to marry me, Ernest. I told him we're getting married."

Ernest sighed.

"I'm afraid of getting sick and dying, Ernest, and I don't want to die a lonely woman. I want to be happy; I want to live some before I die."

"You won't die."

She burst into tears. "Look around this place of filth. When was the last time you had a good meal with soy milk and bread? We have no food, no clean water, no privacy. Everyone is sick with typhoid or dysentery or scarlet fever. We've been here for months. When will this end?"

What could he do? Nothing.

"We've been through so much, Ernest. I've been by your side since you had the bakery. Don't you . . . at least . . . enjoy my company?"

"I can't support you."

"No one is talking about getting rich."

"But—" He couldn't say it. At the doorway, some people gathered a pile of rice straws and dried branches to make a fire. A plume of smoke rose, like a slim figure wearing a fitted dress.

"When I escaped from Berlin, I thought life would be better here. But no, I became a baker to survive. Then I met you. I knew I would be happy again. This . . ." She gestured around, sniffing the putrid air filled with coughs and groans. "This is not the life I dreamed of."

This was not the life he'd dreamed of either. But happiness? It didn't exist. He gave Golda a pat on her shoulder and made his way out. A sharp cry pierced his ears. A new life had arrived; a wave of happy voices rose. People congratulated one another and clapped their hands, and the boy was reciting, "Love is stronger than death."

Ernest's eyes moistened. He had said that line a long time ago. What a surprise to hear this now, in a life of loss, sickness, and sorrows, in a time he doubted the existence of hope and laughter. But it was true—he would always love Leah, his parents, and Miriam, no matter where he was, for as long as he lived.

Golda reached him and threaded her arm through the crook of his, her lips purple in the cold, her eyes pleading. She was losing weight, her plumpness peeling off her like the taro skin. And was that a cough bursting from her throat? A rasp in her chest?

He took her hands—cold and bony—and rubbed them to give her warmth. He had been mired in the dark murk of life for so long, sick of this sickening world for so long. It was tiresome, hollowing, and yet if there was such a thing called love, if there was a way to give happiness, then let him be the one to light the wick of warmth.

He married Golda the next day. For the first time, he entered the shelter for the yeshiva students on Ward Road and listened to the seven blessings he had never heard before. He was calm, transfixed by an inner tree of peace, by the cloud of voices, by the runelike yellow flickers of candles. Because breaking a perfectly good bowl would be a waste, he was given a shard. He stamped on it and heard a chorus of "Mazel tov," and the ceremony was over.

Old Liang and his wife gave them a gift of eight sweet potatoes, enough to last a honeymoon of four days. The Chinese neighbors, in their tattered tunics, came to congratulate them too. Smiles on their sunbaked faces, they sang a sweet song with a lilt. It sounded like the song he'd once played, the song he'd once loved.

Golda, clad in a borrowed white chiffon blouse and a knee-length plaid skirt, sang and danced, her green eyes sparkling like a spring meadow. She was a good Jewish girl, whom his mother would have liked. And he would look after her, share with her the scraped taro skins and sweet potatoes; he would love her, like a new husband in an old world, like a good husband in a bad war, even though it was doubtful that he could love the same way he had loved before.

79

FALL 1980

THE PEACE HOTEL

Ms. Sorebi rests her elbow on the table, the fringe of her leather jacket draping like wilted straws. It has a strange appeal, I have to admit—the jacket suits her.

"When I interviewed the Jews, I was horrified to hear of the conditions in the designated area. The ghetto was horrendous, infested with scarlet fever, typhoid, and all kinds of diseases. Many got sick and died. They told me about the gravesite outside the ghetto and . . . it broke my heart. Did you know they had to reuse coffins?" Her voice cracks.

All the lives we've lost, all the love we've forgotten, and all the decisions we must live by. "I wish I could say war was cruel and we all had to endure. But the truth is no matter what hardship we went through, we eventually forget it after it's over."

Her head turns away, but her eyes grow brighter.

"Do you see why I want to make a documentary now? I want to remember; I don't want to forget."

A beautiful tune is wafting in the air, faint, drifting like a bed of clouds; it has that voice, innocent like a fairy tale, melancholy like the night breeze. It reminds me of the song I loved years ago. "When we'd just met, Ernest played the jazz song called 'The Last Rose of Shanghai.' I loved it, and I still remember the lyrics. It says in English, 'There is a kind of love that strikes like a thunderbolt; it blinds you, yet opens your eyes to see the world anew.'"

I remember it was at that moment that I fell in love with him. He knew my music, and he played the tune like it was his. Had I explained to him the meaning of that song? That the lyrics have Buddhist influence? That a thunderbolt is also a weapon used by the thunder deity in Buddhism? That I firmly believed in karma?

Ms. Sorebi is quiet, gazing at a spot to my right, listening to the music, as if she has become part of my story, as if she can envision all the winding lanes in my memory. Is this a show of hers or her genuine interest in my story? I can't tell, but I like this, this silence, this wordless reflection, this reach of a long lasso to the past.

"Ms. Shao?"

I'm not ready to answer, for I can see him right in front of me. His bright smile, his blue eyes. As if he had never left me.

"I'm sorry, but I'm dying to know. Was that the last time you saw Mr. Reismann?"

80

JUNE 1944

AIYI

I became a widow, a mother, a burglar, a thief, and an occasional garbage-bin diver. I did all tricks without shame, for life in the dank stone-arch-gate room, alone with a child, was hard. There were days when my stomach knotted in pain from hunger and Little Star screamed for food, days when I scrubbed our lice-infested hair with the kerosene from the lamp, days when I fled from the hooligans who tried to rape me, days when I reminisced about jazz and the luxury of my old life.

Let the war end, I prayed. Yet there were few signs of peace. On the street skittered the news of Japanese victories against the Nationalists and the Communists, all dispersed by the puppet government. No one knew anything about the war between the Americans and the Japanese. And the foreigners had all vanished from Shanghai. For half a year, I'd encountered not a single European or American on the streets.

Sometimes I thought of my encounter with Ernest and regretted my coldness. Yes, he had let me go, but yes, I was responsible for his loss. I should have told him that I had given away our daughter and apologized to him.

One night, a clunk from the courtyard awoke me. It was after the midnight hour; the buildings were quiet, and the alleyway was submerged in sleepiness.

I gently unhooked Little Star from my arms and slipped off the bed. My feet brushed against a low plastic stool. I picked it up. I had never faced a burglar before. Whoever was out there was not a Japanese, who would have made a ruckus.

The faint breathing from outside grew heavier as it came toward the bedroom. I swung the door open and flung the stool around. I couldn't see what was in front of me, but I hit something.

There was a groan.

"What are you doing?"

"Ying?"

"Who else did you think it was?"

"I thought it was . . . Why did you come at this hour?" I fumbled for the matchbox, found it, and then looked for the kerosene lamp at the foot of the bed. But I couldn't find it. Little Star must have been playing with it. Then near me came another groan, and the bulk of Ying collapsed to the ground. "Did I really hit you that hard? What's wrong with you?"

He didn't answer, so I lit a match. The light shone on Ying's ghastly pale face. His left shoulder was soaked.

"Is that blood? Were you shot?"

He closed his eyes. "Lower your voice, Aiyi. You're going to get us all killed."

"You shouldn't come here." I had an idea about what he had gotten himself into, and I hated him for it. Finally, I found the lamp. I lit it, went to check the front gate to the alleyway, and pushed the latch to make sure it was locked firmly. Then I returned to Ying.

"Are you going to help me? Give me the opium. Here. In the bag." He kicked a green canvas satchel near his feet, which I hadn't noticed earlier.

"No."

"Please."

Begrudgingly, I unbuttoned the satchel. Inside was a boxy leather bag, a pair of binoculars, a small bag of peanuts, and a pistol. Already I could smell the unique flower scent. I held a small amount of mud-like putty, the size of a red date.

He grabbed the putty and bit into it. With the putty, he wouldn't feel a thing. "Now take the bullet out."

I folded my arms across my chest. "Why should I help you? So you can go out and shoot our people again? I know you work for them."

"I don't work for them." The putty was working; his voice was swelling, losing its edge.

"I saw you walk into their building. I know what you're doing. I know who you are."

"Do you?" In the faint kerosene lamp light, he was smiling, and it was not the energetic, comical smile that he used to give. "I'm not going to tell you anything more. But I'm not a traitor. I only want to save my country. I will never betray my country."

Should I believe him?

"Will you get the bullet out?" He gazed at the light, and I could see he, like Emily, my father, and many addicts before him, was swimming in the transitory realm of fog and oblivion.

I held the kerosene lamp, leaned closer, and dipped my right thumb and forefinger into his shoulder. Soft flesh closed on me; blood spurted. I felt the metal among the viscous pool alongside hard bones and dug out the bullet.

◆

Near dawn, when the alleyway stirred with squeaky rickshaws, Ying awoke. There were still traces of drug on his face, but his eyes were alert. He groaned, examining the knot I'd made on his shoulder, and shook his head. "You are doing a poor job as a nurse, and as a maid. Where did you get that costume?"

"It's my protection. I couldn't find anything else to wear. Are you going to tell me how you got shot?" Little Star stirred near me.

He was still groggy as he recounted events in a low voice. He had received important intelligence that a Japanese truck was loaded with sophisticated radio equipment transported from Japan. Ying and his resistance force had ambushed the truck and successfully detonated it, destroying all the equipment, but many of his people died. He'd blown his cover and was shot. But it was worth it, he said, for during the ambush, he had learned key information regarding the war.

"What information? Can you tell me?"

"Sorry. It's top secret. But you should be proud. I almost killed that son of a bitch."

I didn't know he had been after Yamazaki.

"He's in charge of the military base in Hongkou. I want his head. I want his ammunition and his radio transceivers. I want all the Japanese dead."

Fifteen months had passed since Cheng's death. "I miss Cheng. I was so stupid; I didn't know how much he meant to me."

Ying twisted his head away, his throat contracting. All these months, Ying had carried his grief over Cheng's death, the sharpened ax. "Where's Peiyu? Where are the other children?"

I told him of Peiyu's leaving for her parents in Jiangsu and how I'd discovered Little Star under the bed. "I've written to her, but no replies. The post office is still closed."

"Well, I'm glad you're looking after the little one. Where's my bag?"

I leaned over and gave him the satchel. He could barely use his hands, so I lifted it, put it on his lap, and untied the leather strap. It was a Japanese military device, a radio transceiver, marked with kanji that said IMPORTANT MILITARY INTELLIGENCE DEVICE. Ying held the device and turned a switch. "Glack, glack, glack" was all I could hear.

It's top secret, he had said.

꧁

Now two people relied on me. I decided to raid Sassoon House since the private villas and houses had been thoroughly emptied. I had not gone to the hotel after the attack on the Settlement, but I'd heard since then the hotel had started billeting Japanese soldiers.

Walking down the broad Bubbling Well Road, I reminded myself to speak English when encountering any Japanese patrolling soldiers so I could pass as one of the European maids from a neutral country with my outfit. But I only encountered one soldier on the entire street, who showed no interest in me. Many checkpoints were unguarded; the racecourse was empty as well. All of a sudden, the Japanese Imperial Army seemed to have left Shanghai.

I wondered if they had lost the war. But there were no victorious Nationalists.

When I came to the hotel's main entrance with the canopy, I stopped short. The sleek modern building was cloaked in black soot; vines of filth climbed the smooth white bricks. The canopy that had been adorned by golden lambency from the Lalique chandelier had collapsed to the ground. All three main entrances were shut; darkness loomed inside. The cobbled street was littered with trash, broken bottles, wreckage from automobiles, and dunes of metal and shrapnel.

The beautiful, elegant, luxurious Sassoon House, a pearl on the waterfront where I had slept in a suite, listened to my favorite jazz, talked to Sassoon, and met Ernest, was no more.

I went to the contractor door near the entrance for carriages, hoping to be lucky. A man in a double-breasted black coat with a holster and a pistol stood at the small door. The hotel guard, someone the Japanese hired to watch the hotel. A local, I could tell.

"Where are the Japanese soldiers?" I asked him in Shanghai dialect to let him know I was a local so he would be friendly.

He glanced at my maid's outfit and replied in the same dialect, telling me the entire Japanese regiment that had been stationed in the hotel for almost two years had been sent to central China as reinforcements to fight the Nationalists and the Communists.

I smiled and walked away.

But I watched the guard for a few days, figuring out his routine, trying to find a chance to sneak inside the hotel. One day when he left his post to drive away some beggars, I slipped inside the building.

It was dim inside. In the once-glorious hallway formerly paved with golden light, the sleek marble floor was a dark field; the rich-colored wallpapers were peeled off, the expensive Lalique chandelier stolen, and the sconces, vases, and paintings were also missing. There was nothing valuable left for me to take. I walked into a room nearby and searched in the cabinets and the bathroom. In a drawer I dug out two smoke-drenched sheets, a hotel robe, and a mosquito tent; in the moldy bathroom I was rewarded with a half-used lavender soap bar. I packed them all in the pillowcase I brought. I would sell all but keep the soap for myself.

On the way out, I went to the Jazz Bar and flicked the light switch on—it still had electricity. The bar was empty as well: the piano, stools, mirrors, tables, chairs, bottles of liquor, and picture frames were all gone, and torn newspapers and magazines in Japanese were scattered on the floor. A sour smell of vomit and mildew hung in the air.

I found two packets of cigarettes and a gramophone buried in a pile of trash. With the cigarettes in my pillowcase, I lifted the gramophone and ran my fingers over its cold surface, its smooth edge. I could hear the tempting beats of jazz flowing from inside, the divine tune of "The Last Rose of Shanghai," and I remembered, too, the evening when Ernest came to our table while I sat with Sassoon and drank his Cobra's Kiss.

What's your favorite song? Ernest had asked. It was that moment that my life had changed, only I hadn't known it. What if he'd never come to my table? What if he'd never played the piano?

We were what the tangle of the past made us, which trapped us, forcing us to be ensnared in a future we could never be set free from.

I'm sorry, he had said.

Hot tears ran down my cheeks. He had lost his sister, and I lost my daughter. It was time to forgive him, but what good would it do me? He could never give me back my daughter.

8 1

ERNEST

He awoke on his bed, her image vivid in his mind. She smiled, her eyes two crescent moons. *Take my hand,* she said, her slender fingers stretching, fine filigrees of spinning gold. *Are you happy? Will you forgive me?* he wanted to ask, drinking in her smile, her blooming heat; instead, all he said was *I've missed you, oh, how I've missed you.* She lowered her head to kiss him, but the moment he felt her lips, her face diminished and dissolved in the dim fog.

He sat up on the edge of the bed, sweating, his chest bare. The summer air in the room was stifling, torrid; the heat clung to him like cobwebs. He grabbed a towel hanging on the headboard and slung it across his neck. The bamboo mattress had stuck to his back, leaving a groove beneath his shoulder blades, and sweat trickled from his neck to his lower abdomen. But the dream, so real, so vivid, still enveloped him, making him hard.

A streak of light pierced through the crack of the wooden boards used as a wall. He stared, tracing it, pale like the skin on her calf. Once upon a time she'd lived with him from sunrise to sunset; but now she only came to meet him before sunrise. He lowered his head and put on his loafers. They were worn and damp from humidity, lumpy from overuse. His toes wiggled against the leather; it felt as if he had stepped inside a lump of wet clay.

Coughing, he tried to stand up, but a pain stabbed his head. He sat down again. He had been running a fever for two days. Not a surprise since everyone was sick with something. He would shake it off. He cupped his mouth and coughed quietly so he wouldn't wake Golda sleeping behind him.

After the wedding, Golda had pawned a gold ring, the last of her jewelry. Gold was worth a great deal these days because of inflation, and she was able to purchase a few more luxuries: a small table, a tin pot to cook meals, and a bamboo mattress to keep cool in the summer. And they had rented this small attic room, their new home.

Married life had been good for him, and he had settled in, like a beetle in a dark corner. Golda gave him a mezuzah from the yeshiva students; he nailed it on the doorpost below the attic roof. She swept the floor and he wiped the table; she stewed the cabbage and he took out the trash. He made love to her on the small table as she asked, on the bed while she was on hands and knees; he listened as she talked about her favorite play, *Tevye the Dairyman and His Daughters*, and her passion for acting.

He was thankful for the marriage, for Golda, who had not only given him the joy of living but also a purpose. He was resolved to be a good husband. When he came across a stalled jeep loaded with beer and jars of radishes, he had stolen them, shared radishes with Old Liang, and then drank the beer with Golda on their bed. *Lehayim,* she said as she raised the bottle of beer before kissing him with her beer-flavored lips.

"You're up." Golda sat up from the bed and yawned, her flaming hair cascading to cover her pale, freckled face. She murmured, asking if he was going to the cobbler's, where he had found a job as a helper. He received twenty *fabi* as his weekly wage, with which he bought a loaf of bread in a shop owned by Goya. Bread was Golda's favorite, and they made it last for the entire week.

A torrent of coughs overtook her. He rubbed her back. She was sick, too, her face flushed. The rashes on her back had spread to her neck, but the skin around her lips was pale. He bent over and kissed Golda's forehead. His apology for his dream.

He would never forget Aiyi and her face, which illuminated the house of his yearning like a warm candle in a cold night. But he was now a married man. A yearning for the past was a betrayal of the present. It was true that he would never forget Aiyi, their heart-throbbing moments, and their impulsive plans, but life had rent them apart, and he and Aiyi were now two distant stars, emitting their own light and running on their own courses.

82

AIYI

"Look, Aunt. What are they doing?" Little Star asked as we walked down a street in the Old City. It had been a week since I visited the hotel, and I had sold the gramophone near Ciro's. To sell the cigarette packets, I had come to the Old City God Temple, where many gamblers, before starting their games in the gambling houses nearby, were usually generous.

I followed her gaze. Along the dilapidated city wall, a group of children dressed in black tunics were all tied together by a rope around their waists. They looked to be no more than ten, with long hair, bare feet, and stagnant eyes; obediently they stood in front of a man with a long braid who inspected them, lifting their chins, unbuttoning their tunics and peering inside. Finally, the man handed a coin to the old man holding the rope, who untied a girl in the cluster and pushed her to him.

The worthless girls near the Old City God Temple, abandoned by their families, sold and used at a young age. I had seen them before and had barely given them a thought. Now a shiver ran through me. My Little Star. Had she not been saved by me, she would be one of those girls along the wall. But a stab of pain pierced me as I thought of my daughter. She should be eighteen months old, barely walking, barely talking, a mouth to feed. Also nothing of value. Who would keep her, a girl of mixed blood?

I burst into tears. I could hear her soft cries, and I could see her wrapped in a bundle, staring at me with Ernest's eyes. "Let's go, Little Star. Let's go home."

"Why are you crying, Aunt?"

"I'm scared."

"Why?"

The child I didn't have a chance to hold. Had I kept her, I would have grown to love her, protect her, feed her just like Little Star. Where was she?

Before dawn, the hour safest for a single woman to walk on the streets, I walked to the train station in the northwest to see the price of the train tickets to the Jiangsu province, where Peiyu was with her family. No matter how much it cost, I wouldn't be able to afford it, but once I knew the price, I could start to save. But the train had stopped operating, I saw. The Japanese had recently bombed the train tracks.

I was heartbroken. I had given away my daughter, thought little of her, and now I wanted her back and I couldn't find her.

When I returned home, I passed a cinema in the Settlement. The front doors were closed and defaced, and the posters on the walls were torn to dusty tatters. But I could still make out the image: Marlene Dietrich with golden curls in *Shanghai Express* and one of the stars of *Gone with the Wind.* Gable, whose arms used to embrace Leigh, looked forlornly at a space of empty plaster on the wall.

I'd still care for you if you married a hundred times, Ernest had said.

Tears welled in my eyes. We hadn't had a chance to watch the movie after all. *You shouldn't have said that, Ernest. It was bad luck; I told you not to say that.*

I still wanted to watch that movie, and he was the only one who could understand how much it meant to me. Would he wish to see his daughter too? When he saw me last time, he'd showed no hatred, no accusation, only regret and love.

Perhaps I should find him; perhaps he would help me find our daughter.

Before me, the sun was rising, a salted egg with gray shells. The pale rays swept the smoke-painted roofs and stretched a long feathery arm through the dusty air; the wind was rising, fresh without last night's scent, and it dipped low and brushed my cheeks like a loving hand. I heard a newborn's cries, a beautiful piece of music, faint, lingering, and in my mind, I saw Ernest's face, polished, glinting through the fog like the eye of the sunrise.

83

ERNEST

Mr. Schmidt died.

A special permission, given by the Japanese authority, was granted to the grieving stateless people so they could leave the designated area and travel to the graveyard. Ernest, Golda, Sigmund, and others climbed into a bus.

Ernest sat by the window, shivering; his fever had gotten worse, and his head was pounding in agony. It was August, the weather mild, but he felt chilled, despondent, and possessed by an uncanny prescience that they would all end up dead. Mr. Schmidt's favorite phrase came to him, unbidden. *We are the lotus flowers in a pond, a shallow bloom.*

The bus crossed the Garden Bridge, dropped into a ditch with black water, groaned, dragged itself out, and went on and on. Finally, it stopped at a patch of burial ground near an endless field of black, barren rice paddy. It was hard to tell whether this was a public cemetery or an unknown town at the outskirts, and Ernest was certain once they left, locating the graveyard would be impossible. So this was the closest to a decent burial for people like him, and there would be no shiva after the burial either.

Ernest got off the bus with the others. It rained mildly, not pouring as it had been a few days before. As one of the pallbearers, he carried the casket with Sigmund and two others. The casket tilted and lowered as they struggled to pull out their feet stuck in the mud. Finally, they made it to the resting place at the end of the lot near a dead oak tree.

Someone in a long white robe recited a string of words with a heavy nasal sound. Ernest listened, determined to remember the verses, to remember Mr. Schmidt—he had asked to borrow his toothbrush in the Embankment Building, the first friend he had made, and he had been a companion, a father figure when they started the business, a partner when the business thrived.

Golda came beside him and leaned on him. She had just recovered from the terrible chills and coughs and started to feel better. The heels of her shoes were caked with mud. She didn't have other shoes; no one had extra shoes.

"He was the first friend I made, the first man I hired in the bakery. He was good at talking to people . . . Miriam . . ." And her. The terrible afternoon. The cold rain felt good on his face.

"You're thinking about the Chinese girl." Golda's face was wet with rain, her green eyes clear like gems.

He lowered his head. "I'm sorry."

Golda picked up a lump of mud and formed a ball in her hands. "Well, I might as well tell you this. She came to see you and gave me her address. She was pregnant. Don't look at me like that."

She came for him? She was pregnant? "When was that? Why didn't you tell me?"

"What's the point? The Japanese would have killed us all if you continued to see her."

"But she was pregnant! You didn't tell me. I was looking for her. If you told me sooner, gave me her address, I could have—"

"You're being ridiculous, Ernest."

The rain fell into his eyes like nails. They had a child, and yet he had let her go. No wonder she was so cold. What had he done? He could have had it all. It would have been the three of them: Aiyi, the baby, and him. They could have lived in the apartment with a balcony, could have laughed and drunk whiskey; he could have lived in a dream.

If only Golda had told him.

His head hurt too much, and the wet coat wrapped around him like a pall of ice. He wanted to weep, to be left alone, right there near the grave.

The prayer ended. Time to lower Mr. Schmidt to the ground. Ernest lifted the casket. It tilted forward, and Mr. Schmidt in his shabby white shirt rolled out into the grave with a splash. The casket was to be saved and reused.

People lowered their heads and walked around, laying balls of mud on Mr. Schmidt as the rain pattered down. Rage rose in Ernest's chest, consuming him. He knelt on the ground, steeled his fingers, and thrust deep into the muddy earth. He began to dig, dig, and dig. His nails broke, his knees chafed; the coldness of the mud made him shiver, and the rotten odor made him gag, but still he dug. He wanted to make the grave decent, deeper, for a man was not a plant, not mud, not a bunch of bones and flesh. A man was an honorable being. A man should cry, but also laugh; should suffer, but also forgive; should dream, but also remember. Above all, a man should be given a chance to make things right again. If only he could make things right again.

On the bus back, Ernest rested his head in his hands, the mud working into his matted hair. He wept, but he didn't know what saddened him more: Mr. Schmidt's death, or the loss of Aiyi, or the lost opportunity to care for his child.

When he looked up again, the bus had stopped. Everyone had left, including Golda. He wobbled out. It was still raining. Above his head, a Zero fighter's engines boomed.

Rain soaking his thin jacket, he shuffled back to his attic room, his head pounding in agony. When he reached the attic, he held the doorframe to stop the pain in his head. Golda was scouring their tin pot. It slipped from her hand and fell on the floor. She let out a frustrated cry.

All the bluster and blame. What was the point? She was his wife, and he was obligated to treat her properly. He picked up the pot and handed it to her.

She burst into tears, always so theatrical.

"It's all right," he said.

She hit him with her fists. A thousand streaks of defiance, of remorse, of anger, of devastation seemed to burst in her eyes, but she didn't utter a word. She just hit and hit. A punch on the chest, a swipe on the nose, and a cut of her long nails scything his neck. He took them all, resisting the pain in his head. When she was done, he put the tin pot on the stove.

That evening, he had many hot, webbed dreams, and he sweated, drowning in waves of perspiration. The pain in his head, his chest, and his limbs became unbearable, and he moaned, delirious. Golda's voice drifted, and then Old Liang's.

"It's sweet wormwood; it'll get rid of the fever." Something bitter poured down his throat. But this was it, he sensed it. His time had come.

When he woke up, the attic was quiet. Golda was lying next to him, her skin pale save for the rashes on her neck and face. Her eyes closed, she looked peaceful.

She was gone.

He would never figure out what took her life. Maybe it was scarlet fever, maybe typhoid, maybe something else. For the second time in two days, he took the funeral bus to the burial ground, Golda inside

Mr. Schmidt's casket. After she was lifted out, he covered her with the straw mattress that had belonged to both of them.

He squatted beside her, bowed his head low, and wept. He had done his best to make her happy, to be the husband she'd wanted; it hadn't been enough, but that was all he could do.

Leah. His parents. Miriam. Mr. Schmidt. Golda. A litany of death. A tune of life lived and lost.

She had made him a better man. Her beauty had been his banner in riches and his food in poverty, her dramatic flair had outshone his bleak self, and her neediness was a bowl that demanded hard work and constant attention to fill. But she had been true to herself, a mirror of veracity he trusted.

I want to be happy, she had said, a declaration she'd believed in, a chance she had given him, a hope he should live by.

He made a cup with his hands, gathered the water-drenched maple leaves, the sunbaked black mulch, the rusty shrapnel, and the broken twigs, and showered them onto her. The current of debris fell through his fingers like the passage of a spirit. When his hands were empty, he held them in the air, remembering the grit of the wood, the fine texture of the earth, and the wetness of his fingers.

All would wither, all would vaporize, and all would be buried in mud and in silence, but he remembered that at least during an endless whistle of the cold wind of life, a happy interlude, fleeting as it was, had happened, and he had been part of it.

84

AIYI

"See these?" Ying, holding a pair of binoculars with his right hand, looked up at the sky where six fighters circled. "They're not Zero fighters. They're bigger. They're American B-29 Superfortresses. I have no doubt about that. Shit. Shit! Yes! Yes! They're B-29s!"

He did a jig, tossing his head and shoulders as though a thousand fleas had crawled on him. His victory dance, which he did whenever he won loads of money at mah-jongg. Good thing his wound in his shoulder had healed. I was not interested in fighters, but I needed to ask him about finding Ernest. Since I saw the girls near the Old City God Temple, I had been dreaming about my daughter. Last time I saw Ernest, he was in the ghetto, the restricted area which outsiders couldn't enter. Ying was resourceful. He could enter without causing suspicion.

"And that's good news?" Little Star was scratching her head furiously, watching the fighters in the sky, so I beckoned her to come to me.

I couldn't tell a Zero fighter from a B-29 at a distance. I only knew the Zeros, flying at a terrifying speed of more than 350 miles per hour, had the rising sun emblem emblazoned on their bodies and wings. They dominated the Shanghai sky, shooting down Chinese fighters as easily as a swatter flattening flies. For the past three years, fighters from the

Nationalist air force had attempted air raids against the Zeros numerous times, but every single fighter from the air force was shot down without hitting a Zero.

"Remember the top-secret information I told you?" he said.

Little Star wouldn't come so I brought the stool to her, sat down, and secured her between my legs. Pressing her head lower, I combed through her hair with my fingers, searching for lice and their plump eggs. How she got infested with lice after I'd just washed her hair with the kerosene, I had no idea. Now my head itched. "I don't think you trusted me well enough to tell me that."

"It has nothing to do with trust, and I still can't tell you too much. I heard the Americans had bombed Tokyo once, but the aircraft crashed in the Zhejiang province. The distance to Tokyo had been an obstacle for the fighters. But the Americans are coming back with more pilots and B-29s! Do you know what this means? If we have the Americans help us, we can rout all the bastards and win this war!"

He had just said this when another fleet of aircraft soared in the sky, chasing the Superfortresses. They were much faster, catching up even as I watched; then they fired. Black smoke burst from a B-29. Ying tossed the binoculars into the satchel and cursed.

"Listen, Ying." I caught two lice and crushed them expertly between my nails. Juice burst between my nails. "You're recovering well. You'll be out and about soon. Can you do something for me?"

He went into the bedroom and rolled underneath the bed, where he'd made a sound barrier with the sheets I'd stolen from the hotel.

"What is it?" he asked.

"Can you find someone for me? You know him. Ernest Reismann. He used to be my pianist." A bunch of brown lice eggs, plump, appeared between my fingers. I positioned my thumbs around them and crushed them.

He came out and stood in front of me. The frown on his face made him look like an ill-tempered child. "Did Cheng mean anything to you?

He's only dead for a little more than a year, and you're thinking about the foreigner?"

Little Star looked up at me, then Ying, and slipped out of my grip. Suddenly, there was nothing I could hold on to.

"Don't you have any loyalty, little sister?" His tone told me the same old message—I, the little sister, the youngest, must obey.

I said quietly, "Do not talk to me like that."

He growled.

"Do you remember once we flew a kite together, Ying? You, Cheng, and me. How old was I? Nine? Ten? You made a hawk, and I painted it in red. You were good at making kites, and Cheng was good at running. We went to a field of flowers. I thought they were sunflowers, but I was wrong, they were rapeseed flowers, with small blossoms, slim stems, and delicate petals. Oh, how beautiful the field looked, a rioting yellow, so sharp, like an ocean of paint. I sat in the field of rapeseed flowers, but you wanted me to fly the kite with you, and Cheng shouted at me to run ahead of him because he didn't want to leave me out of sight. But I couldn't catch up with him. He was too fast. Then the wind blew up my skirt, and I tumbled down the field and broke my leg. Remember that? I broke my leg."

Now across China all rapeseed flowers had disappeared, flowers eaten, stems chewed, roots cooked.

"I don't know why I'm telling you this, Ying. I just want to say I remember this, an episode of our childhood, the things we did, the memories we have."

When people came into your life, there was a reason for that; when they were gone, there were explanations for that. But we must remember them, for if we remembered well and reflected right, then we would be lovers, siblings, cousins, and friends in the next life. Karma, like Mother said. *Yuan*, like what I told Ernest.

"I know he meant a lot to you, Ying."

He kicked the wall. "You have no idea what he means to me. He was more than a brother to me."

"I knew."

"How would you know? No one knew. No one. Not even Cheng himself." He twisted his head away, but he was sobbing.

The firecracker of a man, my brother, a fearless spy, a secretive man, an enigma. I put my hand on his shoulder.

He sniffled, walked into the bedroom, and shut the door.

Whenever I raised the topic of Ernest, Ying clammed up.

He talked to me about other important events of war at least, turning on the transceiver's switch, the volume a buzz of a mosquito. In June, the Allies had staged an attack on Normandy, and they successfully captured the ports in France. In July, the British began their fight to drive the Japanese out of Burma. Paris was free from the Nazis by the end of August. Also, the Allies had achieved momentous victories in New Guinea and were ready to take control of the Philippines.

Yet victory was scarce in my country. In the same summer the Allies landed in Normandy, the Japanese deployed more than 360,000 troops to attack Changsha, a vital city with important railroad networks that connected the south and central parts of China, Burma, and India. But months of resistance by the Nationalist army failed. Relentless, Japan swooped down to the neighboring cities. In a series of devastating defeats, the Nationalists lost thirty-eight cities in the Henan province in thirty-seven days. All over Shanghai, the few newspaper stands sold stacks of papers printed with exultant headlines. "Great Victory to the Empire of the Sun!" "The No. 1 Plan of Japan Has Succeeded." "Mission of Controlling Central China Has Completed." "Japan Has Conquered Central China!"

"I need bombs," Ying mumbled one day under the bed. Yamazaki was still alive, he said, working in the military base, following his emperor's order, actively destroying China.

"You should go shopping." I couldn't hold back my sarcasm, irritated by his stubbornness.

"I need men too!"

"Are you going to help me find Ernest or not?"

He released a loud groan and turned to his radio transceiver. "No."

85

FALL 1980

THE PEACE HOTEL

"I saw him at the border of the ghetto. It was a surprise. I wish I had forgiven him." The music. It's gone.

Ms. Sorebi clears her throat. "I've been waiting for an opportunity to tell you this, Ms. Shao. After our meeting yesterday, I tried to find more information about you, and I went through the photos I brought in my hotel room. Guess what I found."

She digs into her handbag and takes out a manila folder. From inside she retrieves two photos and places them by my hand. "I hope these will bring you fond memories. I might be able to use them for the documentary as well. However—forgive me, Ms. Shao—it appears I have more questions."

I put on my glasses and squint. The photos are black and white. The first photo is me inside the Jazz Bar with Sassoon. The caption, in Sassoon's handwriting, says, *Shao Aiyi, the owner of One Hundred Joys Nightclub, 1940.* The second photo is an image of a woman and a little girl beside an old-fashioned rickshaw, dated 1946. The woman appears to be dirty and tired, like a refugee, but anyone can tell this is still me.

The girl next to me has messy hair and wears a tunic that looks like a trash bag.

I don't want to make a fool out of myself, but tears run down my face despite my effort. "I can't believe it. This picture. She's perfect . . . Where did you get this?"

Ms. Sorebi takes a napkin from a table next to us and hands it to me, her eyes glowing. "As I've mentioned, I found a treasure trove in Sassoon's collection in Dallas, Texas. He took many photos. There were photos of Mr. Reismann playing the piano, photos of Sassoon himself and his friends at parties, photos of street scenes. This picture of you and the little girl appears to be part of a street scene in Shanghai. But look at the child. She looks about four, and she is the spitting image of you. And you said you regretted giving your daughter away and you were looking for her."

"Yes, I was looking for her, my daughter . . . I have done the most unforgivable thing, I gave her away . . ."

She leans over. "Now, Ms. Shao, I can't help asking, is the girl in the photo the daughter you were looking for?"

86

JULY 1945

AIYI

Over the past few months, I went to the rattling Garden Bridge a few times by myself. Standing by a building with a collapsed wooden door, I watched the sentry tower on the other side of the bridge; inside it a Japanese soldier was drinking from a canteen and another, carrying a rifle with a bayonet, was checking people entering the area. Behind them were low wooden houses and narrow lanes, where several foreign women with blond hair wearing black skirts were picking at cabbages.

The ferries had stopped running.

One afternoon, Ying came out from under the bed, cradling the transmitter. After clicking the switch off, which had been lowered to a whisper, he jumped, his arms sweeping wildly in the air. His victory flea dance again. For months, he had been secretive, listening intently to the radio and then hurrying to leave the house.

"Are you going to tell me?" I asked, sitting on the stool beside the charcoal stove. I should wash Little Star's hair with the kerosene again, but I was feeling sick. It was probably because of water or the sour noodles I'd eaten. All morning, I'd had a racking pain in my stomach that made me unable to stand straight.

Ying whispered in my ear. "I just received a message, an important message."

The Americans had shifted their strategy in the Pacific theater. Their B-29 bombers would soon mount a massive attack on the Japanese in Shanghai while the Imperial Japanese Army poured their forces into central China to protect those thirty-plus cities they had won. The Japanese had even pulled the majority of their forces from the east coast, including Shanghai. Only a few Japanese soldiers, led by Yamazaki, stayed in Shanghai.

"He's alone. Alone in Shanghai. His days are numbered. I'm going to kill him." Ying put a pistol in his belt and covered it with the coat. "You must leave Shanghai."

"Why?"

"Didn't you hear what I said? The Americans will bomb Shanghai! They are helping us drive the Japanese out. While they attempt to take over the sky, my people will attack the Japanese on the ground. So together with the Americans, we'll rid Shanghai of the Japanese."

"Why would the Americans help us? Besides, the Japanese are powerful. They have the military base in Hongkou and their warship . . . Don't forget the warship."

When the Japanese attacked the Settlement almost four years ago, the *Izumo* had bombed the British HMS *Peterel* and captured the American USS *Wake*. Equipped with many machine guns, the warship was heavily guarded; any crew and ships, even sampans loaded with animals for sale, that approached within a radius of half a kilometer would be shot. And destroy the base? That was as unlikely as destroying Tokyo.

"That's why we'd help the Americans. My men have a plan. We will destroy the warship and the Japanese military base and distract the Zero fighters. Everything is in place."

"I thought your men died during the truck attack."

"Many patriotic people are willing to fight, little sister. Not perfectly trained, but they'll do. I can't tell you anything more. I'm going to a meeting. Will you listen? Leave Shanghai. Take Little Star with you."

"Where should I go? There's nowhere to go." All the cities around Shanghai were occupied. "Where's Little Star? She was right here. Have you seen her?"

"She'll come back soon enough. Out stealing, likely. You trained her well." She was five, already deft at making fire and stealing bits of coal. "Go south. To the Zhejiang province. You have to leave Shanghai, Aiyi."

"I don't know . . ." If I left Shanghai, my last connection to Ernest, my hope of finding my daughter, would be lost.

That evening, I lay in bed, feverish, shivering, coughing.

"Are you going to die?" Little Star asked me.

"Not yet."

Not before I found Ernest and my daughter.

The next day, Ying returned home a different person, deflated, depressed. All his energy that had spurred the flea dance was gone, and he covered his face with his hat, puffing in anger. The meeting had been ambushed. Some of his men were shot; the others were caught and sent to jail. It was his luck that he was pissing outside and missed the shooting.

"Fuck, fuck, fuck! There must be a mole."

A pain was crushing my chest; it hurt to cough. "What are you going to do? You're only one man. You can't attack the base and sink the warship alone."

He gave a heavy sigh. "Time is running out. We can't win this war without the Americans, and the Americans can't defeat the Japanese without us."

87

ERNEST

When he left the small shop with bread, Ernest noticed a young Chinese in red suspenders in the corner. He had been there for several days, chewing on a toothpick or something, watching the jail across the street. Once in a while, he pressed down his brown-and-green plaid cap. The man reminded him of a petulant godlike youth in fine suits and a purple tie. Aiyi's fiancé, Cheng. But the youth in suspenders was not Cheng.

Ernest's thoughts drifted to Aiyi. Last time he saw her, she was alone, poorly dressed, and seemed hungry. He wondered if something happened to her, Cheng, and her family. And their child. He hoped she was treating the child well, and he longed to know whether it was a boy or a girl. With all his heart and soul, he wished someday he could meet his child, the proof that he still had something precious.

He turned onto a lane to his attic room.

He felt tired. Each day he took the same route from the cobbler to his attic: the dingy cobbler, the bread shop, the jail, a rice shop, an apothecary, a deserted dentist's shop, and then the row of wooden buildings that held his attic. Climbing on a narrow and steep staircase, he entered the room and ate half of his bread. Then he helped Old Liang scrape taros downstairs. Before dusk it would be time for bed; before dawn he would awake.

The sky, a vast ocean of gray brine, didn't change. The sound of Japanese fighters, a constant drum above the roof, didn't change. Part of him believed his entire life would be spent like this; part of him hoped he was wrong.

A sleeve of wind, vibrating with music, brushed his face, smooth like a woman's fine hair. Entranced, Ernest turned away from his usual route and walked toward it, the low, mourning tune like nothing he had heard. He padded toward the wooden sign that marked the border of the area, walked toward the towering stone gate decorated with a curved pediment etched with smooth carvings, a vestige of the neoclassical buildings at the Settlement, and peered down the dim narrow alley inside, where a few people, their faces coated with grime, squatted.

The dirgelike tune continued, enticing him to walk into the alley. He ducked under the barricade of damp tunics, long trousers, and red underwear, passing the men staring at him expressionlessly.

The tune grew louder with each step, and he stopped, breathlessly, outside a small gate. Through the gap of the gate, he could see a court-yard where a girl with braided hair did laundry in a bucket and two men knitted a rope. Near them an old man was fiddling a guitar-like instrument with two strings. Each time he pulled the bow, a melancholy tune waltzed in the air.

Just like that, the memory of music galloped toward him: the tender notes of Schumann's *Kinderszenen*, the intricate murmurs of Scriabin's preludes, the epic thrust of Beethoven's Piano Concerto no. 5, *Emperor*. And jazz. The music of freedom, the music of his success, the music of love.

Hot tears ran down his face, tumbling, rumbling, wetting his chin and hanging on his bony jaw. His shoulders trembled and his entire body shook. He cried, like a child who lost his way home. Since Miriam's death, he had never hummed or wanted to play the piano again. And now, listening to the melancholy tune, after two years of being a prisoner, he realized he had forgotten what music had meant to him. He had forgotten it was once his life, forgotten it had helped him survive; he had forgotten it was a sacred land of joy and sorrow, the art of remembering and forgetting, the language of love and forgiveness.

Would she forgive him? Would he ever listen to music with her again?

He would do anything he could to see her, one more time, and his child, just once. And he promised he would be the balm to her pain, the building blocks to her happiness. If she were mad at him, if she felt like she should strike him, shatter him, he would willingly be torn apart to make her happy again.

He ran out of the alleyway, laughing; he could feel the keys under his fingers, hear the sound of the piano, and smell the air of music. He had wasted much time, so much time.

He went to Goya, asking for permission to leave the area. The gaunt, detestable man asked for a payment and berated him when he had none to give. Ernest went to the metal Garden Bridge, where a Japanese soldier in the sentry tower inspected a caravan of trucks entering the area, and asked for permission to leave. The soldier sent him back to Goya.

He would keep trying.

Three days later, when Ernest walked toward home with a loaf of bread under his arm, the Chinese youth in suspenders appeared again. The man looked up, catching his gaze. Ernest gripped the bread with two hands—many robbers and thieves these days. Then a prick of memory stabbed him. He jerked and went back to the youth, his heart pounding with excitement.

"Excuse me. You look familiar. Do I know you?" Then he remembered. He had seen the youth in her club. He was always beside Cheng, drinking and smoking.

The man pressed down his cap and squinted at him. "What are the chances?"

"You're . . . Ying. That's your name, isn't it? Yes. That's you! Aiyi's brother." He was a hard man, his gaze sharp with hostility. "This is the designated area. What are you doing here, Ying?"

"None of your business."

"Do you know where your sister is? I've been looking for her."

Ying struck a match and lit his cigarette. "Why should I tell you?"

He cleared his throat. "I'd love it if you can do me a favor. I'd love to see her again."

"Why should I do you a favor, foreigner? Haven't you done enough damage already?"

Ernest didn't know what to say, but he couldn't walk away from the last connection to her. "So, I noticed you've been here a few times. Did someone you know get thrown in jail? Can I help you?"

Ying looked at the jail and then him. Suddenly, his hard eyes flashed with interest. "You can certainly help. I need a tank. Will you steal it for me?"

"A tank?" It was inconceivable to steal a bike, let alone a tank.

"I don't have men left. You're the only one I got."

"Me?"

"How's this, foreigner? If you steal the tank for me, I'll tell you about my sister."

"What do you need a tank for?"

"To end the war, foreigner."

Ernest tried to laugh. "I wish I could help, but I don't know where to find a tank."

"At the base. I'll tell you everything you need to know."

388

"The military base?" He would be shot the moment he walked in the base. He didn't know how to drive a car, let alone a tank. He glanced at the row of shanties, the jail's brick building, and the metal railing of the Garden Bridge at the end of the street. "Look, I know you want to end the war. It's a fine idea; I'd like to see it end too. But it's suicide."

"If you want to see her, you'll do it."

"I can't."

"Coward."

Ernest sighed and was going to say something when Ying swung his arm and locked his hand around Ernest's neck. "It's all because of you, foreigner. She ruined her life for you. She was a sweet girl, but she changed ever since she met you. Her husband died for her, do you know that? Her husband, he was like a brother to me." His voice was full of resentment, and something intense flashed in his eyes.

"Cheng died?" The memory of the godlike youth lingered in his mind. His strikingly handsome features. His fine suits and a purple tie. The last time he'd seen him, Cheng had beat him and kicked him out of the club. He was a fierce rival, whose manliness and wealth Ernest thought he could never match, more of a man than he had dreamed of becoming, and he had never asked, out of selfish reasons, why Aiyi chose him over Cheng.

"Fuck you, foreigner. You want to die in this filth? Go ahead. We're all going to die anyway." Ying withdrew his arm.

Ernest coughed, rubbing his neck, yet a lump of pain lodged in his chest and refused to leave. The price of life, the loss of a man like Cheng, her grief, his grief. He wanted to scream to repel the foulness of war, the indignity that plagued them, and he ached to see her, to comfort her, to hold her hand, to say something like *love is stronger than death* or say nothing at all.

He turned around, facing the shanties, his attic room, the military base with the fence of barbed wire in the distance. He had no weapons, no experience; he would infiltrate the enemy base alone and charge at death alone, but he was no longer lonely.

"How do I break in?"

88

FALL 1980

THE PEACE HOTEL

I clutch the photo with two hands. "These are precious, Ms. Sorebi. Thank you for showing them to me. I've been looking for my daughter for many years, but sadly, she is not my daughter."

"Are you sure?"

"But look at her, how beautiful she is. You were right. My Little Star was about four years old."

"Little Star? Oh. I see . . . That explains the resemblance. Well. My apologies. But it says it's 1946. Shouldn't she be six?"

"Well, she suffered from malnutrition. And I can tell you the year is wrong. It wasn't 1946. It should be before 1946, or before the summer of 1945."

"How can you tell?"

"I lost my foot in 1945. Besides, my Little Star suffered terrible burns during the aerial raid. She barely survived."

"Could you talk about the raid, Ms. Shao? I was going to ask you that. The Japanese surrendered after the atomic bombs, but I heard there was a massive bombing by the Americans in the summer of 1945 in Shanghai in an effort to end the war. A great fire engulfed the city. Many people perished."

I pick up a transparent prawn dumpling, but it slips from my hand and falls to the floor. "I was sick that day. My memory is foggy, and I still can't figure out how everything happened. Yes, the entire district was in flames. And Little Star . . . I had stupidly left the front gate open the morning of the raid, and she had wandered out when the bomb hit. When I found her, she was burned beyond recognition. I nursed her back to life."

"What about your birth daughter then? You said you were looking for her. Did you find her?"

I need to be careful; I can't afford to mess this up. "Let me ask you something. Have you heard of the Doolittle pilots?"

"The eighty pilots who bombed Tokyo after Pearl Harbor?"

"Yes, eighty pilots. I heard two drowned. Eight were captured by Japanese and became war prisoners, and the rest died. Jacob DeShazer, a bombardier, was among the captured. He endured repeated tortures in prison camp, thought he was going to die, and vowed that if he survived he'd become a preacher and return to Japan to preach. He was rescued after the war, so he returned to Tokyo and handed out missionary flyers at the Shibuya train station to spread God's word. A Japanese took a flyer, read it, and contacted DeShazer, saying he'd like to follow his path to become an evangelist. Do you know who that Japanese man was?"

"Who?"

"His name was Mitsuo Fuchida, the lead bomber aviator of the Imperial Japanese Navy that attacked Pearl Harbor."

She rubs her temple. "I haven't heard anything like this. A story of karma, I believe? But does this have anything to do with you, Mr. Reismann, and your daughter? I'm confused. The interviewees said Mr. Reismann died, so I believe you wish to preserve his memory by making the documentary. Is that right?"

"That's part of it, Ms. Sorebi. Karma, yes. My mother believed in that, and so do I. Who would have known the niece I saved during the war would save me in the end?"

"Could you be more specific?"

"I never gave up on finding my daughter, Ms. Sorebi. It was also Ernest's last wish. He lost all his family members during the war, as you know. But I couldn't find her, after all these years of searching. My niece helped me. She hired private investigators and followed every trail we had, flying all over the world to find my daughter. One day, she was on a flight from Hong Kong to Sydney on Cathay Pacific, flipping the pages of the in-flight magazine, when she saw information about an exhibit on Shanghai Jews. She took a chance, went to LA, and saw Ernest's profile in the special exhibit—and your biography and your name."

She looks more confused.

I need to drink some water in order to continue, but I don't want to lose a minute. "Yes, I can tell you all about my daughter: She grew up with two sisters. All brunettes. She blended right in with her new family in the Texas suburb with her brown hair. When she was fourteen, her parents died in a car crash. A relative let slip that she was adopted. She became a foster child.

"She studied law at college but dropped out. She ended up with no bachelor's degree but a mound of student loans. She married her high school sweetheart but later divorced. No kids. Then she remarried a salesman at Sears. He had an affair and broke her heart. She divorced again. She has a darling boy, a nine-year-old who loves horseback riding. He wrote his teacher Mr. Morton as Mr. Moron all over the school's hallway, and he was suspended. She was unable to make a mortgage payment and lost her house. She decided to move out of Texas and went to LA, where she became a documentarian. She took an offer from a museum to make an exhibit for Shanghai Jews and highlighted Ernest Reismann."

Ms. Sorebi leans over. "Holy shit! How did you know all this about me, Ms. Shao?"

89

AIYI

Ying was up to something. All day long he fiddled with the transceiver under the bed. At night he disappeared. When I mentioned Ernest, he replied irritably that he had been looking for him but was unable to find him. Many refugees had caught dysentery or infection and died. It was likely Ernest had died too. "You know how filthy the area is," he said in a grave voice.

I didn't believe him, yet thoughts were puddled in my mind. The pounding headache and fever stole my energy. What Ying said could be true.

When he returned one evening, he tied up the corners of the sheets and packed what little we had—the kerosene lamp, the two round tin containers that held strips of dried sweet potatoes, and the empty whiskey bottle, which we refilled with boiled water. He tossed the bundle onto my lap. Everything was packed. Little Star was dressed. The rickshaw would come to the alley and take us to a wharf at dawn the next day.

❧

I had a terrible night. I dreamed of Ernest playing the piano—the rhythm, the energy, and the clarity. Oh, only he could play jazz like this; only he knew what music meant to me. But then it changed. Its legato sound drew out like a trail of tears, and it was unmistakable—it was the song of farewell. I awoke, perspiring, before dawn. Little Star was still sleeping, but perplexingly, the music lingered. I went out to the courtyard, to the dark alleyway, to the street, shivering and coughing, following the sound of the piano. One last time.

Each step shook my head and triggered a stabbing pain in my stomach. I kept walking, looking for Ernest sitting by a piano. But it was confusing; my vision was foggy. It seemed there were shadows of early scavengers picking at trash, rickshaw pullers huddling at the poles, and men holding flashlights, cutting the tires of a moored double-decker bus.

The music was still in the air, faint, like a shadow in fog, a leaf in a storm, and now it was familiar, energetic, just like the old times. Elation raced through me. Ernest must be nearby. I could tell because the music grew louder. And louder. And louder.

And all of a sudden the shadows on the street fled—the rickshaws, the men holding flashlights, the scavengers. I froze. What I heard was not the sound of the piano; it was the siren.

And on the edge of the black sky, where the dawn's light had just squeezed through, a fleet of bombers, like bats, sailed through a bed of pale clouds and dove toward the Huangpu River, the art deco buildings, the Customs House, and the high-rises on the waterfront. American B-29s. Ying hadn't lied—we must leave Shanghai. I should wake up Little Star before it was too late. But as I was about to turn, the bats roared over the high-rises and veered north.

The siren grew shrill. It came from the north, the Japanese military base.

Panic struck me. Ying had been lying after all. The American planes were not bombing us in Shanghai; they were targeting the Hongkou district, where Ernest was confined.

90

ERNEST

The base was only guarded by a few dozen soldiers, Ying had said, because the majority of the army had been transferred to central China. Once Ernest drove the tank out of the base, Ying would take it from him. He would not be shot, because the Japanese would be distracted and engaged with the incoming American bombers.

At first, it appeared just as Ying had said.

The siren shrieked the moment the fleet of American bombers appeared. Within seconds, harsh and stark lights glared on the military field, and the personnel in khaki and green uniforms—the fighter pilots carrying goggles, belts, and equipment, the soldiers holding rifles—raced across the vast field. The sound of engines revving echoed, shaking the ground.

But there were hundreds of Japanese troops, not dozens, and all acted in a chillingly orderly manner. Ernest crouched in a trench, camouflaged with a flat wooden board, outside the high wire fence of the base. He would enter the base by climbing through the trench, which had been dug for him beneath the fence.

The tank that he needed to steal, Ying had said, was a captured American M18 Hellcat, equipped with a seventy-six-millimeter main gun and a Browning heavy machine gun, a perfect weapon to destroy the warship. But Ernest saw two tanks on the field, one smaller than the other. Both had a star emblazoned on the hull. With all their power, the metal beasts had open tops, no protection of a cupola. He had no idea which one was the Hellcat.

He grew nervous. He needed to crawl through the trench, enter the base, and steal the tank near the crew of pilots and soldiers, then drive it out of the base. It was a mission suitable for a trained soldier, not him. He was not a fast runner and no good at combat; he didn't know anything about American tanks.

His bottom grew wet from the damp soil; he slipped down, tempted to crawl back, return to his attic, and lie to Ying that something went wrong, that he had tried but failed.

Above the ground, the wire fence rattled; the ground shook. He remembered once he had been close to the barbed wire in an internment camp, trying to see Miss Margolis. That had been three years ago; he'd been twenty-one, determined, unshakable in his faith. It was with Aiyi's help that he'd finally found Miss Margolis and saved the refugees. He smiled. This was for Aiyi then. Once he stole the tank, he would see her again.

He flipped onto his stomach and crawled. When he reached the other side, he hoisted up and saw that not far from him, near the fence, were five motorcycles with sidecars. Beyond the motorcycles, a file of soldiers cranked two leaf-green Zero fighters' engines to life, and above the base, a fleet of American B-29 Superfortresses zoomed.

He couldn't spot the tanks—they had been next to a Zero fighter, but now they were gone. Snapping his head around, he realized a file of Japanese soldiers had blocked them. He climbed out of the trench, and crouching, scurried along the motorcycles for cover. A soldier carrying a fuel hose attached to a fighter was walking toward him. Ernest jerked around before he was spotted and dashed to a nearby staircase and ran down. It was an underground tunnel, fortified with cement, large and spacious, able to fit a double-decker bus. He didn't know where it led or how deep it was, but he feared that if he ran too deep inside, he might not be able to get out.

He had just turned around when a shout came from deeper in the tunnel. He ran up the stairs and reached the ground, where he saw a soldier climb out of the open top of a tank to bow to an officer on a motorcycle with a sidecar. The engine of the tank was running.

He leaped toward the tank, climbed on one of the seven round wheels, and fumbled for a handle to mount. But there was no handle on the rear slope. Desperate, he dug into a steel roller, hoisted himself up, and tumbled into the lidless turret, his head knocking against the gun mount inside the turret. The massive main gun swiveled; the tank rattled, the wheels digging into the ground.

The soldier who had started the tank and the officer ran toward him. Was that Yamazaki? Ernest's heart chilled. It was Yamazaki, who pointed at him with the black barrel of a rifle.

Fear raced up Ernest's spine. Without a lid on the tank, he was an easy target. He pounded the buttons in front of him and grappled with the lever to propel the metal beast to move. Nothing happened. He put all his weight on his foot and pulled the lever again. The transmission roared and the machine pitched, thrusting him forward just as a bullet grazed his hair. His heart jumped to his throat. He was going to die before seeing Aiyi for the last time.

Then the tank rambled forward at a surprisingly fast speed, rammed into the row of motorcycles with sidecars, and grazed the wire fence, setting off a blaze of sparks.

"No!" he shouted, but the tank kept jolting forward, slamming into the landing gear of a Zero fighter, hauling it through the vast field. The plane's crew screamed, jumping aside. Shots popped around him like fireworks.

Suddenly all shots ceased, replaced by staccato shouts of warning. He smelled it. The fuel.

He had slammed into the fighter fuel tank, or perhaps he had run over the fuel hose. Now he must find the entrance to the base and get out of here before it exploded. Crouching, he struggled with the lever, searching frantically among the maze of smoke and sparks for the entrance. *Where is the entrance?* His body bounced in the air as the tank thrust forward, a cacophony of running engines and clashing metals booming in his ears. He peered through the swirling waves of dust, looking for the building with a gate.

Nothing but a thick wall of dust and smoke.

And the tank sped on, a wild metal beast.

Rivers of sweat ran down his face; the pungent smell of fuel and smoke choked his throat. "Shit!"

He must have pushed something wrong; desperate, he tried to reverse his action. But when he took his hands off the lever, the tank threw him, and he smashed against the inside of the turret. Struggling to rise, he managed to hold on to the opening, just as the tank crashed into a building. Bricks exploded. A dull sound rang in his ears; his vision blurred.

When he could see again, a man ran toward him in the suffocating smoke. He had a massive bag on his shoulder, and he was waving at him wildly. It was Ying, who had promised to wait for him outside the base.

"I'm here, I'm here!" Ernest waved, raising his voice above the booming of the tank, which, to Ernest's relief, had slowed down considerably.

"Stop the tank, damn it!" Ying was shouting by the side of the tank, digging into his bag.

"I'm trying!"

"Try harder!"

He fumbled for the lever, jammed at it. "It won't stop!"

Then he saw what was in Ying's hand. A machine gun. Aiming at him. He would shoot at him? After he stole the tank for him?

"Duck, Ernest!" The flame shot out of the machine gun. Ying fired—not at him, but at something behind him.

Ernest turned around. A raging mountain of fire had engulfed what used to be the base, and an orange cloud flooded toward him, torching his body. He cried out in agony, and unbelievably, he heard a scream answer him—a scream from another tank, right behind him, charging at full speed.

"No!" he shouted as a massive force rammed his tank, and he was tossed up in the air.

91

AIYI

A violent volley of gunshots rose, and a choking storm of smoke engulfed the metal bridge and the rows of buildings behind it. I couldn't see the tower or the guard on the other side of the bridge. Holding my painful stomach, I shuffled along, crossing the shaky bridge, waiting for the shouts or the click of a gun that would shoot me when I least expected it.

None came.

I crossed the bridge, passed the wooden board with the sign THE DESIGNATED AREA FOR STATELESS PERSONS, and limped as fast as I could. "Evacuate, Ernest! Evacuate!" I burst into a wooden building near me, holding on to the doorframe to stop my head from spinning. It was deathly quiet inside. I staggered out, gasping, feeling woozy.

A low hum came overhead; the black silhouettes of Superfortress B-29s skittered in the sky, dropping something that looked like a string of mah-jongg tiles.

Boom. The ground throbbed beneath my feet, and all around me the bare tree stubs, the telegraph poles, the wooden buildings, and the brick walls crashed like a pile of bones. A torrent of shrapnel, flashing and whistling, hurtled by and scissored the wires above the roofs; a violent wave of heat and rubble hurled toward me.

I was thrown back and knocked into something. My face burned, my throat burned, my legs burned. I couldn't get up, lift my hand, or scream. But how strange the world was. People seemed to be doing a jig on the bare trees, on the top of the roofs, on the broken beams, and on the crushed telegraph poles. They screamed but were unable to free themselves. From the caverns of collapsed buildings, children crawled; on the smoky street, people ran in circles.

They were foreigners, Chinese, children, men, and women. My head feverish, I scrambled to my feet.

"Cross the bridge, everyone cross the bridge!" I shouted, waving my hands, fanning away the thick smoke and dust, and pushed whoever came my way. Stunned, they went, their heads crowned with white ash and black soot, their faces splattered with blood.

But some were caught in the destructive roar. A bald old man, a foreigner, gaunt and feeble, moaned on a pile of rubble near me; a child in a gray short cotton dress bawled, crying for her mother; and a blonde woman sat on the ground with nothing in her eyes. I shoved her to walk toward the bridge; I shoved the child too.

The old man was sinking in the rubble, his groans barely audible. I climbed up to reach him. *Hurry, hurry.* But he was too far. I lay flat on the pile, reached farther, grabbed his hand, and pulled; he was heavier than I had expected. With some struggle, he finally crawled out, slid down the rubble, and landed on the ground. Exhausted, I had to lie there for a moment to gather some strength. Where was Ernest? I still hadn't seen him. Was he nearby? I got up, but my foot was trapped by a web of boards. I pulled. The pile beneath me rumbled, and I sank to my waist. Frightened, I cried out frantically. "Help! Here! I'm here!"

A voice replied in the black air laced with debris and soot, but all I could see were fuzzy figures in the dusty haze, rushing around—so close, yet so far away.

No one could see me; no one could help me. My body ached, my strength was running out, and the burning heat and smoke mixed with sizzling fuel wrapped around my throat like a hot towel. Above my head came another heavy hum.

I screamed.

Silence answered, followed by a salvo of gunshots in the distance. The mound of rubble quivered again, and I tumbled deeper down to my chest, pinned between the smoldering beams, broken bricks, and coils of scalding metal. I panted for breath, to loosen the clasp around my chest, just as a thunderous sound roared near me. A shell detonated.

Before me, the entire row of wooden buildings crumbled, a crimson blaze ricocheted from behind the rubble, and then everything vanished. Everything, except the thick coat of smoke.

Something lurked in the smoke.

The vague shapes of two beasts. One was overturned, the gun motor sparking fire and the steely wheels rolling on a metal belt; the other stalled, with a running engine. Near the tanks, surrounded by the raging fire, were two figures. One I loved to see; the other I hated.

Yamazaki, the metal clips on his boots flashing like shards, was kicking Ying on the ground.

"Stop, stop!" I screamed.

Yamazaki didn't stop—crazy, like a rabid animal, his face red in the fire. Abruptly he paused and stumbled sideways, turning to face something across from him—another figure. I could only see his back by the sputtering fire, but I would have known that back anywhere. My heart leaped with happiness.

"Ernest! Ernest!"

His entire body was covered with red welts, burns, blisters, and ash. A piece of shrapnel had struck his right arm, the arm with the wounded hand that had pounded out note after note. He crouched, wavering, facing the man who had killed my husband, the man who was going to kill my brother. But Ernest should know—didn't he know?—he was not Yamazaki's match.

But recklessly, he drove himself toward Yamazaki like a spear, knocking him to the ground with such a force that both folded over, slammed into the overturned tank, and crashed in a heap. Ernest, to my greatest joy, got up on his feet first. His face bathed in blood, he struck my enemy with his left fist, again and again; it was hard to believe, but every delicious blow from Ernest made Yamazaki groan until he finally lay flat on the ground. Panting, Ernest fell to his knees. He looked utterly spent after having been powered on a spurt of energy to kill Yamazaki. But Ernest didn't see that, behind him, Yamazaki was crawling to a long rifle near the rubble. He grabbed it and sat up.

"No!" Gathering all my strength, I heaved; inch by inch, I pulled myself out. I was close to swinging my legs out, close to freeing myself and helping Ernest. But suddenly a rush of air swept my feet, and I dropped through the crosshatched boards to the bottom of the rubble.

From outside my prison of detritus came the sound of the world ending.

Gunshots.

Then silence.

I saw nothing; I heard nothing. I was beyond tears.

With the last of my strength, I crawled. Through the burrows of splintered piles of wood, through the cavern of dark smoke. The sharp shrapnel rent my skin, the ragged edges of stones and bricks crunched against my bones, and the smoldering metal coils ensnared my flesh. I kept crawling.

The air outside was pungent, scalding, and chalky like ashes. The earth burned, sticky like blood, soft like melting skin. The sky ruptured, a crimson, bleeding wound. Where was he?

A hand grasped mine, and I looked up, ready to spit on Yamazaki.

"Aiyi?" said a voice, faint, but exploding in my ears.

I gripped him with two hands. *Ernest!*

His eyes were swollen and bruised and his cheeks were coated with blood and ash, yet it was the most beautiful face I had ever seen.

"I thought . . . I thought . . . What happened?"

He gave a wan smile. "Your brother."

Behind him, in the shower of dust and sparks, I saw Ying, a silhouette, holding a machine gun. He had shot Yamazaki before he could fire at Ernest.

And Yamazaki, the murderer, my nightmare, was finally dead, half of his face blown away by the bullets.

"I didn't know you were in the rubble, Aiyi. How did you get there?" A trickle of blood flowed down Ernest's face.

I had many questions too. How had he ended up with Ying, how had the two come across Yamazaki, and what had they done with the tanks? But I only nodded and nodded.

"I thought I would never see you again . . . I thought . . . I've missed you." He wept.

I put my hand on his face. So close he was. So real he was. It was as if he had never left me.

"Get out of here. You two, get out." Ying was shouting. His face was ruined, blood gushing from behind his ear.

"What is it?" I asked.

I didn't hear Ying's reply, for his voice was swallowed by the noise of a bomber emerging in the sky and from the warship on the river as its machine guns blasted. Ying shouted again, "Ernest, Aiyi, you need to get out of here before the bombing starts. I'll take care of this."

I tried to get up, but my feet were weak and painful. "Ying, let's all go together."

"I can't, Aiyi. Go; go with Ernest. I must destroy the warship." He steered the gun motor on the tank and fired at the warship. A detonation boomed somewhere. A fountain of sparks and water bloomed; the sky roared with a downpour, soaking us from head to toe. Ying laughed hysterically—the tank's shell had struck the warship. One of the three funnels, like a smoky finger, slowly bent.

But sparks flashed from another gun turret on the warship. The American fighter that could end the war wobbled in the sky like a kite, leaving behind a trail of smoke. The Japanese warship had shot the fighter.

"Damn it!" Ying fired another shell. "Aiyi! Go now before it's too late! Go!"

I crawled to Ernest. "Let's go, Ernest."

He had slipped to the ground, and his voice was so feeble I could barely hear it. "Aiyi, I did all I could, and now I don't have anything left in me. You must get out of here while you can. I've seen you for the last time. I can die happy. Go. Go before it's too late."

I wept. "You can't. You have to come with me, Ernest."

"Promise me. You'll look after our child. Is it a boy or a girl? I wish I could see the child. It would be lovely. My child. How lovely."

"Our child . . . I gave her away, Ernest. I'm sorry. I don't know where she is. You can't stay here. You must go with me. You must find her for me."

He grabbed my arm. "You gave her away?"

"I'm sorry. I'm sorry. You must help me. You have to get up. Get up, Ernest. I can't walk. I don't want to die here. I need to find our daughter. Please, please."

Gunfire spluttered near me. I looked up. Something dark floated toward me—an American bomber. It grew bigger and bigger, and I could see the black goggles against the window.

Ernest screamed, and the next thing I knew he was on his feet and I was in his arms.

Something exploded; a wave of heat rushed toward us. Ernest, screaming, just ran and ran, toward the bridge.

I looked back. My brother. He was a spy, he could drive a tank, he could destroy a cruiser, he could kill, he could do anything, and he could, no doubt, escape from a fallen bomber. But I couldn't see him, or the mountain of rubble that had trapped me, or the two tanks. For the land had become a massive field of fumes and flames, a sizzling pyre of wood and metal, a painted field of yellow earth with rapeseed flowers, where a blazing fragment, like a scrap of crimson cloth, shot up in the air like the red kite that we used to fly.

Tears poured out of me.

When Ernest stopped, I saw we had crossed the bridge. Absolutely exhausted, we dropped to the ground and leaned against a fallen house. Throngs of people, whom I had helped evacuate, crouched nearby—the bald old man, the girl in a short dress, and the blonde woman among them. Some families, holding one another, roamed to the park nearby.

I felt cold. My hair was scorched and almost burned to the scalp in places. My arms were bare and so was my chest. And my foot. Some rusty wire had pierced through it, and it was stuck at an awkward angle. Had Ernest not carried me, I would never have been able to get out alive. "We'll find her, Aiyi. For as long as I live, we'll keep searching until we find our daughter."

What more could I say? I still felt guilty, but I was not hopeless. Despite the war, despite all my losses, despite everything, I was the lucky one. I had been loved and was still loved, and I was ready to love again. I embraced him, skin to skin, and I saw what he saw, I felt what he felt, I wanted what he wanted.

When the winds of life had sent him to me years ago, I had not asked the reason why; now there was no need to ask. I threaded my fingers into his, and together we stared at the mountain of fire that had swallowed my brother. Above it, in the smoky sky, the Zero fighters and the noisy American bombers had vanished. In the distance, the gun turrets of the cursed cruiser were finally smoldering, and the river lapped, its yellow foam writhing in the moaning wind.

92

FALL 1980

THE PEACE HOTEL

"Because you're the person I wanted to meet the moment I got the call from my niece, because you're the person for whom I've been searching for decades—because you are my daughter," I say. I look at this woman, whose pictures I have gazed upon countless times with a magnifier, her bright black eyes—that used to be blue when she was a newborn—piercing me like headlights in fog.

When I saw her eyes in the pictures that Phoenix gave me, it was a surprise, but I knew it was common for babies to change their eye color. Now she's sitting right across from me, a grown woman, and I can see the lips that were Ernest's, the fine crease under her eyes, and the jet-lagged look on her face. "You look so much like your father, with his lips, the shape of his eyes, and brown hair. If you study Ernest's photos, you'll see how much you resemble him."

She rubs her arms as if cold. "Well, Ms. Shao, I wish you were right, and I'd love to be the daughter you're looking for, but I'm afraid you're mistaken. I was born on August 23, 1945. After World War II."

I shake my head. "You were born on December 12, 1942. There were two women in the bedroom when you were born. One didn't want you; one didn't know how to keep you. I've regretted that for almost forty years of my life."

"I can show you my passport. It has my birth date."

"Sweetheart, there were no real birth certificates in China until recently. All papers were forged. Whatever your adoptive parents got was not authentic. And I suppose the birthplace on your certificate is Hong Kong?"

She scratches her head.

"If this is helpful, I know you have a patch of birthmark on your right ankle."

Her eyes widen. "How . . ."

"I've spent years searching for you. I was told your parents were doing business in Hong Kong, where they adopted you. Phoenix found their names, their pictures, and your name through the adoption agency. Here." I take out a photo from a wallet in my Prada bag.

"Gosh. They're my parents. They look so young. And that's . . . that's . . ."

In the photo, a white woman wearing a skirt is holding a toddler in her arms, and standing next to her is a man wearing a white suit.

"That's you, isn't it? The toddler? You recognize yourself? You must have lots of pictures of yourself as a child. I wanted to tell you that you were my daughter yesterday, but I wasn't sure how you would respond. I asked you to make a documentary so you could listen to my past with Ernest. If you have doubts, we can always do a paternity test of some sort. But really, anyone who knew Ernest can tell. Haven't you come across his pictures when you were researching?"

"We all look alike in black-and-white photos."

I give her another photo I saved. "We took this photo before Ernest passed away six years ago."

"I thought he died during the war."

"Did your interviewees tell you that? He lost touch with his people after the bombing. It's no wonder they thought he died. But he had a good life after the war." I stare at the photo in her hand. Ernest and I were smiling at Canada Place, a cruise ship behind us. He was fifty-three years old, with generous blue eyes and wispy gray hair that came from years of yearning for the daughter he never had a chance to meet. It was our sixth cruise to the Bahamas. His right hand, tanned with age spots, had developed arthritis and gave him a paralyzing pain that could only be eased by strong medication. He never played the piano again, and the same troublesome hand would lead to a sailing accident that took his life.

My daughter scrutinizes the photo for a long time, and I wonder if she'll exclaim again, but she puts it down, gets up, and picks up the suede hat from the table. "Excuse me."

Is she excited? Angry? Preparing to leave Shanghai? I can't let her get out of my sight, not after all these years. I turn my wheelchair to follow her, but my daughter disappears from the restaurant.

A long moment passes before my daughter returns, her boots tapping the marble floor. She sits down across from me, clenching a ball of tissues.

"Ms. Shao, I don't know what to say. This is beyond my imagination. I have a lot of questions, if you don't mind. If I am the daughter you're looking for, I think I should be grateful and excited. I still believe there's a good chance you're making a mistake. But the birthmark on my ankle. How did you know?"

She's crying, dabbing her eyes with the sodden tissue. I take a napkin from a table near me and give it to her, as she did for me earlier.

She laughs, but tears are still rolling down her face. "I'm sorry. This is all too much. I don't know how to say this. This is crazier than a documentary! So you asked me to make the documentary, but your intention was just to let me listen to your story, is that right?"

"I still hope you'll make a documentary to honor my husband. Your father. Will you do that?"

"Of course. I want to make a documentary about . . . your husband. So you married him. What happened after the aerial raid? Tell me everything."

"I've told you about Phoenix and how she was terribly burned."

"Phoenix is Little Star?"

"Plastic surgery helped her face, but you can still see the scar tissue."

She nods. "What did you do after you united with Mr. Reismann?"

"I got tetanus from the rusty wire, and my foot had to be amputated. As soon as the pain eased some, I looked for you with Ernest and Little Star. Ernest had Little Star and me sit in a wheelbarrow and pushed us all the way to the Jiangsu province. It took us three months, and it was a bittersweet union. Peiyu was pleased to see her daughter alive, and she told me she gave you to one of her relatives in Shanghai, not far from where my home used to be. So we decided to go back to Shanghai. But Little Star wouldn't let me go. She couldn't remember Peiyu very well, and she was frightened to be left there. So I asked for Peiyu's permission to look after her. She agreed. So the three of us—Ernest, Little Star, and I—went back to Shanghai to find you, but another family lived there. We were told you were sent to an orphanage. Ernest searched every single orphanage, joss house, and hospital in Shanghai. It wouldn't be too hard to find you, he said, since you had his eyes and that birthmark. But the civil war started, and Ernest, Little Star, and I immigrated to the US with the help of Mr. Blackstone, the host family of Ernest's sister."

"So you married Mr. Reismann, forgot about the daughter you gave away, and never came back to Shanghai again."

"I couldn't, my dear. After the Communist party took over, I was named a traitor for marrying a foreigner and banned from entering

Shanghai. Then the Cultural Revolution swept across the country. Any news about you and the family who adopted you was cut off."

"How did you and Mr. Reismann end up in Canada?"

"We led a happy life in Austin, Texas, the three of us, but I was an outsider, to say it nicely. I was wheelchair bound and perhaps one of the only two Chinese women in Texas. The other one I knew was Claire Lee Chennault's wife, Anna Chen. They called me ma'am and then told me I was not welcome in grocery stores, concerts, parks, or restaurants. I was housebound, a prisoner. That was why your accent brought up many bad memories for me at first.

"Ernest thought it was not worth living there, so we moved to Vancouver. Vancouver was quieter, had more Chinese people. We started a small restaurant, which became a successful chain, which led us to invest in more restaurants and hotels. Ernest was a capable businessman, as you've learned, and I made by hand all the dumplings from my wheelchair. Now we have the international hospitality company that manages a broad portfolio of hotels, restaurants, and resorts, the Shao Holdings Company." Which she knows.

"Do you have other children?"

"Sadly, I couldn't have children after you. My body suffered too much during the war."

She looks toward the window, toward the void between the sky and the earth that must be the size of the absence of a mother in her heart. A moment later, she says, "My adoptive parents were kind to me. They loved me as their own. If my aunt hadn't let it slip, I would never have known. But when I lost my parents and found out about the adoption at fourteen, I thought my world was over. I tried to find out who my biological parents were. That was why I came to Shanghai years ago, since my aunt mentioned Shanghai. But I found no proof, and the near arrest was enough to stop me."

I listen; I have waited for this for so long.

411

"After so many years, I'd given up. As I was growing up, people said I looked Italian, European, or even Latina. I didn't know what to say, but I had a feeling I might have Asian blood. I tried not to dwell on that, though. Sometimes it's better to forget about your origin. It's easier, you understand? Because this feeling . . . this thought that I was not wanted, that it was probably better off if I hadn't been born . . . Do you understand what it was like?"

What else can I say? The unforgivable sin that I have committed and can never atone for?

"It's like—" She stops, covering her face, but then she speaks again through her hands. "It's like your heart is a leaky bottle that you're trying to fill. All the love, joys, and happy moments go right through it, and it can never be filled up."

I have tears in my eyes. "If I could alter time, I would not have left you. If we could go back to those years, I would spoil you like a doting Chinese mother. My daughter, I can never make up for the lost years, for what has been missing in your life, for what has been missing in your heart. But I wish to tell you that you were missed and you were loved, since the moment you were given away, for every moment of your life, even though you never knew, even though we were continents away."

She puts down her hands and looks at me, her face a river.

ACKNOWLEDGMENTS

This book was written after the losses of my mother and my father-in-law. I was confused and depressed but didn't know it. Many struggles, detours, and false starts took place because of that. I'm deeply thankful to all the people who helped create this book.

I'm incredibly grateful to my brilliant editor, Jodi Warshaw. Thank you so much for your patience, your vision, and your faith in me. I cherish the opportunity to work with you.

Thank you to my agent, Rachel Ekstrom Courage, for your devotion, your phone calls, and your excellent feedback. Many thanks, too, to Maggie Auffarth for your astute comments on an early draft. To Tegan Tigani, for your peerless intelligence and insight—your editing skill is in a class by itself. To my copyeditor and my proofreader, the warriors behind the pages, thank you so much for saving me!

Thank you to Andrea Peskind Katz, the founder of Great Thoughts' Great Readers, who urged me to write a novel about Jews in Shanghai. It's fair to say that without your suggestion, this novel would never have been written. I'm so grateful for our talks and texting and your lavish encouragement and support along the way. You're a friend a writer can only dream of!

Thank you to my boy, Joshua, for the tank. I promised to acknowledge you, so here you go. You have walked around the neighborhood with me, distracted me, and enthralled me with your magic talks of World War II bombers, fighters, and pilots, and much more.

Thank you to Mike Leibling for your generous guidance, your open-mindedness, and your subtle but wonderful British humor when I needed it. To Dianna Rostad, for reading anything I wrote, for the tears and laughter, and for your decades-long friendship. To my dear friend Janie Chang, for your gentle talks, our shared heritage, and the dim sum.

Thank you to Rabbi Geoffrey Dennis for helping research the bat mitzvah tradition in the US in the 1920s. Without your help, the details of Miriam's momentous ritual would be told differently. To Sofie Delgado and Sabrina Moormann, for helping me with the German passage in the novel. Thank you to my talented friends at Tall Poppy Writers—Amy Reichert, Ann Garvin, Aimie Runyan, Hank Phillippi Ryan, and of course all the others I don't have a chance to add here—for all the lovely conversations, the expert suggestions, and many thoughtful comments and generous help on my publishing journey.

Thank you to the librarians at Flower Mound Public Library, especially Vickie Doss, for putting in my hands many books I requested through the interlibrary loan service. I'm grateful for your enthusiasm and diligence.

Thank you so much to my Jewish family for your enthusiastic embrace of my books and your steadfast support—you probably will never know how much your acceptance means to me—and to my family in China and my precious Annabelle for cheering me on.

Last but not least, my endless love and adoration to Mark, my husband, my secretary, my technical support. I hope you'll read my books someday, and I want to let you know that you're my favorite song, and you'll always have my ears.

FURTHER READING

Many scholars and novelists have written informative books on Shanghai and Jewish refugees in Shanghai during World War II, which I found extremely helpful during my research:

- *Empire of the Sun*, by J. G. Ballard
- *Exodus to Shanghai: Stories of Escape from the Third Reich*, by S. Hochstadt
- *Flyboys*, by James Bradley (a great book that illuminated the mentality of the Japanese soldiers during World War II)
- *The Last Kings of Shanghai: The Rival Jewish Dynasties That Helped Create Modern China*, by Jonathan Kaufman
- *Love in a Fallen City*, by Eileen Chang, translated by Karen S. Kingsbury
- *Remembering Shanghai: A Memoir of Socialites, Scholars, and Scoundrels*, by Isabel Sun Chao and Claire Chao
- *Shanghai Refuge: A Memoir of the World War II Jewish Ghetto*, by Ernest G. Heppner (to honor Mr. Heppner, whose book I read at least ten times, I named my main character after him)
- *Shanghai Grand: Forbidden Love and International Intrigue in a Doomed World*, by Taras Grescoe

- *Strange Haven: A Jewish Childhood in Wartime Shanghai*, by Sigmund Tobias
- *Ten Green Bottles: The True Story of One Family's Journey from War-Torn Austria to the Ghettos of Shanghai*, by Vivian Jeanette Kaplan
- *Voices from Shanghai: Jewish Exiles in Wartime China*, edited and translated by Irene Eber

ABOUT THE AUTHOR

Weina Dai Randel is the award-winning author of the novels *The Moon in the Palace* and *The Empress of Bright Moon*, a historical duology about Wu Zetian, China's only female emperor. *The Moon in the Palace* won the RWA RITA Award in 2017, and the series has been translated into seven languages and sold worldwide. Born in China, Weina came to the United States at twenty-four. She holds an MA in English from Texas Woman's University in Denton, Texas, and has worked as the subject-matter expert for Southern New Hampshire University's online MFA program and as an adjunct professor for Eastfield College. Interviews with Weina have appeared on WFAA's *Good Morning Texas* as well as in such publications as the *Wall Street Journal, Huffington Post, Los Angeles Review of Books,* RT Book Reviews, and BooksbyWomen.org. She lives in Boston with her loving husband, two children, and a family of chipmunks in the backyard. For more information, visit www.weinarandel.com.